# HOMETOWN HOTTIE

WESTON PARKER

STAR KEY PRESS

## Hometown Hottie

**Editor:** Eric Martinez
**Cover Designer:** Ryn Katryn Digital Art

# FIND WESTON PARKER

# 1

## NOVA

My hands curled into fists at my sides.

What the *hell* was Frank Louison doing, not so discreetly, taking pictures of my family's land on his phone? He turned the device horizontal, lifting it up to get a panoramic shot of the ranch with the majestic mountains as a backdrop. Red Stone Ranch had been in my family for three generations. From the serrated mountains that made up our border, to the grasslands where the cattle grazed, and the river that flowed gently through it all, there wasn't an inch of it I didn't know.

I knew its secrets, where to find its treasures, and most importantly for the situation I was in at the moment, I knew how to protect it. As I strode through the colorful tents in the parking lot on the edge of the property, I waved hello to some of the vendors who were setting up for our Saturday market, but I didn't stop to chat.

Later, I would check in with everyone, but right then, I wanted to set Frank straight. He could keep his grimy hands and his greedy eyes off my family ranch.

"This is private property, Frank." I snatched the phone right out of his hand, scrolled through the pictures he'd taken, and deleted them all. "You're not supposed to be here. You're trespassing."

The developer spun to face me with a charming and *almost* disarming smile on his face. Key word *almost*. He splayed his hands wide in a show of innocence before extending one to reach for his phone. I pulled back, and he arched an eyebrow.

"Give me my phone, Nova. You want to talk about private property rights?"

I glanced down at the screen one more time to make sure all his photos of my home were gone. Then I smacked the phone into his waiting palm and met his gaze directly. "Here. Take it. And don't get any ideas going and taking more pictures. You don't have permission. Now," I added, nodding toward the parking lot, "please leave."

He pouted, turning on the playful charm. "Don't be like that. I came for the market, and the view from here is so beautiful, I couldn't resist. I'm hardly the only one."

Inclining his chin toward the shoppers starting to arrive for the day, he pointed out a few different groups of people pausing for selfies before they hit the stalls.

I sighed and turned my gaze back to him, my eyes narrowing. "Those people are here to buy fresh local produce and handmade goods. You're here for the ranch, and that's not for sale."

Frank reached for the sunglasses hanging in the V of his shirt and slid them over his squirrely eyes. "There's nothing like the smell of fresh bread in the morning. How is that little bakery of yours doing? It seems to have become a popular place for the people around here."

"It has. Thanks for asking." I lifted my chin a little higher in the air.

Frank had a few inches on me, but he was a big-city boy with shiny shoes and manicured nails, a transplant who'd smelled the development opportunities in Wyoming and had moved to Silver Springs with the intent to put up high-rises and condominiums.

In other words, he was here to threaten our way of life, and any man with shinier nails than mine didn't belong anywhere near here. He didn't intimidate me, and his false charm and idle flirtation weren't going to fool me into convincing my parents to sell our property to him.

Not. A. Chance.

"I'll have to come check it out some time," he said conversationally, that supposedly charming smile back on his lips. "I hear the coffee's good. Maybe I can buy you a cup and we can talk."

"You want to buy me a cup of coffee in my own shop?" I arched an eyebrow and scoffed. "No, thank you. Besides, unless the talk you want to have is you telling me that you're leaving town for good, you and I have nothing to discuss."

He slid his hands into the pockets of his jeans, lowering his head slowly to one side as if trying to size me up. *Good luck to you, asshole. They don't make me in your size—or in any size you can handle.*

"You know, Nova, I'm not the bad guy here. In fact, there are a lot of folks around these parts that think of me as something of a savior. Times are changing, and if you refuse to change with them, you'll get left behind."

"Yup. I guess I'm just an old fashioned country girl." I flashed him a tight smile. "If there are people who think of you as a savior, then go bug them and leave us alone. I'm sure they'd trip over their own feet to worship you."

He turned away from me and waved toward the sprawling land that reached the base of the mountains in the distance. "I can't leave you alone. What you Murphys have got here is prime real estate. The kind that can fetch your parents the money they need to retire comfortably and to leave a little behind for your kids and your brothers."

"My parents will retire comfortably right here, thank you very much, and my kids and my brothers will grow up on this ranch just like we did. Stop wasting your time and go find some other rancher to harass. Preferably four or more counties over."

For the first time today, that suave facade gave way to the real Frank. He yanked his mirrored sunglasses off his face and narrowed his eyes at me, haughtiness written all over his ordinary features.

"You can't bullshit me, Nova. I'm not one of you simpleton towns-people. I know how business works and I know yours has been trending down for years because your father is stuck in the past. At this point, there's no way you can even pay the taxes on this place, and I have a client who's just waiting for your folks to go bankrupt trying to keep it afloat. Your stubborn pride is going to ruin what your family built."

I bristled. He wasn't wrong about Dad being stuck in the past. My father was a good man and a better rancher, but he didn't believe in modern *tricks* like marketing or even something simple like these Saturday markets.

Frank had struck a chord, but that didn't mean I had to admit it. My teeth ground together and I held his gaze without flinching. This man with his pretty nails and expensive shoes would never get my help convincing my parents to sell, and that was all he was here for.

"Now I've tried being polite, Mr. Louison. Us simpleton towns-people are brought up that way, but since it's not working, let me try it in fancy, big-city language, shall I?" I pointed toward his cherry-red pick-up with the brand-new tires that had probably never even seen proper dirt. "Take your pansy-ass truck and get the fuck off my prop-erty before I go fetch a gun."

He eyed me like he didn't believe I would do it, but when I shrugged and started back toward the building, he scoffed down a disbelieving laugh and threw his hands up in front of him, palms out as he walked backward. "Okay, Nova. I'm leaving, but I will be back. That's a promise, not a threat. Your days on this ranch are numbered and you know it. I kind of wish you'd have taken the easy way out."

Not giving him the courtesy of a reply, I planted my hands on my hips and watched pointedly as he marched to his truck, slammed the door, and finally sped off, throwing up a cloud of dust and gravel behind him. My heart was racing a million miles a minute, my palms sweaty as I wiped them on my jeans.

I might have won the battle, but the war was coming. I felt it in my bones as surely as I felt the sunshine beating down on my bare shoul-ders. The ranch had been struggling for years. What we made from the bakery, coffee shop, and market offset that some, but even combined, those businesses didn't do nearly well enough to make a real dent in the growing expenses on the farm.

Frank, our own personal vulture, had positioned himself perfectly. All he needed was for the ranch to go belly up and he'd be picking at our bones with those shiny white teeth of his. Veneers, probably.

*Ugh.*

Dread sank like a stone to the pit of my stomach, weighing me down, but I forced smiles and small talk on my way back to the bakery. Six years ago when I'd come back home from college, it had taken me four months to convince Dad to let me turn one of the old storage sheds into a little bakery.

The business had grown from there and I was damn proud of it, but at this rate, Frank would be the one kicking *me* off the property in a couple years.

I breathed in deep, trying my best to act calm as I chatted to people who sold their wares here every weekend. I had known them all my life. Seeing their smiling faces helped ease some of the worry weighing down on me.

When I finally made it back into the privacy of my kitchen, sweltering heat enveloped me, but I shut the door behind me anyway. My best friend and fellow baker, Cassidy, looked up when I walked in, smiling as always until she saw the look I had on my face.

"Girl, you need to get some sleep." She blew out a low whistle between her teeth. "You look like hell. What time did you get in here this morning?"

"Four, but it's not that." I rocked back on my heels and jerked my head toward the parking lot. "I saw Frank out there."

Her nose wrinkled like she smelled something rotten. "Your gun is under the counter."

I snorted a laugh. "He left before I could shoot him for trespassing."

"Oh well." She sighed dramatically. "Maybe next time."

"There better not be a next time," I muttered.

Sympathy softened her kind brown eyes and a furrow appeared on her freckled brow. "Did he bother you about selling again?"

"Doesn't he always?"

She walked out from around the worn wooden table we used to roll out the dough. "Come here." She pulled me into a tight hug and rubbed my back as she held me. "It'll be okay, doll. I know it doesn't feel like it, but we're doing well here. You'll figure it out, but not if you keep getting no sleep and working yourself to the bone. I've got it from here. You head on home."

"I can't." I squeezed her back and ran through my mental checklist of things to do on market day. "I've got too much work to just crawl into bed in the middle of the morning."

"Yeah, but you've always got too much work," she said, backing away from me and grabbing the rolling pin she'd been holding when I'd walked in. "I'll clean up. You really need to get some rest. Especially after dealing with that snake."

A dry chuckle escaped me and I shook my head. "I can think of better words than that to describe him, but sure. Let's go with *snake*. There are kids outside, so I better not start flinging around the more creative insults I've thought up." *Like he's a shit-munching twat waffle who would sell his own mother's kidneys to make a buck.*

I inhaled and exhaled deeply, trying to gain control of my hammering heart and simmering temper. If I let him upset me, he won, and I refused to let that bottom feeder win.

Frank first appeared in town a few years ago. Everyone thought he was just another developer passing through, but it soon became clear he was a scavenger, and a merciless one. He dug in his heels and started snatching up businesses and properties all over the area.

Despite plenty of opposition from the folks in town, myself included, he wasn't going anywhere and he wouldn't stop until he got what he wanted.

*And now, he has his sights set firmly on Red Stone Ranch.*

Nausea rolled through me and the anger gave way to feeling just plain sick. For years now, I'd barely had a moment to slow down and I never relaxed. My brother Ryan and I had done everything we could think of to try to help our parents, but it wasn't enough. It was never enough.

"Do you remember Carson Drake?" Cassidy asked suddenly. "He

went to school with us back in the day. Played with the NFL until he retired last season? I think he might've been in Ryan's year."

My eyes snapped open and my mouth went dry. Not even my worries about the ranch were enough to keep my body from reacting like I'd stuck my finger in an electrical outlet. "Uh, yeah? Sure, I think so."

Did I remember Carson Drake? That was like asking if the sun had remembered to shine this morning. If the moon would remember to rise tonight.

For as long as I lived, I would remember that name, and not just because Carson had, in fact, been in Ryan's year at school. He'd also been his best friend and teammate—as well as my one-time summer love. Cassidy had zero clue that we'd had a thing, though.

The mere thought of him made me tense. I cleared my throat, trying to sound casual. "Why do you ask?"

She shrugged, arms full of stuff she'd gathered from the table. Then she took everything to the sink and gently lowered it in. "I heard some people at Moe's talking about him the other night. Apparently, he's been investing in the town ever since he got drafted, like, a million years ago."

*Ten years ago, but who's counting?*

Unaware of my mental correction, she turned to look at me over her shoulder. "The hospital expansion, the new wing at the high school, a couple parks, and the new library are because of him. Maybe you should try to get in touch. A guy like that might be able to do something to help you stop Frank from taking your property."

"Yeah, thanks. I'll think about it." *But I'm never, not ever, going to ask Carson for help.* "I should get back out there. Make sure everyone is happy and that they don't need anything. We need to keep 'em all coming back."

She smiled. "They will keep coming back, babe, but sure, go on. I'll handle everything here."

"I know you will."

Cassidy Markus was one of the few people in this world I trusted completely. I returned her smile with a grateful one of my own, then spun around and went to make sure nothing had gotten wildly out of hand since I'd come to hide in the kitchen.

For the rest of the day, I had my hands full with customers of my own as well as those who were visiting the market. Once the parking lot had cleared out and I'd done the cleaning up after, the sun was starting to paint the sky in orange and pink pastels and it was time to go up to my parents' house for dinner.

I trudged inside and looked around for my brother to talk to him about Frank, but he was nowhere to be found. I sighed. He hadn't been much help lately with trying to keep the ranch afloat.

"Where is he?" I asked Mom when she came around the corner, carrying a casserole dish in her hands and wearing a big smile. "Also, hey, Mom. How was your day? Do you know where Ryan is?"

"Oh, he's not joining us tonight." She pressed a quick kiss to my cheek before she continued to the dining room. "He's out with some friends from high school who just moved back to town or something. Either way, you're stuck with us old people for dinner. Go wash up. I'll grab Daddy."

Alarm bells sounded in my brain as she grinned at me. Ryan only had so many friends from high school, and definitely only a few who had left town.

*So who exactly is he meeting with tonight, and why is this the first I'm hearing about any of 'em moving back here?*

# 2

---

## CARSON

"Man, it's weird being back," Vance muttered as we walked into Moe's, the best—and one of the only— bars in town. My friend screwed up his face as he looked around. "How does it look exactly the same as it did before we left? And how does it *smell* the same?"

"People around here don't like change." I clapped him on the shoulder and walked directly to the pitted wooden bar where I'd had my first ever legal beer. The same faded, US flag hung overhead, and the same glitchy TV was mounted on the wall over the bottles.

Unlike Vance though, I found it comforting that nothing had changed. It was familiar. Felt like home, which was exactly what we'd both come back here for—home. "Besides, you knew it hadn't changed much. We were here for that weekend just last year."

"To visit our parents, not to live with them," he said as he drummed his fingers on the counter, looking around with a thoughtful expression on his face until he suddenly grinned. "You know what, though? It's kind of nice knowing we're not leaving again in a couple days. I think it's just going to take a while to really accept that we're back for good this time."

"Agreed." I ordered a pitcher of beer from the kid behind the bar.

He did a double-take when he recognized us, but before I could ask if he wanted a selfie or something, he squeaked and rushed away.

Hopefully to get our beer.

Vance laughed. "I guess that's one thing that's changed. We're real hometown heroes now. I don't think we left the adoring crowds behind back in civilization."

I rolled my eyes at him, in agreement with his assessment but not really wanting to talk about it. Vance and I were the only two players from our state who'd gone on to play in the NFL. We'd been teammates in high school but had gone to different colleges and had been drafted to different teams.

Over the years, we'd kept in touch and remained friends. Now we were both back home at the same time with the same mission. Retired and ready to slow down, we wanted to use our money to help the small town we loved, and we wanted to live out the rest of our days in the place we'd come from.

Escaping my hometown after high school had been great, but only for a while. These last few years had been exhausting and everything about life in the spotlight had gotten really, really old. For the past couple of years, Vance and I had both toyed with the idea of leaving the game with our dignity intact before we'd finally made the leap.

Now here we were, back home and with absolutely no concrete plans to fill our days. We'd figure it out, though. For now, I was just happy breathing in the stale beer scent of our beloved Moe's and I was looking forward to calmer, quieter days with people who wanted me around for more than just my money.

"Well, well, well, look what the cat dragged in." Ryan's familiar voice rang out from behind us. His arms were spread as wide as his grin when I turned to look at him. Well over six feet, he was as tall as Vance and me, and also like us, there wasn't an ounce of fat on him. His skin was deeply tanned from spending his days outside on the ranch and his dark brown hair was messy instead of styled. He took a few more steps forward, whistling as his gaze moved from one of us to the other. "Carson Drake and Vance Abrams. The NFL's very own heartbreakin' superstars are really back in the town, huh?"

Vance pumped his eyebrows at him. "Ready to break some hearts and take some—"

"Don't say it." I smiled at my old buddy and accepted his hug, smacking him on the back a few times before I let go. "How're you doing, man? It's been a long time. They don't have working phones around here anymore?"

Ryan chuckled. "The phones work, but so do we. Some of us weren't just chasing balls and chasing tail and getting paid for it."

Vance pretended to be shocked, pressing his hand to his chest and batting his eyelashes. "Well, I never. What are we doing here then, Drake? I thought we were coming for *le good life*. This doesn't sound like that."

Ryan laughed at our friend, giving him a back-thumping hug too. The squeaking kid brought over our pitcher of beer and two mugs. He looked between Vance and me with huge eyes, and I could practically see the stars in them until he glanced at Ryan.

The kid smiled. "What can I get you, Ry? Are you really with them?"

"Unfortunately," he replied with that grin still on his face. "Thanks, Kevin. It looks like Carson's already got us ready. Just grab me a mug."

I cradled the pitcher close to my chest. "I don't know what you guys are drinking, but this is for me."

Vance patted his rock-hard stomach. "I'd watch the beer gut if I was you. If that's what you're after though, go for it."

I sighed. "Fine, I'll share."

Kevin, the bartender kid, handed Ryan a frosty mug. Ryan thanked him and waved us to a booth near the pool tables that were in serious need of refelting. As we sat down, he frowned at us, the massive grin finally fading. "You two really back for good? I mean, I'm here, so I got your texts, but seriously? You're home?"

Vance filled the glasses.

"Yep, we're home for good," I said. "It was time for us to bow out gracefully while we still could."

"Gracefully, huh?" He lifted both his eyebrows at me. "When have you ever been graceful?"

I laughed and settled back into the booth with the plastic bench covers creaking under my ass when I moved. *Damn, it's good to be home.*

The humor faded from Ryan's eyes again as he looked back and forth between us. I spun my beer on the table in front of me, turning it slowly between my fingers before I leaned forward. "Out with it, Ryan. It's been a while, but you know us so just speak freely."

"I'm just struggling to get my head wrapped around this." He squinted at us. "You worked your butts off for years to get scholarships, to go to college, get drafted, rise up in the league, and now you're just home?"

"You worked your ass off too." Vance shrugged. "Yet, you turned it down before we even got to college."

"Sure, but that's just it. I never got the taste of the bright lights and big cities. Don't get me wrong. I'm damn glad you guys are back. I guess I just don't really understand it."

"There ain't no place like home, Ry," I said honestly. "You just have to be gone long enough for that truth to really sink in."

"It hits you in the nuts like a sack of bricks." Vance brought his glass to his lips and took a long sip of his beer. "How have things been around here?"

Ryan chuckled, shrugging as he took a look around. "Much the same as always, boys. There have been a few new developments, but nothing major. Where are you staying now that you're home?"

"I'm with my Mom," I said. "I want to build my own place eventually, and in the meantime, I wanted to rent a townhouse while I searched for a property, but Momma wasn't having it."

Ryan grinned. "Good old Momma Drake. Let me guess, she told you that over her dead body were you paying to stay someplace else when she has a perfectly good house—"

"Just standing there, mostly empty," I finished for him, chortling. "Exactly, yeah. Vance is at his parents' too."

"Yeah, but the difference is that I've already gone to look at a few places to live. The other benefit about moving back here is that we'll get way more bang for our buck. The old Granger place is on the market to buy for less than I paid for rent in a year back in New York. That big house on two acres of land with everything on it, and it costs a fraction of a fucking penthouse. It's ridiculous."

Ryan rocked his head from side to side, a flicker of something darker in his eyes as he nodded. "That's great, man. The old Granger place is awesome."

"It's probably going to get condemned," Vance joked. "If I buy it, I might as well build my own house because I'm going to have to do a lot of work, but I don't know. I guess we'll see how it goes."

"How about you?" I asked Ryan. "How's your family?"

While I didn't specifically mention Nova, I was hoping he would bring her up. Sitting across from him now, looking into the big blue eyes he shared with his sister, I couldn't *not* think about her. A pang of something shot through me, but it was gone too soon to identify what it had been.

"Same old, same old," Ryan said unhelpfully. "My parents are still on the ranch. Dad still thinks that time stopped moving forward somewhere in the nineties and Mom still makes that mean chicken casserole if you guys are interested in coming for dinner sometime."

"You still staying there?" Vance asked while I kept waiting for Ryan to mention the only member of his family he hadn't brought up so far.

My friend nodded. "We converted the old barn into a shop and apartment for me."

Since he was still silent on the subject, I reluctantly put it out there. "How's Nova?"

God, I had such a thing for that girl back in the day. Ryan had shut it down pretty quickly, though. He even pursed his lips at me now. "She's fine."

Leaving it at that, he questioned Vance about what kind of work the Granger place would need and offered to help him patch it up if he decided to buy it. I took the time to wonder about what had happened to Nova Murphy.

She'd had the potential to be the great love of that part of my life, and I still wasn't happy about the way things had ended with her. Not that I'd spent the last decade longing for her and obsessing over what might have been.

In fact, I'd gone the opposite way for a long time, but shit. Here I was, with her brother right across the table from me, talking about their ranch and their family. It was only natural to be thinking about her.

Wasn't it?

I hadn't seen her since before I'd even been drafted. While I had been home as often as I could make it to visit my mom, I'd never been in town for any extended periods of time and I'd never gone out enough to accidentally bump into the one who got away.

I was sure she'd long since moved on. She was probably married with a few kids by now, and the beer went sour in my mouth at the thought, so I banished it. *Enough. We're catching up with Ryan, not reliving the past right now.*

Still, it looked like Nova Murphy wasn't done haunting me just yet.

When I walked into my mother's house later that afternoon, she was unpacking a beautiful box of pastries, humming under her breath when I joined her in the kitchen.

"How did it go with Ryan?" she asked, picking up the box and presenting me with a multitude of mouthwatering treats.

I swiped one as I nodded at her. The delicious flavor exploded in my mouth. I groaned and reached for another. "It was good, yeah. Where'd you get these from? They're amazing."

"Aren't they?" She smiled. "Nova Murphy opened a bakery a few years ago and it's the best in town. Ryan didn't tell you?"

I shook my head. "Must've slipped his mind."

"Well, it's been years. I'm sure you boys had a lot to catch up on." She gave me an indulgent smile when I reached for yet another pastry, leaving the box in front of me when I sat down at the breakfast bar.

"So, Nova has a bakery now, huh? That's cool. Where's it at?"

"Red Stone Ranch." Mom gave me a weird look. "Did Ryan really not tell you about any of this?"

"Nope," I said around a mouthful of fluffy, buttery pastry. "What is there to tell?"

"Not much, really. I just thought he'd have wanted to brag a little bit about his baby sister. She's been working so hard, trying to help out her parents. She's really stretched herself thin since she moved back after college, but she still volunteers at the library a few times a week to read to the kids. A real angel, that girl. I'd have thought her brother would be more proud of her."

"I'm sure he is."

I changed the subject after that, but Nova lingered on my mind long after I went to bed, tossing and turning as I thought about those big blue eyes and her long, dark blonde hair.

Once upon a time, I'd felt things for her that I hadn't felt before or since, and while I hadn't come back here for her, I wondered if I should pop in at this bakery tomorrow. See what all the fuss was about and maybe, just maybe, get to catch a glimpse of what my life might've been like if things had gone differently.

# 3

## NOVA

S undays and Mondays were my days off. From the bakery, anyway. They were the only two days of the week we were closed, so naturally, that meant I spent them getting caught up on chores around the ranch.

Knee deep in hay in one of the barns, I could've sworn I heard a truck pull up at the main house. Since I wasn't expecting anyone or anything, I didn't go to see who it was. They weren't here for me, and if I didn't finish the mucking today, I'd just have to do it tomorrow—and there were more than enough things on my to-do list for tomorrow as it was.

Getting back to work, I lost myself in the routine, allowing it to clear my thoughts of worry and enjoying the burn it created in my muscles. Twisting my ponytail around itself, I snapped another band around my hair, effectively creating a messy bun to keep it off my neck.

I kept going until I was dripping with sweat, feeling it slide down my spine and my throat. *So that's where all the moisture in my body has gone.*

My mouth was bone dry and I wiped my brow with the back of

my forearm, resting the shovel against the wall before I pulled off the heavy work gloves. *Gah, I need a drink before I pass out.*

Glowing with heat, dirty, and covered in sweat, I headed around the back of the main house and stumbled into the kitchen—only to stop in my tracks once *he* came into view. Tall, handsome, broad-shouldered, and much too familiar even with his back to me, I recognized him instantly.

*Carson freaking Drake! What on God's green earth is* he *doing here?*

As soon as I saw him, my heartbeat turned into a hummingbird trying to take off in my chest and my mouth was still dry but in a whole different way now. Carson had always been built like a superhero. With what he'd wanted to do for a living, being ripped was part of the package, but these days?

*Holy hunkness.*

He didn't look like just any superhero anymore. He strongly resembled Thor, except that Carson's hair was dark as night and his eyes were an electric, almost otherworldly green. Outside of that though, he was definitely godly material.

Meanwhile, I looked like I'd jumped into a muddy puddle and then ran seven hours home. *Shit. Shit. Shit. Shit.*

I'd always known there was a chance I would see him again. With his mother still living in town and his friendship with Ryan distant but intact, it had never been beyond the realm of possibility that he'd appear out of the blue one day.

I just had *not* realized today would be that day, and to say that I was not prepared for it was the understatement of the century. To my mind, there was only one thing to do. *Run!*

My mother was standing in the middle of the kitchen, talking to Carson like he was her long-lost son. I soundlessly slid my feet backward to make a quick escape, but the movement must've caught my mother's eye because she suddenly looked right at me.

"Nova, honey! Look who's here. You remember Carson Drake, right? Come on in. Join us for some lemonade."

My heart pounded against my ribs as he slowly started turning to face me. For the first time in ten *fucking* years, and I looked like a rat who'd been drowned in dirt. *Shit.*

Like a buck in the headlights, I froze when he finally looked at me, my heart the only part of my body that was working. Those gorgeous, impossibly intense eyes burned into mine. A smile spread on his full lips as he looked at me with something like wonder softening his chiseled features.

*Oh, fuck no.*

Finally managing to awaken my limbs, I turned and bolted, not bothering to look back or to explain to my mother that I would not, in fact, be staying for the reunion she was trying to orchestrate.

Past the hammering of my heart in my ears, I heard her hollering after me. "Nova! Are you okay?"

I didn't stop. Didn't even consider it. I just fled right back to the barn and decided to pretend I'd never left it.

Carson hadn't become one of the best quarterbacks in the entire NFL by letting things go, though. A couple minutes later, he appeared in the wide open doorway, hands in his pockets as he strode in and smiled at me again.

"I'm sorry if I scared you back there."

*Aww, crap. That voice.*

The sound of it still made my knees weak. It was a little rougher and a little deeper now than it had been when I'd last heard it, but it was still so much the same that I would have recognized it even in the middle of the loudest rock concert the world had ever seen.

"You didn't scare me." I averted my gaze from his to focus on putting my work gloves back on. "I just, uh, I remembered that I hadn't finished the corner yet."

I tilted my head toward a corner of the barn—any corner—only to find that it was clean when I followed up the head tilt with a glance. *Oh, for crap's sake.*

Another smile played on Carson's lips. "You wanna try again?"

"Yes, please," I said. "Okay, fine. So that was an excuse. Obviously, I've already done that corner, but as you can see, there's plenty of work still to be done."

He made his way deeper inside the barn. Those broad shoulders stretched against the confines of his navy blue T-shirt as he moved. The fabric tugged around his biceps, chest, and abs, forming little lines that drew my gaze to them.

Chuckling when he caught me staring, he pulled his hands out of his pockets and motioned at his abs. "How about this? To apologize for scaring the living daylights out of you, I'll let you cop a feel."

"Jackass," I muttered, fighting laughter as I finally lifted my gaze back to his. "I don't want a feel. I was just noticing that you've replaced most of your muscles with steel. Are you trying to become Superman?"

"I already am." He gave me a playful smirk. "What have you been doing for the past ten years if you haven't seen any of my games? Because you wouldn't have to ask me that if you'd caught even one."

"Oh, you know. A little bit of this and a little bit of that." I stabbed a pile of hay on the floor. "Mostly this. Do you mind, Carson? I really do still have a lot of work."

As I asked the question, my eyes snagged on his instead of just continuing on past them like I had been doing. Looking right into them, I felt that same bolt of electricity shoot through me that used to be there when we were kids.

He and I had always had an intense connection. It was something I'd never had with anyone else, which was probably why I wasn't married and popping out a kid every other year. But I hadn't seen this man in over a decade and it was crazy to think it was still there.

*I probably just imagined it. Like a throwback rush or something.*

"I didn't intend on going into your parents' house, Nova. I came to check out the bakery. Mom gave me some of your pastries, and I needed more. But she didn't mention it was closed today. Your mom found me in the parking lot, dragged me inside, and tried to feed me."

"Yeah, she tends to do that," I said. "I think she hangs out there on Sundays and Mondays with the express purpose of finding hungry people who had hoped to get something from the bakery just so she can feed them."

"Well, I'm not complaining."

"Few people do when my mother feeds them." I smiled. "It was good to see you, but I really should get back to it."

"Of course." He looked so comfortable breathing in the scent of poop and standing in the middle of a barn that it was like he hadn't spent a decade living the high life. "I'll have to come out to the bakery some other time. See you around, Nova."

He tossed his hand up in a friendly wave and left, and my heart caught fire. I was even panting with the force of it, so completely thrown by having him on the ranch again that it felt like it might've been a dream.

It had been real, though. I could still see him as he walked toward a large black truck parked in our drive. When I'd seen him just now in the kitchen, I'd figured he was just in town for a quick visit, but now, I remembered Cassidy saying he'd retired, and Mom had mentioned friends of Ryan's who had moved back to town.

*Carson might be back for good.*

Unease spread through me at the thought. Having Carson back in town might turn my whole life upside down. I doubted it would be good, especially if that connection of ours was still there.

As I watched his truck pull out of the driveway, I thought back to the night he'd kissed me. It was during a bonfire just before he'd gotten drafted. He'd told me that he wanted to date me and I'd wanted to be with him too, but Ryan had seen the kiss and got into a big fight with Carson about it.

Without a word to me, Carson had left and today had been the first time I'd seen or spoken to him since. I had no idea what to do or how to feel about it, but when I finally went back inside to get that drink, my mother wouldn't shut up about him.

He'd always had a fan in her, though, and it looked like that hadn't changed. I hopped up on the kitchen counter, listening to her go on and on and wondering what it was about him that enchanted us Murphy women so.

Whatever it was, that hadn't changed in the last ten years either, and I shuddered to think what my brother would do if he ever found out. *Yeah, I think it's best if I stay away from Carson Drake.*

For Ryan's sake and for my own.

Because I'd lost him once and I wasn't sure I could go through that all over again.

# 4

## CARSON

Back in the room that had been mine as a kid, I unpacked a little bit. It was pretty fucking weird, sliding clothes back into these closets when I'd once felt such a sense of finality and triumph when I'd emptied them.

I sighed, grabbed a pile of T-shirts from the suitcase open on my bed, and dumped them onto the dusty shelf. Staying in this room again was like stepping back in time. In all the years I'd been gone, Mom hadn't touched it at all.

My maroon, navy, and dark green bedding was still on the small double bed, and posters of all my heroes—including Carson Palmer, who I'd been named for—still covered the walls. The desk was clean, but my textbooks from high school and college lined the shelf beside it.

Medals, trophies, and award certificates I'd received back then sat spotless on top of the dresser, the bookshelf, and in frames on the wall, telling me that while Mom had definitely been cleaning in here, she hadn't even taken down the last class schedule I'd taped to the mirror senior year.

I blew out a heavy breath and sank down on the bed, kicking my feet up on the side of my suitcase and folding my arms behind my head as I stared at the ceiling. For a cool decade, I'd been living in one state or another, jumping from city to city during the season and never even thinking about slowing down.

I hadn't put down any roots at all, not even buying a place for the off-season like most of my teammates had done. But now that I was back in Silver Springs, I wanted to do just that. Buy some property. Build a house. Get this new chapter of my life started.

But it felt really damn wrong to be lying on my bed in my mother's house at noon on a Monday at age thirty-one. Kicking back in the middle of the day was bad enough, but add in all those other factors and it felt like the walls were about to close in on me.

Loud voices sounded from downstairs and I sat up, frowning as I tried to figure out if they belonged to who I thought they belonged to.

My bedroom door crashed open, and Vance and Ryan burst through it like a thunderstorm.

"Whoa, it's like a time capsule," Ryan said. "This room hasn't changed at all."

Vance strode in like he'd last been here yesterday, and he nodded toward me in bed. "Carson's even getting ready to spank it. Things really haven't changed."

I laughed and sat up against the headboard. "Yeah, I was thinking about your mom, and I couldn't control myself."

"So it *is* just like high school." Ryan grinned and sat down on the desk.

Vance pulled out my desk chair and sat backward on it just like he always used to. A mental image of the two of them in those exact positions in this room, but twenty years ago, popped into my head.

"No," Vance said. "If it was like high school, he wouldn't be thinking about my mom. He'd be thinking about your—"

I tossed a rolled-up pair of socks at Vance's head before he could mention Ryan's sister. "Can we stop talking about jerking off? My mom is right downstairs."

Ryan guffawed, not noticing Vance's slip-up. Relief washed over me. I didn't want to dredge up that old fight, especially since everyone was in a good mood.

"What were you doing, then?" Ryan asked. "Your mom said you've been shut in here for a while."

I scrubbed my hands over my face. "Anyone else feel like we've gone back fifteen years or so?"

"Oh, yeah," Ryan said immediately. "I've been feeling that way since I found out you two were home, though. Didn't think we'd ever live in the same town again, but especially not this one."

"How am I going to sleep on this tiny thing?" I motioned at the bed, stretching out to show them what I meant. All four limbs dangled off the mattress when I spread out.

Vance started giggling like a little girl. "You look like a turtle on its back."

"You might want to rethink renting a place and buying some furniture you actually fit on," Ryan said. "Or maybe sleep on the floor."

Vance jerked his head at a calendar from the early oughts on my nightstand. "That model standing next to the motorcycle has six kids now. Poor woman has been locked in a custody battle with her rocker ex for years now."

I sighed and turned the "babes and motorcycles" calendar face-down. "Well, thanks for ruining that for me."

Vance nudged Ryan with his elbow. "You still got your bike? The scrambler?"

"I sure do." Ryan smirked. "I bet I could also still kick your ass on it. Still got yours?"

Vance had to think about it before he shrugged. "Yeah, I think it might be under a cover in Mom's garage. I'll have to check, though. I honestly haven't even thought to go in there."

Ryan glanced between us again, sighing as he shook his head. "Well, at least now I know you still don't care about your bike as much as you should. Anyway, are you ever going to tell me why you're really home? You both were living the dream, and you're telling me you just left it all behind for life in Silver Springs?"

"We did." I dropped my elbows on my knees and shrugged.

"We're too old to be taking hits now, man. If I kept going for just one more season, I'd have the knees of an eighty-year-old."

Ryan scoffed. "We're not *that* old."

"Maybe *you're* not." Vance snorted. "We've been in the NFL for a decade, Ry. That's a decade of putting our bodies on the line day, after day, after day. Eventually, it starts leaving a mark. Well, I already reached *leaving a mark* about five years ago. By the end of last season, my body was warning me to take it easy."

"Same," I agreed. "It was just a matter of time before pushing so hard would lead to a permanent injury. A career-ending injury. I just figured, what was the point of success if I wouldn't be healthy enough to enjoy it? I figured it was time to make space for the new kids on the block. The boys with the golden arms who are in their early twenties and who still have strong bones."

"Fair enough." Ryan paused, then let out a soft burst of laughter. "God, I can't believe we're those guys now. The old guys. Yesterday, *you* were the new kid with the golden arm."

"Feels that way." I smirked at him. "Sometimes, it feels like it happened overnight, this whole becoming a veteran thing. One day, we were fresh out of the draft, and the next, we were fresh over the hill, in football years. It's insane."

"Yeah, it really is," Vance said, then inhaled deeply and cracked a smile. "Is that your mom's famous mac and cheese I smell? Man, it really is the good old days in here."

"Life was a lot simpler back then," I said. "There are worse things than being back in the good old days."

Ryan grimaced when I said it. It was just a flash and then it was gone, but that flash made it clear that he was still a little bit bitter about everything that had happened back then. Probably a little of it had to do with his sister and me, but I had a feeling it was more about everything else than it was about that.

The guy had been just as good a football player as Vance and me —if not better. All those dreams we'd dreamed growing up, he'd dreamed with us. He'd put in the same hours we had. Kept to the same rigid training schedules and diets.

But when the time had come, he'd rejected a scholarship at a big school to go into the trades. While Vance and I had gone to play football as planned, Ryan had stayed behind to work for his family. I still didn't understand it.

It had come out of nowhere back then, and even though we'd lost touch at times and resumed it at others, I still didn't know what had really happened. If it was still hurting him, though, I wasn't about to push. Not yet.

"So you've still got your bike," I said. "I'm willing to bet you have a few new stories about her."

Sufficiently distracted, Ryan grinned and launched into a few colorful descriptions of trips he'd taken over the years.

They stayed for a couple hours and we shot the breeze, and when they left, I went to hunt down my mom in the kitchen. Weird as it might be to be home, having her so close after so long was a definite benefit.

Her jet-black hair was now shot through with streaks of silver, and crow's feet were etched into the skin around her eyes. It was clear every time I looked at her how much time had really passed. How many years had gone by when I'd barely gotten to spend any time at all with her.

"Did you get to visit the bakery?" she asked as she sat down at the breakfast bar with me, wearing her standard jeans and a white blouse with puffy sleeves. "Oh, no. Wait. Nova wasn't open, was she? I'm so sorry I forgot to tell you, honey. Please tell me I didn't waste your time by sending you to a closed store."

"You could never waste my time, Mom," I said without a word of a lie. "I went by there, but most of the baskets in the windows were empty. They seemed pretty sold out."

"She always is," Mom said fondly, her eyes crinkling in a smile. She glanced at the empty pastry box next to the garbage bin. "Nova's place is wonderfully popular around here. She changed our lives the day she opened it. She bakes with the town's recipes but without us having to make it all ourselves. It's been a real game-changer."

I listened with interest, trying to hide the intensity of it behind going to get myself some water. "That's great. I'm happy if it's going well with the Murphys."

Mom smiled sadly when I glanced at her over my shoulder. "I never said that, but at least her businesses are doing well."

"So what else has she been up to all these years?" I asked off-handedly, knowing that my mom knew the answers I was craving.

She knew everything about everyone. Not because she was a gossip but because people loved talking to her. A pillar of the community, salt of the earth type of woman who always just wanted to help.

"That's what she's been up to," Mom said. "Since she got home from college, anyway. Armed with a degree in Agriculture from Oklahoma State University, she came back to twist George's arm to let her open a bakery on the ranch."

A faraway look crept into Mom's eyes, her mouth twisting in sympathy. "He and Mara sure got lucky with those kids, both sticking around just when they needed help most."

My insides were burning about curiosity to find out more. Ryan and Nova were both proud people. Too proud to ask for help and too stubborn to accept it even if they needed it, but damn.

It didn't sound like life had been kind to them while I'd been gone. I just didn't know yet what all it had thrown at them or how they had made it through.

# 5

## NOVA

After a long day of farm chores, I kicked off my boots on my little front porch and walked into my cottage by the creek, looking forward to a nice, cool shower. My muscles were aching, my skin was a little hot from all the sun I'd gotten, and my head was gloriously quiet.

Humming to myself, I made my way past my kitchen and across my living area before ascending the stairs to my loft-style bedroom. All the stress, the work, and the worry of a ranch was so worth it when this was what I got to come home to.

Dad and I had built my cottage with our own hands after I'd come back from Oklahoma, and not a day went by when I wasn't grateful for my tiny slice of heaven when I walked in. It was nothing fancy. Most folks these days would call it rustic, but I loved my wooden sanctuary by the water.

Set in a grove of trees right up against the riverbank, I had a cozy deck overlooking the water and the mountains. I also had a fireplace, a living room with a small, round dining table, a bedroom, a bathroom, and all the privacy I needed even though my parents and my brother also lived on the same property.

Striding over to the sliding doors leading out to the deck, I opened them to let in some fresh air. The sound of the bubbling stream outside greeted me as the water flowed past. I breathed in the scent of earth and pine, feeling tension ease from my shoulders.

I heard an engine outside, moving closer until it cut off right in front of my door. The serenity of the moment was broken. I turned to see who it was, and Ryan's heavy footsteps coming up the few stairs to my porch answered the question for me.

I groaned. *So much for my long, cool shower.*

I walked into my kitchen instead. Like everything else about my cottage, the kitchen was small, but it was open-concept with a country-style layout. A center island had my stove in it and my pots and pans hung from rails above.

Dad had mounted plenty of shelves. We'd left them open instead of installing cabinets, but we'd done it to save money, only finding out about a year later that open shelving had become a trend.

I grabbed a bottle of whiskey and swiped two glasses off a shelf just as the door swung open and my brother walked in. Ryan took after my father. They were both built as tall and as sturdy as horses, with dark hair and a constant five-o-clock shadow on their jaws despite how often they shaved.

I was the spitting image of my mother, with light hair and fair skin. She and I could've been sisters, but Ryan had gotten nothing except her eyes. My eyes. We'd also both inherited our father's stubborn streak.

My brother didn't stop walking until he could reach the bottle I was holding out toward him. Then he kept right on going, taking the glasses and the bottle with him as he strode out onto my deck. I followed, both of us kicking up our feet on the table outside after we sat down.

It was something of a ritual for us. We did it at least once a week, both of us looking out at the land we loved so much for a few silent minutes before we even said anything.

After he poured us each a generous drink, he finally glanced at me. "I heard Frank came by again."

"Yep." I leaned back against a cushion Mom and I had made

ourselves for my chairs out here. Every inch of this cottage and every-thing in it was *me*. Mine. And Frank would tear it all down to build a resort or something. The very blood in my veins turned bitter at the thought of it. "He'll go away eventually. We just need to keep saying no."

My brother raked a hand through his thick hair, his head shaking. "We're going to have to do more than just say no, Nova. It's getting to that point now where we can't just keep thinking it's all going to work out in the end."

"It will work out in the end," I said. "As long as Dad *lets* us work it out."

He barked out a dry laugh. "You know he's not going to let us do that. Which is exactly why we're in this situation."

I couldn't argue with that. Ryan and I both loved our father as much as we did the ranch, each other, and our lives, but the man was stubborn as a mule. A quiet moment passed between us until I spoke again. "Did you go check the eastern border fence today?"

"Yep. It's coming down. Again."

I groaned. "I really thought it was going to hold for longer than this. I just fixed it last month."

"It doesn't need fixing anymore, Nova. What it needs is to be replaced," he said in a hushed voice, like he was scared even saying it out loud would make the fence fall down for good. Although with the state of things around here these days, he probably wasn't wrong. "That entire section between Murphy's Rock and the Ridge is fucked. You can only repair something so many times before it's time to let it go, and it's time to let that go."

Worry formed a rock at the center of my chest as I did a few quick calculations in my head. "We can't let it go. Do you have any idea how much it's going to cost to replace even just that section?"

"Yep."

"We don't have that kind of money, Ry. It's rocky over there, which makes it even more expensive. My best guess is fifteen thousand or up."

"Up," he said.

My stomach flipped. "We definitely don't have that kind of money."

"Nope."

I made a face at him as my eyes narrowed. "Are you going to add anything useful to this conversation?"

Frustration zapped across his features, hardening them as he shot a glare in the direction of the distant main house. We couldn't even see it from here, but I knew that was where he was looking. "What do you want me to say, Novie? That we don't have the money? We don't have the money."

As I turned back to the view of the sun dipping behind the mountain, a shaky breath rattled out of me and fear gripped my insides in its icy clutches. "We're going to lose it, aren't we? All of it."

I saw my own emotions reflected back at me from Ryan's eyes when they met mine. "Probably, yeah. Unless we can convince Dad to expand. I still think we should turn some of the grazing land into hay, wheat, and corn fields. It's not an immediate fix, but at least it'll provide some decent income once we get it going."

"I know." Ryan had been saying that for months now. I looked into it and he was right. Our father, however, didn't want to hear it. "If he keeps refusing to build cabins for tourists, we could still start a social media page. Advertise the business. Build a brand. Again, though, it'll also take time. None of our ideas are immediate fixes."

"It doesn't matter because Dad's not going to go for it anyway." We lapsed into silence for a beat, but Ryan suddenly grew tense, his mouth opening and closing like there was something he wanted to say but he was having trouble with it.

"What?" I asked. "Talk to me. If you've got another idea, tell me what it is and I'll help you pitch it to him."

"It's not an idea so much as it is taking an offer." My brother turned his head to look at me fully. "Frank's offer, actually."

Disbelief so intense that it made my ears ring smacked me in the face. "Excuse me?"

He sighed, raking both hands through his hair as he held my gaze, his own blues as haunted as mine right now, but he pushed on anyway. "Just hear me out, okay? It's a last resort, but I've looked into it and that offer he made Dad really wasn't bad. If we sell all but a third of the land, we could keep our houses and your bakery intact. Dad would have to downsize the cattle, but we'd still have some. We'd also be able to keep the sheep and hogs."

Indignation raced through me, but as much as I hated what Frank stood for and what he represented, I hadn't heard any of the people in town complain that he'd swindled them. As far as I knew, most people liked him as much as dog shit on their shoe, but even then, he was known for making fair offers.

He would have been run out of town a long time ago if folks started talking about him tricking people out of their properties.

I didn't even know what he'd offered Dad. I'd never asked, but if Ryan thought it was a good price and if Frank would be willing to buy only two-thirds of the ranch and let us keep the rest, then perhaps it was something we had to consider.

It would be futile anyway. Dad would rather run this place into the ground before selling off the land that had been in our family since before the town had settled. Still, it was a possibility Ryan and I could keep in our back pockets as a last resort—just like he'd said.

Desperate times called for desperate measures, and times had never been more desperate for the Murphys.

I nodded slowly as I looked at my brother again. "Okay, if the time ever comes, I'll have your back. We'll pitch the idea to Dad together. At least it would mean that we wouldn't lose it all."

Ryan gave me a sad smile. "We still might, Novie. You never know. It kind of makes me wish I had gone to play football back in the day, you know? I thought I was helping by staying here, but right around now, retiring with a fat bank account sure sounds more useful than helping with chores."

My heart sputtered. "Speaking of which, I heard that Carson's in town."

"Vance too," he said, but he didn't seem too interested in talking about it. "Will you pass me the whiskey?"

I picked up the bottle but didn't hand it over just yet. "You could've given me a heads-up that Carson was back, asshole. It would have been nice if I'd been able to brace for impact."

Ryan plucked the bottle from between my fingers and waved me off with his free hand. "Why should you care that he's back? You guys haven't even talked in, what, ten years?"

Instead of pouring himself another drink like I'd expected him to, he pushed the chair back with a soft scrape and stood up. "You know what? You look like you need a shower and some rest, and so do I. We'll talk tomorrow, okay?"

I didn't bother walking him out. Ryan came and went from here like it was his place. I bit my lip and tightened my grip on my drink as he left.

As much as I hated to admit it, my brother was right about this. Why should I care that Carson was back? After he'd left without a word and never contacted me again, he'd made himself pretty clear. We'd had a thing, but that was all it had been.

A thing. A fling—and not even a full-fledged one at that.

The best thing I could do was forget that he'd come home at all. I'd resolved to do just that the other day, but I hadn't been able to stop thinking about him. As I downed the rest of my whiskey and trudged upstairs to my bathroom to finally grab that shower, I pushed Carson Drake out of my mind.

That boy—man, now—was hot as Hades, but just as much trouble. There was enough trouble in my life as it was. The last thing I needed was to invite more by allowing him into my head or my heart again.

It was over between us and it had been for a long time. All it needed to do was stay that way.

# 6

## CARSON

First thing Tuesday morning, I headed back to the bakery. For a girl who'd barely crossed my mind in at least eight years, Nova sure was back in full force. It was almost funny how fast it had happened. Maybe she had never really left my thoughts, and she was just waiting patiently for me to rediscover her.

As Red Stone Ranch came into view, I frowned and leaned forward, blinking just to make sure I wasn't imagining things, but no. The bakery was right at the very edge of the property, with just a parking lot between it and the road—and there was already a line out the door.

*Holy shit. I'm impressed.*

I steered off the road onto the gravel of the lot, driving all the way to the ass end before I managed to find a spot. After I parked, I joined the line and chatted with some locals as we slowly shuffled our way forward.

Occasionally, fans would approach me. Even though I was retired, I understood my success and good fortune were all because of them. I had trained hard and I had sacrificed my body on the field, but if no one bought tickets, none of it would have mattered. The least I could do was sign whatever they wanted me to sign and pose for pictures if they wanted one.

In between, I enjoyed talking to the people in line that I'd known before. They filled me in on bits and pieces about everything that had happened in town while I'd been gone. They thanked me for the donations I had made to the community.

All while inhaling the most delicious scents in the world, which was both heaven and torture. I'd eaten this morning, but my stomach was snarling by the time I finally made it inside.

The bakery was on one side of the building. On the other, a coffee shop led out onto a patio that had been built at the back. Glass sliding doors all around meant the entire space could be closed if it was cold, and it had a homely, country feel to it.

I grinned and looked around for Nova, surprised when I saw Cassidy Markus emerging from the kitchen instead. She squeaked when her gaze landed on mine, and I chuckled, holding my hands out as I approached her. "Can I take that for you? It looks heavy."

"Car—" She cleared her throat, glancing down at the basket of bread in her arms like she was only just remembering that it was even there. "Carson Drake. It's good to have you back in town, but I'm not letting you touch these loaves. You'll have to wait like everyone else."

I grinned. "You saw right through my devious plan. If I promise not to steal any, can I help?"

She handed over the basket gratefully and wiped some flour from her hands onto her apron. "Well, I'm Cassi—"

"I remember you, Cassidy," I said, laughing as I followed her to the shelf the basket had to go on. "We had AP math together, right?"

Her eyes grew wide as she stared up at me with a slight crease between her eyebrows. "I didn't even realize you knew I was in that class."

I shrugged and tapped my temple. "Well, I'm a jock, and my head has taken a few hits, but there's a few things still rattling around in here."

Cassidy flushed a bright, glowing red, stammering when she

finally managed to find her voice. "I wasn't trying to say you forgot. I meant, like, you never knew in the first place."

"That's okay. I know what you meant. We ran in different circles, but it's a small town. It's not like we were friends, but I knew you were there." I chuckled and slid the basket into place before I turned to look at her again. With her sleek, high ponytail and those soft brown eyes, she hadn't changed a bit in the last decade. Unless I was very much mistaken, Ryan used to have a crush on her. I wondered if that was still true.

It might've been true for me too if Nova hadn't captured my attention so completely back in the day. "Is she here?"

"She?" Cassidy asked, raising an eyebrow.

I nodded. "The woman of the hour, I mean. My mom said she started this place?"

"Nova?" Cassidy grinned at me. "Yeah, she did. This place. The coffee shop. The market. It's all her. I'm just here to help her bake and to tend the counter when she's not around. I don't know when that girl sleeps. But no, she's not here. She went to the library for read-aloud."

"Right. I heard about that, too."

Cassidy smoothed a hand over her ponytail, pulling it over her shoulder. She kept staring at me, her expression becoming increasingly more curious. "Do you want me to tell her you came by?"

*Shit.* "No, thank you. That's okay. I was just wondering if she had some recommendations on what to get."

Cassidy jerked her head, motioning for me to follow her. "Now, I know you're fresh off the boat from the big city, and some of the folks over there might argue with me about this, but Nova's bear claws are better than anything you've ever had."

"Load me up." I grabbed a box to fill and added some other pastries to it while she led me to said bear claws. "Let me take some home to my mom as well then."

"Your mom was the one who insisted she make these," Cassidy said lightly. "It's been a really popular addition to our menu. Here you go."

"Thanks for letting me jump the line," I said, winking at her.

"Thanks for helping a girl out. And come back sometime when Nova's here and tell her how much you like her bear claws."

Someone else grabbed her attention and she left, practically jogging back to the counter as she took over from a younger girl who seemed frazzled. I packed my box, paid, and left. As I devoured some in the truck on my way to the library, I marveled at how good the pastries were.

I wasn't sure when I had decided to go to the library, but it was my destination. I had gone to the bakery and Nova hadn't been there, and now I was stalking her at a read-aloud. *Not my finest moment, that's for sure.*

There was something about Nova that sucked me in, though. There always had been. She just had this magnetic force about her that I couldn't resist. On the other hand, I'd never really tried to resist. I was a gut-guy. If my gut said to do something, I generally listened.

Right now, it was telling me to track her down. I didn't think she was in danger or anything quite as dramatic. I just wanted to see her. That was all there was to it.

As I pulled up in front of the library, I grinned when I noticed the renovated facade. Pride for the part I'd played in making it possible puffed up my chest a little bit.

They'd done a good job plastering and repainting it and giving it a bit of an upgrade while maintaining as much of the original look and structure as they could. I stuffed another pastry in my mouth, realizing that I was going to have to start working out just as hard as I used to if I wanted to keep eating like this. Then I climbed out of the car, jogged up to the steps, and went inside.

Nova sat in front of a group of little kids and some parents in a nook right off the foyer, reading animatedly and making everyone laugh. I stood right out of her sight, skirting around the shelves surrounding the nook and then watching her from close to the librarian's desk.

"Little Red Riding Hood ran through the woods," Nova said emphatically, making her eyes big at the kids as she ducked like she was dodging tree branches. "She was a smart and savvy girl, who kept her coat tight around her so she didn't catch a cold, and her eyes were wide open, not missing a thing. She took note of landmarks so she wouldn't get lost in the woods and she was careful not to get turned around."

I chuckled softly, glad I'd decided to stay out of sight for now. She was so wrapped up in the story she was telling—not really reading— that she hadn't noticed me at all and I was getting a kick out of seeing her like this.

Nova was a true country sweetheart, a girl who loved her ranch, her family, her town, and its people so much that she would never even mention leaving. Her long blonde hair was braided into pigtails today, but not those elaborate braids that took hours to accomplish.

When I'd known her, Nova had never spent more than a few minutes on her hair. Same with her face. She had a beautiful, heart-shaped face with a smattering of freckles across her nose and naturally long, black eyelashes.

I'd always thought she didn't take so long to get ready because she was already so fucking gorgeous that she didn't need to spend hours getting done up. Now, I had a feeling that it was because she'd just never had hours to spend on stuff like that.

Even back when she was a kid, she'd worked hard on the ranch. Her golden skin and curvy but toned body proved it. Her muscles were lithe and defined under her hourglass figure. Sitting on a large beanbag as she read, she wore faded denim jeans with little rips and tears everywhere that I was willing to bet hadn't been put there by the manufacturer.

Behind me, the librarian stood with two parents whose son had just run to join the group, and although I was focused on Nova's animated storytelling, I couldn't help but overhear when they started talking.

"She's a real gem, that girl," the mother gushed. "Joshie refuses to miss her read-aloud. We're practically at the point where we're counting down the days until Tuesday."

From the corner of my eye, I saw the librarian chuckle as she leaned in. "He's not the only one. All the kids love her. It's just a shame her family is going through what they're going through at the ranch. One of these days, we might just lose her because of it."

I half turned, keeping my attention mostly on Nova but now also making sure I could hear every word they were saying. I shouldn't be eavesdropping, but I couldn't resist. Neither Ryan nor Nova had mentioned anything to me about what they were *going through* at the ranch, and they were my friends.

I was concerned. And okay, I was curious too. My mother had hinted at problems and now these people were discussing it as well. Clearly, it wasn't really a secret that they were in trouble. It seemed the whole town knew, and I wanted to know what was going on too.

The man's face hardened. "It's not helping that they've had that developer sniffing around. I wish he'd just leave 'em alone. Money troubles are hard enough without having a jackass like that preying on you in your weakest moments."

My eyes narrowed and my pulse spiked. They were being preyed on by a developer and they hadn't mentioned it to me?

I didn't like that. At all.

Especially not because they had money troubles and I had money. Money that I wanted to invest in this town and they both knew it.

Sighing softly, I shook my head and left, keeping a low profile by shuffling my way back around the shelving so no one would see me. Ryan was one of my oldest friends and I knew he was proud, but shit. I needed to pay him a visit soon and see if there was anything I could do to help.

The Murphys were an institution in this town and with its people. Even if they hadn't been my friends as well, I would have wanted to help. The only question now was whether they'd let me—or whether that legendary pride would stand in their way.

# 7

## NOVA

A soft snick sounded as I turned the key in the lock, smiling at the end of another successful day in the bakery. I was dog tired, my feet aching and my arms like jelly, but when I turned and saw my parents out on their early evening stroll around the property, I broke into a jog to catch up.

"Hey, guys," I called to their backs, taking a moment to study their profiles from this angle.

They walked hand in hand with the sun setting over the mountains and the fields stretching out ahead of them. Dad was tall and dark, his hair shot through with streaks of silver these days, while Mom was as blonde as ever, petite enough to fit perfectly under his arm when he slid it around her shoulder.

At the sound of my voice, they stopped walking and waited for me. A fond, loving smile broke out across Mom's lips when I caught up to them, and she reached out, brushing some stray flour off my shirt.

"If only the flour was seeds and we were sowing them for your bread to grow from the earth," she said wistfully. "What a blessing that would have been. The best of both worlds. We'd have your bakery stocked to capacity every day without you having to work so hard to keep up."

I chuckled, falling into step with them as they started moving again. "It sure would be interesting to see baked goods pop up from the ground, but I'm not sure what we would've done about pest control."

"Or looting," Dad grumbled from Mom's other side. "If the whole property was just littered with Nova's creations, we'd never be able to keep people off it."

"Always the pessimist," Mom said as she fought a smile and turned her head to press a kiss to his shoulder. "It would've been something, though. Wouldn't it?"

"Something of a riot," he joked as he winked at me over the top of her head. "How'd it go today, kiddo?"

"So well. We sold out of everything. Again." I grinned at him. "How would you feel about expanding the coffee shop into a full-blown restaurant? We'd have to be open at night, but—"

"You work too hard as it is, honey," Mom interjected, nudging me with her hip as she sent me a soft smile. "If you start a restaurant, you'll never sleep again."

"Besides," Dad said, taking her side without skipping a beat. "We couldn't be *more* proud of you. My chest would burst. Is that what you want, to have my heart pop if I became even prouder?"

I pushed down a laugh. "Of course not. I'm pretty confident it wouldn't actually pop, though. I don't think that's how it works."

Dad chuckled as he shrugged. "How would you know? Unless you're a doctor now, too."

"Oh, I'm a doctor, alright," I retorted playfully. "I've successfully completed my doctorate in common sense several times over. That's how I know."

Mom let out a soft giggle as she shook her head at us. "You two have the most absurd arguments, but I love it." She glanced at me, worry filling her eyes as she looped her arm around mine. "If you really want a restaurant, honey, we'll support you, but even longer hours?"

She blew out a heavy breath, silent for a moment as dirt crunched under our boots and a light breeze washed over our faces. Dipping her head toward the sky, she inhaled deeply, closing her eyes before smiling at me again. It was a soft, reluctant smile, but I appreciated that she was pushing through the worry.

"We're so proud of you baby. You've been working so hard for so long, and we never want to stand in your way, but restaurants are a tough business and you're already selling out of everything almost every day. We could probably keep up with the increased meat supply, so it's not that. I just worry that you'd lose what little bit of a life you have left if you do that."

"Work is my life," I insisted. "This *ranch* is my life. My home. Increased meat supply means more money for the farming operations. That's a good thing, right?"

"Not if it steals the last bit of time you've got left for yourself." Mom sighed and looked at Dad, who was staring at our mountain as he shook his head.

"The farming operation isn't yours to keep afloat, sweetheart. Our family has fallen upon hard times before and we've always made it through. This is no different. Ranching flows through our veins. We'll pull through."

Frustration bubbled through *my* veins. Ranching might be in it too, but the frustration was definitely stronger right now. The Murphys had always pulled through. He was right about that part, but we'd done it by being smart and staying with the times.

With the attitude he'd taken that everything would be okay as long as we worked hard, I wasn't sure we were going to make it through this time. I didn't mind working hard. In fact, I couldn't help it. It was my duty to my parents to save the farm, but I'd meant when I said this place was my home and I'd be damned if someone like Frank sold it off to the highest bidder and turned it into high-rises or worse—a mall.

Ryan had made a good point the other day about only selling two-thirds of the property. As a last resort, it made sense, but we weren't there yet. For now, our neighbors were other ranches and there wasn't a condo in sight.

I would fight tooth and nail to keep it that way, but pigheaded confrontation with my dad wasn't the way to change his mind. I could tell him he was wrong, but if I did, he'd only dig in his heels. With him, Ryan and I needed a rock-solid plan and we needed to pitch it together.

Besides, I didn't really want a restaurant. It was just an idea I'd been toying with for a little while, but honestly, I didn't think it would make much of a difference to the overall expenses on the farm either.

"You guys have a good walk," I said once we started nearing my cottage. "I'm meeting Cass in town for a drink. I'll see you tomorrow, okay?"

"Okay, honey. Be safe." Mom gave me a quick hug and brushed a kiss to my cheek, and Dad ruffled my hair like I was still six years old.

"Don't stay out too late, kid. You need your rest."

I smiled, fighting the urge to roll my eyes at the old man. "You got it, Daddy. Love you both."

"We love you too, baby." Mom cuddled into Dad's side as they resumed their walk.

Back in my cottage, I washed up before I headed out to meet Cassidy at Moe's.

I pulled into the parking lot, gravel crunching under my tires as I slowed to a stop. Green neon lights winked at me from the sign above the door. Country music spilled out from inside, and since it was a warm night, there were groups of people gathered near the open doors, swaying to the rhythm as they sipped their beers and smoked the cigarettes they'd stepped outside for.

As the primary hangout in town, the bar was always busy, but the parking lot was a little fuller tonight than it usually was on a weekday. Women in skimpy outfits sauntered around and the guys acted macho, walking around like they were carrying watermelons under their arms and their chests a little more puffed out.

I chuckled as I took it all in from my truck. Then I hopped out, wondering what Moe's had done to draw the larger crowd. Probably another drink special, which made me wish *I* could run those too. A night like this had to rake in serious amounts of cash.

Adding it to the mental pile of ideas to make more money, I walked in and found Cassidy bundled into a tiny booth at the back. She waved at me and I wound my way through the bodies packing the interior and dropped down opposite my friend. Angel that she was, she had already ordered us each a beer.

"Crazy night," she said, speaking up to be heard over the sound of chatter and music. "Do you have any idea what's going on?"

"Ladies' night?" I guessed. "Maybe they've changed it to Wednesdays?"

She shrugged a shoulder, not looking convinced, but then she let it go and turned her attention to me. "I've got some good news. We sold out of pastries before ten a.m. and a lot of people are asking if they can start placing orders. I thought it might be something you'd be interested in."

"Definitely," I said. "I could use all the money I can get, but we'd have to work out the logistics. It's a relief that we're still selling out, though. I was wondering if it was going to last."

Cassidy raked a hand through her loose blonde hair, a thoughtful haze in her eyes until she blinked it away. "It's not helping much, is it? The money the bakery is bringing in, I mean. We can work out logistics all we want, but is it going to help?"

"It has to," I replied, hating that she was so worried about it all. "It'll help, Cass. Every bit helps. Ryan and I are trying to save up for some advertising for the farm to try to drive business, but it's insanely expensive. If I start taking orders and we have regular clients whose money we can count on, that could be a game-changer."

She gave me a cautious smile. "Well, I'm onboard, but only if you promise to think about getting extra help. You can't keep doing it all, babe. It's just too much."

I waved her off, deciding not to keep fretting about it tonight. It was bad enough that the situation on the ranch *always* came up. I didn't want to become *that* person who couldn't talk about anything else.

"We'll work it out." I brought my bottle to my lips and took a long sip. "In the meantime, what's new with you? How was the date with Bobby?"

Her nose crinkled as she laughed. "It was a disaster, and not the beautiful kind. I don't even know why I bother. Dating is the worst. I think I should take a page out of your book and stop doing it. At least for a while."

"Nah, don't do that. Mr. Right is out there for you. You just have to be patient until you find him."

A commotion at the doors made me twist in my seat to see what was going on, and Cassidy suddenly let out a dreamy sigh. "If only one of those two could be my Mr. Right, I'd be as patient as I needed to be."

*Those two* were Carson and Vance, and they were also the reason for the commotion. As soon as they walked in, people flocked to them, which made me wonder if they were also the reason for the busy night here at Moe's.

If word had gotten out that they were frequenting the place now that they were back, it explained why so many more people had turned up tonight, hoping to catch a glimpse of our very own superstars. I rolled my eyes and turned back to her.

"Don't tell me you're also buying into the whole *hometown heroes* thing." I gave her an exasperated look. "They're the same guys we used to know."

"Sure, but now they're famous, rich, and more ripped than ever." She shot me a beaming smile. "You've got to be the only woman in town who's not especially happy that they're here to stay. Fresh meat. Fair game. Hot as hell. They're causing something of a feeding frenzy."

I laughed, but she wasn't wrong. All those scantily clad girls were vying for their attention, draping themselves all over them at the bar and pressing their *assets* into their faces. Part of me felt a little sorry for them until I saw the expression of glee on Vance's face.

I couldn't see Carson's, since he had his back to me, but it wasn't that far-fetched to imagine him looking the same. The thought irked me, but I pushed it away. He wasn't mine and he never had been. I just had to work on ignoring him and all the strange emotions he stirred up in me.

This town was plenty big enough for the both of us—as long as I could stay in my lane and not let his return keep plaguing my brain. Cassidy distracted me successfully, launching into all the different stories she'd heard of what women around town had done in their attempts to get the former NFL stars' attention, and as long as I didn't focus on the fact that Carson was one of the stars in question, it was amusing to hear about their antics.

As we were talking, Cassidy suddenly grabbed my arm and leaned in with excitement shimmering in her eyes. "Carson Drake keeps looking over here. At you, Nove. Why is that? Did he taste your bear claws and fall in love?"

# 8

## CARSON

Considering that Moe's was where everyone our age hung out in this town, it wasn't a huge surprise to see Nova here tonight, but it still came as a pleasant one. Positioning myself so I'd be able to see her without being overly obvious about staring at her, I sipped my beer and tried my best not to roll my eyes at the way Vance was soaking in all the adoration we were getting.

I stayed put for a while, watching as she laughed with Cassidy, not once looking over at us. *Go figure that the woman I want attention from is the only one not giving it to me.*

That was Nova, though. Always doing her own thing. Eventually, I got bored of waiting for her to spare me a glance and made my way over there, knowing I was playing with fire but not caring. Ryan wasn't out tonight and all I was going to do was say hi. No law against that.

Cassidy saw me coming and jumped up almost immediately, grabbing their empty beer bottles from the table and flashing me a coy smile when I reached them. "Hey, Carson. I'll be back in a few. Just need to get some more drinks. Have fun."

She even winked at me as she walked away, and I laughed as I took the seat she'd just vacated. "What was that all about?"

Nova's eyes sparkled with unshed laughter and maybe a bit of exasperation as she shrugged at me. She looked gorgeous as ever in a plain yellow sundress and her hair cascading in loose waves down her shoulders. She wasn't done up, her makeup almost nonexistent and her hair simply loose rather than crunchy with hairspray or straightened to twigs.

I appreciated the effort women made just as much as the next guy, but there was something about her being so comfortable with going natural that just got to me.

She shrugged. "Cass got it in her head that you were staring at me. I think she's not so subtly trying to give us some time alone."

"I was staring at you," I admitted easily. "Remind me to thank her later for giving us a couple minutes to catch up."

"Catch up, huh?" she asked, unable to fight the disbelieving smile that tugged at the corners of her lips. "Why would we need to catch up, Carson? It's not like we were ever friends."

My hand flew to my chest and I gripped it. "Ouch. That's not the way I remember it. I remember us being friends. Good friends, in fact. The best, for a while there."

"That wasn't friendship, Drake. It was hormones." She cocked her head at me, that smile still playing on her beautiful mouth as she looked into my eyes. "Since that's not something we should talk about, what exactly do you want to catch up on?"

"We could talk about it," I said, sliding my forearms onto the table and holding her gaze intently. "You know as well as I do that it wasn't just hormones, though. I mean, come on. At the very least, it was a thing."

"I see the big cities have made you real eloquent," she teased before she let out a soft sigh. "A thing, huh? That's a good way of putting it."

"We could always talk about revisiting that thing," I suggested, my hands itching to close the final couple inches between my fingers and hers.

She shook her head, chuckling and playful rather than taking it seriously. "Do you remember that time my brother kicked your ass for kissing me? Something tells me it'll be a lot worse if he catches you doing it again."

"I can take him," I said confidently. "Besides, I've never regretted it. It was worth the black eye, but I didn't come over here to talk about that or him. I just wanted to check in with you. Find out how you are."

Her eyebrows inched up. "You did? Uh, okay. I don't know how to do this though, Carson. I don't know how to be your friend."

"It's easy," I said. "Just tell me how you've been. Pretend I'm Cassidy or something."

"Pretend you're Cassidy," she mused out loud, swiping her tongue across her lips. "Yeah. Okay. I'm game to give it a try. I've been good. Busy. Thank you for asking. How about you?"

I grinned at her. "See? That wasn't so hard. I've been good too, Nova. Thank *you* for asking. Not so busy these days, but hoping to get busier soon. What's been keeping you so busy?"

"Life," she said without elaborating. "What are you hoping to get busy with?"

"You," I joked and laughed when she made her eyes big at me. "What? You can't blame a guy for trying. You left the door wide open on that one."

"Touche." She glanced at the beer I was holding before she snagged it from between my fingers, took a sip, and glanced at the bar where Cassidy was still waiting to be served. When she looked back at me, I arched an eyebrow and she shrugged. "What? You wanted to be friends. Friends share. I know your mother would've taught you that."

I groaned. "Did you have to bring Mom into it?"

She grinned at me. "It's a small town, Carson. The moms are always in it. There's no avoiding that."

My head tilted as I looked right into her eyes. "That's not entirely true. We managed to keep ours out of it back in the day."

"Only because it never became more than a thing," she replied easily, giving back my beer as she jerked her chin toward the bar. "Vance is calling you."

Blinking hard, I remembered there were other people around. He was, in fact, calling me back over. Sighing as I stood up, I left the beer on the table in front of her. "I'll see you around, Nova. Keep that. It looks like Cassidy might be a while. Excellent bear claws, by the way. I'll have to stop in again soon and see what else you've got."

Reluctantly backing away, I shot her a final smile and went to rejoin my friend. Vance had extricated himself from the gaggle of girls who had been surrounding him when I'd left, and he lifted both eyebrows at me now, shaking his head when I reached him.

"What the hell were you doing looking so cozy with Nova Murphy?" he asked as we took our places at the bar once more. "Don't you remember what happened that summer we came back to visit from college and Ryan caught you two kissing at the bonfire? Because I remember. It was a damn bloodbath."

"No, it wasn't." I motioned to the bartender for another beer and then signaled that I'd like two more and pointed at Cassidy's head. He jerked his chin in a nod, immediately striding over to the fridge to fill my order.

When I looked back at Vance, he huffed out a breath. "Back off, Drake. Seriously. Don't invite that kind of trouble in right now. We came back for life to be simpler, not to make it even more complicated."

"Nova is a grown woman," I said. "I can flirt with her if I want to. As long as she flirts back, right? Ryan can't decide who she can and cannot talk to anymore. She's long out of high school and I'm not the college guy back to break hearts for the summer this time."

Repeating what Ryan had said to me that night still put a bitter taste in my mouth. I'd never meant to come back to take her heart and break it with a meaningless summer fling. It'd never been like that, yet he hadn't given me the chance to tell him what it had been like.

On the other hand, I'd understood even then where he'd been

coming from. His sister had been in high school and I'd been going to college practically on the other side of the country. Not only that, but I'd had my heart set on playing professional football and it hadn't been like I could do that from here.

Ryan had known that I'd leave after that summer, and he'd been scared of me taking his sister's heart with me. So I'd backed off because I'd known it too. I had known I would be gone and that it would be years before I'd really be back here, if I ever would.

But that had been then, and this was now. Vance was still looking at me like I was crazy, a resigned expression tightening his features as he shook his head at me once more. "Don't do it, Drake. Just don't. There are plenty of other women in this town who are just itching to warm your bed for a night. It doesn't have to be Murphy's sister." He motioned at all the women who were making eyes at us as if he was trying to prove his point.

"What if I'm not just looking for a hookup?" I asked.

Vance snorted as he tried to hold back a laugh. "What are you saying, Carson? You saying that the guy who's never had a serious relationship and lives for the game is suddenly looking to settle down?"

"That's not the only game I lived for before," I said. "I left football behind. Why can't I leave the other game behind, too?"

He made a confused face at me. "Why would you? Look around you, man. Opportunities for hookups abound."

"That's not what I want anymore," I said, surprising even myself that I'd said the words out loud, but it was true. I wanted more, and I glanced at the table where Nova was now talking to Cassidy again. I wanted more and I wanted it with her.

Again.

Vance, however, was definitely not buying it. "That's exactly what you want, Drake. You want to hook up with her because you were headed that way back in the day. Before Ryan put a stop to it. Thing is, it feels wrong to think of her as just a hookup because of who she is, so you're justifying it by thinking you want more. You don't."

"That's not it."

He gave me a knowing look. "That *is* it. I happen to know for a fact that you weren't pining for that girl all the time we were gone. She's not your high-school sweetheart that you never forgot, and you guys weren't star-crossed lovers just waiting for the right time. This is not some sweet story about second chances and reunions. It's your cock wanting the one girl it can't have. That's all there is to it."

Before I could argue, Vance's hand landed heavily on my shoulder and he gave a beautiful blonde at the bar a pointed look. "Be my wingman with her. Maybe she's got a friend who can help take your mind off Nova."

I wasn't super interested and I really didn't want Nova to see me doing something that would probably look like hitting on other women, but Vance wouldn't take no for an answer. "Come on, Carson. Do this for me. If you don't want her friend to distract you, then fine. But at least help me with her."

"You don't need help," I said. "All you need to do is walk over and I'm eighty percent sure you've got it in the bag."

He rolled his eyes at me. "Way to be modest, dude. Just come on and help me. Get out of your head. You and Nova have a history, is all. And look, I get that we're both going to have to face our pasts now that we're home, but don't drag her into it. The way I hear it, the Murphys have got more than enough going on without having to worry about you wanting to get your dick wet."

He took me by the shoulders and started marching us both toward the blonde. "So just forget about her and help your old buddy for a few minutes. Clear your head, and then think about what it is that you really want."

I gave in, but only because he'd made a few good points. Not the worst of which was that the Murphys had enough to worry about. I could argue with him until I was blue in the face about him being wrong about what I wanted with Nova, but ultimately, it wasn't just as simple as going after her.

Until I was absolutely sure that my *feelings* were really that and not just some throwback to the past, or to get what I hadn't back then, I had to keep a level head. I also had to be wingman for my best friend. Even if it was only so that I would be seen doing it in case word ever got to Ryan that I was seen *getting cozy* with his sister first.

*Man, when did the simple life get so damn complicated?*

# 9

## NOVA

At four a.m., I was up and baking for the morning rush. Exhausted after staying up late helping with farm chores, I smelled the scent of burning sugar. Cursing, I raced to the oven, noticing the stream of smoke spilling out of it and realizing that I'd burned a tray of pastries. I clenched my jaw in an attempt to quell the rising tide of frustration.

With a deep breath, I grabbed an oven mitt, jerked the door open, and yanked the tray out. A scream lodged in my throat as I glared down at the pastries that were now little more than blackened heaps of charcoal.

They were completely unsalvageable and it was going to cost me at least an hour to start another batch all over again. I didn't have a choice, though. My frangipane tartlets were a seasonal favorite and they'd been the first item we'd sold out of every day for the last couple months.

With a loud growl, I headed over to the freezer and pulled out some more of the homemade sweet shells. At least I'd made some extras in the hopes that I'd be able to whip up another batch of these to replenish the first once it sold out.

*So much for planning ahead.*

As I checked on everything else to make sure I wasn't about to ruin any other goods in the meantime, I tried to get my head on straight. It wasn't in the right place and it wasn't just because I was tired.

Carson was distracting me just by being back in town and I was starting to feel pathetic for being so affected by the knowledge. *No man should make me burn my tartlets just by being around. I should be stronger than that.*

I usually was, and it was bugging me that I couldn't force him out of my head. No matter what I tried, if I blinked, his face was there. It was probably worse because I wasn't at all used to it. When he'd left this town, I'd thrown myself into finishing high school with the best grades possible. Then I'd thrown myself into college, then opened up my businesses on the ranch. Not to mention all the chores.

I hadn't made time for guys and romance, and I hadn't wanted to. But now Carson was back and all those idle, girly daydreams I'd had when I'd scribbled "Mrs. Nova Drake" all over my notebooks were back in full force.

*And yes, I did do that in high school. Thank you very much. I had to make up for never doing it in middle school, after all. Every girl deserves a crush that makes her doodle. Even if she is a late bloomer.*

Shoving a mental middle finger up at the part of my mind that still judged me for those actions, I poured all the negative emotions into remaking the tartlets. By the time I was done with those and had caught up with all the other baking I'd had to do, it was seven a.m. and Cassidy had shown up.

As soon as she walked into the kitchen, her brow furrowed and her face fell. "Are you alright? What the hell happened? I can practically see the thunderclouds over your head."

"I'm fine. Just tired and frustrated." I forced a deep breath and followed it up with a tight smile. "I burnt some of the frangipanes, so you're going to have to pull the new batch out of the oven when they're done."

"You got it," she said, concern darkening her eyes as she stared into mine. "You burnt them? That's a first."

I groaned. "I know. I guess I just wasn't focusing."

Cassidy inhaled deeply, shut the door behind her, and strode over to the pantry. "I'll get started on a new batch of shells for tomorrow morning, but you need a break, girl. No one can do it all, not all the time. I've been saying this for months now, but take a damn break. Get some proper sleep and don't even think about the bakery for the rest of the day."

"No can do." I checked my watch and headed for the door to switch on the lights in the coffee shop and start the machines. "I've got the read-aloud in less than two hours and I don't want to miss it. I look forward to them too much."

She sighed, laughed softly, and made a weird squealing sound at the back of her throat. "You know what you are? Incorrigible. I'm sure Mrs. Norris would forgive you for missing one session. She knows how hard you work."

"We're a whole town full of hard-working folk who like to be kept busy, Cass. Mrs. Norris herself is the librarian by day and church volunteer at night. Or, I mean, not at night. Just whenever she's not at the library, but it sounded cooler that way."

"Sure, but that's also because she sleeps at night. Unlike you, who comes back here to mix dough and batter after mucking out stalls, and feeding hogs, and—"

"Okay, that's enough." I pointed at the oven. "Remember about the tartlets. Please. I can't lose another batch today."

"You won't," she promised. "Enjoy the read-aloud. I hope you enjoy it more than sleeping."

I nodded as I backed the door open with my butt. "I really do. I know you didn't mean it, but I really, really do."

She made another exasperated hum, and I spun around and got to work in the coffee shop. Once the peak morning rush was over, I double-timed it to the library, arriving just minutes before the read-aloud was supposed to begin.

Only to find none other than Carson Drake sitting on my beanbag.

I frowned, glancing between him and a blushing, smiling Mrs. Norris. "What's going on? I'm not late, am I?"

"Oh, no, honey. You just have a buddy for this hour." She beamed at him like he was a platinum-encased superhero, singlehandedly teaching the world how to read. "Carson has even picked out a book you can read at the same time. Isn't that lovely?"

"Lovely," I repeated tightly, but I wasn't agreeing with her.

My eyes locked on Carson's as I silently asked him just what the heck he was doing at *my* read-aloud. Amusement flared to life in his gaze and he patted the spot beside him. Slinging my bag off my shoulder, I dropped it on the floor and made a point of taking the other beanbag.

Mrs. Norris put her hands together as she smiled at us. "Thanks to both of you for being here. I'll let you decide how you're going to go about it before the kids arrive."

She bowed out, leaving me to glare at the unwelcome intruder who had better find a different timeslot if he wanted to read to the kids at this library. "What are you doing here?"

He shrugged, that amusement still dancing in his eyes as he smirked at me. "Reading to children. You?"

I shook my head, utterly confused about what was happening right now. "What *is* your deal, Carson?"

"My deal? I'm a retired football player who wants to give back to his community. What better way than starting here, with the children I might inspire to chase their dreams one day?"

"No, that's not it." I stared at him, taking in that chiseled jaw and the perfectly innocent green eyes gazing back at me. But he was no innocent. Dressed in dark-wash jeans, expensive sneakers, and a T-shirt so tight it might as well have been painted on, he looked like he was going on a date—not to a read-aloud. "You knew I was going to be here, didn't you?"

Not that I thought he'd gotten dressed up for me or to impress me, but what I suspected was that he was here to mess with me. Whatever he was doing later had nothing to do with me, but here and now, he hadn't come for the kids. That much, I was sure of.

"You've never had a philanthropic bone in your body," I said, not harshly. I was just stating a fact. "I know you've been giving money for all kinds of things around town, but giving time is something entirely different."

"Yes, it is." He nodded agreeably, but those eyes still hadn't left mine and his annoying bulging biceps kept rippling as if he was moving them around on purpose. "That's kind of why I'm doing it though, Nova. I've been giving money for a long time, but I could never do anything else. Now, I can. So here I am."

Once again, I shook my head. It wasn't that Carson was a bad person. Not at all, in fact. I just didn't think it was a coincidence that he'd ended up here, at my read-aloud, when he could've chosen any other day and time of the week—other than Tuesdays at ten a.m., that was. Because that was mine too.

"What do you want from me?" I asked. "Why do you keep ending up in the exact same place as I am?"

"I don't want anything from you, Nova. I'm just doing my part for my town. Just like you are. Are you really pissed about me showing up to the read-aloud? Or is there something else going on with you?"

"There's nothing else, Carson. I just don't understand how you keep showing up everywhere I go. It's unnerving."

"Unnerving?" He held my gaze for a long moment before his eyebrows slowly started rising. "Or a challenge of some kind that you're going to rise to?"

As those electric eyes drilled into mine, I realized he was right. I was feeling weirdly territorial over my spot here at the library. Probably because it and a few other things around town were all I'd had while he'd been off gallivanting all around the country.

For some of us, this town had always been enough, and yet somehow, he was the returning hero and people were acting like he should be lauded for it. I wasn't jealous. People had been plenty nice about my own return when I'd come back from college.

Maybe I was just a little bitter? I didn't really know how to put words to all the feelings swirling around inside, but what I did know was that no one did read-alouds better than I did. So if he wanted to turn it into some kind of competition, then it was on.

And he had no idea what was about to hit him.

# 10

## CARSON

Before I even knew what was happening, Nova and I were doing the read-aloud like we were competing for some grand prize. She was even more animated than she'd been the other day and I was feeding off the energy radiating from her, playing off the cues she was giving and loving every minute.

The back and forth, give and take rhythm we had going was seamless, as if we'd spent hours rehearsing it, and the kids were completely captivated. As we read a story about two giants, I was pretty captivated myself.

With Nova, everything always came so naturally. Like she and I were two halves of the same whole or some shit I never would've been caught dead thinking just a month ago.

By the end of it, even the parents burst out in applause and several of them crowded around us.

"Are you going to be reading together again next week? That was wonderful." The question had come from a hopeful-looking mother, who beamed at Nova before glancing shyly at me.

Another parent nodded, then gestured at the little girl who'd inched her way forward until she'd been sitting in the very front row.

"Please say there'll be a repeat performance. I've never seen Ella so interested in a story before," he said, mainly focused on me. "I didn't know you were a man of so many talents, Mr. Drake. Thank you for giving your time."

"It's *her* you should be thanking." I tipped my head toward Nova. "She's the mastermind. I'm just along for the ride."

"So you will be reading together again?" another woman asked, repeating the original question.

Nova opened her mouth—presumably to say no—but I beat her to it. "Yes, we absolutely will be doing it again. Anything for the kids. Right, Nova?"

Her throat worked like she was swallowing down some vile things she'd been about to say, but then she smiled and nodded at the parents. "Thanks for bringing the kids. We appreciate it. See you next week."

Before anyone could say anything else, Nova picked up her purse from the floor and hurried out into the parking lot. I chased after her, shielding my eyes against the bright sunshine as we broke free of the building.

"Wait, Nova," I called, jogging to catch up. "Do you want to go grab some lunch? We can plan our next session and choose a book together this time."

Her hand was already on the door handle of a beat-up, light blue truck I recognized as having belonged to her father when we were kids, but she spun to face me. There was a fire in her eyes as she shook her head at me.

"Unlike you, I still have a job, Carson. I need to get back to it."

She locked her gaze on mine for another moment, opening her mouth like she was about to say something else, but then she must've decided against it. Opening the door instead, she climbed into the old truck and slammed the door before she sped off, probably racing back for the lunch rush at the coffee shop.

I'd never experienced said rush myself, but Mom had told me it could get pretty hectic there. I sighed and walked over to my own truck, muttering to myself as I opened the door. "I'm retired. Not unemployed."

While I'd been hoping for lunch with Nova, I was okay with going home to spend time with my mom. She was outside doing yardwork when I pulled up, and my heart nearly stopped when I saw her teetering on a stepladder while she tried to trim a plant.

"Fuck. You're going to break your neck," I muttered before slamming to a stop in the driveway and jogging over to help. "Are you okay up there, Mom? I'm not gonna lie. It looks like you're trying to hurt yourself."

She chuckled. "I was just fine doing this while you were away, sweetheart. I'll be just fine doing it now."

"Maybe, but the difference is that now, you don't have to take the risk. Let me do it for you." She glanced down at me and handed over the trimming shears before she climbed off and motioned for me to take her place.

I took over, my heart still pounding with fear over what could've happened to her. I knew she'd managed while I was away, but she'd also been ten years younger when I'd left. Also, I had no idea why I was this upset about it, and evidently, neither did she.

"What's bothering you, baby boy?"

"Baby boy?" I wagged a finger between the two of us, even though I was now on the stepladder. "Have you seen me lately? I'm, like, twice your size. At least."

She waved me off. "You'll always be my baby boy, which is also how I know for sure that something really is bothering you. You wouldn't have bothered with the semantics if you were okay. Did something happen?"

"No, not really," I said as I tilted my head back to focus on the greenery I was supposed to be trimming. "I, uh, I just volunteered at the library with Nova today, and she didn't like it very much. She doesn't seem to like *me* very much anymore, actually. I'm just not sure why."

Okay, I had a feeling I did know why. It had been ten years, but back then, I'd been kissing her one minute, and the next, I'd been in my truck, on my way home, and she hadn't seen me since. Not until last week anyway.

I'd brooded about it a bit at first, but then I'd gone back to college. The draft had happened. Life as I'd been imagining it had gotten started. Eventually, I just didn't think about her so much anymore, and then I didn't think about her at all.

Nova had been here, though. All along. I knew she'd had a lot of other stuff going on and I didn't think that she was hung up on me at all, but she did seem to be pissed at me, and that was the only reason I could think of why she would be.

"Nova is such a darling," Mom said, pulling me out of my thoughts. "She's as hardheaded as her dad and her brother, though. As proud and as stuck in her ways. If you're trying to get close to her, you may want to find a different way than to threaten something she thinks of as hers in this town."

"I wasn't threatening anything," I protested, though I could understand why she might have seen it that way. On the other hand, I kind of felt like everything I did was threatening to her in some way these days, and that, I just didn't understand. "I didn't mean to threaten her place at the library. It's not like I want to take over the read-alouds. I just thought it would be fun to do it together. The kids loved it."

Mom peered up at me and pressed her hand to her forehead to keep the sun out of her eyes. "Like I said, honey. If you want to spend time with her, maybe try not to be in her way. The question I'm interested in hearing your answer to, though, is why you're in her way at all?"

I wasn't trying to be in her way and I knew I shouldn't have been anywhere near her, but she really was like a magnet to me. I couldn't explain it, but it had always been that way between us. Nova and I just *worked*.

She got me in a way no one else ever had—or had even bothered to try to—and she was the one woman I'd never felt like I needed to put on an act around. Nova didn't need me to be that guy. Not the football player or the cool kid who had to pretend not to give a damn.

Back in the day, she was the only one who'd known about my fears and who had listened when I'd talked about my dreams—and not just those that involved football. I was comfortable with her but because it had always felt like she accepted me for exactly who I was.

She hadn't wanted or needed the bullshit. Not even on the days that I had needed it.

As I thought it over, my mother fixed me with a questioning look. "I'd love to see you settle down and get married. I'm itching for grandkids and I can't wait to see you as a dad, but if you're not ready for it yet, I suggest you stay the hell away from Nova Murphy, baby boy. She's the girl you marry, not the one you fuck around with before you find the one."

My jaw dropped. "Did you just say *fuck around with*?"

Mom smirked at me. "I might be old, Carson, so maybe that's not what you kids call it anymore, but I call it like I see it. Even if I never did it in front of my elders. Whatever name you want to put to it, the point remains the same. There are people you can mess around with and people you wait until you're ready for, and Nova is someone you need to be ready for."

Still gaping at my mom, I wondered just how much she really knew about what had happened ten years ago. I had never flat out told her, but obviously, she knew something was up with Nova and me. She'd never said stuff like this to me about any other girl.

Then again, it was possible she was saying it precisely because Nova wasn't any other girl. What I'd told Vance the other night had been true. I was ready to settle down, and while I'd dated and had a few casual girlfriends, they'd all lacked a spark I'd been looking for since I'd been young.

A spark I'd only ever felt with Nova.

But she was off limits. As off limits now as she'd ever been before. I was only just starting to really mend my friendship with Ryan and he didn't want me anywhere near her.

Which meant that spark or not, if I couldn't fight these urges to be near her, I'd lose my friend. That had been true all along though, and it had never stopped me before. Partially because I hadn't let it. Not until it had really mattered and I'd agreed that the timing hadn't been right.

But now? I didn't know. It seemed to me that all bets were off. While I knew which of the Murphy horses I should've been backing, everything in me wanted to back—and mount—the other.

*And yep. Just like that, the simple life has definitely gotten really fucking complicated.*

# 11

## NOVA

Out on the ranch, sweat poured down my temples from under my cowboy hat and snaked down my spine. I'd been looking for almost an hour and I still hadn't found my brother.

The unforgiving sun beat down on me and I could only pray that my sunscreen worked as hard as I did. When I finally rounded the bend to Murphy's Rock, I heaved out a sigh of relief and dug my heels into Badger's side.

My trusty chestnut responded, perking up now that he knew we were close. "That's it, boy. We're going to rest in just a minute. Just one more minute."

Ryan was fixing the problematic fence—again—bent over and cursing as he hammered at a crooked post. When he heard the rhythmic clip-clop of Badger's hooves, he straightened up and twisted, peering out at me from under the rim of his hat.

"Nova? Is everything okay? What are you doing out here?"

I tugged gently at Badger's reins and pulled him to a stop before I gracefully dismounted. After finding him some shade, I let him graze with Ryan's mare, Hatric, and dug into my satchel to toss a bottle of coldish water to my brother.

It had been ice cold when I'd left, a peace offering of sorts, but that had been an hour ago. As he caught it, he arched an eyebrow at me. "Nova? Did something happen?"

"Everything's fine," I said easily before twisting the top off my own bottle and taking a few long gulps. "I just thought I'd bring you some hydration. How's it looking?"

He kicked at the offending fence post and blew out a deep breath. "Exactly like you think it is. I've done what I could for now, but it's not going to hold."

I eyed the fence and the work he'd done to patch it up. Deciding that this was as good a time as any to tell him why I'd really come looking for him, I jerked my chin at the fence. "I might have an idea that might help us get the money we need to fix it, but I'll need your help."

"That's a lot of *mights* in one sentence, Nove." He gave me a skeptical look. "What's the idea?"

"Well, I've been thinking that we should move forward on marketing the ranch. Dad is never going to give us the go-ahead, but I think this is a prime example of it being better to ask for forgiveness rather than permission."

He tugged his shirt out of his waistband and wiped his face. Then he took another long sip of his water before he fixed his suspicious blue eyes on me once more. "I'm not sure we'll ever get forgiveness, but I'm listening. I suppose facing Dad's wrath is better than losing the ranch. What have you got?"

"You need to act like a cowboy for a few videos," I rushed out, waving a hand at him, referring to the exact way he looked right then. "All you have to do is be really, really good looking, preferably shirtless and sweaty. We could even make a quick video of you just doing what you've been doing all day."

My brother scowled at me. "What the hell are you talking about?"

Sliding my phone out of my satchel, I quickly navigated to a few videos I'd found online of other ranches who were doing the same things. "Check it out. They're using those to get attention, but they're selling their meat in subscription boxes with the ads. Some of them are getting thousands of views a day, and all they're really doing is making videos of their day-to-day lives and posting them online."

"Let me get this straight," he said slowly as the first clip ended. "You want me riding around naked on horseback? And you want to film it?"

"I want to save the ranch!" I protested. "You wouldn't have to be naked. I already told you we could even just make our first video of you right here and right now. As soon as you get back to the work you're going to be getting back to anyway. All I need is, like, a minute of you doing what you were doing before I rode up and we'd have something to post."

Ryan stared at me for a beat, then broke into loud, guffawing laughter, even doubling over as he shook his head. "I'm not doing that, Nova. I'm sorry. I want to save the ranch too, but not like that."

"Why not?" I asked, and unlike him, I was being serious. "People are signing up for these subscription boxes like they're hotcakes. I've been following this one ranch in Montana for a couple months and you won't believe all the changes they've already made. They've got a brand-new website with an online store that had to have been designed by a professional. All the areas they use regularly in their videos have been upgraded and renovated. They've also been teasing new developments on their property and their engagements are through the roof."

"Things aren't always what they seem on social media, Nova. You know that. Those 'upgrades' might be one renovated stall or even just a green screen for all you know. Besides, even if it is working for them, that's not to say it will work for us."

I shoved the phone at him again. "Look at that, Ryan. There are ranches all around who are doing it, and I mentioned the ranch in Montana specifically because that was the first one I saw, but there are even people doing it in Crystal Springs. That's less than fifty miles from here."

He didn't take the device from me again. His face was no longer set in a scowl but it still didn't look like he was about to agree. "If there are already so many people doing it, then who's to say it would help us at all?"

"Grass-fed, organic food is all the rage right now. We'd got mutton, lamb, beef, veal, and pork. Hell, all we need are a few chickens and we'd be a one-stop shop. People would never have to get their meat from anywhere else ever again. There aren't a lot of ranches who can say that."

I put up my hand to show him I wasn't done yet when I saw him open his mouth to interrupt. "Plus, we already sell all our own meat in dishes at the coffee shop, and we could link the reviews of those to our posts. Potential buyers would see that our meat is really great quality and that even the locals rave about it."

Ryan drank down the last of his water, then handed the bottle back to me. "You got any more of that? I ran out just before you got here."

"Sure, but only if you agree to let me make a real quick video of you before I leave."

He laughed. "Not a chance. Keep your water. I've got my truck and I happen to know exactly where I can refill my own bottles. So thanks, but no thanks."

I handed over the spare bottle I'd brought along for him instead of pushing the issue. As he took it, he blew out a long breath, his eyes resting heavily on mine.

"Look, Nova. I'm not saying it's a bad idea. It's not. I can tell that you've really done your research on this, and if it's working for other people, then it might just work for us. That being said, I just can't do it."

"Why not?" I gave him a pleading look. "If we get even a tenth of the orders it looks like that place in Montana is getting, then we'd be able to fix the fence in a couple months. With cash money. You can't tell me that's not worth posing for a few videos."

Ryan's reddened brow lifted, his nostrils flaring as he turned to take in the length of fence immediately behind him. "Cash money is good. Great, actually, but I've been working on a few ideas of my own."

"Like what?" I asked. "We talked about this just the other day and neither of us knew what to do next."

"Yeah, I know, but then I heard about these investors who specifically look for going concerns worth pumping their money into. I've been talking to Dad about trying to find one for Red Stone. It would allow us to modernize our facilities and to expand your market. All without compromising any of the stuff Dad is so worried about compromising."

"Like our ownership of this ranch?" I huffed out a breath. "Investors don't give money for nothing and they certainly don't do it without collateral."

"Maybe not, but as long as we can give them their piece of the pie, they'd never call in that collateral. A lot of our equipment is going. Dad knows that. He also knows that I've fixed what I could but that some of it is on its last legs. It's going to need replacement and soon, and he also knows that we won't even be able to find some of those relics we've been using at auction, which means that a certain level of modernization is going to be impossible to avoid."

"Okay, so he's finally willing to compromise," I said. "At least a little. If he's realized that modernization is unavoidable, even to a certain extent, then we might be able to sell him on using the money we make from subscription boxes to do the upgrades we need to do."

"Or we could find an investor who's willing to give us the money to do it," he reasoned. "Obviously, cash money without any strings will always be better, but not like this, Nova. Not by making me prance around on a horse waving my dick in people's faces."

"We're not talking about porn, Ryan." I wrinkled my nose. "You wouldn't be waving your bits in anyone's face. All we're talking about is flashing your abs and flexing your biceps a bit."

"But an investor—"

"We don't have that kind of time," I said emphatically, the emotion of it clogging up my throat as I stared at him, silently begging now. "Finding an investor could take months. Then there's negotiations to be done. Visits, inspections, and all kinds of corporate red tape and due diligence that any investor worth his salt would insist on. Meanwhile, we've got Frank breathing down our necks and bills that are piling up. We just don't have that kind of time, Ryan."

I hadn't been expecting him to jump on this opportunity, but I needed him to understand that it was fast becoming a Hail Mary. And that if he had just said yes, I could've already had our first video. We might even already have sold our first subscription box before the day was out.

That was the beauty and the power of social media—and I fully intended on harnessing it. Now I just had to convince my family to let me.

# 12

## CARSON

**M**iracles do happen.

I grinned as I drove onto Red Stone Ranch, excited to finally get to help out. When Ryan had reached out this morning, I'd nearly fallen out of bed. That was how surprised I'd been to get the call. But here I was, ready to get the job done.

He'd said to meet him at the barn. Something about *old doors* and *a two-person job*. I didn't really know what we were going to do, but whatever it was, I was in.

At least I had been until I walked into the barn with that huge grin still on my face and ended up smack bang in the middle of a Murphy Battle of the Wills. Ryan was on one side, his arms crossed over his chest and his features set into a deep scowl. Nova was on the other, her arms crossed even tighter and her eyes narrowed to slits as she glared at her brother.

"What is it, Ry? Are you embarrassed? Don't be. Women all over the country are going to be salivating over you, and all the men are going to want to be you. The manly man who fixes stuff and farms. Who cares about the few people in town who won't understand what we're doing?"

Ryan's jaw clenched as he gave his head a firm shake. "It's not about being embarrassed. It's about making a fool of myself for no good reason. I know this has worked for other ranches and it really is a great idea, but there's no guarantee that it will bring in any business at all. Let alone enough business to actually cover any of the expenses we'll be incurring."

She tossed her arms out to her sides, exasperation rippling across her face like a living thing. Her eyebrows lifted and tugged together, her mouth twisted, and her nostrils went wide. "What costs? I'll be making the videos and editing them myself. I got a free subscription to a website that makes it pretty easy. I'll also be running our pages and uploading the videos, managing the orders and the payments, and for the time being, I'll even pack the darn boxes myself. So what costs, exactly, are you so worried about covering?"

"Boxes cost money, Nova! Have you seen those things? They've got to be a product of their own. Plus, it's not like you can just box up meat and ship it. There's refrigeration to consider. Packaging. And have you even thought about what happens if so much as one chunk is delivered rotting?"

Her chest was heaving, her cheeks flushed as she stared him down. Neither of them seemed to have noticed me yet, and I was starting to feel like an intruder, so I cleared my throat and took a step forward.

"Hey, guys," I said carefully, glancing from one sibling to the other. "What's going on here?"

Nova opened her mouth to tell me, but Ryan dropped his arms to his sides and marched over. "It's nothing. Come on. We'll need to start by taking off the door completely so that I can get to the hinges. Thanks for coming, bro. Have you had any coffee? We can go grab some before we get started."

"Let's do that." I'd clearly walked in on something important, and I was eager to find out how I could help.

From the bits and pieces I'd heard, I was pretty sure I knew what was going on. Frankly, I didn't know why Ryan was so against it. Marketing and promotion had been part of my job for the last decade, and I'd enjoyed it.

Sometimes, it got a little annoying, but in general, I'd found it pretty fun. As long as you were doing it with the right people and the photographer didn't have a stick up his ass, it was a good time.

The way Ryan was still scowling though, I knew better than to give my opinion before he told me his side of the story. He led me to the barn they'd converted into an apartment for him, and as I walked in, I realized it was the first time I was visiting.

Surprised by the size and the fixtures, I looked around, hands in my pockets, and let out a low whistle. "Jeez. When you said you lived in a barn, I wasn't expecting this."

I'd known the roof would be high, obviously, but between that and the windows they'd put in just under it, the space was airy and filled with natural light. It seemed huge, with a shop area set up for him toward the front and a living area with a kitchenette toward the back and on the left.

Beyond the kitchen, they'd put in a back door that led out on a deck capable of being enclosed in the winter. The stairs had been reinforced and ascended to his bedroom. Pine partitions rose up from the corner, and I assumed that was where the bathroom was.

All things considered, it was a really nice, cozy place with a TV mounted on the wall, rugs on the concrete floors, and tools all over the place. Ryan headed for the coffee machine and smiled as he leaned against the counter once he'd spun to face me.

"Thanks. Dad, Nova, and I put it together ourselves. It was a ton of work, but I like to think it came out alright."

"It's great, man," I said genuinely, already starting to get all sorts of inspiration for the place I wanted to build myself. Striding toward him, I took a seat at the breakfast bar that separated his kitchen from his living space and fixed him with a questioning look. "So, what was all that about?"

He let out a heavy sigh and ran both hands through his hair. "I'm sure you've heard about it anyway, since no one in this town knows how to mind their own business, but the ranch is having a tough time at the moment."

I rocked my head from side to side. "I've heard some, but I'd rather get the real story from you."

His eyes latched on mine, and for the first time, I saw the storminess of worry swirling around inside them. "The real story is that we're in a tight spot. A real tight spot. Our production has remained the same since Dad took over the ranch from Grandpa in the eighties. Meanwhile, times have changed. Advancements have been made and life has gotten a hell of a lot more expensive."

"It sure has."

Ryan nodded slowly. "With a little bit of modernization, we could increase our output and even start growing our operations, but Dad doesn't want to hear it. He's old school, but we need to do something new, or we're going to lose the place."

I frowned. "Maybe I'm just being ignorant or maybe I was gone too long, but what exactly is the problem with old school?"

He let out a dry chuckle. "You sounded a bit like my dad there, but the problem is that everything around here is ancient. If we could upgrade the structures to include more energy effective heating measures, we could save a bunch of money just from that. The same goes for updating our breeding programs, the pens, the buildings, and streamlining the infrastructure we've got. We also need to look at expanding our farming operations to grow crops so we can supplement the income we get from ranching. Raising cattle, hogs, and horses at the rate we are just isn't enough anymore. If we could afford to buy a few more heifers and sows, then maybe, but we can't afford it."

"Okay, I think I'm starting to get it, but what is your father so set against? Growing crops or what?"

"Everything. He says our infrastructure may be old, but it's working so there's no reason to spend a bunch of money on upgrades. He also thinks that growing crops is absurd because he's a rancher, not a farmer, and he's not willing to release any of the grazing land to me for crops."

I grimaced. "So basically, he's dead set against changing anything. Is that right?"

"That's about it, yeah. He just wants to keep plodding along exactly like we have been, but realistically, if we do that, then we're dead in the water."

I knew he wasn't going to accept it, but I had to offer. "Look, man, if you need some money to buy a few new heifers, why don't I give it to you? You can pay me back from the proceeds of their calves and we can start small. See how it goes."

He shook his head firmly, cutting me off. "I don't want your money, Carson. What I do want is for you to help me fix the doors so the animals don't freeze to death once winter gets here. I'd have asked my dad, but it's heavy lifting. He'll never admit it, but it'd probably break his back if he tried."

"Yeah. Okay. You got it."

Ryan fixed our coffee and told me a little bit more about the plans he and Nova had for the ranch while we drank it. Before we got to work, his dad called, saying that he had to speak to him. He took off, and I took the opportunity to track down his sister.

The bakery was closed today, but her truck was in front of it, so I started there, knocking on the door before I walked in. "Hey! Are you in here?"

"I'm in the kitchen," she called out. "Carson, is that you?"

"Yeah, it's me." Without the scent of fresh baked goods in the air and with no customers, the place seemed bigger than it had before. I moved past the shelves of local produce and the empty stands and baskets that usually carried her breads and pastries, really looking around now that I didn't feel like I was about to be trampled.

The bakery and farm stall opened up to the coffee shop near the back, with a beautiful view of the land and the mountains from the tables. Most everything was made of treated wood, with red and white checked tablecloths in the coffee shop, giving a real country feel to it all.

Nova stuck her head out the kitchen door, wiping her hands on her apron as she frowned at me. "What are you doing here?"

"I came to talk to you," I said honestly, deciding to just lay all my cards on the table. "Ryan just told me a little bit about what's been going on with the ranch. It sounds rough."

"It is." She motioned for me to follow her back into the kitchen, where she sat on a low stool and gestured for me to do the same. "Why did you come here if you've already talked to Ryan?"

I saw the flicker of irritation that sharpened her features when she said her brother's name. Leaning forward, I spread my legs and rested my elbows on my knees. "He told me about the problems you've been having and what you need to solve them. What he didn't tell me was what you were arguing about this morning."

She blew out a frustrated huff of air as she shook her head. "We were arguing about him being too shy to show some skin on video. Somehow, he got it in his head that I wanted him to be naked on horseback, which isn't true. I just need a few shots of him shirtless and being a rancher."

"For subscription boxes," I guessed out loud now that she'd confirmed my suspicions.

Nova dropped her chin in a curt nod. "Yep, and I know there's no guarantee that it will work, but there's also no guarantee that it won't. It's not going to cost a damn thing to at least try, but he's not budging."

I cocked my head at her as I wondered if she'd forgotten who she was talking to. "You know you could always ask me for help, right? That's what I came back for, to help my town."

"What?" She squinted at me. "I can't ask you for help. You're a pro ball player, not a rancher."

"Sure, but just my face and endorsement alone could already be the turning point for your business." I looked her right in the eyes. "I know you've been pissed at me since I got back, and I know that you and I have some stuff to sort out, but this is separate from that. Ryan may not be comfortable posing shirtless and sweaty, but I am. Hell, at this point, I've probably done more promotion than I've played football. Tag me in, coach. I'm here and I can do it. I want to do it. All you have to do is say the word. Just think about it. You know where to find me when you're ready."

# 13

## NOVA

It was a great day at the market. We were getting busier every weekend and I'd been noticing more and more people driving in from out of town. It still wasn't enough to cover the debts we had, but it was something.

Clear blue skies stretched to infinity overhead. The sun was out, and we even had a band playing on a small stage they'd set up for themselves outside the bakery. While they belted out some of the most popular songs country music had ever known, even I had to admit that this market was a raging success.

The vibe was incredible. We had more vendors than ever before, with colorful tents covering every inch of the parking lot today and streams of people moving between them. Every time I inhaled, I got a whiff of the scents of grilling meat, baking bread, and sweet treats wafting in the air.

My mood couldn't have been any better as I moved from stall to stall, mingling and handing out samples from the tray I was carrying with me. I didn't stop smiling once, so damn happy and proud that the market was growing the way it was.

It was a win for the entire community and anyone within driving distance who either wanted to sell or buy anything produced locally.

Despite the ever-growing hole the ranch was in, this was a triumph that I was going to savor.

As I looked across the parking lot, my gaze landed on a pair of electric green eyes and it sent a jolt of energy through my entire being. *Carson.*

With his dark hair stylishly mussed and a winning smile on his face, he shook hands with folks and made small talk, but those eyes remained connected with mine. My pulse spiked and my heart flipped in my chest as I smiled back at him.

For just that moment, time seemed to stand still. My surroundings melted into the periphery until they weren't there anymore at all. I felt an invisible tether between us and it was so intense that it brought tears of joy to my eyes—until my brother popped up right next to Carson and the whole illusion shattered.

I blinked hard and immediately averted my gaze, a little startled as I crashed back down to earth. *What the hell was that?*

A little out of sorts, I spun around and muttered to myself under my breath. "Refill the tray. Yep, the tray needs to be refilled."

I wasn't one to get my head lost in the clouds, but damn, I felt like I had gone for a quick flight. Hurrying back to the bakery, I breathed in and out, and in and out, trying to regain my composure.

I pushed open the door and stepped inside. Thankfully, as soon as I did, I was distracted from whatever the hell had just happened by the chaos inside the store. Cassidy was doing her best to get to everyone, but it was clear that she was getting overwhelmed and our customers were getting impatient.

Every table in the coffee shop was filled. A line of people waited for her to ring up their purchases from the shop while others seemed to be looking around for help on the floor. I swallowed hard. *Shit. This is why I can't afford to get distracted.*

I also couldn't afford to hire more help, which meant that Cassidy and I were on our own. Abandoning my tray of samples on the counter, I answered a few questions on the floor as I crossed it, then grabbed a notepad and apologized profusely as I started taking orders from the patrons in the coffee shop.

"That's quite alright, dear," an older woman said as she flashed me a kind smile. "You're very busy today. That's a good thing. No need to apologize."

I grinned back at her, once again feeling grateful for the community I belonged to. This town and people like this woman were why I had never dreamed of leaving Silver Springs. Why would I move to some city to live life in the fast lane, surrounded by traffic and assholes, when I had this amazing place? Why search for paradise when I had already found it?

"Thank you," I said sincerely. "We really appreciate your understanding, but I'm bringing you a pecan pie tartlet anyway. It's on the house. A small symbol of our gratitude."

I'd been planning on using all those tartlets as samples outside, but the people in here really deserved something in return for their patience.

As I passed out tartlets around the room, I caught sight of Carson suddenly appearing behind the counter. He tied an apron that barely fit his broad frame around his waist before he started shelling out pastries and cakes.

Cassidy's jaw slackened, and so did mine, but she quickly blinked away her surprise and got back to work. I, on the other hand, wasn't able to stop staring quite yet. As I watched, he laughed with customers and took pictures with them.

Everyone seemed to love that he was there, and at the same time, he was ridiculously efficient at helping the people in line. For the next twenty minutes, I shuffled plates and made drinks, answered questions from people in the shop, and popped into the kitchen every so often to fix a sandwich or fill an order, but when I looked again, we were completely sold out.

Disbelief rattled through me.

Carson spread his arms wide and gave the people still waiting the most adorable, apologetic smile. "I'm so sorry, guys, but that's all we've got for you today. Please feel free to browse around the store. We might not have any freshly baked goods available, but there are plenty of other delicious treats and don't forget to pick up your farm fresh steaks and bacon before you leave."

My eyelashes fluttered in shock.

People chuckled and nodded, immediately breaking from the line and starting to browse the few other things we had. Several groups walked straight to the freezers lining the back of the store between the bakery and the coffee shop, stocking up on meat just like he'd told them to.

In all the time I'd had this place, meat had never been a huge seller. This wasn't a butcher shop and that wasn't what my customers came here for. When I'd had the fridges and freezers installed, it had been more so that I had the meat I needed for the items on the coffee shop menu. I had put them out on the floor in case, but shit.

A few words from Carson and it looked like I might just find myself in the meat business soon. As he helped Cassidy ring up the remaining customers, I realized I owed him a great big thank you.

I hadn't asked him for this, but he'd made a huge difference to me today and I had to swallow my pride because of it. I'd been grouchy with him ever since he'd come to town, but he hadn't done anything to deserve it other than surprise me with his return.

A sheepish smile spread on my lips, and I handed my notepad over to Cassidy to take care of the patrons remaining in the coffee shop. Without a word, she took it, understanding what I meant and leaving me alone with Carson.

"So, uh, I've been a bit of a witch to you lately, haven't I?"

Carson lifted the apron over his head and shrugged. "You had your reasons."

I held his eyes with my own and tried to remember what those reasons had been. "Maybe, but thank you for all your help today. Really. I can't tell you how much I appreciate it. We were drowning before you arrived."

"You managed just fine for years before I got here, Nova. I'm happy to help, though. Any time." He folded the apron over his arm before handing it back. "Just, uh, if I'm going to be doing this again, do you think you can find me one of those in blue? I'm not sure dusky pink is a good color on me."

I laughed softly, taking the apron and hugging it to my chest. "Any color is a good color on you, but sure. We'll make sure to keep a more manly one just in case you get bored at the market again and decide to come help out."

"Like I said, any time. I'm available." He looked at me like he meant it as more than just an offer to man the counter in the bakery. "My schedule is pretty wide open these days, so put me to work. I'd be happy to do it."

He sounded like he really meant it. He wanted to help. He wasn't just full of hot air and he wasn't trying to pull anything. Carson Drake, who had been my brother's friend since they'd been four years old, was back in town. Sure, he'd made his mark on the world and he'd built a real name for himself, but he'd always been a good guy with a good heart.

Good arm and instincts on the field aside, he was just *him* again now. For the first time in a long time, I felt like I really knew him as I stared into those eyes.

Emotion threatened to choke me, so I darted my gaze toward the tip jar instead. "I don't know how much we made, but help yourself. You deserve to be paid for what you did here today."

He scoffed. "Murphy, I've been so bored since I got home, I'd have paid *you* to let me do that. I'm not taking your money."

I glanced back at him, chuckling as I shook my head. "Fine, but it's your loss. You could've used it to buy your mom some flowers on the way home."

"Thanks, but she's got enough flowers. She doesn't need any inside as well. I swear, that woman is going to break a hip one of these days with her vigorous gardening style."

"Vigorous gardening?" Laughter thickened my voice as I frowned at him. "What on earth is that?"

"Drive by my house any day of the week and you'll see for yourself," he said easily. "Seriously, though, thanks for letting me help you. It was nice."

"Nice, huh? Well, there's always plenty to do around here, so if you ever get bored again, just come by and we'll be happy to work you to the bone."

"I've been trying to get you to do that, but it's good to know the message is finally sinking in." Glancing around, he lowered his voice, the humor fading from his eyes. "How's everything going with the ranch? Has Ryan gone topless yet?"

I laughed despite how dire the situation was. "Please don't describe it that way around him or he'll never agree."

He smiled. "I told you I'd do it. I'll pop my shirt off right now if you want. Get your phone out."

His cheery demeanor was a ray of sunlight breaking through the dark clouds surrounding me. He grabbed the hem of his T-shirt like he was about to yank it off.

I giggled and clamped my hands over his thick wrists. "No, you crazy fool. Keep your shirt on."

"Are you sure? We can put beefcake on the bakery menu."

I groaned and rolled my eyes. "Leave the beefcake under wraps, please."

He nodded and let go of his shirt. "Fine, I'll save it for another day, but you have to get a drink with me later to celebrate a great day of sales. Deal?"

"The bakery is sold out, but the market is still going on. I don't know when I'll be done."

He motioned toward the vendors outside. "It looks like everyone is nearly sold out. I've been seeing the number of people out there dwindling for a while now and some people have even started packing up their stalls."

I glanced where he was pointing. He was right. While I'd been so wrapped up in what had been happening here, it seemed the market really had wound down.

"A drink?" I looked back at him, and against my better judgment, I nodded. "Sure, Carson. Let's grab a drink. We definitely have something to celebrate. The newest employee at my bakery."

"I'll drink to that."

# 14

## CARSON

"I'm really excited to see this place," I said as Nova and I walked into the new brewery that had opened just a few weeks before I'd come home.

It was one of my business ventures and I'd been dying to see how it had turned out in person. Nova grinned up at me as we stopped just inside the door, taking in the trendy concrete floor and counter-tops, the kegs and barrels, and the solid mahogany bar that ran the entire length of the back wall.

Numerous taps were mounted on it and the scent of hops and fried food hung in the air. She lifted her eyebrows as she brought her gaze back to mine. "Wow. I thought you said you haven't been keeping busy."

I shrugged. "Investing is not keeping busy. I've never even seen this place before. Last I heard, they were busy installing the final fittings."

She ran her fingers through her ponytail, toying with the ends of her smooth blonde hair. "And you're okay with that? Giving money to people to do whatever they want?"

"Sure. Why not?" I inclined my head toward two open seats at one end of the long bar. "The partners I've got here want me to be more involved, and eventually, maybe I will be, but for now, I'm focusing on settling back in."

Nova followed me to the high-backed chairs, taking one and pointing at a tap marked *Silver Pale Ale*.

"I'm trying that," she said immediately. "I love a good pale ale."

I looked at her again once I'd sat down, marveling over the fact that I was actually here with her, back in town with no plans to leave and not dreaming about it either. "Since when do you know anything about beer?"

"Since I turned twenty-one a little over six years ago and stopped having to be nervous about drinking it," she said playfully. "It's amazing how much a person can learn in over half a decade."

I laughed. "That's fair. What else have you learned, then? I keep thinking I know you, but maybe that's not true anymore."

"It's true enough." She gave her order to the bartender when he came by, and I did the same thing before I turned back to her. Getting comfortable, she settled into the chair and crossed her legs. "I guess that depends on what you want to know. At heart, I'm still the same person, but I'm also smarter, wiser, and a lot more jaded."

"Okay, we're starting there," I said immediately. "Why are you more jaded?"

She chuckled and rolled her eyes at me. "Whoa there, cowboy. Stop looking like you're about to punch someone on my behalf. If someone needs punching, I'll do it myself, but aside from that, there's no one to punch. Just life, you know?"

"Yeah, I think I do." I accepted my beer when the bartender pushed it over to me, and I asked him to keep the tab open.

Once he was gone, I focused back on the blue-eyed mystery who looked so much like the girl I used to know. She was a full-fledged woman now, though. The more time I spent with her, the more I realized there was a lot of depth to her.

Yet, she was still just as easy to hang out with and talk to, and it still felt like I knew her. I just didn't know all the details anymore.

"Tell me about you, superstar," she said conversationally after taking a sip of her beer. "It feels like all we've done since you've been back is talk about me. What about you? What was life like away from here? Was it everything you wanted it to be?"

"Yes and no." I wrapped my fingers around my glass, watching the bubbles as they rose to the surface. I took another sip, swallowing while I thought about how to finish answering her question. "When I first left, it was a little weird. Cities are loud and busy. It took me some time to get used to the fact that it never seemed completely quiet."

Her eyes widened a little bit. "Really? Never?"

"Never," I said. "Well, I mean, if your apartment is properly soundproofed and stuff, then sure, but even then, the quiet just isn't the same. Plus, it took me a really long time to get used to not seeing the stars shining as bright as they do here."

"Constant noise and no stars." Her nose wrinkled adorably. "Yep. I'm never leaving. It's official."

I laughed. "I don't think you'd like it much, but not because of that. Everything is a bit cramped. Even the parks and the fields are caged in by buildings. It definitely took some getting used to. Mom told me you went to Oklahoma State U, though. So you must know all this."

"Sort of, but Oklahoma City is no New York. Besides, it's not like I've never visited a city. I just never saw myself staying wherever I was while I was there. I'd imagine that's a whole different kettle of fish, moving in and knowing you were there for good."

"It must be, but I wouldn't know. I always knew it wasn't for good."

She arched an eyebrow at me. "Always? That's funny because the way I remember it, you talked about leaving here and never coming back."

"Yeah, but that only lasted until I left, and I don't mean for college. When I started college, I knew I'd be back, but once I got drafted, things changed. Suddenly, I was gone and I didn't even know when I'd be able to visit again. That put things in perspective a little bit."

"Okay, I guess I can see that being true. I felt the same way when I went to college. It was temporary. I wasn't always sure I'd be back here as soon as I graduated. I thought about getting some work experience somewhere else first, but I never doubted that Silver Springs was where I'd settle to live my life."

"Same," I said, smiling. "Seems we still have a lot in common."

"We both love the town we grew up in. That hardly seems like a big thing to share. I think most people love their hometowns, even if they don't necessarily want to live there."

I chuckled and held my glass up for a toast. "Here's to loving Silver Springs and making it the place we both want to settle."

"Hear, hear." The glasses clinked as we brought them together. She held my gaze as we each took a sip. Once she'd swallowed, she tilted her head at me. "Is that why you retired so early, then? You got homesick?"

Surprised laughter tore out of me. "I guess you still don't know how to ease into stuff, huh?"

She shrugged, humor sparkling in her eyes as she stared back at me. "Who's got the time to ease into everything? If you ask me, people are too delicate about things these days. If I want to know something, I'll ask. Why try to wrap it up in a pretty little bow?"

"It's called tact, but you've never had that much of it," I said. "Okay. I'll play, though. Do you want the football answer or the life answer first?"

"Well, since I don't want to be accused of not being delicate enough with you again, let's go with the football answer. Something tells me that's the one you've rehearsed the most."

"I don't need you to be delicate with me, but okay. The football answer is that ten years in the NFL is enough. As a player, you get knocked around like a punching bag. It takes a toll. I'm still healthy enough to play a few more years, but I wanted retirement to be my choice. I didn't want a career-ending injury to force me out."

She pretended to clap her hands in a round of applause. "All that rehearsing paid off. That was flawless. Now give me the real answer."

"I got to the point where my heart was here instead of on the field. Vance and I talked about home a lot and the more we talked, the more we missed it. Eventually, I was counting the days until the season would end and I'd be able to come back home, and then I realized that I'd rather not have to leave again."

Those gorgeous blue eyes drank me in before she nodded. "I think you were really being honest with me right then. First time?"

"Saying it out loud? Yep."

She smiled. "I'm glad you stayed true to your heart, Carson. It takes a big person to walk away from something they love."

"Sure, but that doesn't mean I'll never play again. I'm thinking of volunteering at the elementary school. It could be fun."

"Elementary school?" she asked. "Don't you think your talents would be better off at the high school?"

"Maybe, but I think it's going to be a while before I'm ready for that. The stress. The pressure. The competitiveness. Before I dive back into all that, where hopes and dreams are crushed with one wrong hit, I think I'll start small. Where it's all fun and games."

"Well, I hope that works out for you. I don't think you realize how bored you'll get with that, but go for it. The kids would love to have you."

"Thanks. Speaking of kids, I seem to recall you saying you couldn't wait to settle down, get married, and have a couple. Why haven't you done that yet? Wasn't that your dream? The house with the white picket fence and as many kids as you could handle?"

Her fingers wound together on her lap, and her eyes dropped to them as she drew in a deep breath. "Guess I'm not the only one with no tact, so yes. I'll be as honest with you as you just were with me. That was the dream, but it's not exactly one I can live all by myself. It hinges on finding the right guy to marry, and that just hasn't happened for me yet."

"It will," I said confidently. *Maybe it already has, but that's a discussion for another day.* "So I know I was joking about it earlier, but seriously, have you given more thought to using me in your videos instead of Ryan? Or have you guys come up with a different plan?"

"A different plan?" She shook her head. "There is no other plan. Nothing that will help as fast as we need it to, anyway. There's a developer trying to buy the property to sell it to a client who'd probably turn the ranch into a hotel, and the problem is that if things keep going the way they are, we might not be able to keep it from happening for much longer."

"It's that bad?" I had thought everyone was exaggerating a little bit. The Murphys had been one of the families who'd founded this town, and people really cared about them. Because of that, I'd thought that it couldn't be bad enough that they'd ever actually lose the property.

As I looked into Nova's eyes now, it was dawning on me just how rocky things were. Money problems made people freak out like nothing else ever could. I'd figured things were rough but that it was more of a cash flow problem than anything else.

Of course, I'd also known about the developer and I hadn't liked the thought of him sniffing around, but I hadn't realized just how close he was to getting what he wanted.

While all these thoughts raced through my head, Nova let out a long, defeated breath and nodded. "It's that bad. My parents really aren't in a good place financially, and honestly, I'm not sure my dad truly understands the gravity of the situation."

Suspicions and rumors now confirmed, I leaned forward and waited until she was looking right at me. "Whatever I can do to help, Nova, just tell me. Seriously. You can't lose the ranch to this asshole. The town won't survive becoming a tourist destination."

Predictably, she waved me away. "We'll work it out. I just wish I knew how to get my dad to see that this isn't like all the other times. All ranches have their highs and lows. I get that, but this isn't just a low anymore. It's rock bottom. Ryan and I have been trying, but..."

"He doesn't want to believe it's true?" I guessed.

She shrugged a shoulder and took another sip of her beer. "That's the biggest problem of all. There are so many ways to generate more money with that land, but if we don't act fast, we're going to run out of time and what little money is left to do them."

I mentally ran through all the plans I'd heard of from them in just the last couple weeks, and I knew she was right. There were a few ways out of this yet, but they needed their father to be onboard. "What about your mom? Can't you get her to veto him?"

"Nope. Mom would be game to try anything, but you know how stubborn my dad is. He's got blinders on about the depth of shit we're in and no one is going to change his mind. Not even my mother."

I winced. "Shit. I'm sorry, Nova. I really hope he comes around before it's too late."

"Don't we all." She blew out another deep breath, then perked up and patted the bar. "Enough of that. I thought this was a celebration, not yet another pity party. Let's celebrate, shall we? Things with the ranch will work out or they won't, but there's no point in talking it to death tonight. Tell me more about what it was like to play ball professionally. Was it as intense as you thought it was going to be?"

I looked at her and believed that she was actually interested. Just like always, she wanted to know about me and my real feelings. A lot of things might've changed about Nova Murphy, but the one thing that never would was that she made me feel more like myself than anyone else. For that, I would always want her in my life.

No matter how much her brother hated the idea.

# 15

## NOVA

A few days after my celebration with Carson, I climbed into my truck feeling good about the week ahead. The last market had been such a hit that I was receiving even more inquiries than ever before about space for new sellers. At this rate, I was going to have to convince Dad to let me use more than just the very edge of the property.

I didn't want to get too excited because it still wouldn't solve our problems, but it felt good to know that I was helping others while also helping myself. Smiling, I turned over my engine and set off to pick up a few crates of strawberries at a farm about an hour outside of town.

I'd found this place a couple years ago and they had the best quality produce in the whole county. I always waited on pins and needles for the call because everything I baked during this season sold out in an hour—tops.

Since I wasn't the only one who loved their stuff, it was important to get there as fast as possible after receiving *the call*. It had come in about an hour ago, and even though it was late afternoon, I couldn't wait for the morning.

Naturally, since I was in a hurry and on the clock, I'd barely cleared the city limits before my car started shaking in a very particular way. *I have a flat. Fucking Mondays.*

Pulling over onto the shoulder, I hit my hazard lights and hopped out. My rear tire had a hole in it the size of Montana. I groaned, wondering what on earth had happened to it. My trip to the strawberry farm would have to wait.

I kicked the tire for good measure, but when that didn't magically fix the problem, I got back in behind the steering wheel and slowly cruised back into town. Thankfully, the auto shop was on the main street and I made it there without running off the road. To my surprise, though, Carson freaking Drake was talking to one of the mechanics outside.

*Okay, this town is small, but it's not that damn small.* I glanced up at the sky. A particularly puffy cloud floated overhead and I wondered if someone up there was trying to send me a sign. *Out with it, universe. Why are you doing this to me?*

Carson turned at the same time as the mechanic, a wide grin breaking out across his face. He put his hand up in a friendly wave. I waved back as I climbed out, hoping he wouldn't come over, but of course he did, following the mechanic when he approached me.

"What seems to be the problem, Ms. Murphy?" Dave, the mechanic, asked before he spotted the flat tire and winced. "Oh. There's your problem. You've got a giant hole in your tire."

I nodded. "Thank you, Dave. I figured that much out. But I don't have a spare, and I need to be somewhere this morning."

"I can probably patch that up for you. Let me give it a gander." He dropped to his haunches at the back of the truck and started doing his thing.

Impatience bubbled in my stomach to be back out on the road, but I managed to flash Carson a tight smile anyway. "What are you doing here?" I asked. "You really are following me, aren't you?"

He chuckled. "Last I checked, I got here first, which means that this time, it seems you were following *me*. Stalker."

"Ha, you wish." I ran my hands through my hair as I glanced at Dave. He was still busy, though.

Carson inclined his head toward a sedan currently lifted on a stand in the shop. "My mom's car is getting some work done. I was just checking in. Not having her car is driving her crazy."

"I know the feeling," I mused.

Dave pushed up from his haunches and gave me a look that said a thousand words. "I'm afraid you need a new rim, Ms. Murphy. The bad news is that we don't have any in stock. I'm going to have to order it, but the good news is that it shouldn't take more than a couple of days to get here. You'll have your truck back before the end of the week."

I gaped like a fish out of water. His words sank in and so did the devastation. It would seem silly to anyone else, but I *had* to get those strawberries before they sold out for the season. The couple who owned the farm would only hold my order for so long.

They would never hold it until the end of the week. They had far too many people breaking down their doors this time of year.

"What's wrong?" Carson asked. "It's just a couple days. It should be fine."

"It would've been, but I have a really important order to pick up right now. I was heading out there when my tire blew up."

"Let me drive you," he said easily. "I was done here anyway and it'll be faster than going back to the ranch and borrowing your parents' or your brother's car."

"Yes, absolutely. Thank you." I didn't even give it a second thought. For once in my life, I wasn't going to look a gift horse in the mouth. "It's about an hour away, though. Is that okay?"

"Just point me in the right direction," he said cheerfully, sweeping an arm out toward his truck and nodding at Dave. "Thanks for the update, man. Do whatever needs to be done and send me your invoice, okay? It's been years since that thing has had proper maintenance done."

"Will do, Carson. See you around."

"See you," he replied before bringing his hand to the small of my back and letting it rest there.

A spark of electricity zapped through me even though his skin wasn't touching mine. Goosebumps broke out across my flesh and left me feeling a little breathless.

*Jeez. What is* wrong *with me?*

"I'll order that rim and get back to you about when you can pick up your truck, Ms. Murphy," Dave said to me.

I bounced my head in a jerky nod to thank him before letting Carson lead me to his truck.

After he opened the door for me and then closed it once I'd gotten in, he jumped in behind the wheel and got us underway. "Where am I going?"

I rattled off the address, still feeling the weight of his palm on my back even though it wasn't there anymore, and then I reminded myself that I was a full-grown woman who knew how to control myself.

*Get your shit together, Nova. This is ridiculous.*

I forced myself to inhale and exhale deeply a few times to calm my racing heart. It worked, and the butterflies were replaced by a buzzing sense of relief. "Thank you so much for this. I know it doesn't seem like the end of the world, but I need those strawberries."

"Strawberries, huh?" He flashed me a lopsided grin and glanced at me before his eyes went back to the road. "I seem to remember you being a miracle worker with those growing up."

I thought back to all the hours I'd spent in my mother's kitchen, watching Carson come and go from our house before and after football practice and always feeling like I needed to have something special ready for him after the serious workout he'd gotten on a daily basis. And okay, Ryan was there too, obviously, but not too much of my efforts were for him.

I probably should've been ashamed about that, but I wasn't. "If you thought I was a miracle worker with those, you should see what I can do with the ones we're about to pick up. They're juicy and succulent, and not one of them tastes watered down. They're the kind of strawberries that are worthy of the name."

"Does that mean there are strawberries that aren't worthy of the name?" he asked, brow furrowing. "I mean, I get juicy and succulent. That sounds great, but a strawberry is a strawberry, right?"

"Wrong," I said in no uncertain terms. "I'll let you try some of these when we're on our way back. You'll be kicking yourself for ever thinking that a strawberry is just a strawberry."

He laughed, his head dropping back a little but his eyes still focused on the road. As I looked at him, his shoulders still shaking with laughter, my stomach filled with joy. He looked so young and carefree, his dark hair still thick and longish but swept away from his handsome face and rippling a bit as he shook his head.

"I'm going to trust you on that one," he said easily. "I always imagined you going to culinary school, and now you have a bakery. How did you end up getting a degree in agriculture when all you've ever wanted was to be in your own kitchen?"

I shrugged. "There are dreams, and then there is reality. Not all of us are lucky enough to have those two things line up the way they did for you."

"The ranch?" he asked.

I nodded. "Same as with Ryan. We both want to help, so I pursued agriculture while he learned how to fix things. It might not be my passion or his, but I still get to bake and he still plays football in the park sometimes."

Carson got a little quiet after that, but we reached the farm in no time, and mercifully, my order was packed and waiting. He helped me load the crates onto the bed of his truck, then snagged some of the berries and popped them into his mouth.

We climbed back into our seats.

"Well, there goes at least one tart," I scolded him playfully. "I'd tell you I was going to charge you for it, but we used your gas to get here, so consider us even."

"Hey, you told me I could try some," he protested. "Those are good, by the way. Amazing, actually. I hate to say it, but you were right. Those really are worthy of the name *strawberry*."

"Ha." I grinned at him, feeling a lightness creeping over me now that I had the produce and the crisis had properly been averted.

"Hold on a sec, will you? I'll get us something to snack on for the road."

After grabbing a tiny box out of one of the crates, I settled back into my seat and winked at him. "How about this? If you can catch it, you can eat it."

"Catch it?" he echoed as we got back on the road. "I'm game, but if we crash, we're sharing a hospital room while we recover."

"Guess I'll have to aim well." I plucked out a strawberry and threw it into his mouth as he drove.

Carson grinned triumphantly after catching it, and he gave a little moan as he swallowed it.

I felt the moan in parts of my body that weren't supposed to *feel sound*.

"That was great," he said. "Let's try it again."

I tossed another strawberry into his mouth. Again, he hummed a pleasurable sound as he swallowed it. The deep, low groan filled the cab of his truck, making a shiver race through me. I suddenly remembered hearing noises like that from him while he kissed me.

My cheeks flushed with heat and my breathing sped up a little, but I kept going, throwing strawberries into his mouth. Hard as I tried, I couldn't keep my body from reacting to him. To the sounds he made and the beautiful grin on his face every time he succeeded. To the way the muscles in his forearm rippled every time he shifted gears and the amusement in his voice whenever he spoke.

I'd never had chemistry like this with anyone else, and even though I missed every last one of the strawberries he tried throwing into my mouth, it was still there, crackling in the air between us. It grew even while we laughed and chatted, and when he leaned over to wipe some berry juice off my lip while we were stopped at a traffic light, I felt like I was about to combust spontaneously.

Carson's eyes darkened as they hooked on mine with his thumb still lingering on my mouth. The thought that he still felt that chemistry too was enough to make my panties damp. Back when we'd been kids, he'd also set my body on fire, but even that paled in comparison to how I felt now.

Everything I'd ever felt paled in comparison to the feelings racing through me.

I held his gaze. There was something so real and raw about this moment, and yet, a relationship between us was still taboo. I didn't know how it was possible that the only guy in the whole world I *shouldn't* want was the same one who made me feel like he was the reason none of my other relationships had worked out.

Like he was the one I was meant to be with. Like he was the reason I was about to jeopardize my relationship with my brother.

All to taste those strawberries on Carson's lips.

# 16

## CARSON

I was about to kiss her when the light changed. Both of us saw it happening in our periphery and it shattered the moment. Nova broke eye contact with me, sat back in her seat, and faced forward.

Internally, I cursed and ranted. *Why does our timing always suck so bad?*

I swore, this girl and I could never catch a break. Not ten years ago and apparently not now either.

For the rest of the drive to the ranch, neither of us said much. I was lost in thought, wondering if the universe was trying to tell me something, and Nova stared out the window, also seeming deep in thought.

Our bad luck continued. Ryan was there when we arrived at the bakery. *Whoop-dee-doo. Thanks, universe. Just keep piling it on, why don't you?*

He eyed Nova in the truck with me and came over. "What's going on, guys?"

"My truck's in the shop. Carson gave me a ride to pick up an order of strawberries." She jumped out of the truck, rolling her eyes at her brother. Then she walked around the back and picked up the crate. "Thanks for all your help today."

She aimed the last sentence at me, then spun around and headed inside. I reeled a little bit as I watched her go. She couldn't exactly acknowledge what had almost happened between us with Ryan right there, but I was baffled about how she could be acting like it hadn't happened at all.

"Grab one of those, will you?" I said to my friend, struggling but eventually managing to tear my gaze away from Nova's back as she disappeared into the bakery.

"What happened to her truck?" He lifted two of the crates and waited for me to do the same before we followed her.

"She got a flat on her way out of town," I explained. "I ran into her at the auto shop and offered to give her a ride."

"As long as it was just a ride in your truck and she wasn't riding *you*, I guess that's okay," he muttered.

Nova must've heard him from where she'd already deposited the first crate of strawberries in the kitchen, and her eyes narrowed at the comment. I could sense her frustration and I had no doubt she could feel the sudden tension between her brother and me.

*For fuck's sake. She's twenty-seven now. Not seventeen anymore.*

Either way, it seemed he was just as protective as ever—which meant I really had no chance with her. I dropped off the crates I'd been carrying in the kitchen, lingering inside with her when Ryan headed back out to collect more.

"I'm sorry he's so on edge when it comes to me," she murmured, those blues filling with real remorse as they held mine. "He's just protective. Don't take it personally, and really, thank you for your help today."

"You're welcome." I was annoyed with Ryan for being an ass, but if I had a hot younger sister who my friends were sniffing around, I probably would have been the same way.

Swallowing the frustration, I took a deep breath, shook it all off, and smiled at her instead of brooding about her brother. "If you ever need a product tester, call me. I'd love to taste the magic you're going to make with those."

She grinned. "See, I would, but I don't have your number."

Instantly, my hand shot out, palm up, and I curled my fingers. "Hand it over and I'll give it to you."

"You shouldn't let my brother hear you saying stuff like that," she joked, but also not really.

Part of me was already bracing for him to come flying at me and smash a strawberry crate on my head. Just for trying to give her my number.

When that didn't happen, she handed me the device and I keyed it in. "There. Now you have it. Call me, okay?"

"I'll think about it." She smiled. "I'd better put all these strawberries away. Goodbye, Carson. Thanks again. For everything, I mean. I'm starting to wonder what we did around here without you."

Blood pounded in my ears when she said it. Her eyes lingered on mine for a beat before she walked outside. I followed her. My heart was doing a really weird hop-skip-jump thing as I stared at her back on our way out.

"I'll see you guys around." I started toward my truck but stopped when Ryan glanced at me and held up a hand. "What's up?"

"Moe's later?" he asked. "I need a beer after this."

I chuckled. "Same here. Let me just go get cleaned up and I'll meet you there."

He nodded, hoisted a couple more crates, and carried them in with Nova in tow, calling after him to be careful. I got into my truck. Just before she went inside, she paused in the doorway and turned to wave at me.

She smiled and my lips curved up too as if I was physically obligated to mimic her. Then she finally disappeared into the bakery and left me sitting in my truck with my heart racing and my cock pressing against the fly of my jeans.

I drove away from the ranch, and for the first time in over a decade, I felt what could only be described as butterflies in my stomach.

*Fuck, that's weird.*

With the radio on in the background, I was vaguely aware of a storm notification coming through, but I was too wrapped up in Nova to pay much attention to it. "Forecasts are warning that it's going to be a big one. Starting at eight p.m. tonight, there's a warning in effect for high winds, flash floods, and tornadoes. Authorities are asking residents to take all proper precautions and to remain indoors. Stay safe out there."

Having seen much worse than that around here before, I shrugged it off, not allowing the possibility of some wind and rain to derail me from my thoughts. There was definitely still something there with Nova. Something real that wasn't just about me wanting to get into her pants—unlike what Vance had been worried about.

I was driving down my mom's street when my phone rang. The number of one of the local realtors I'd reached out to popped up. Hitting the button on my steering wheel, I shook my head to clear the mental cobwebs. "This is Carson."

"Carson! I'm sorry for bothering you so late. I've found a few properties with development potential for you to take a look at. All the owners have confirmed times for viewing, and if you're available, I'd like to show you some places in the morning?"

"Sounds good," I said. "Text me the time and address of the first property and we'll take it from there."

He agreed, and I grinned like a loon after I hung up. *Things really do feel like they're falling into place pretty nicely now that I'm finally here.*

When I got home, I gave my mother a kiss on the cheek and checked that she and the house were alright before I washed up and headed to Moe's. Mom had weathered her fair share of storms alone while I'd been gone, and thankfully, she'd already battened down the hatches just in case this one got ugly.

I looked up once I was back in my truck, but apart from a few clouds drifting in, it didn't look like much was going on up there. About an hour later though, that changed.

Sitting around a table near the window with Ryan and Vance, we watched the storm roll in. Lightning streaked across the sky, and thunder rumbled so intensely the booth we were sitting in vibrated.

Vance regaled Ryan with tales of weird situations he'd gotten himself into with women while he'd been on the road.

"Maybe they were right about it being a bad one," I commented during a lull.

They glanced out the window, but none of us thought much about the storm—until the rain came. A bone-jarring thunderclap pierced the air, and the next thing we knew, water pelted down, splashing against the window and hitting the roof with such force that the noise became almost deafening.

Ryan tensed as he glanced down at his phone. "Shit. I'm sorry, guys, but I need to get back to the ranch."

"Need some help?" Vance asked without hesitation.

I tossed a few bills on the table and stood up too. "A couple extra sets of hands won't hurt. What's going on?"

"Dad's worried about the wind. He said there were trees falling over." His jaw hardened, and his eyes took on a glazed look, like he was mentally going over the checklist of things we'd need to do once we got there.

As we left Moe's, thunder cracked the sky open above us, and all the lights blinked out. Vance cursed. "Fuck. Let's speed this up, boys. We need to get there before all hell breaks loose."

Wholeheartedly agreeing with him, I ran to my truck and fell in behind them on the road. My windscreen wipers moved as fast as they could but I could hardly see a thing. It was like a wall of water coming down. I leaned forward, slowing as much as I dared and squinting in the hopes that I'd be able to see better.

A difficult drive later, we finally got to the ranch. Ryan opened his window and waved a hand to show me to pull over. I did and rolled my window down, frowning.

He shouted to me over the wind. "I can't get a hold of Nova! Can you go check on her? I need to make sure my parents are okay. They're not answering their damn phones now either."

I nodded and quickly shut the window again. My whole side was already soaked. Lightning raced across the sky above the mountains. It lit up the inky black night for a second. Rivers of rain ran over the dirt road and trees bowed in ways trees should not have been able to bend.

*Crap. George was right to be worried about the wind.*

A tremor of fear ran through me as I headed up in the direction of Nova's cottage. So far, I'd only seen her place from a distance but I knew where to go. Pressing my foot down a little harder on the gas, I pushed my truck faster, still battling to see through the rain. Every time I hit a bump, the whole truck jolted, but I didn't slow down.

She knew better than to not pick up her phone with a storm like this raging outside. *If she's hurt, I won't be able to handle it.*

When the little cottage finally appeared in the faint glow of my headlights, I hit the brakes, and the tires slipped a little before I came to a complete stop. Dragging in a deep breath, I grabbed a hoodie from the backseat and positioned it above my head. Then I opened the door and sprinted across the soggy ground.

Mud splashed against my jeans. My feet squelched in it as I ran, but it didn't slow me down much. As soon as I got on her porch, I banged on the door, praying that she heard me and that I wouldn't have to break it down. I would if I had to, though. Nothing would keep me from her if she needed help.

I was soaked to the bone, my hoodie drenched despite the short distance I'd covered, but I was barely aware of it. Each second ticked by like an eternity while I waited for her to answer.

She finally opened up and gave me a confused look. "What are you doing out in this chaos?"

Relief coursed through me. "You're okay! Shit. We were worried. You didn't pick up your phone."

A flash of light tore through the night, and this time, it struck nearby. A boom followed instantly. Nova stepped aside to let me in, and I slammed the door behind me.

I'd made it here safely. Nova was fine, but the storm was far from over. If things kept intensifying the way they were, the destruction would be catastrophic. At least I was at her side, where I could keep her safe.

I had no right to feel the way I did about Nova, but I would die before I let anything happen to her.

# 17

## NOVA

Riding out a wild storm didn't seem so scary now that Carson was standing in my little cottage.

A minute ago, I'd been hunkered down by myself with my pajamas on and a blanket wrapped around my shoulders as I used a flashlight to track down all the candles I had stashed around my kitchen. I didn't look glamorous or sexy, but my appearance hadn't even crossed my mind until he showed up.

Being faced with a dripping wet, ridiculously hot former NFL player had a way of putting things into perspective.

I tugged the blanket tighter around me and wondered if I could sneak away to change out of my *Bambi* PJs. They were super comfortable but not my first choice when entertaining a handsome guest.

He shoved his hands into his drenched hair and swiped a wet sleeve across his brow in an attempt to clear some of the water there. I wasn't the only one who needed to change their clothes.

Snapped out of my uncharacteristic self-consciousness, I shook my head. "Service has been spotty since the storm rolled in. I didn't even realize anyone had tried to check on me."

"Your brother was fit to be tied when you didn't answer."

"Yeah, he was so worried, he sent you to check on me instead of showing up himself." I shook my head and laughed. "Not that I'm complaining. I appreciate you coming out here. Now take off your clothes."

"You want me to take off my clothes?" He arched a brow at me and held my gaze as he reached for the button of his jeans. "If you insist."

I rolled my eyes. "You're dripping all over my good rug from Target. I'm going to get you a towel and something of Ryan's to put on."

He shrugged and kicked off his muddy shoes. Then he flicked open the button on his jeans and dragged down his zipper, completely calm and casual but moving slowly. As if he was waiting for me to change my mind. My entire being flushed with heat, and the storm outside paled in comparison to the emotions raging inside me.

He started pushing down his waistband. I bit my lip, my eyes begging to lower to his crotch to watch it happen, but I kept my gaze firmly locked on his. "Well, I guess you could keep them on, but you're not sitting that wet ass on my sofa."

He chuckled and shoved the jeans off but mercifully kept his black boxer briefs on. In my peripheral vision, I saw how the material hugged his muscular thighs and I was tempted to ask him to turn around so I could see his ass. As he stepped out of the soaked jeans, I finally remembered that he needed something to dry off with.

As well as clothes to put on.

"I'll be back." I ducked my head and turned around, heading down the hall to my linen closet and hoping he hadn't seen just how much I was blushing.

After grabbing two towels, I dug into a box filled with Ryan's old clothes and I pulled out a pair of sweats and a T-shirt. Then I dragged in a deep, calming breath before I went out to him again. When I got there, he was on the phone in front of the door that led out to my patio. With his back to me, he didn't see me walking toward him, his gaze intently focused on the storm raging outside.

The phone was on speaker, and he held it next to his face. "So they're okay?"

"Yep," my brother's voice rang out. "They're fine. Apparently, cell service has been coming and going. Dad, Vance, and I just went out to check, and more trees have come down."

"Okay," Carson said. "What can I do to help?"

"Stay with Nova," Ryan replied in a gruff voice that made it sound like he'd rather have said anything but that. "You guys are stuck up there together until we can clear the road. There's a tree blocking it not too far from my parents' place. We tried heading there to grab you two so we could all ride it out together, but it must've come down just after you went past."

"There was a lightning strike," Carson said. "Just after I got here. It could've been that."

"Could've been any number of things, but figuring out what caused it doesn't help us get to you guys. Sit tight, okay? That'll be our first priority once it starts clearing up."

"Don't worry about us," Carson said. "We're fine here. Any news on the power?"

"Just that they're working on restoring it, but it's probably going to take a couple hours." Ryan blew out a heavy breath and silence stretched for a long minute until my brother finally spoke again. "Carson."

"Ryan," he said patiently. "You don't have *anything* to worry about, okay? We're good here. *Nothing* is going to happen."

He emphasized the words like he was trying to reassure Ryan that he and I weren't going to do anything, and even though I'd been happy to ogle his strong back and firm ass while he was standing there in only his underwear, I was kind of upset about the reassurances.

I understood that he was just trying to set my brother's mind at ease about us being stuck here together, but surely, I should get a say in whether or not something was going to happen between us. Irritation spurred my feet back into motion and I ignored those powerful thigh muscles as I strode up to him and smacked the little bundle of towel and clothes against his chest.

As I did, his free hand came up to secure them and his eyes darted to mine. He gave me a grateful smile and kept listening as my brother spoke. "Yeah, okay, bud. Just, uh, be safe and don't do anything stupid. If I get any updates about the storm or the power, I'll text you. I just don't know if—"

The line went dead and I smirked. "See, spotty service. Dry off and get dressed. I'll track down the rest of the candles."

I'd already lit some, which didn't help with the *not ogling him* thing. Even the worst looking people were all pretty and soft in candlelight, and Carson was not one of those people. Even so, he'd just conspired against me with my brother. He didn't deserve to be ogled right now.

He dried off quickly with one towel, then used the other on his hair and to soak up the puddle that had formed around his feet. Once he was done with that, he changed into the clothes I'd brought him while also trying to call his mother.

The phone was still on speaker, so I heard his first few attempts fail as I moved around the room, lighting a bunch more candles. Finally, as I was heading to the stove to boil some water for hot drinks, the line connected.

Carson grabbed the phone off the back of the sofa, his jaw tense when her voice didn't immediately flow through the speaker. "Mom? Are you there? Are you okay?"

There was some crackling. Then she came through, the connection a little broken at first. "I'm fine— Mrs. Norris—down the street."

His brow furrowed as he stared at the phone. "Mom?"

"I'm here," she said cheerfully just a moment later. "Oh, there we go. That sounds better. I'm fine, honey. Mrs. Norris and Earl from down the street are here with me. Eleanor got caught in the rain, so she decided to hunker down here, and Earl was trying to save a tree." She chuckled. "We've got snacks, wine, and candles. Where are you? Are you alright?"

"I'm fine. I came out to Red Stone Ranch with Ryan and Vance, so

I'm with Nova. She's fine too. She just wasn't picking up her phone. We're all good, but we're stuck here until the storm dies down enough for Ryan and George to move some downed trees."

"You're with Nova?" she said, sounding weirdly delighted.

I smiled as I filled my stove-top kettle and set it down on the hob. This turn of events had me feeling things as well.

"Yeah, it's a bit of a long story," he said. "But everyone is safe and dry."

"That's wonderful, darling. They're predicting that it could go on all night. It could easily carry on into the morning, too. I'm sure you two will keep each other safe and *occupied*."

Carson groaned. "Thanks, Mom. I'll talk to you later, okay? Stay safe."

"You too, baby," she said, still excited as if she couldn't imagine any news better than what she'd just heard.

I fixed us each a cup of tea and carried the mugs over to the living room. Carson sat down on the sofa. When I handed his over, he grimaced at me. "I'm going to assume you heard all that."

"You did have her on speaker," I said as I wrapped my fingers around my own mug and sat down on the sofa kitty-corner to the one he was on. "Do I want to know what that was about?"

He sighed, eyes on mine as he shook his head. "Probably not, but I'll tell you anyway. My mom knows I came home to settle down. She knows I want a family, a wife, and all those other things I couldn't have the way I wanted them while I was playing and on the road all the time."

My heart fluttered. "Okay, but what does that have to do with me?"

Those green eyes sparkled in the candlelight as he stared right into mine. "My mom has always liked you. I think she's hoping that we'll fall head over heels in love in the time it takes the storm to clear."

If we had been any other pair of people stuck together for only a few hours, I'd have found the idea of falling in love so fast laughable.

But Carson and I weren't any other people. With us, it was definitely within the realm of possibility that it could happen.

*Well, for me, anyway.*

I blew out a long breath through my nostrils and reminded myself of what he'd said. Nothing was going to happen between us tonight. So while it was sweet that his mother was so excited, it didn't make a lick of difference if he wanted all those things. He didn't want them with me.

*Besides, I don't have time for any of that anyway.*

A stab of disappointment speared my gut, but I refused to let it show. "I love your mom, but somehow, I think she's a little off-base tonight. It must be the storm."

Unless I was imagining things, I saw my own disappointment flickering in his eyes for a second until he blinked it away. Smiling instead, he leaned back on the sofa and brought his cup to his lips, taking a small sip and swallowing it down. "Okay, so now that you know the truth about my homecoming and my mother's dreams, what about you? Why did you wait so long to be a baker and why haven't you allowed yourself to find love and have kids?"

"Wow. We're jumping to intense conversation tonight, huh?" I tried teasing, but it fell a little flat. We'd touched on this briefly the other day at the brewery, but right then, I felt like he could see straight through me.

If I was being completely honest, I had been using the ranch as a distraction because no one had ever made me feel like he did, but I couldn't go there. Not while we could be stuck here together all night or maybe even longer. It would probably make him hellishly uncomfortable if he didn't feel the same way, and he wouldn't even be able to escape.

Besides, I didn't want him to feel pressured into doing anything with me when he'd just told Ryan he wouldn't. "I've answered that question already. I just haven't found the right guy. As for being a baker, I didn't wait that long. I went and got a degree that could help my family, and as soon as I could after I got back, I opened up the bakery."

He cocked his head, those freaking eyes still super intent on mine. "I don't think that's the whole truth. Is it? Or are you just not ready to tell me the rest of it yet?"

"That," I murmured, my heart galloping in my chest as I wondered if he already knew the rest of it even if I hadn't said it.

Carson let out a soft groan, still looking at me as he moved forward on the sofa and leaned over to set his cup down on the coffee table. I scooted forward too, as if tethered to him with an invisible but unbreakable force.

"Nova..." He trailed off, his hands coming up to cup my face. I leaned into his touch, my lips already buzzing with the anticipation of what was about to happen.

"Don't overthink it," I whispered as I slid my hand around the nape of his neck and gently pulled him closer to me.

"We should not be doing this," he breathed but he didn't stop. His fingers gripped on my cheeks and around the base of my scalp as he brought my mouth to his.

Our lips touched and angels sang. I swore I heard their chorus of relief and joy as my fingers pushed into his hair. His tongue came out to probe my lips. Sparks flew through me, my body and heart electrified.

I parted them for him, moaning. He kissed me passionately, like this was it. Like we were making each other some kind of promise we could never break.

And then the power came on and ruined the moment. My spirits sank to my shoes. So often, it felt like our stars were aligning and then something like this would happen, making me question it all. If Carson and I were meant to be together, then why on earth were we always forced to break apart right when we were on the verge of something wonderful?

# 18

CARSON

*eriously?! Fucking seriously?*

S I blinked against the sudden brightness in the cottage, my body and soul raging against the interruption and begging me not to let it put a stop to the kiss. Nova wrenched her mouth away from mine before I could pull her closer to me again. Her hands dropped away from my head, and her body shot backward as she scooted all the way to the opposite end of the sofa.

"Damn it," I muttered. "I thought it was supposed to take a couple hours."

Her cheeks were flushed, her lips slightly swollen, and her breaths coming hard and fast, but she shook her head, her eyes wide as she suddenly got up. "Yeah, uh, the problem must not have been as big as they were expecting. Who knows?"

Tucking her loose hair behind her ears, she started blowing out the candles. Then she suddenly paused and tilted her head. A crease appeared between her eyebrows. "Hey, do you hear that?"

"Hear what?"

"Exactly." She glanced at me, moving again now to continue extinguishing the candles. "The rain is letting up."

*Fuck.* "No. What? How is that possible? I thought this storm was supposed to be huge."

"I hate to break it to you, but it was. With that amount of wind, the worst of it has probably just blown over. It might keep raining for a while, though. Besides, it's been hours since it hit. How long did you want it to last?"

*Approximately as long as you would've had enough food to sustain us both, and then I only would've wanted it to let up enough to replenish our supplies before it started up again.* "Yeah. no. I guess you're right."

I glanced at the slim grandfather clock in the corner of the room. It had been almost five hours since Ryan, Vance, and I had arrived at the bar. Time had flown, but it was gone—and so was the worst of the rain. Any minute now, Ryan was going to call to tell me they were heading out to start removing the trees blocking the road, and once that happened, who knew how long it would be before we had some time alone again?

"Nova—"

My phone started ringing and I flinched. If I didn't answer it, he'd head straight here. Fallen trees be damned. If he so much as suspected that I wasn't picking up because I'd fallen into bed with his sister, that would be it. He'd ramp his damn truck over the logs and come storming in here guns blazing.

"You should get that," she said softly, all the candles now blown out as she glanced at my muddy boots. "Do you need dry socks before you head out?"

"Uh, okay." I inhaled deeply and answered. "Hey, man. Are we in the clear?"

"Yep. I'm heading out to get the tractor now. Dad and Vance are already on their way. If you take the road down from Nova's toward the bakery, you'll find them."

"I'll be there in a few," I said, then glanced at Nova. "Before you freak out when you see it, I'm wearing some of your old clothes. Mine were soaked through,"

"Thanks for the heads-up. We're good, bro. I'll see you in a minute."

He hung up and I turned toward her just in time to see her features tighten like she was hurt. I frowned. "Are you okay?"

"Yeah. Fine." Her voice was too tight for it to be true, but their dad and Vance were already waiting for me. I didn't have time to dig into whatever was happening.

"Okay, then." I took the dry socks she'd fetched for me and quickly sat down to put them on. "Thanks for all this. Do me a favor and stay put, okay? Your parents are fine. The power is on. Vance and I will help your brother with whatever needs to be done before we take off. There's no reason for you to go out there."

She scoffed and shook her head at me. "I'll be just fine, Carson. It's not like this is the first storm I've ever seen."

"Yeah, but it could turn back," I said. "It's just safer if you stay here."

She rolled her eyes. "Uh huh. Thanks."

I put my boots back on and stood up, crossing over to her but stopping just short of actually letting parts of our bodies touch. "Look, Nova, I'm not telling you what to do. I'm asking you to please stay here where it's safe."

"I need to check on the bakery."

"I'll do it. Just as soon as we've cleared the road. I'll call you with an update, okay?"

Instead of responding, she just shrugged and held my gaze for one more second before she scoffed again, turned around, and marched to the door. "You'd better go before Ryan gets angry. God forbid we upset my brother, right?"

Confusion raced through me, but she pointed at the open door. I left, my head shaking as I wondered what the hell had just happened. It kind of felt like we'd gone back to how she'd acted when I first got home, and I had no idea why.

Jogging through the rain to my truck, I climbed in and turned over the engine. Turning my attention to the chaos around me, I headed out to meet up with the others. Leaves and branches carpeted the ground, with some trees down along the side of the road as well.

Water shimmered on the fields, letting me know that the flat parts were probably lakes at this point.

I sighed. It could've been a lot worse, but damage was damage and fixing it cost money. Even buying extra feed for the animals if they couldn't graze normally by morning would be expensive, but I couldn't worry about that now. Hopefully, it wouldn't be necessary, and everything would be just fine in a few hours when the rain had stopped completely and the water had a chance to drain.

My headlights landed on George's truck when I turned around a bend, and my eyes widened when I saw him and Vance wrapping thick chains around the downed tree.

They were wearing heavy raincoats, and when I stopped to join them, George grinned and went back to his truck to fetch another.

"Here," he said when he came back and handed it over. "We figured you'd need to borrow one of mine. Thanks for your help tonight, Carson. I appreciate it."

"No problem, sir. Just tell me what to do and consider it done." I pulled on the coat, popping the hood on and tightening it around my face after zipping up.

"Get on that side and help Vance. We're trying to secure it before Ryan gets here."

Vance smirked at me when I joined him, waggling his brows even as he fiddled with the metal. "You have fun with Nova while I was stuck talking strategy with George and Ryan? They're tackling the damage control like a head coach, man. I felt like I was back in the locker room."

I chuckled. "They have to. The more they can mitigate the damage, the less it will cost them to fix."

"You haven't answered my question."

I crouched down and tried to slide my hand between the muddy ground and the stump, rolling my eyes at my friend. "It was fine. There was no *fun* being had. We just talked, is all."

"Pity," he joked. "Seems like a wasted opportunity to me."

Ryan arrived with the tractor and even Vance shut up as we really got to work. By the time we'd removed all the trees that had fallen into the roads and cleared the debris, it was nearly morning, but I'd made Nova a promise.

I needed to go check on the bakery before I headed home. Ryan and George grinned at me as they each gave me a firm handshake, then went to make sure the animals had made it through okay. Vance gave me a pointed look once they were gone.

"Whatever you're doing with her," he said. "Be careful. We grew up with him and when he finds out, he'll go nuclear. He's her family, Carson. That means something. It means a lot actually."

"I know," I assured him. If only he understood how very aware I was of all that, he definitely wouldn't have told me again. "I *am* careful. Get home safe, Vance. The sun is going to start coming up soon, but until it does, it'll be hard to spot debris on the roads."

"Same to you," he said before he drove off.

I got in my truck and drove down to the bakery only to find that Nova was already there. Thankfully, the structure seemed to have made it through intact and everything seemed fine. The outside area was a bit of a mess, but I was pretty sure the entire town would look the same way. As for Nova being here, already busy cleaning up, I didn't know how to feel about that.

I had asked her to stay put.

"What are you doing here?" I jogged over to her and slid my hands into the pockets of Ryan's sweats so she wouldn't see the tremor that was running through me at the thought of everything that could've happened to her out here all alone.

She frowned at me. "I'm cleaning. We need to be ready to receive customers soon. Pastries and breads don't bake themselves and I can't have people pulling into a parking lot that looks like a tornado hit it."

I shook my head at her. "You could've been crushed, struck by lightning, caught in the rain, or got hurt on your way down here."

She stared blankly. "It's not even raining anymore. And all those things could've happened to you too. Why do you care anyway? You're obviously done helping my brother, so you should probably get home now."

"Why do I care?" I echoed as my eyes narrowed. "Didn't we *just* kiss?"

"Yeah, well, why don't you go talk to Ryan and see how your best friend feels about us making out?" With that, she marched back into the building and shut the door in my face.

Letting out an incredulous huff of air, I followed her, opening the door and shutting it again behind me. A lot of other guys might've just walked away after something like that, but I couldn't. I didn't even try.

I'd walked away once before after we'd kissed and I believed in learning from my mistakes. I caught up to her as she was striding into the kitchen, and I gently circled her wrist and tugged her into me. She squeaked in surprise but didn't try to pull away as she turned her head up to mine.

I hadn't been planning on doing it, but when I saw her eyes dart to my lips, I kissed her again before pulling away to look at her. "I will talk to Ryan. If that's what you want, I'll talk to him."

"I don't know what I want, Carson," she said, her voice sharp but soft and her eyes shining with something I couldn't quite place. "I'm frustrated and I'm scared about what all this means. I was already feeling overwhelmed enough with just trying to keep the ranch afloat, but now you're back and everything just feels so much more complicated."

I opened my mouth to tell her I felt the same way, but she wasn't done yet. "All this time, my family has been my number-one priority, and now I'm kissing you and that puts my relationship with my brother in the line of fire. I can't…"

She took a step away from me, the expression in her eyes haunted. She dropped her face into her hands, inhaled and exhaled deeply a few times, and then pushed her fingers into her golden locks as she lifted her chin up again.

I practically saw the thoughts racing through her head even though she didn't voice them all. It didn't take a genius to figure out that she was feeling desperate to maintain control over at least one part of her life.

She probably also felt a bit foolish. Frankly, I understood the sentiment.

Was it really possible to catch feelings so fast after such a long time? I didn't know, but I was willing to risk it. When Nova spoke again, it became clear that she wasn't.

"Please don't say anything to Ryan," she said, her voice hushed now like she was pushing through pain to say what she was. "This means nothing and Ryan and I already have so much on our plates right now. Let's not make it worse."

Struck by her words, I looked into her eyes. She seemed to regret saying it, but that didn't make it better. Or not true.

Nodding slowly, I started to turn away from her and she tried to reach for me, but I backed up.

She winced. "I didn't mean it like that."

"You're right. I should head home. Check on my mom. Good luck with all this, Nova." A minute ago, I'd thought that I couldn't walk away from her again, but if what we had wasn't worth fighting for to her, then it was best I leave.

I really did need to check on my mom, but more than that, maybe the universe was onto something with all the roadblocks it kept putting in our way just before we did something we could never take back.

And maybe it was right.

# 19

## NOVA

A few days after the storm, the ranch was finally starting to look better. We'd all been hard at work with the cleanup and all the hours we'd put into it were paying off.

The only remnants now were ditches in the dirt roads that had been formed by the water. Ryan would be dealing with those next week, which meant my extra work was basically done.

As I strode to my parents' house to check if there was anything else I could do to help with the damage, I should've been smiling at how well the ranch had held up against the onslaught of the elements this time around.

High winds and that much rain might've destroyed some of our infrastructure without all the maintenance we'd been doing, and I should've been proud that our patch jobs had stood up to it all, but I wasn't. I didn't feel much of anything, really.

Ever since Carson had walked out of the bakery that morning, I'd been listless. Glum, as my mother had put it when she saw me yesterday.

As much as I was trying to shake off what had happened between Carson and me on that dark, stormy night, I was having trouble forgetting those kisses. I was having even more trouble forgetting how I'd felt during and then how very badly I'd felt after.

Yet, despite the emotions constantly swarming around deep inside me, fighting for dominance over which deserved my attention more, I was weirdly numb. Like I just hadn't been able to keep up and had shut down a little instead.

Sighing as I got to my parents' house, I tried to put a smile on my face, intent on keeping up appearances while I was here. As soon as I pushed open the door and heard Ryan making some kind of heated argument, however, all of those other worries faded and my heart leaped into my throat.

"That's a huge chunk of the property, Dad," he was saying. "Not only that, but it's the part that includes Nova's house, the bakery, and the parking lot, which, in case you missed it, is where she holds the market."

"Yes, I realize that," Dad said gruffly while I felt like I'd been punched in the stomach by a jackhammer. "We can always build another cottage, though. There will be more than enough space on the land we keep to build her an even bigger, better place, and we'll have the money to do it."

"I don't want a bigger place," I said as I stumbled into the room, my knees threatening to give out.

My parents looked stricken when they realized I'd overheard them. My mother's mouth dropped open and my dad grimaced.

"Let's just get you into a chair and then we'll talk about it, honey," Dad said.

Mom shot up and took my arm, sympathy and understanding shimmering in her eyes as she led me to a chair and sat me down. Once I was there, she offered me a sad smile. "None of us want any of this, sweetheart. I'll bring you some iced tea, okay? Just talk to Daddy."

I blinked stupidly, my brain unable to process what I was hearing. Dad turned his gaze back to Ryan's, his expression becoming as hard and stubborn as my brother's as they faced off with one another.

"Both of you have been on me for months about doing something to save the ranch, and Frank has given us an offer we'd be idiots to refuse. I thought you'd be happy about this. Relieved. This is what you wanted, isn't it?"

"Frank?" I whispered. "I thought you said you'd never sell to him."

Dad glanced at me, a heaviness in his eyes I'd never seen before. "I wouldn't have, and I know you don't think I've been listening to you, but I have been and you've made me see things clearly, darling. I'm only sorry it took me so long, but at least it's not too late. Frank has a buyer who's willing to purchase that strip of land from us immediately."

Tears rose from deep inside, making my throat hurt with the effort of holding them back. "Why that part? Why would you sell off my bakery? My house? Why does it have to be that?"

"With the money we make from the sale, we could relocate the bakery to a storefront in town," he explained. "I tried to negotiate about which portion of the land we'd be willing to sell, but Frank insists that the buyer wants that part in particular."

"What for, though?" It made no sense to me. "If this buyer has so much money, can't they build their own renovated barn for whatever they want to use it for? Their own cute cottage? That's my bakery. My home, Dad. I know it's your property, but it's my home. I don't want a storefront in town or a bigger house."

Ryan was beside himself with rage. He rolled his fingers into fists at his side and shook his head. "Just hold off on this, would you? Don't sign anything yet."

"I'll hold off as long as I can." Dad heaved out a long sigh and brought his hands up to scrape his palms across his salt and pepper beard. "I just don't know how long we can afford to wait. If this buyer is as serious as Frank has made him seem, he's going to want the paperwork as soon as possible. Maybe we can convince him to wait, but I don't know. I'll do what I can."

Dad gave Ryan a look that made me think he felt sorry for him for some reason. Sure, we were all feeling sorry for ourselves, but this was different. This was like Dad thought Ryan should've known something that he didn't.

"Who's the buyer?" I asked, feeling desperation well in my chest. It mingled with the confusion created by that look.

Dad's gaze darted to mine. His shoulders tensed and his spine slowly straightened as he looked into my eyes. "It's Carson Drake."

My head started spinning, my ears rang, and my heart turned to stone. Ryan saw red, letting out a burst of humorless laughter and turning an unhealthy shade of purple. "No. Fuck no."

He took off then, not saying another word to our father as he stormed out of the house. For a moment, I didn't move a muscle. I just sat there, frowning and wondering where on earth he was going. Then I realized that wherever it was, it wouldn't be good.

Ryan was pissed, scared, and probably feeling betrayed by a childhood friend. My brother wasn't prone to lashing out, keeping things bottled up to the point of constipation instead, but he sure looked ready to lash out today.

Jumping to my feet, I chased after him, my limbs still feeling like jelly but I couldn't let that stop me. Not if it might save him from making an enemy out of a friend. A friend who wanted to buy a very particular portion of our property. As hurt and confused as I was, I wouldn't let Ryan alienate him or make it worse.

I was shocked that Carson was the buyer, but something in my gut said we didn't have all the facts. Or maybe I just didn't want to believe it. Either way, I would get to the bottom of this and it wouldn't be by using my fists to do the talking.

"Where are you going?" I called to my brother as I raced past my mom.

She stopped in her tracks, my glass of iced tea in her hands, and watched both of her children burst out of her house.

Ryan didn't stop moving, practically sprinting to his truck and shouting his response at me over his shoulder. "I'm going to talk to Carson. That guy has gotten everything he's ever fucking wanted. He doesn't get to have this."

Despite my own heart feeling like it was breaking, I frowned and struggled to keep up both physically and mentally. "What are you talking about? He has money and he's looking for a property to build a house on. If Frank told him that was for sale—"

"Why are you defending him?" Ryan spat at me, finally stopping once he reached his truck. He threw the door open and spun to face me with one hand on the steering wheel. "I get that he's the fucking golden boy. Always has been. He's a goddamn hero around here, but he can have that. He can have the hero worship, and the adoration, and everyone else in this town throwing themselves at his feet, but he can't have this. I won't let him have our fucking ranch."

My heart pounded in my chest. I'd stopped only a few feet away from my brother, and as I folded my arms, staring him down, I saw the bitter hatred swirling around behind his eyes. I'd known they'd had their problems. Their friendship had been frayed and in turmoil ever since that night at the bonfire, but with this new insight, I was starting to wonder if that kiss had only been the final straw.

It sure seemed that there was a lot of other stuff going on that I'd never even thought about. "Look, I'm not saying we should let him have any part of the ranch, but what is this really about, Ryan? I don't know why he would even think that strip of land is available for purchase or why he wouldn't have come to us about it directly if he wants it, but he used to be your best friend."

"Sure." Ryan shook his head. "He *was* my best friend until he kissed my sister, left, and thought sending money back to his mom every now and then would make things right. And now this? I'm sorry, Nova, but I can't accept that."

"No one is saying that you should." I hadn't realized how much Carson leaving had affected my brother until this very moment.

All these years, I thought they'd had a spat because of that kiss and had then grown apart a bit because of the thousands of miles separating them from one another. Now, however, I was learning that there were other issues between them. Or maybe it was just that Ryan missed him.

Carson and Ryan had been like brothers once upon a time, and through the years, I'd often heard him make offhanded comments about how Carson might have approached this or that. How much easier something would've been if Carson had been around. He told their old stories at Moe's whenever he got even a tiny bit tipsy and I knew he'd kept track of Carson's pro career, and at any given time, he'd known how his friend was doing.

I'd gotten in the way of that once, and not wanting to do it again was why I'd sent Carson away the other day.

I squeezed my brother's forearm. "Let me talk to him, okay? I'll find out the truth. Just don't jump to any conclusions. I don't trust Frank as far as I can throw him, and I know you don't either, so let me find out what's really going on before you break his nose or something."

Ryan's gaze was fixed on mine, searching until he finally asked the question. "Is there something going on between you and Carson again?"

"No," I said firmly and without flinching. It wasn't a lie, even though I wanted it to be. "I just don't want you to wreck a lifelong friendship over the word of a developer who is a master at manipulating people. I'll go talk to Carson. You go back inside and I'll let you know what I find out as soon as it happens, okay?"

He stared at me for another beat, then blew out a breath as the fight melted out of his posture. "Yeah, okay. Just call me as soon as you know anything."

"I will."

Ultimately, their friendship was and always had been more important than a crush. Now all I had to do was convince myself that it was nothing more than that, and then it would all be fine. *I* would be fine and maybe, just maybe, I might even finally be able to move on.

# 20

## CARSON

Leaves crunched under the rake as I swept them across my mom's front lawn. We were still clearing the debris from the storm on her property after having helped a few of her neighbors first. In this neighborhood, where I'd grown up, most of the owners were getting on in age and Mom had proudly offered her services, along with her NFL superstar son's.

My head shook as I added leaves to the giant pile I'd made, but I was still smiling as I wiped my brow with the back of my forearm and took a drink of water. Honestly, I loved that she was so proud of me, even if I did often feel like shit over having left her alone for so long.

My phone rang, jerking me out of my reverie. The number of the realtor who'd wanted to show me those properties popped up on my screen. Obviously, we'd never gotten around to going to the viewings the other day, what with everyone scrambling after the storm.

"Hello?"

"Carson!" the guy said on the other end of the line. Frank something or other. I could never remember his name. "I heard you were okay after that storm. It was a whopper, huh? I'm glad we're on the other side of it now."

I frowned. Being on the other side of one storm simply meant we were on our way to the next, but I didn't say it. As far as I knew, the man was a transplant from somewhere else and he probably hadn't been around here very long. "Yeah. Sure. I'm glad you're okay too. What have you got for me?"

"I'd like to meet you at a few places today if you're available," he said. "The first is just outside town and there's another opportunity that may come soon. I'll take you there, but it's closer to town and a darn nice piece of land, if I have to say so myself. The owners are getting older and they might be willing to sell, which means you'd get a great deal on an insane amount of acreage."

"Sounds good. Text me the address of the first place and I'll meet you there in about an hour?" With blues skies and bright sunshine having returned with a vengeance after that storm, I was drenched in sweat and feeling like I was glowing. I needed to shower before I went anywhere.

"I'll see you there, buddy," he said before he hung up.

I huffed out a breath and slid the phone into my back pocket, refocusing on the last of the leaves I had to rake. I had a severe dislike of people who acted like you were their friend after they'd only spoken to you on the phone a handful of times.

I wasn't this guy's *buddy* and I was starting to get a strange vibe that made me wonder if I could trust him. Something about him was also nagging at me to remember why I felt this way, but I let it slide for now.

He was showing me a couple properties that were on the market. It wasn't like I was getting in bed with the devil. After adding the remaining leaves to the pile and bagging it all up, I sped through a shower before I headed out.

Mom was at the library, helping to clear the parking lot, and I locked up behind me and waved at Earl as I passed his house. He gave me a friendly wave back and I grinned again, glad that I was starting to feel at home here once more.

Frank had sent me a pin location and I'd put it on my GPS, but it took me a little further out of town than I'd been expecting. Not too far, but closer would certainly be better.

"Your destination is on the right," the disembodied voice said through my speakers, and I slowed, pulling up on the lawn outside what appeared to be a small property with a very overgrown garden out front.

Tall trees lined the edge of the property, making it hard to see past the foliage to catch a glimpse of what was going on beyond. An obnoxious bright red truck sat in the drive on the way up to the house, and a slick-looking guy with a weasel face and a skintight suit climbed out of it. He grinned and tossed his hand up in a wave as I climbed out.

"Carson," he said, spreading his arms open wide before he reached up to pull a pair of sunglasses off his eyes. "It's nice to finally meet you in person."

"Yeah, you too..." I trailed off because I'd forgotten his name again, but I stuck out my hand to shake his when he offered it.

"Frank," he said magnanimously, that grin not faltering at all. He gave me a weak handshake before motioning toward the property. "Right, so the owners of this place have moved to California to be with their daughter. They've got someone looking after the property until it's sold, but you'll have to excuse the state it's in at the moment. I'm not sure he's cleaned up yet."

"I get it," I replied easily. "I grew up around here. I can look past some mess in the garden."

He chuckled. "Of course. Let's go take a look at it, shall we?"

I nodded and fell into step beside him. He fished a bunch of keys out of his pocket. As we walked up the drive, I looked around eagerly, hoping that this would be a first-time lucky situation. The yard between the road and the small, ramshackle house really was a mess, but that didn't bother me. Neither did the size or general lack of maintenance of the house itself. I'd preserve what I could and recycle the materials that were usable, but other than that, I was looking to build from scratch anyway.

"As you can see," Frank said as we approached the house. "The owners were struggling to keep up with everything around here for at least a few years before they moved, so I'd recommend tearing it all down. Since you're looking to build, that's not a problem, is it?"

"Uh, no, but I'm not sure I'd tear it down just for the sake of tearing it down. Someone built a whole life here. I'd like to respect that as much as possible."

He hummed but didn't respond. "This other property I'm taking you to see after has a lot more potential than this one. There's a river and two beautiful, relatively new structures that are completely usable as-is but could be incredible features to keep and incorporate into your place. There's also a lot of grazing land if you want to keep some livestock, existing access roads on the property, and the mountains run across the back of it, so that makes for some excellent hiking opportunities."

My heart tripped over itself, but I couldn't put a finger on why. It all sounded too good to be true, for starters, but there was something else that was bothering me about this sales pitch. As he showed me around the property, which I thought had a lot of potential itself, he kept going on and on about the other property, like he wasn't actually trying to sell me on this one at all.

The whole thing left a bad taste in my mouth, but when we were done, I appeased him and followed his truck to this supposed utopia I was going to love so much. On the way back to town, I drummed my fingers on my steering wheel, wondering why he started slowing when we approached the property line of Red Stone Ranch—and that was when it hit me where we were going.

I slammed on brakes and pulled over immediately. That was what had been bothering me. *Frank the realtor is Frank the developer that has been trying to sell the ranch out from underneath the Murphys.*

Frank stopped too, and I got out with a frown as he strode up to me. I had half a mind to grab the collar of his shirt and toss him against the truck while I demanded answers, but I managed to keep myself from letting the violence take over.

"What the fuck is this, Frank?" I snapped, my features dropping into a scowl. "I know this place, and I also know that's it's not for sale."

He held his hands up like he was trying not to frighten a scared baby deer. "It's not for sale *yet*, but it will be. If you know the place, you also know that the owners are getting older and they're drowning in the expenses of maintaining the property. I'm offering them a lifeline by buying pieces of their property one by one. As they let go of those pieces, I'll sell them on to developers who will be able to help this land achieve its true potential in a way the current owners will never be able to do."

So that was his scheme. He'd just given me the full rundown and it was more horrifying than I'd thought. He was planning on pushing them off their property bit by bit, splitting it up, and selling it off. Nausea rolled through me.

I might have the guts to tell him off about this, but how many others had he already brought out here? How many people already intended to buy these parcels of land as soon as they became available?

"Some might say that the current owners have already developed it to its fullest potential," I ground out. "Not that it matters because, like I said, this property isn't for sale."

"Not *yet*," he reiterated. "Mr. Murphy is coming around, though. Don't you want to get in on prime land right next to town before it officially goes on the market? A location like this will sell itself within a week, tops, Carson. Think about it and let me know?"

*Go kick rocks, asshole.* "I've already thought about it, and I don't need you as a realtor anymore. Stay away from the Murphys, Frank. Trust me when I tell you that they're not people you want to mess with in this town."

With that, I climbed back into my truck and sped off, leaving him in the literal dust. I wanted to go talk to Nova about it immediately, but after what had happened the other night and the morning after, I wasn't sure she even wanted me around.

Frank had said that George was coming around, though, which meant that something had changed between now and then. That night, the property definitely hadn't been on the market and he hadn't intended on selling, but now, Frank seemed certain it would be for sale soon.

Unease wound itself like vises around each of my internal organs. Whatever he'd told George to get him to consider his offer, I had a feeling it hadn't been the whole truth and George was in a damn dangerous position.

Determined to think it through before I went to them and accused Frank of planning an ambush, I pointed my truck in the direction of Moe's. I needed some time before I went home and had to face my mom for dinner. Time to think of how I was going to break it to her that my childhood best friend was about to have his home—and the reason he hadn't chased his dreams—yanked away from him without ever seeing it coming.

# 21

## NOVA

I took Ryan's truck when I left the ranch, but I didn't go directly to Carson's mom's house. I drove around for a while first, trying to clear my head and sort through my own emotions before I went to talk to him. In the space of an hour, I'd gone from listless, to shocked, desperate, and angry, to confused, to level-headed, and now, I was back to being angry.

It was best to let it pass before I went and did exactly what I'd been afraid Ryan would do—make matters worse. For hours, I just drove around, grappling with everything that had happened in the last few weeks. Ever since Carson had come back to town, my quiet existence had been thrown into a washing machine stuck on the spin cycle, and even though the ranch's troubles existed long before his return, they seemed to have been ramped up to a whole new level.

When I finally made it to Mrs. Drake's place, I parked on the street and cast my gaze around their friendly, cute front yard. I'd always liked this house. It had always seemed so warm and welcoming, but today, I dreaded having to go in there. I dreaded what I would learn once I did.

If Carson really had made an offer on my strip of land on the ranch, I wasn't sure I would ever get over the betrayal. I knew he didn't owe me anything and that I'd never even really been his friend, but shit. The least he could've done was to tell me that he wanted to purchase that piece of the ranch from us. I would've been angry and said no, but at least I wouldn't have been blindsided. In the end, I might've even considered it.

Selling a part of the property to Carson, knowing that he was only looking to lay down roots and build a house, was a lot better than selling to a developer who'd want to build a fucking mall. But he *hadn't* come to me and I *had* been blindsided, and the way I felt right now, I'd sooner chain myself to my cottage and spend the rest of my life starving, thirsty, and unable to move rather than to surrender an inch of what was mine to him.

In my fit of righteous indignation, I slammed the car door shut behind me. Mrs. Drake must've heard it because their front door suddenly opened up and she came out. She smiled brilliantly when she saw me, stepping aside to let me in before I'd even made it to their porch.

"Nova Murphy! What a pleasant surprise. How are you, darling?"

I had no quarrel with his mother, so I swallowed my burning anger enough to smile in return. "I'm okay, thank you, Mrs. Drake. How are you?"

She waved me in and walked me to the kitchen. "Oh, we can't complain. It won't help anything, will it? How's the cleanup coming along on the ranch? Carson told me you had some downed trees? Thank goodness, no one was injured."

"We were very lucky," I said, glancing around in the hopes that her son would make himself known. He didn't.

"Would you like a cup of tea?" she asked.

I shook my head. "Thank you, but I only came by to have a quick word with Carson. Is he here?"

"I'm afraid he's not, but he will be soon." She checked on something in the oven before she glanced at me over her shoulder. "I've made a lasagna. It's almost ready and he won't want to miss that. Why don't you join us for dinner? Not to brag, but I've been told my lasagna is some of the best there is."

"I'm sure it's incredible, but I don't want to impose. I'll just, uh, I'll give Carson a call and talk to him over the phone instead."

"Nonsense." She strode over to a cabinet, pulled out another plate, and handed it to me with a smile. "Stay. I insist and I'm not taking no for an answer."

Supremely uncomfortable, I jerked my chin in a nod. Once a woman in this town started insisting, everyone who'd been brought up right knew that your ass was staying put. "Alright. Thank you. Can I help with anything?"

She shook her head, humming a tune under her breath and seeming excited to have me here. "Let me just get the salad out of the fridge and then you and I can dish up. If Carson knows what's good for him, and I know he does, he'll be walking through that door any minute now."

She fetched a fresh, colorful salad from the fridge and kept humming under her breath as she carried it to the dining table. She'd already set places for herself and Carson. I'd never felt like more of an intruder than when I carried my plate from the kitchen and waited for her to set another.

If I had come here with good intentions, I would have dug into her lasagna like I was Garfield. People around here were gracious hosts and they loved feeding each other, but I didn't deserve her delicious cooking. Not when I'd come here planning on yelling at her son and telling him to shove his offer up his ass, where his head clearly was.

"There we go," she said cheerfully as she stepped away from the added table setting. "Have a seat. I'll bring the rest."

"Are you sure I can't help with anything?"

Once again, she waved me off. "You're a guest, Nova. One I've been looking forward to having, so you just sit down and make yourself comfortable. I'm glad we're going to have the opportunity to talk for a bit."

My stomach churned as I sat down. *The opportunity to talk about what, exactly?*

Thankfully, I never had to find out. Just as she came back with the food and started making me a plate, Carson walked in, slamming to an abrupt stop when he saw me sitting at the dinner table with his mother.

Those bright green eyes flashed with unpleasant surprise. His dark eyebrows tugged together as he rocked back on the heels of his expensive sneakers. "Nova? What are you doing here?"

"That's no way to greet a guest, honey," his mom admonished him playfully. "Go wash up. You're late as it is."

"Sorry," he muttered, a hand clutching his hair. He turned and disappeared down the hall. If I didn't know any better, I'd have said he was stressed and thrown off his game by my appearance, but I doubted I had the power to make the mighty Carson Drake feel that way.

*Oh, great. Some of Ryan's bitterness has seeped into me. This is not good. Keep it together, Nova. Just keep. It. Together. Don't ruin lasagna night.*

Unfortunately, my mental pep talk wasn't working. I was in a downright catty mood by the time he sat down at the head of the table.

"So, have you found a property yet to build your big, fancy house on?" I asked, the attitude clear in my voice.

His foot found mine under the table and he gave me a pointed look that said very clearly to shut up. "No, I haven't."

"That's not what I heard," I said, unable to back down and keep the peace.

He tapped his foot against mine like a warning, and my eyes narrowed. Sliding my foot out from underneath his, I kicked him in the shin. Carson grunted and he dropped his fork with a loud clatter.

Mrs. Drake frowned at him. "What's wrong, honey? Is everything okay?"

"It's fine." He picked the fork back up and dug into his pasta like he was afraid that if he stopped chewing for just a single second, he'd say something he'd regret.

With neither of us very excited to see the other, dinner was tense as hell, despite the amazing food. His mother attempted to keep things upbeat, but the mood remained off. With a final, questioning glance at her son, she rearranged her features into a smile and pointed it at me.

"You were still telling me about how the ranch was doing after the storm," she said. "You said you all were lucky. Does that mean the damage wasn't too bad? And the animals, they made it through okay?"

"Yes, ma'am," I said. "The horses were a little skittish for a few days after, but luckily, my brother and I were there to reassure them."

Her eyes got soft and fond as she nodded. "You two always have had a touch with them."

"It helps that they know they can trust us." I cut a glance at Carson. "We don't have any ulterior motives. What you see is what you get."

He made his eyes big at me, jerking his head to show me to stop while his mother's attention wasn't on him. She nodded at me some more. "They do seem to have a real feel for people, don't they? I've always said that dogs and horses are the best judges of character there are."

"They're definitely better at that than I am," I said honestly, sending Carson a quick arch of my eyebrow before I glanced back down at my food. "This really is delicious. Thank you, Mrs. Drake. I appreciate the invitation and I hate to eat and run, but I'm going to have to head out soon."

"There's dessert! You have to wait for that, at least. I won't make you stay for coffee, but my chocolate mousse might make you want the recipe." She winked at me.

We all lapsed into silence as we finished eating. As soon as she left the room to fetch the chocolate mousse, Carson leaned over the table, his gaze intent on mine. "We need to talk about all this in private. Taking stabs at me in front of my mother isn't going to fix anything."

"Talk in private about what, Carson? You don't want your mother to know that you're trying to buy a huge chunk of my family's property and didn't even have the balls to tell us about it yourself? What, you thought the offer on the table was good enough to buy our silence? It's not, and besides, it's not like she won't know whose property it really is the first time you take her out to see it."

"It's more complicated than that," he said quietly, those eyes imploring me to stay put and shut up. "I'll explain everything, I promise. Just not right now."

His mom walked back in then, and we sat through an uncomfortable, tense dessert with her.

Carson stood up as soon as he'd shoveled in his last bite. "Thanks so much for everything, Mom. It was amazing, as always, but Nova and I have to go. Now."

She blinked a few times in rapid succession before she smiled at us and motioned toward the door. "You're excused. It was good to see you, Nova. Come by again, okay? I feel like we've hardly had an opportunity to talk."

I didn't want to lie to her, but Carson hurried me out of there so fast that I didn't have to. I didn't have time to do anything other than say "thank you" over my shoulder as he took my arm and marched us out of the house.

As soon as the front door shut behind us, I yanked free of his grasp and turned to look up at him, hoping that I was finally going to be able to get the truth. "What the hell, Carson?"

## 22

### CARSON

Until a few weeks ago, I hadn't seen this girl for a decade, but even I knew she was ready for a fight as soon as she spun on me. Well, actually, I'd known she was ready for a fight as soon as I had walked in and seen her sitting down with my mom, but either way, if it was a fight she was after, she was going to have to pick it elsewhere and not with me.

"What the hell, Carson?" she snarled.

I sighed, slid my key fob out of my back pocket, and hit the unlock button.

Since she'd only just wrenched herself free of my gentle grasp, I didn't touch her again, but I did nod toward the truck. "Come on. Get in. We're not doing this here."

Her eyebrows shot up as she scoffed. "Like hell, we're not. I'll do this wherever I damn well please. You're trying to buy my house *and* my bakery, and you don't even have the decency to give me a heads-up. You knew Dad would consider it if it was *you*, didn't you? You—"

"Not here," I ground out, kicking into motion and walking backward toward the truck, my gaze firmly locked on hers. "If you want your answers, you'll come with me. I'm really not doing this here."

I spun around and headed for the driver's side. Nova let out a puff of air. Then her hurried footsteps smacked against the paving of the driveway as she followed me. Without a word, she climbed into my truck but turned her back on me, her arms crossed. I backed out and headed toward a bluff that looked out over the town.

It was the old party spot, the exact place where I'd kissed her for the first time a decade ago, and as I parked, my heart still skipped at the memory of how it had felt to finally have her lips against my own. It had been a hell of a rush—until Ryan had jumped in. Then it had just become hell.

As soon as I'd looked into my friend's eyes, I knew I'd crossed a line I shouldn't have been anywhere near. I'd known he would be pissed at me, but not like that. The way he'd looked at me that night, not only with anger, but the hurt and the betrayal?

It had stayed with me for a long time.

The lights glittered below as the town got settled in for the night. I remembered the last glimpse of this exact view as I had climbed into my truck, knowing that I wouldn't be coming back here for a long, long time. Now here I was, once again with Nova by my side, and it felt like no time had passed at all.

Obviously thinking about the same night I was, Nova scoffed down a laugh as she finally turned to face me. "What, are you going to kiss me and run away again?"

*Yeah. Okay. That's it.*

Now mad myself, I narrowed my eyes and turned so my back was resting against the door and my body was fully facing hers. "Let's get one thing straight. You might have jumped to conclusions because you're always ready to believe the worst about me, but I was never going to take your family's property from you, Nova. I contacted a realtor when I first decided I was coming home and asked him to find some properties for me. This afternoon was the first time I saw the guy, and as soon as I realized whose property he was trying to sell me, I fired him."

Her nostrils flared, all that fight still simmering like furious embers in her eyes. "I'm not ready to believe the worst about you.

Why else would I have gone to your mom's to talk? And if all that's true, then why did my dad know that you're the buyer and how does he have an offer on the table? I don't want to believe it, Carson, but it's looking like you're lying right now."

"I'm not," I said forcefully. "I don't know what he told your dad or why. Hell, I don't even know how much Frank offered your dad for the property, supposedly on my behalf, but I do know what he's up to now and you're not going to like it."

Her breath caught and she shrank into herself, something that looked a lot like fear taking over from the fight. "What are you talking about? What is that snake up to?"

"Pretty much exactly what you think," I admitted. "Pushing you off it piece by piece. Subdividing and selling each part on to different developers as he goes along."

"You're sure?"

I grimaced but nodded. "He's not going to stop harassing you, Nova. If you were thinking that he was just going to go away, he's not. I'm sorry to have to be the one to tell you this, but he's gunning for that property. Hard. The way he's selling it and tried to push it on me, I won't be surprised if he's already got a whole line of developers just waiting for word of it becoming available."

All the color seeped out of her cheeks. Her brow furrowed and she let out a shaky breath. "Shit. Fuck. Okay. Thank you for telling me. I'm sorry I thought you were being dishonest."

"Frank really told your dad I was the buyer?" I asked, the corners of my eyes tightening. "Where the fuck did he get that from? When did he say this?"

She shrugged. "I don't know. I found out about it just after lunchtime today, but it sounded like Ryan knew earlier. Not that it was you. Just that Dad was considering an offer."

My teeth gnashed together. "What a dick. I wish I could say I was surprised he'd pull something like that before I even knew he wanted to show me a property, but I'm not. These guys tend to go off on their own tangents when they're trying to win over big-money clients."

"I knew something was going on, though. Once I got over the

shock of hearing your name come out of Dad's mouth, I mean. I knew there had to be more to it."

I exhaled deeply through my nostrils, wishing I could reach for her but not following through. "Will you be honest with me about your family's financial situation? Just how deep in the hole are you?"

"I'm not telling you that," she said immediately, her eyes refocusing on mine. "Why would you even ask that? You're not a bank or an investor."

"No, but I could be." I kept my voice calm and even. "Before you jump to conclusions again, just hear me out, okay?"

"Okay," she said slowly and softly. "I'll try, but I should warn you that I'm pretty close to my breaking point right now and this line of questioning isn't helping."

"The questions might not help, but *I* want to," I said. "I want to help, which is why I'm asking. I guess the question I should be asking is whether you're willing to risk losing everything rather than letting me help you?"

"That's not up to me." She met my eyes, a glimmer of doubt in hers. "I'm not sure I should be telling you this, but after a few things I heard from my brother earlier, I doubt he'd take your help even if the alternative is losing everything."

I sucked in a harsh breath. I'd known Ryan wouldn't readily accept my help, but what the hell could he have said to her that made her think he'd rather lose the ranch than come to me?

It stung to know that one of my oldest friends didn't trust me enough to let me help him save a ranch I loved just as much as his family did, but either way, this wasn't personal. It was business. At least, that was how I had to try spinning it.

"After I fired Frank, I gave it some thought," I said, pushing past that sting of hurt. "I honestly don't believe that he's going to let it go. Not if someone doesn't buy the entire property from him before he can start selling off pieces or unless your parents magically find a way to start thriving again."

"It's not magic, though," she protested, but it wasn't me she was fighting against right now. "It's just good business, but Dad doesn't see it that way. We could be thriving."

"Okay, that's great, but what happens until then?" I asked, but it was a rhetorical question. "Once I realized that he wasn't going to stop pushing until you were gone, I went back to him and told him to draw up an offer. For the entire property. I'll buy it from him and gift it back to you, free and clear. No harm, no foul."

"No harm?" she squeaked. "You'd be out a ton of money and I don't know if we'll ever be able to pay you back."

"That's the point of a gift, though, Nova. You don't have to pay someone back for it."

She shook her head. "Sure. If it's a scarf or some bath products for Christmas, then it's no harm, no foul, but a whole ranch is hardly the same as a pair of novelty socks. It's not something you just gift to someone."

"Fine, then I'll gift it to Ryan and you. That way, it'll be in your names, where it was going anyway, and you could operate it however you pleased. Work your not-magic, turn it into a thriving business with all the ideas you have, and pay me off in installments once you're able to."

Instead of simply saying no again, she looked deep into my eyes. "While you were giving this so much thought earlier, did you ever stop to think about how Ryan would feel about all this? He doesn't want your help, Carson."

I blew out a sharp breath. "Yeah, I kind of figured he didn't want it, but he needs to get over himself for once in his life and allow me to be a friend. Either that, or his whole family could lose everything you guys have spent generations building up."

Unsurprisingly, Nova leaped to his defense, but I had to admit that the angle with which she came at me caught me off guard. "You say that he needs to get over himself, but he's been doing that every damn day for the last ten years, Carson. He got over himself for the first time that day when he turned down a scholarship to stay behind while you and Vance danced your tight asses out of here. He got over himself again when you got drafted. He got over himself to cheer for you in every game you played and he got over himself while watching from a distance as you got to live his dreams."

My mouth dropped open, but she wasn't done yet. "Don't you dare tell me that he needs to get over himself *for once in his life*. I know that it wasn't your fault that he didn't go, Carson. I also know how hard you tried to convince him to change his mind, but at the end of the day, he did it for us. For his family, so don't you dare accuse him of not choosing to protect everything that our family has spent generations building up."

"I wasn't—" I started, but then I realized that it was exactly what I had been doing. I'd gotten so caught up in how pigheaded he was for not wanting me to help that I had accused him of not caring if they lost it all. "I'm sorry."

With tears welling on her eyelids, she swallowed hard and turned back to the window. "Take me back to the truck, please. I need to get home."

Obviously still fuming, her shoulders were rigid and her spine was ramrod straight all the way back to my mother's house where she was parked. She didn't say another word, but I'd have given her all the money for the ranch just to have known what she was thinking.

I stopped next to Ryan's truck and wondered when she'd be getting hers back. She didn't climb out immediately. Instead, she turned slowly to look at me again, defeat now shining dark in her eyes. She drew in a deep breath like she needed it to give her courage.

"I'm sorry about the other night," she said in a voice so quiet I barely heard her. "I didn't mean those words the way they sounded. Thank you for telling me about Frank's plan, but we've got it from here."

I wanted to reach out and take her hand, asking if she would've given me a chance if things had been different back then. If she would give me a chance now.

But I didn't take her hand or ask my questions as I watched her get out of my truck. One thing she'd gotten right that night was that both she and her brother had more than enough on their plates right now. The last thing they needed was to have me crashing into them while they were juggling everything that was most important in their lives.

# 23

## NOVA

Feeling like there was a weight tied to the bottom of my soul, I went to find Ryan once I got back to the ranch, but he wasn't there. He wasn't at his place, my place, or our parents'. Figuring that he'd probably gone down to the bar, I heaved out a heavy breath and headed to the bakery.

There was no way I was going to be able to fall asleep right now and there was a lot of work to be done, so I spent a few hours being productive and allowing the repetitive motions of my baking to drown my thoughts.

After midnight, I stumbled to my bed and stripped down, not even bothering with pajamas as I collapsed onto the mattress and waited for sleep to steal me. Exhausted as I was though, it didn't come. I wasn't entirely sure it would.

Unable to get Carson out of my head, I pondered texting him. To say what, I didn't know, but I kind of just wanted to talk to him. These days, I felt like every time I turned, he was there. I just didn't know if that was a good thing or a bad thing.

I knew what Ryan would think and what Ryan wanted *me* to think, but despite the guilt that still plagued me about those kisses, I just couldn't convince myself that Carson's rock-like presence in my life all of a sudden was bad. Ryan had sacrificed a lot, but none of it was Carson's fault.

Was I about to throw away a great man just because my brother had a bee in his bonnet?

At some point while I was thinking it all over for the umpteenth time, I must've finally drifted off because the next thing I knew, my alarm was screaming at me that it was time to wake up. I groaned as I rolled over in bed, feeling like someone had rubbed sand in my eyes. I forced myself to get up and felt mildly more human once I'd had a long, hot shower.

As always, the morning routine at the bakery not only woke me up but cheered me up a little bit, and as I was setting up for Cassidy to take over for the day, I even finally found my brother. Or, more accurately, he found me—and he looked awful.

*Luckily it's too early for customers. If he pitches a fit, at least we won't have an audience.*

Ryan knocked on the outside door and I went to get it. His eyes were so bloodshot and watery that it looked like he'd spent all night crying. Even before I opened the door and caught a whiff of whiskey wafting off him, I suspected that he'd drowned his sorrows in copious amounts of alcohol all night long.

"Coffee?" I offered as I stepped aside and let him in.

He groaned and gave me a nod. "The strongest you've got. Also, if you've got any whiskey, make it a dirty coffee."

"I'm afraid the dog that bit you took all its hair with it. I don't have any," I said sympathetically. "I can help with the caffeine, though."

"I'll take it."

Ryan's dark hair was sticking up at all angles, and it was damp, which told me that he'd already showered, but I wasn't entirely sure it had sobered him up. Especially after I told him what Carson had told me, and all Ryan did was shrug.

The expression in his eyes was lifeless and flat as he sipped his coffee. "Maybe we should take him up on his offer."

"What?" I was so surprised that my voice came out high-pitched.

Ryan winced and held his forehead. "Keep it down, will you?"

"Sorry, but what? You want to take Carson's offer? I thought for sure you were going to tell him to go fuck himself."

My brother shrugged again, his shoulders slumping. He drained his first cup of coffee and pushed the mug across the counter to me for another. "Trust me, I wish I could, but if he buys the ranch, your bakery could stay here. You could stay in your cottage. The weekend market will keep running the way it always had. I hate to say it, but it might be our best option. *Your* best option."

I could tell that he truly hated the idea, and I understood where he was coming from. Ryan was a proud man. Always had been. Like my father, they didn't talk much about their emotions and they didn't sit around crying about stuff. I knew how much it would be hurting him just to be saying what he was.

"What's changed?" I asked. "A week ago, you wouldn't have even considered this, so what's going on?"

"We don't have any other options," he said on a pained groan. "Man, this conversation is making me feel sick, but I'll pay Carson back eventually, and we'll get to keep the ranch. He gets to be a hero again, and I won't be the jackass that lost our family's land, forcing us to share a house in a city someplace far away from here."

"Why would we move to a city?"

He snorted. "None of us would be able to stick around here if we lose the ranch, Nova. It'd hurt too much."

"Okay, but why would we all be sharing a house? I don't like Frank at all, but so far, the offers have been alright."

He shut me up with a pleading look. "You're zeroing in on the wrong thing. The point is, if we take Carson's offer, none of that will happen and we'll be able to stop worrying about money all the damn time."

"What if Carson doesn't allow us to pay him back?"

Ryan frowned. "You just said he'd have paperwork drawn up or something like that."

"Yeah, he offered, but you know he's gonna fight it when it comes down to paying him back. Even if he does let us pay him back, he'll probably just find some roundabout way to pump it back into the ranch. Tell us to buy him a herd of cattle or something and to raise them for him."

"Raising a herd of cattle doesn't cost as much as the damn ranch."

"Now *you're* focusing on the wrong thing." I shrugged. "It'll be something like that. He'll say that he's paying us for our time or whatever. He won't just let us pay him back. I just want you to be prepared for that."

Ryan fell silent, chewing the inside of his lip before he sighed. "Are you sure there's nothing going on between the two of you?"

"I'm sure. We're just friends." I shook my head. "No, we're not even that. We're acquaintances who talk because you two are friends."

"Then how do you know that he won't just let us pay him back?" he asked, looking me right in the eye. "How do you know that he's going to find some way to get around it? I suspect those things, but I've been his friend since we were kids. We never hung out with you together, and as far as I know, you have no reason to know him that well—unless you do. Unless you somehow know him a lot better than I think you do."

"What I know is I don't want to lose the ranch, so maybe focus on that, you weirdo," I teased, but he kept staring at me, waiting for some kind of answer. "Would it be a problem if there was something going on between us?"

I'd kept my tone light and still teasing, but Ryan got up anyway. "Thanks for the coffee."

Without another word, he turned and walked away. I gaped as the door swung shut behind him. He hadn't even said goodbye. Hadn't stopped to add anything else. He'd just left.

*Then again, he did have the last word. Maybe that was good enough for him.*

I sighed, running my hands through my hair. He got in his truck and drove away. His fresh coffee was still standing in my machine and I slid it out, drinking it myself as I sat down behind the counter and wondered when our relationship had become like this.

Growing up, Ryan had always been protective of me, but it had never been this way. It'd never been to the point of shutting me out or trying to control my life. As my older brother, he'd always beat our mom to the band-aids when I scraped a knee and he was the one who comforted me if I spilled my drink and cried.

Growing up, he'd always been the person I'd turned to. About everything. If I was having a tough time at school, I spoke to my brother about it. When things were great, I told Ryan first. As soon as I had news, he was the one I called.

Yet, something about me catching feelings for his best friend had disrupted all that. I hadn't gone to him when I had my first serious crush because it had been Carson.

I hadn't asked him for his advice when my heart had been so sore after Carson had left because neither of us had spoken about the other thing.

Instead, when it came to his best friend, my brother turned into a helicopter parent, breaking it up when he caught us kissing and threatening the boy if he tried it again. Even now, it wasn't even a matter open to discussion.

It was just a firm no—that wasn't even worth being told to me directly because he'd already said it to Carson. It was ridiculous.

I missed the fun my brother could be. The good times we'd had and the laughter we'd shared, but it didn't feel like there would be any getting back to that. Now that Carson was back in town, it felt like that version of my brother was totally off the table.

Just the other day, I'd been thinking about their friendship and how much Ryan had missed Carson. Now that I was missing Ryan, it wasn't as simple as getting myself out of the way. Or maybe it was, but the part of myself I would have to leave behind in order to do it was my heart, and I just didn't know how to shove that aside.

Not without resenting my brother for it for the rest of my life.

# 24

## CARSON

My mother frowned at me from across the counter at our breakfast nook, cradling her coffee in her hands. She stared into my eyes with doubt shadowing her own. "I don't know if I should answer that question, sweetheart. The situation on the Murphy ranch has nothing to do with us. It's the *Murphy* ranch, and we're not Murphys."

"I know, but look, I'm just trying to help. Besides, it's not like I'm asking you to show me their financial statements. All I'm asking is for you to give me some background about how it got so bad."

She got a pinched look on her face, taking a long sip of her coffee before she shook her head at me. "It's not that simple, Carson. Talking about this feels wrong. Why do you want to know? How are you going to help if Ryan won't talk to you about the extent of their troubles himself?"

"I don't know yet, but I want to try. I just can't do that if I don't know what went wrong."

"What went wrong is that George didn't want to hand over the ranch to his kids to bring into the modern era." Her nose wrinkled. "Damn it. I didn't want to say it that way, but there you have it. Everyone else started modernizing years ago. The first wave of it happened while you guys were still at school, but George held on to the old ways. The longer it took him to get onboard, the more he fell behind."

She blew out a breath, cocking her head at me as she narrowed her eyes in question. "Just what are you going to do about any of this, darling? Everyone has tried over the years to talk a little bit of sense into George. Even Mara, but no one has gotten anywhere with him. What makes you think it's going to be different when it's coming from you?"

"Because I'm not going to give him advice on modernization or tell him what he should be doing with his business. He's the rancher. I'm just a kid who played football and got paid for it. I won't presume to know better than him, but the Murphys need money and I've got some that I've been itching to invest in this town."

"Well, maybe you need to consider satisfying that itch someplace else." Mom gave me a serious look as she got up. "I know that Ryan has been your friend for a long time, but that boy has been through enough to last several lifetimes. Don't go complicating his life unless you're damn sure what you're doing is the right thing."

She carried her cup to the sink and rinsed it, then came over to give me a kiss on the cheek. "I'm heading out, sweetheart. You have a good day, alright?"

"You too, Mom," I replied as I finished my own coffee, my mind already a million miles away.

*Maybe you need to consider satisfying that itch someplace else.*

My mom's warning echoed through my mind, and I briefly contemplated it before shaking my head. There was no place else I'd rather invest than in the Murphys. I'd already done a bit for the larger community with the upgrades to the library and the school, and I was in talks with the city council about fixing up some other local points of interest.

I'd also invested in a variety of businesses, bought some stocks, and put some money away for a rainy day. *Don't go complicating his life unless you're very damn sure what you're doing is the right thing.*

This was the right thing, though. I felt it in my bones. This was why I had arrived back home exactly when I had. I couldn't shake the feeling I needed to do this.

It wasn't even really that I wanted to. I did want to, but it was more than that. Deeper. Somehow, I just couldn't let it go. I couldn't let it be when I knew what they were going through. That family had been too good to me over the years, and sure, they'd been the same with every child who had regularly darkened their doorsteps, but still.

I felt like I owed it to them to help out now that I was in the position to do so. Grabbing my phone, I put in a call to Vance. If there was anyone who would talk me out of it fast if he thought it was a mistake, it was him.

He was the only one who really had any inkling of how much money I'd made and how little of an effect buying the ranch would have in the greater scheme of things. When he picked up, I grinned. "Want to meet me at the gym?"

"Yes," he said without hesitation. "It's way past time we hit that place again. I'll meet you there."

We hung up without saying goodbye, both of us suddenly too eager to bother with niceties when we'd be seeing each other in a few minutes.

As soon as I walked into the gym that had been opened while we'd been gone, I felt my worries starting to lift. I'd only been here a few times since I'd been back, but it was a gym and the clanging of the equipment and the scent of cleaning products and chlorine were as familiar to me as my mother's house. I inhaled deeply, hitting the pool first while I waited for Vance to arrive.

Cutting through the water helped me calm down, and by the time I climbed out, Vance was just finishing up on the treadmill. "How you doing, bud? You're looking a lot better than you have been the last few times I've seen you."

I flipped him off. "Thanks for nothing, asshole. Why do I even bother with you?"

"Because you love me." He batted his eyelashes, then laughed as we walked to the neon light on the wall that read *weightlifting*. "Seriously, though. What's up? You've been quiet lately."

"I'm just wrapped up in business that isn't mine," I said honestly. When he arched an eyebrow at me, I sighed and gave him the answer he was looking for. "Murphy business. Someone tried to sell me their ranch. So in my defense, I didn't go looking for it this time and it found me anyway. Makes me think there's a reason I keep finding myself near them."

"Near Nova, you mean," he said, stopping as he decided which piece of equipment to tackle first.

I shook my head and pointed at the bench press machine. "I'll spot you, and no, it's not just Nova. Although at this point, Ryan is in the way."

"Of you and Nova? He's always been in the way of that."

I rolled my eyes, chuckled, and shook my head. "He's in the way of the help I want to give them. He's too proud to take it and I'm worried that if I push, I'm going to end up ruining a friendship that's only just getting back on track."

"It might be worth a shot talking to him directly." Vance lay on the bench and wrapped his fingers around the bar. "He might give you some grief for it, but that's better than him feeling like you're trying to go behind his back."

"Fair enough. I'm not trying to go behind his back, though. I talked to Nova about it first because she showed up at my house. Apparently, the realtor told them I was gunning for the stretch of property that includes her house, the bakery, and the market area."

Vance's eyes went wide before he started laughing. "Wow. I bet she was *not* happy with you."

"Not even a little bit," I said. "At least we know what the realtor's plan is now, but it's not good for the Murphys."

"You're not a Murphy." He started pushing at the bar, his muscles flexing. Then he lifted it out of the cradle and slowly lowered it to his chest. "Has it ever occurred to you that this isn't your problem to fix?"

"Yep, it's occurred to me, but I can't seem to stop. This is Red Stone Ranch we're talking about, man. You and I practically grew up there. What would we have known about discipline without George's chores whenever we went out there? Where would we have been without the dedication he beat through our thick skulls one responsibility at a time?"

Vance grunted and lifted the bar back into place. "I'm not arguing with you, bro. Being on that ranch taught us a lot and those are lessons that helped us achieve everything we did."

"But?"

"But you're still not a Murphy. I don't want to see them lose that place either, but ultimately, it's theirs to lose."

I didn't like it, but he wasn't wrong. At this point, I was sure all the Murphys knew I was willing to help them out. If they wanted me to, they would come to me. Until then, I wasn't a Murphy and this was none of my business.

My friend seemed to sense the change in my mood and grinned. "Do you remember the blonde from Moe's that night?"

"Vaguely." I frowned. "Why?"

"I've been hanging out with her," he said as we swapped so I was the one on the bench and he was spotting me. "Her name is Jessie and she's a true blue country girl. She's even taking me horseback riding later this week."

I burst out laughing before I'd even lifted the bar once. Vance bent over and scowled at me. "What's so funny?"

"Nothing," I said but sat up. "Maybe we should do a set of deadlifts first. I'm not going to be able to do this if you keep making me laugh."

"I still don't know what's so funny."

I chuckled some more. "I was just picturing your fat ass on a horse. Poor beast. You better start taking this workout a little more seriously, man. All this homecooked food and cold beer is getting to you."

He gave me a playful shove. "Pots and kettles, Carson. Pots and kettles. Let's do this before we both reach the point of no return."

I nodded, ready to lose myself in the workout and clear my mind of all things Murphy. There was no exercise that would make me forget about Nova, but the rest of it? I would give it time to come to me, and if that didn't happen, then I'd try and try again.

# 25

## NOVA

**M**emorial Day weekend was one of the only weekends the bakery wasn't open. On the Thursday before, Cassidy and I were fighting for our lives against the holiday rush. She manned the counter while I replenished the stocks and served the customers in the coffee shop.

After wiping sweat off my brow with the back of my arm, I slid another tray of pastries out of the oven and set them down to cool. Then I picked up a basket of bread and carried it out to the shop. Mrs. Norris waited for me at the kitchen door, giving me a coy smile as she held up the paper bag she'd already collected for hers.

"I figured I had a better chance if I stayed right here until you came out."

I laughed, dead on my feet after a hectic morning but thrilled that business was going so well. "Have at it. Take as many as you need."

She plucked a loaf out of the basket and winked at me. "If I take more than one, I might get tackled for it on my way out. At least I have mine now. Have a good weekend, honey. I'm glad you're taking a break."

"So am I," I said truthfully.

It had been ages since I'd done it, but Cassidy and some of our girlfriends had convinced me to go to the lake with them this weekend. Normally, I'd have spent the time I had off helping out around the farm, but my friends had twisted my arm.

I desperately needed a break and Cassidy's parents had a lake house with plenty of room. Better yet, they were letting us have it free of charge and I would be driving out there with Cassidy, so it was going to be a vacation that didn't cost me an arm and a leg.

It was going to be a huge party and I couldn't wait. Excitement thrummed through me as I said goodbye to Mrs. Norris and dropped the basket into its stand, grinning at the clamor and chatter of the customers surrounding me.

"We're almost sold out," Cassidy said when I checked in on her. She flashed me a happy smile. "Those last few trays are going to go fast."

I grinned at her. "Everyone in the coffee shop has finished eating and I've handed out all the bills, so we should be finishing up in less than an hour."

She squealed, tossing her arms around me and giving me a quick squeeze before she turned back to the cash register. "Bring out the rest, honey. I'm ready to bust out of here."

"You and me both."

For once, that was completely true. Faced with a few days of freedom, I had no idea how I was going to fill my time, but I was looking forward to being bored for a change. Not that I thought my friends were going to be allowing any boredom this weekend, but they also counted lying around on the shore drinking cocktails as an activity, and in my book, that was perfect.

Another hectic hour later, we were completely sold out of everything and Cassidy was practically shooing the last of the customers out the door. Once she shut it with a definitive click behind them, she tugged the ties of her apron loose with an exaggerated flourish and smiled. "That's a wrap, boss. Don't stick around here too long, okay? I'll pick you up first thing in the morning, so you need to be packed, ready, and rested."

"I promise." I gave her a quick hug before she left. Singing some girl-power ballad at the top of her lungs, she lowered herself into the flashy little sports car her parents had bought for her birthday last year.

I chuckled as I watched her go, but I had to admit I loved her energy. As soon as she was gone, though, I doubled back to the kitchen. I stayed behind to do inventory and put in an order for the goods we'd need next week, but I had also been working double time on a secret project.

That tray of pastries I'd baked earlier had cooled down nicely and I smiled as I popped them into boxes to take along for the weekend. I'd spent all morning making extras so that I had some yummy treats to bring up to the cabin for everyone.

*Can't show up empty handed.*

As I boxed up the last of them, a truck pulled up outside and I sighed. *Shit, I hate turning people away, but I really don't think I've got anything left to sell.*

When I walked out of the kitchen and saw who was at the door, I realized that wasn't going to be a problem.

Carson stood on the other side of the glass, wearing cargo shorts and a light blue T-shirt that hugged his powerful frame. Sunglasses covered his eyes, but his dark hair was pushed off his handsome face, and he seemed relaxed, which meant he probably hadn't come here trying to convince me to let him gift us the ranch again.

My heart rate sped up as I approached the door. He pulled his sunglasses off and his eyes met mine. A smile I couldn't stop curved my lips. That electric green color that had stolen my breath so many times shimmered with laughter, and when I opened the door, he pressed his palms together in a praying motion.

"Please tell me you have some of those strawberry pastries left. I'm craving them and I promised my mom I'd bring her some for the weekend."

I wrinkled my nose and gave him an apologetic smile. "If you wanted those, you should've been here three hours ago. I always sell out of them first thing in the morning."

"Damn it." He let out a defeated sigh, his face falling. "I knew I should've come sooner, but Vance and I were helping out with some work being done on the football field at the high school and I guess I was hoping the gods would intervene on my behalf to make you keep some for me."

"I'm pretty sure I was too busy to notice any signs the gods may have sent," I said, then stepped aside and waved him in. "However, your mom did feed me the other night, and if she wants them, I could probably whip up another batch real quick."

He perked up, eyebrows twitching. "Really? You'd do that for us?"

"I'd do it for *her.*" I chuckled and shut the door behind him. Then I motioned for him to follow me to the kitchen. "Well, for anyone who wants a pastry badly enough to look like their puppy has been kicked when they find out I don't have any left. Plus, I owe your mom. We ran out of there pretty fast the other night. She must think I'm a rude, ungrateful brat."

"Nah. My mom adores you. There's no way she'd ever think that, but if it's motivating you to make the pastries, then sure. That's what she thinks."

I pushed back another burst of laughter and went to gather the ingredients from the pantry. As I came back with my arms full of everything I needed, Carson was waiting on my side of the table.

"Put me to work," he said. "The least I can do is help."

I arched an eyebrow at him. "Have you ever baked before?"

"Only with you." He held my gaze for a moment and it was like I could feel that tether between us trying to pull me closer to him.

Naturally, that meant that I broke eye contact immediately. *No one wanted a gorgeous guy looking at them like that when they couldn't have him. Right? Now I'm talking to myself.*

I cleared my throat and grabbed a couple mixing bowls. "Right. Okay. Yes. You can help. Can you empty the flour into this bowl and make a well in the middle for me?"

"Sure." He grabbed a container and held it out to me.

"I said flour, please."

He shrugged and continued to offer me the wrong container. "This *is* flour."

"Then why does it say 'sugar' on it?" I asked, arching an eyebrow at him.

He grinned and shook his head. "To confuse people?"

"Nope."

He finally located the flour and then proceeded to simply dump it into the bowl. A cloud of white puffed all around us, and I laughed as Carson waved a hand in front of his face. "Shit. I didn't know that was going to happen."

"Are you sure you want to help?" I asked.

"Absolutely. What's next?"

With both of us now covered in a fine layer of flour, I figured it was best to keep him away from the dry ingredients. "Make the well and then crack those eggs into it. I'll take over from there. I'm just going to chop some strawberries first."

"Shouldn't I do the chopping? Holding a knife seems more manly than cracking eggs."

I chuckled. "It might be more manly, but it's also more dangerous."

A minute later, I found out I'd been wrong. Having Carson around flour—even if just to crack eggs into it—was more dangerous than him holding a knife. For starters, no eggs had ended up in the well and there had been a few more clouds of flour for every egg he cracked.

"You're a beautiful man, Carson Drake, but in here, you're a big, burly mess in a very snug kitchen area. I think it'll be better if you get out of my way." I motioned at the flour we were both covered in as I moved in beside him. "I'll make the pastries and you can help by keeping me company."

"You got it." He wiped the back of his hand over his jaw, leaving a clump of the mixture behind on his cheek.

Giggling at how he looked, I reached up to brush it away and suddenly realized that we were now standing chest to chest. In an instant, all the humor faded from the air around us and the tension that was always there when we were together was right on the verge of snapping again.

As I looked deep into his eyes, somehow unwilling to look away again, his hand landed on my hip and I leaned in, wanting nothing more than to kiss him again. My hands acted of their own accord, flour be damned as I ran them over his chest and shoulders.

Carson had always been big, but he seemed larger than life now with his legacy following him around, a constant, unseen presence that was evident in the hard strength of his body and the way he carried himself.

He certainly wasn't the boy I'd fallen for when we were young, and yet, nothing had changed between the two of us. "We can't do this."

I breathed the words, my heart pounding. My entire body screamed at him to do it when he dipped his head like he was going to kiss me. Instead of that, however, he simply pressed his forehead to mine and the pained expression on his face told me that this was killing him as much as it was killing me.

Both of us wanted this, but neither of us wanted to be the one to give in. It would be too big of a betrayal to my brother. Carson must've had the same thought because a moment later, he stepped back, giving me space—and air that didn't smell like his cologne.

With his long strides eating up the distance, he crossed to the other side of the kitchen and leaned against the counter there, gripping it like he physically needed it to keep him from coming back. Our eyes remained connected and I saw how difficult this was for him.

It wasn't any easier for me. I wished the moment hadn't ended so soon, but this was for the best. Finally drawing in a deep breath, I nodded and wordlessly went back to work. Painfully aware of him watching me, I made the pastries in silence, glad that these didn't have a long baking time.

Once they were in the oven, I cleaned up, wondering if I should break the silence but really not knowing what to say. Carson moved like he was going to help me with the dishes, but I shook my head at him.

If he came within three feet of me right now, I wouldn't be liable for my actions. So instead, he just watched while I did that too, and then he took the boxes from me once I'd filled them with fresh pastries. As I walked him to the door, everything just felt so unfinished between us, but I took the easy way out.

"Don't eat all of those in the truck," I said, my voice slightly hoarse and husky from disuse. "Save some for your mom."

He stopped when we reached the door, waiting for me to open it before he flashed me the tiniest grin ever. "Thanks for this, Nova. I'll make sure to tell my mom about the effort you made for us."

"No problem. Have a good weekend. Goodbye, Carson."

It seemed like he had something else to say, but he must've decided against it because he turned to leave instead. Just before he walked out the door, he finally looked at me again over his shoulder. "Oh, I'll, uh, I guess I'll see you at the lake. Probably."

My heart lurched and my eyebrows shot up, but he was gone before I could ask him what he'd meant. As far as I knew, this was supposed to be a girls' trip, but if Carson was going and we did see each other there, at a place where the drinks would be flowing and I wouldn't be able to hide behind work or chores, I didn't know if I was going to be able to keep my distance.

And if I didn't, then this explosive situation between us was about to get out of hand. *Maybe I shouldn't have let them convince me to go to the lake after all.*

But I had and I wasn't the type to let my friends down at the last minute. So I was going, and apparently, Carson was too. *Let the games begin, I suppose.*

# 26

## CARSON

Before we headed out for the weekend, Vance and I went to the Murphy ranch. We were packed and ready, but we'd wanted to talk to Ryan before we left.

"You know it's unlikely that he's going to allow you to help like this, right?" Vance asked as we pulled up next to Ryan's place. "I know you two were like brothers at one point and I realize that you feel like you have to help, but this might not be the way to go about doing it."

"Maybe not, but no one has given me any better ideas. It's time to take the bull by the horns or bow out."

"Since when is Ryan a bull?" Vance smirked at me. "Although I guess you've gotten to know a whole different side of him since you fell for his sister."

I scoffed. "This has nothing to do with Nova."

He made a sound of disbelief but left it at that since Ryan had just walked out. He stopped on the porch of his house and frowned when he saw the two of us sitting in a truck outside. He pulled off the work gloves he'd been wearing, then cocked his head at us as we climbed out.

"Boys. It's good to see you, as always, but am I missing something? Was I supposed to meet you?"

Vance slid his hands into his pockets, hanging back to give me the floor as he grinned like a loon who was excited for the show he was about to see. I cleared my throat, gesturing toward the shed I'd seen him glance at when he'd walked out.

"Anything in there we can help you with?"

His head inclined further. "You came out to help me with chores?"

"Sure." At least this way, he'd have no choice but to talk to me. "You got anything for me?"

He snorted in an attempt to hold back laughter. "Always. I'm not about to turn down a couple extra pairs of hands, but why did you bring Vance?"

"Hey," he protested, finally shuffling forward. "I have hands."

Ryan glanced at him with an amused expression. "Yeah, you do, but you and I both know Carson came here to talk to me about the offer he made my sister. Did he drag you with him for moral support?"

"Nope, but we're leaving for the weekend when we're done here and I want to get on the road as fast as we can. Why waste good drinking time on not drinking?"

"You never change." Ryan chuckled, starting toward the shed and not waiting for me to follow. He already knew I would. "So, you really spoke to Nova about the situation on the ranch instead of me, huh?"

"It was kind of hard not to, considering that I got home to find her about to have dinner with my mom," I said. "Did she tell you that I didn't know this was one of the properties Frank wanted to show me?"

"She sure did," he replied, taking all of this a lot more calmly than I'd thought he might. "The guy is a snake. If it'd been anyone else, I'd have thought that maybe you were bullshitting, but with Frank, I completely believe that he'd try selling off pieces of a property he doesn't have the right to sell."

"Yeah, well. He's a developer. He knows you've got prime property here, and unfortunately, he also knows that you're going to have trouble hanging onto it if something doesn't change soon. That's any developer's wet dream."

Ryan exhaled through his nostrils before he shrugged. "Yeah. I fucking love this town, but sometimes, I wish it was just a little bit bigger. It's pretty damn inconvenient having everyone in our business all the damn time."

"It's only because everyone around here loves you," I said. "They care about your family and people talk about those they care about."

"They also talk about those who're having a tough time while they sit and watch how it plays out," he said. "I appreciate you coming out here to clear the air, but you should know that I'm not mad at you. Hell, I even considered taking you up on the offer for a minute there."

I stopped moving completely, my eyebrows jumping up. My mouth dropped open and my heart started pounding. "You did?"

"Yep." He handed over a shovel from the shed. "Thing is, Carson, I don't want a handout. If you really want me to even consider this, it's got to be on the condition that Nova and I pay you back once we turn things around."

"I just want to help, and this way, at least Nova gets to keep her house and her bakery. You don't have to pay me back."

He shook his head. "We know we don't have to, but we want to, and again, if you really want to help, it'll be a loan, not a gift."

"How about we make it a gift, and if you want to, you can push all the profit you would've given me back into the ranch and name a barn after me or something? Or maybe buy me a herd of—"

"Nope." He strode toward me with his own shovel now in his hand, his jaw set and his expression firm. "Don't argue with me about this, okay? I know you want to help and I don't really know the words I need to thank you for it, but we're not a charity."

"Of course not." I frowned deeply. "You know that's not how I see you at all."

He nodded slowly. "Well, I hoped you'd say that because it means that if we take your money, we pay you back. That's business. You making a donation is charity."

I groaned. *He's just as hardheaded as his sister.*

Knowing I was fighting a losing battle, I finally relented. "Fine, but for the record, I already told Nova you guys could pay me back."

"I know, but we also figured you'd try to find a way to get out of taking the money when we eventually get there, so I thought I'd put a stop to that notion right here and right now. If we do this, you'll let us repay every cent. With interest."

My mouth twisted. "Interest? No. No way."

Ryan sighed and held out his hand. "Then give me back that shovel and go on your merry way for the weekend. I appreciate the offer. I really do, but I won't just take money for nothing. Not only will my parents never go for it, but in the end, it'll cost us our friendship. I'll always feel like I owe you something."

I hung onto my shovel with one hand and stuck out the other. "Deal. No backsies. You take the money from me now and I take it back from you when you've got it."

His eyes narrowed as they dropped to my outstretched palm. "The terms of when and how we'll repay you will have to be clearer than that. It can't just be something vague like 'when we've got it,' or else you'll just keep saying that we don't have it yet and put what we do have back into the ranch."

I rolled my head back and sent a furious glare at the sky. "Okay. Okay. I get it. I did tell Nova that I'd have paperwork drawn up and I will. We'll have a smartass lawyer draft us proper terms that I won't try to find a loophole in."

Ryan's face split into a grin. "You're seriously willing to agree to that?"

"I am." Too bad they knew me so damn well. "Are you going to shake my hand already?"

"One last thing." He reached out but didn't smack his hand into mine just yet. "We do this privately. Frank doesn't get anywhere near this deal."

I made the final move and grasped his hand, giving him a firm shake. "Now there's one thing we wholeheartedly agree on."

Relief softened Ryan's features as he nodded and released me.

"Alright, then. Obviously, I still have to talk to my parents and see if they were serious about selling before, but if they were and they're willing to do it this way as well, then it's a done deal."

Relief of my own coursed hot and heavy through me. "Let me know how it goes with them. I really want to get this done. It'll be a huge weight off my shoulders."

"You're telling me," he said easily, once again impressing me with how well he was taking all this. *I guess it helps that he had so much time to think about it before I came to him.*

I was feeling pretty good about it all until Vance spoke again. "You going up to the lake this weekend, Ry? It's supposed to be a big party."

*Fuck.*

Ryan shook his head, though. "I've got too much work to do here. Is that where you guys are going?"

"Yep," Vance replied cheerfully. "We rented a cabin. I'm trying to woo one of Cassidy's friends, though I only figured out recently that she went to school with Cass and Nova. Jessie, you know her?"

"The blonde?" He nodded, but I noticed he wasn't looking at Vance anymore. He was now watching me carefully, like he was starting to put it together that Vance and I were going to the lake—with his sister and her friends. "Yeah, I know her. Sort of, anyway. As well as I know any of those girls, which isn't very well. They're Nova's friends. Not mine."

*Oh, shit. Shots fired.*

Vance glanced between the two of us, seemingly realizing that he might've stepped in it and backtracking as fast as he could. "Jessie wanted to take me home to meet her parents already, which is way too fast for a guy like me, but a weekend at the lake? That sounded like my kind of getting-to-know-you exercise."

Ryan turned toward me with his jaw tightening and suspicion darkening his eyes. "So let me see if I've got this straight. You two rented a cabin at the lake to spend the weekend with my sister and her friends?"

"Vance rented it," I said. "I'm just going along for the jet ski it comes with."

Neither of them looked like they believed me. Ryan slowly turned back to Vance, a contemplative gleam in his eyes. "This cabin you rented. You got space for one more?"

"Sure, man," Vance replied without giving it a second thought. "We'll give you the directions and you can come up later after you are done with your chores."

Inwardly, I groaned. This should've been great news, a weekend with both of my best friends and zero responsibilities, but instead, I was disappointed that Ryan was coming, and I hated myself for it.

*Yeah, I have to be the shittiest friend who has ever lived, but I was really looking forward to spending time with Nova without the possibility of Ryan interrupting us.* With the wind knocked out of my sails, I forced a grin to my lips and jerked my head at the truck.

"Hurry up then, gentlemen. Those beers we've got in the back won't stay cold forever and I've got a hot date with a motorbike that drives on water. We'll see you there later, Ryan."

# 27

## NOVA

Cassidy and I arrived at her parents' fancy lake house to find the party already underway. Jessie, Amber, and Harriet had driven up an hour before us, and clearly, they'd put the time they'd had here so far to good use. They'd already opened all the stacking doors to the deck, opened the infinity pool, and put on music that flowed through the built-in sound system.

A gentle breeze rolled over my skin as Cassidy and I walked into the house. Natural light flowed in through the large windows her parents had installed. With all the doors now open, it almost didn't feel like we were inside at all.

Jessie let out a loud whoop when she saw us from where she was standing behind the island in the kitchen. A blender already whizzed up a batch of margaritas in front of her. Wearing a bikini and with her hair pulled into a high, messy knot on top of her head, she let go of the button, grabbed two cocktails she'd had waiting for us, and grinned as she handed them over.

"Welcome, ladies," she said in a sing-song voice, pulling us into gentle hugs so she wouldn't make us spill our drinks while doing it. "I'm so glad you're finally here. This is going to be the best weekend ever."

"No doubt," Cassidy replied excitedly, sighing as she stepped out of Jessie's embrace and brought the glass to her lips. "You're a queen, Jess. Thank you for this. You have no idea how much I needed it."

"Uh, I think I do." She winked at us. "All of us needed it just as bad, which is why we're here, right? To take a well-deserved break for a change."

Amber walked down the hallway, a bottle of suntan lotion in one hand and a margarita in the other. Her bright red hair was also pulled up but into a sleek bun. Her bikini was barely there, and when she saw me wondering where the rest of the fabric had gone, she laughed and rolled her eyes.

"I'm not getting tan lines, girl. Those are not hot and I'm here to make the best of the sun while we can. Where's Harriet?"

I frowned. "I don't know. I haven't seen her. We just got here."

As if to prove my point, I glanced at my bag still lying at my feet. "We haven't even put away our stuff yet."

Jessie let out a long-suffering sigh. "She's on the phone. Apparently, there are some meetings happening today that she insists she needs to sit in on."

"What?" Cassidy picked up her own bag and marched toward the hallway. "Come on, ladies. Let's go steal her phone after Nova and I change."

Our gracious host sashayed down the hall. I chuckled and followed after her, already starting to feel like I'd left my worries a million miles away. Between the fresh air, the music playing, and my friends, I couldn't bring myself to stress about anything right now.

Shedding all that horrible tension like an old skin, I darted into the room Cassidy pointed me to and finally allowed myself to relax. I changed into my favorite red bikini I'd had since high school. Sipping my margarita, I rejoined the others in Harriet's room.

Our raven-haired friend was on the phone, as we'd been told, and as soon as we all burst in there, she made her eyes huge at us and shook her head, mouthing a very firm, *No*.

Cassidy pumped her eyebrows at her while Jessie went around her back, her hand reaching out to snake the phone away from Harriet's ear. She pressed it to her own ear and made noises that I suspected were supposed to sound like Harriet was breaking up. Then she ended the call.

"Guys," Harriet complained, already stalking toward Jessie to steal the phone back from her. "That was important. I need to keep my finger on the pulse of this merger or I'm going to lose it."

"You won't," Amber said lazily, inspecting her nails until she glanced up at our friend. "You weren't even saying anything, babe. I hate to tell you this, but they probably didn't even realize you weren't on the call anymore. We, on the other hand, notice when you're not around. You're on vacation, right?"

"Of course, but—"

"No buts," I said firmly, snatching her phone from Jessie but hanging onto it for now. "Take it if it's really important, but it's a vacation weekend. Try to relax. You deserve it."

She sighed and nodded, but when the phone pinged in my hand, she grabbed it, furiously unlocked it, and concentrated intently as she read her email, despite the groans that had broken out from the rest of us.

"I think this calls for the pontoon boat," Cassidy decided out loud. "There's no way she can keep working once we're on the water."

She, Amber, and Jessie went to the kitchen to stock the cooler. Harriet replied to the email and I waited for her. Eyeing my beautiful friend with her Snow White features all scrunched up with worry, I frowned. "Is there something going on at work? Something that's not just work, maybe? You seem extra stressed."

She waved me off. "I'm a female mergers and acquisitions lawyer. I'm always extra stressed. This is nothing. How are you?"

I shrugged. "About the same as you, except that I've decided to take a real break this weekend."

Finally shoving her phone into a waterproof backpack, she hiked the bag over her shoulder and looked out her window at the lake. "A real break, huh? Are you going to be able to do that with Carson Drake right over there?"

My heart skipped, but I tried to play it off. Harriet and Amber knew about my history with Carson. Mostly because they'd both been at the bonfire that night and they'd picked up the pieces after he'd sped away.

I'd already realized that Cassidy and Jessie were probably going to find out about this weekend—if Jessie didn't already know as a result of her blossoming relationship with Vance. Even so, I didn't want to turn it into a *thing*.

None of them had come here to counsel me through my misguided feelings for my brother's famous best friend. So I lifted my shoulders and smiled. "I don't mind that he's going to be here. I didn't know he was coming until yesterday, but I came to spend time with you guys. That's it."

"Vance and Jessie are getting hot and heavy," she mused as we walked out of the room. "Those guys are bound to spend a lot of time with us this weekend, so we might've come to spend it together, but together now means with them too."

"Nah. I'm sure the lovebirds will lock themselves in a room soon enough and we won't see much of Carson once Vance disappears."

We joined the others in the kitchen.

She chuckled and took my arm, rolling her eyes at me. "Girl, it's not like any of us are going to mind seeing *much* of Carson Drake."

Jessie perked up at the sound of Carson's name. A beer had replaced the margarita that had been in her hand before. "I can't wait for them to get here. A whole weekend at the lake with Vance is going to be amazing."

"And us," Harriet said dryly with an amused smile playing on her lips. "We're here too, so it's a whole weekend at the lake with all of us."

Jessie laughed and pretended to blow her a kiss. "Of course. That was what I meant. Now let's take this party out on the water, girls. Amber has been dying to get started on her tan."

"Can you blame me?" Amber asked mildly, holding both of her arms out to her sides. "I'm so pasty, they can probably see me from space."

"As long as you do it with a drink in your hand, I'm happy," Jessie said cheerfully, shutting the cooler filled to the brim with drinks and ice. "I've been itching for a good party weekend for years. I mean, how long has it been since we've all been able to just kick back together like this?"

"Years," I confirmed without even having to think about it. "Let's go then. It's a gorgeous day and we don't want to waste any more of it inside."

A chorus of whoops rang out and the group of us headed down to the dock. We carefully climbed onto the pontoon boat and helped Jessie load the heavy cooler without incident. Cassidy was a pro at handling the boat, and she took us out to the middle of the lake, where she cut the engine.

I kicked back in the padded bench seat and let the sun warm my skin. Tension drained from my shoulders and the gentle waves rocked me like a baby. The day couldn't be more perfect.

"Harriet!" Cassidy snapped when she saw our friend was back on her phone again, her face buried in it once more.

She looked up and gave everyone an apologetic smile. "Just this one email. I tried to ignore it, but this idiot is like sand in my vagina."

A chorus of groans echoed around the boat. I shook my head but left her to it as Amber, Jessie, Cassidy and I spread out on the boat to work on our tans. Harriet's first email turned into another, and another, and eventually, we harassed her about it so much that she hid it in her backpack. She grabbed a hard seltzer from the cooler and damn near chugged it all in one go.

I laughed. "There's the Harriet I remember."

She wiped her mouth and glanced around like she was looking for something. "I wonder when the boys are going to get here. I'm ready for a little eye candy."

"Hey, you leave Vance alone," Jesse said playfully. "Keep your eyes on Carson."

Harriet frowned. "I don't know about Carson. Do you all think he still has feelings for Nova?"

"What?" Cassidy screeched, sitting upright and swiping her

sunglasses off to gape at me. "He had feelings for you? And you never told me?"

I groaned. "Yes."

She shook her head and looked almost impressed. "Well done, you sneaky bitch."

"But it's not like that," I said, not sure what it was like, but I felt the need to defend myself for some reason.

Amber remained perfectly still in her position so as not to risk ruining her tan, but the arch of her perfectly manicured eyebrow said it all. "You guys are unfinished business, Nova. It's likely that he still has feelings for you. Unless you've finished said business since he got back into town?"

Jesse cheered. "Aww yeah! Get it, Nova."

I rolled my eyes. "I'm not getting anything but older and grouchier."

Cassidy gave her head a firm shake. "No. Nope. Hold up. Let's pause for a minute. Can someone please tell me what happened with Nova and Carson, and why am I only hearing about it now?"

My cheeks flushed with heat that had nothing to do with the sun as Harriet and Amber told her what they'd seen at the bonfire way back when. I filled in the gaps in a squeaky voice and begged them to leave it in the past—where it belonged—but they weren't having it.

"He's so dreamy," Amber said once I was done telling the story. "That part hasn't changed. Have you guys seen him since he got back?"

She didn't ask the question to anyone in particular. I shrugged, Cassidy and Jesse nodded, and Harriet shook her head. Amber sighed. "I might've taken a shot at him if I didn't know that his heart already belonged to Nova."

"It doesn't," I protested, but I had to admit that it was nice to be able to talk about this without having Ryan throw a temper tantrum about even just the possibility. "No part of him belongs to me. Least of all his heart."

"Pity," Harriet said thoughtfully. "It's a good heart. I'd take it anytime if I could. That's part of what makes him so dreamy, isn't it? The fact that he's actually a good guy?"

I hummed my agreement.

None of them even knew what he was trying to do for us with the ranch, and I preferred to keep it that way, considering that I didn't know yet what my parents were going to say. But the girls weren't wrong about him.

The low hum of an approaching engine alerted us to the presence of another craft, and the next thing I knew, *their* boat came into view. Ryan was at the helm, with Vance lounging in the back. I hadn't even known my brother was coming with them, but I shouldn't have been as surprised—or as disappointed—as I was.

Then I saw him.

Carson was behind them on a jet ski and I tried not to stare, but his abs were on display and his smile had never looked whiter. His wet skin glistened in the sun, highlighting the hard lines of his arms and chest.

He soared over their boat's wake, jumping through the air with his strong legs braced for impact and his tanned arms expertly maneuvering the jet ski back to the surface of the water. Fully aware that my friends were going to have to mop up my drool if I didn't stop staring, I suddenly couldn't stop thinking about that moment in my kitchen yesterday.

I kicked myself for letting that moment pass us by without seizing it.

He pulled up beside us. Warmth and joy filled my entire being now that he was here, the picture finally feeling complete in a way it hadn't before.

I knew Ryan would feel betrayed if Carson and I got together, but I was starting to realize I would be betraying my heart and Carson's if we didn't at least give it a shot.

Now I just had to decide whether I was going to be selfless or selfish—and I already knew which of the two I wanted to choose.

# 28

## CARSON

"Come get on our boat, Jess," Vance called to Nova's friend as soon as they stopped beside the girls too. "Ryan is a better captain than Cass. You'll be safer with us."

The blonde tipped her head back and laughed. "I'll go with you, but not because I agree. Cassidy is an excellent captain, and better yet, I packed this cooler myself and we're not running out anytime soon."

"A girl after my own heart," Vance crooned, getting up and offering his hand to help her climb over.

Meanwhile, Cassidy had been staring at Ryan with something of a challenge written across her dainty features. "At least I can drive a boat with my clothes on. What happened to your shirt?"

Ryan grinned at her and even winked, in a good mood for once. "I left it at the cabin. Consider it a gift to you."

"A gift?" She scoffed, but I saw the humor in her eyes. "In that case, I hope you kept the receipt because I'd like to return it."

"Oooh," Harriet cheered from the side. "Shots fired. Get him, girl."

Cassidy winked at her friend before smirking at Ryan. "No offense, but I've been behind the helm of a boat practically since I was born. My parents even have pictures of me on this very lake when I was a baby with my tiny, chubby baby hand on the throttle."

He raked his gaze across her, and I knew what he was thinking. She might've had a chubby hand as a baby, but there sure wasn't anything chubby about her now. As it turned out, Cassidy had been hiding a pretty good body under that apron she wore at the bakery. She was all woman now, compared to the flat-chested, curveless creature she'd been back in high school.

Nova noticed her brother checking out her friend, and she scoffed quietly as she hid her face behind her hair and shook her head.

*On that note.*

"I'm going to take Nova for a ride," I called out to him from the jet ski, finally allowing myself to look at her fully now that his attention was so firmly fixed on her friend.

Of course, as soon as I said her name, his gaze snapped to mine and I braced myself for the scowling to start again, but it didn't. Miraculously, he pumped his eyebrows at me as he nodded. "Feel free to dump her in the lake if she starts mouthing off."

Nova rolled her eyes and got up, giving me my first real look at her in a modest but unbelievably sexy bikini. I recognized it from back in the day and the sight of her in it made my mouth water just as much now as it had then. It hugged her boobs, the cups cutting down between them to where they met in a cute little center bow. While she probably wasn't in danger of accidentally showing a nipple, it was still skimpy enough to get my blood pumping to my cock.

It grew against the Velcro fly of my swim trunks, but I didn't bother trying to stop it. With the jet ski in the way and me sitting down, no one would notice. Besides, with her full curves on display and that tiny scrap of a triangle the only thing covering her pussy, it would've been pointless to try getting rid of the effect she was having on me.

"If anyone is getting dumped in the water, it'll be Carson." With a sweet smile at her brother, she flashed him her middle finger and jumped on the jet ski with me. I whisked us away before Ryan could change his mind. Adrenaline rushed through my veins as her arms wrapped around my waist and her legs molded around my hips and thighs.

I ripped us around the lake and she held on to me for dear life, but I heard the delighted laughter coming out of her as we took to the air only to land again with a carefully executed slide. With the wind in her hair and feeling like we were flying, I knew she was having a good time and that made me feel happy.

If anyone deserved to cut loose like this, it was her. It was also a real thrill to get to be the one she was cutting loose with.

"This is amazing," she shouted into the wind.

Since she wouldn't hear me if I tried to respond, I lowered one hand to her forearm where it sat against my belly button, squeezing it before gripping the throttle again. It was a busy day on the water and I stopped a few minutes later to make waves for a group of kids on inner tubes before dashing away again.

When we slowed to wait for a boat with a guy on water skis behind it to pass, she poked me in the ribs. "It's my turn to take you for a spin."

"I don't remember saying you could have a turn," I joked even as I made way for her to climb over. She sat down between my legs and I slid my arms around her waist with a groan. Having her in the driver's seat wasn't going to be the most dangerous part of what was happening right now.

She turned her head to glance at me over her shoulder, and I saw the blush that had risen on her cheeks. Assuming that she now knew I was at least half hard, if not more, I smirked at her. "What? Do you blame me?"

Her lips parted and her tongue popped out to swipe across them before she sighed. "No, I guess I don't."

Without another word, she faced forward again and took off. Not the best driver, she dumped us into the water soon after hitting a big wave of her own creation. I hit the surface and skidded a little bit before coming to a stop. Then I laughed as I watched her sputter while wiping water away from her eyes.

Nova always had been a good swimmer, though. I didn't have to worry about her. After watching her for a moment, that long blonde hair now soaked and slicked back, I sliced through the water with powerful strokes of my arms and got back to the jet ski in no time.

I got back on and held out a hand to fish her out. "Come on, but I think I'm taking over from here."

Treading water, she flashed me a playful grin and shook her head. "No way. If you want me to get back on that thing with you, come get me."

With that, she dove under the water and swam away, her long legs visible despite the slight murkiness of the surface. I sighed and watched her bob around for a moment before I jumped in after her. *She really is trying to kill me. That's the only explanation.*

The warm water enveloped me. I hoped it would give me the strength not to do anything stupid, but then Nova launched herself at me as soon as my head broke free and I caught her, holding her to me even as she writhed and splashed trying to get free.

"Damn it. I had the upper hand." She laughed. "How did you turn that around on me so quickly?"

I tried to ignore the sensation of her thigh sliding against my crotch as she struggled, loving the feeling of her hot, wet skin against my own and trying to ignore that too. "What are we doing here, Nova?"

My voice came out as something of a low growl, and she giggled. Biting her lip, she turned to face me and finally stilled as her gaze met mine. "You came to get me, remember?"

Those blue eyes sparkled with laughter, but there was a heat in them that I wished I hadn't seen. Torn between kissing the shit out of her and behaving like the good little boy I wasn't, I finally sighed and spun her in my arms so she wouldn't be looking at me like that anymore. Then I towed her back to the jet ski. "Ryan will kill me if you drown on my watch, so whatever you were planning, it's not going to happen out here."

"Do you really think you could make me so weak that I would drown?" she teased, but I heard the huskiness in her voice and I groaned.

"I know I can make your legs shaky and your knees weak. I also know I could make you scream my name and no one but me would hear it over the roar of these engines." With that, I dumped her like a wet rat on the jet ski. "Unfortunately, I can't do any of that either without getting killed."

The laughter faded from her eyes. Her lids were hooded and her pupils were slightly dilated as she stared back at me. I let out another groan and shook my head at her. "I'm going to need a minute."

Ducking under the water, I pressed at my erection with the palm of my hand and willed the damn thing to cool down enough that I'd be able to climb out. It took more than a minute, and when I eventually joined her on the jet ski, she let me drive without protest, not saying a word as I steered us toward Cassidy's house.

I beached the craft on the shore by the dock. When we arrived, Ryan and Vance were hanging out with the girls. They were all standing around a firepit, with Ryan and Cassidy bickering over who was going to be the grill master tonight.

"It looks like we're staying for dinner," I said quietly to Nova, glancing down into her eyes and fucking wishing that I could close the two feet of distance between us.

"Looks like it," she replied, sending me a small, uncertain smile. "How did Ryan end up coming with you?"

"Vance," I explained.

She let out a long exhale and nodded, glancing at her brother. He pointed at the firepit, probably trying to make some kind of point. When she looked back at me, she smiled. "I'm glad you guys brought him. He really needs to get away more often and he looks happy. More like himself."

I glanced at him, nodding my agreement. We joined them and Ryan immediately tried to win both of us over to his side. "Tell Cassidy that there's no way she can cook a steak better than me. I'm the master, and therefore, I should be the one to do the grilling."

"Bullshit," Cassidy retorted. "Just because I'm a woman doesn't mean I can't grill a damn steak. You go make the salad and I'll cook the steaks."

Ryan snorted and I reached into the cooler for a beer. I tossed one to Nova, knowing that I had a heated gleam in my eyes, but shit, I couldn't help it. Not when she was still in that bikini I'd had so many fantasies about.

"I'm staying out of this," I said as I took a seat on one of the nearby lounge chairs.

Nova went inside to take a shower. As hard as I tried not to, I found myself waiting for her to come back out. I also found myself wishing I could've gone with her. When I realized she was probably naked right then, I got hard all over again. Then Ryan howled with laughter—not at my bulging cock thankfully—and my arousal died an instant death at the reminder of why we couldn't be together.

*Fuck. This really is going to be a damn long weekend.*

Spending the evening with her was torture, and I was relieved when the guys and I finally got back to our own cabin and opened beers on our porch. Ryan smirked at Vance, launching right back into giving him grief about shooting his shot with Nova's friend.

"It's Jessie, bro. In my eyes, all those girls are still, like, twelve. What the hell are you doing with her?"

This had been going on since we'd left Cassidy's parents' place, and Vance grinned as he turned the tables. "Says you. I saw the way you were looking at Cass all day, man, and you definitely weren't looking at her like she was twelve."

That was true. He'd solved the grill master problem by hauling her over his shoulders and dumping her into the water off the edge of the dock. Everyone else had been delighted, howling with laughter, and even Cassidy had seemed a little thrilled when she'd finally come out of the water.

"You guys fight like an old married couple already," Vance said as we settled on the deck under the stars. "You might as well call it like it is and tie the knot already."

Ryan grumbled an incomprehensible reply and washed it down with beer, but I noticed that he hadn't flat out denied that there was anything going on between him and Cass. My eyebrows inched up and I grinned at him. "The plot thickens, huh? What's going on, Ry? Are you secretly hooking up with your sister's best friend?"

Part of me hoped he was. All this felt like old times and I was happy, but I still couldn't get Nova out of my head, and if he really was crushing on her best friend, then maybe he would understand eventually. Would he really be that upset if I pursued Nova anyway, though? Or would it end our friendship just as we were getting it back on track?

I didn't have the answers, but as I sat there and shot the breeze with them, drinking beer and feeling like all was well, I couldn't shake the feeling that Nova should've been here too. At my side. Where it felt like she belonged.

# 29

## NOVA

Doing nothing but lying in a hammock in the sunshine was pure and absolute bliss. I wasn't reading. I just existed and I was pretty sure it was the closest I'd ever come to heaven. Sighing happily, I focused on the sensation of the sun warming my skin and the scents of earth, and motor oil, and gas from the boats on the lake that wafted through the air.

With Carson on my mind—and just across the lake—my body felt like it'd been suspended in a cocoon of relaxation. I closed my eyes. A smile ghosted across my lips as I remembered luring him to me in the lake yesterday, and I was pretty sure I was just about to fall into a slightly naughty dream about it when a weight suddenly jumped onto the hammock with me.

My eyes flew open just as Cassidy nestled in beside me, resting her head on my shoulder and turning it so her gaze was on mine. "I'm pretty sure Ryan was flirting with me yesterday."

I blinked rapidly at the sudden change in direction of my thoughts. It took me a second to catch up, but when I did, I smiled at her. "Yeah, I noticed that too. You should go for it."

"That was blunt," she said, sounding mildly surprised. "Are you sure? I mean, he's your brother. It could be weird for you if we got together."

I chuckled. "Unlike Ryan, I'm fine with people doing whatever makes them happy as long as they're honest with each other and clear about what they want. Besides, I think he'll be way nicer to everyone if he just gets laid already."

She swatted me, giggling, then shook her head and rolled onto her back. We lay in silence for a beat, both watching the clouds as they drifted by before she spoke again. "Are you ever going to seal the deal with Carson? Now that I finally know about you two, so many things make sense. He's the guy you've been waiting for, isn't he?"

"I haven't been actively waiting for him," I said slowly, trying to explain it in a way that would make sense even to myself. "I didn't set out to wait for him, at least. It was just one kiss and a whole lot of chemistry back in the day. I would've been crazy to be stuck on him for ten years, waiting for him to come home when I never even knew he was planning on it."

"But?" she said when I didn't continue.

I sighed. "But I think I *have* been waiting to feel that way again. I've been waiting for a guy who makes me feel the way he used to, and no one ever did."

"So what now?" she asked. "You weren't waiting for him, but does he still make you feel that way?"

"Yes." I winced as I admitted it for the first time out loud. "He really, really does. I don't know how to explain it, but it's true."

She laughed. "You don't have to explain it, babe. I get it. I've seen the way you two look at each other, like you're both in pain and longing for something. It just didn't make sense to me until I found out that you used to have something. Why didn't you ever tell me about it?"

"There was nothing to tell," I murmured. "I had a crush on him and he kissed me one whole time. That's hardly the stuff to obsess over, so I felt silly about it. I also thought that it would pass and it did. I guess I just never forgot the way he made me feel, you know? I wasn't hanging onto him so much as the idea of being capable of feeling that way, but now he's back and it's a mess. Again."

"It wasn't silly." She reached for my hand and squeezed it. "The heart wants what it wants, Nova. If yours wants Carson and he wants you, then maybe it's time you did something about it."

"I want to," I confessed, baring my soul about this for the first time ever. "I really, really want to, but it's more than just giving in to the chemistry and lust. That's what makes it so complicated. I like having him around too much. I like talking to him and laughing with him. I don't just want to screw him. I want to be with him, but that's crazy."

"Why is it crazy?" she asked as a confused frown furrowed her brow. "He couldn't keep his eyes off you last night, my friend. Somehow, I don't think all he wants is to screw you, either. I think he wants the same things you do, and that could never be crazy."

"Except for the Ryan of it all."

She rolled her eyes. "Why would he be all that upset if you got together, even if it was just casual? You're both grownups now. I'm pretty sure you'd both consent, so what does it have to do with Ryan at all?"

"It's because I'm his little sister and Carson is his best friend. He sure seems to think that gives him the right to an opinion."

"So? I'm your best friend and he's your older brother, but that didn't stop him. What's good for the goose is good for the gander, hon. I'm pretty sure that makes you even, right?"

"You have a point, but I still don't know. I think I've been too conditioned to think of him as off limits to really be able to see it objectively."

"Objectively, you're both completely single. You're not related. Neither of you is in a position of authority in relation to the other, and legally, you've both been adults for a long time. There really is nothing standing in your way. If your brother has a problem with it, then he needs to grow the hell up."

Music started playing inside again, filtering out to us. Jessie appeared on the deck in another bikini and carrying a tray of ice-cold mimosas. "It's nearly noon, girls! That means we're about three to four hours too late to be starting with these, so we'd better catch up."

I laughed and went to join the others for a day next to the pool. All around us, people were doing the same thing we were, and a few hours later, it had turned into one big party. Our yard was covered in people in swimsuits and the music was blaring. Fires were lit as the afternoon wore on and the drinks kept flowing.

Tipsy and having the time of my life, I danced around with Harriet and Amber, not really sure where Cassidy and Jessie had disappeared to but not worried. The girls and I had spent most of the last couple hours in the pool, alternating between swimming, dancing, and working on our tans—all while sipping on delicious cocktails we whipped up ourselves.

"I need to get some water," I shouted to my friends over the music, then left them on the deck and made my way through the throngs of people to the kitchen.

As I opened a bottle of water, Carson appeared, seemingly out of thin air and looking like a sweaty, tousled Greek god. He was shirtless again, a fresh glow on his skin saying that he'd spent the day in the sun just like I had. His dark hair was messy and windswept, and his eyes twinkled like gemstones in the low light of the kitchen as the sun started dipping low on the horizon outside.

I hadn't even noticed he was here until now, and it threw me a bit to suddenly find myself looking at the man I'd spent all day and all night last night thinking about. "You're here."

"Am I?" He brought a bottle of beer to his lips and drank down a long sip before grinning at me. I watched, transfixed in my tipsy state by the bobbing of his Adam's apple as he swallowed and then by the rugged beauty of that grin.

*Nova! He said something. Respond.*

I jerked my gaze away from those lips and looked at him. "I'm pretty sure you are here, yes. If I'm dreaming and none of this is real, you wouldn't be here."

"Wouldn't I?" he asked, his voice a little rougher now. Then he rounded on me, moving closer and penning me in against the kitchen counter. When he spoke again, his lips were against my hair and I shivered. "If you were dreaming, I think I would be here, but none of these other people would be. It would only be the two of us."

"Keep dreaming," I retorted, pushing the words out past my suddenly bone-dry mouth.

He chuckled, the sound reverberating through me and making me feel all tingly before he pulled back to look into my eyes. "I'd love to, but I didn't bring the jet ski to hide what will happen if I do."

My lids slammed shut and I dragged in a sharp breath. I didn't think we were going to talk about that again, but here he was, casually bringing up the raging erection he'd had yesterday when it'd only been him and me on the water.

"Carson." I inhaled deeply, opening my eyes again to find him giving me that same pained look he'd had on his face in my kitchen the other morning.

He pushed away from me, putting a good three feet of distance between us. "Yeah, I know."

I swiped my tongue across my lips, willing my heart to stop racing so much. I needed to think clearly. "Where are Vance and Ryan?"

He shrugged. "I don't know. We got here a couple hours ago and I lost them almost immediately. Haven't seen a trace of either of them since, so I'm starting to think they're either behind closed doors somewhere or they've taken off for a walk or something."

The party raged on around us. I knew I should've told him that it had been good to see him but that I should get back to my friends. Those weren't the words that came out of my mouth, though. *Flipping cocktails have taken control of my tongue.*

"Do you want to come have a drink with me?" I asked. "If we're both alone, we may as well be alone together."

He nodded slowly, then smiled and swept a hand out in the direction of the yard. "I think I saw two spots opening up around the fire. Our cooler is there and you'll have choice of beer, beer, and beer."

"Beer sounds good," I said, falling into step beside him and staying close to his side so we wouldn't get separated in the crowd.

At some point, his fingers twined around my own and my heart went absolutely berserk, slamming, and racing, and skipping, and jumping, but I didn't let go of his hand. Not now that I was finally holding it after so many years of dying to do just that.

Wordlessly leading me to the firepit, we took two seats off to the side. Almost instantly, we were surrounded by a wall of people. Most of them had their backs to us. Carson seemed to have blended in here, with no one paying him more mind than they did anyone else.

The benefit of all that was that we were fairly safe behind all these bodies. Even if Ryan did come back to the party from wherever he'd gone, it was unlikely he'd see us here together, with me sitting close to Carson with a goofy smile on my face and stars in my eyes.

"How was your day?" he asked, leaning in closer to be heard above the music. "We took it easy, but I think Vance was counting the minutes until he could come see Jessie."

I giggled. "I think Ryan might've been counting the minutes, too. Were you?"

"Yes," he said against my ear. His hand slid onto my thigh and yet another shiver raced through me.

I was at the precipice. Filled with liquid courage and after Cassidy's pep talk, I wanted to take him inside. I wanted to kiss him— and more. But we talked for another little while before I finally managed to get the words out.

"Should we go somewhere quieter? It's really getting loud out here."

"Sure." He nodded, reluctantly letting his hand slide away from my thigh.

I missed the weight and the heat of it there immediately, but that was why I was doing this. *So that I can feel the weight and the heat of him everywhere.*

Hopefully.

Taking him back inside the lake house, my heart was hammering in my chest. I led him upstairs to the bedroom I'd been staying in. There was enough space that everyone had their own room this time around, and I'd never felt so lucky to know I had my own *lockable* door.

Once we were in there, I closed the door behind us, drowning out the worst of the noise from below. Leaning against the door, I was unsure of what to say or do at this point. It was suddenly so quiet and we were suddenly so alone.

Carson turned around, not seeming nearly as uncomfortable as I was in the soft light of dusk that filled my room. "Are you keeping me prisoner up here?"

I reached behind me and flicked the lock on the door. His eyes went wide and dark with understanding. In that same instant, he let out a low, raw growl, and then we were closing the distance between us, crashing together someplace in the middle. He didn't waste any time, one arm snaking around my waist and the other capturing my face. Then he bent his head and kissed me fully.

I melted into his touch. We were both frantic. All the tension was finally bursting and I was going for it. Nothing was going to stop me now.

# 30

## CARSON

Part of me couldn't believe what was happening right now, but that part shut up real damn fast when Nova moaned into my mouth and roped her arms around my neck. Just because one part was having trouble believing this was real didn't mean that the rest of me wasn't onboard.

All the way onboard. With whatever it was she wanted to do.

The locking of the door thing made me think it was something she didn't want anyone to walk in on, but with our luck, the house was about to catch fire or her brother was going to burst through the window. Another possibility was that she was going to end this wild, passionate kiss just as suddenly as it started. When none of that happened, I tightened my grip on her and hoped like hell that this was our time.

Not wanting to hesitate anymore just in case the universe turned against us again, I kissed her harder, finally getting to do it the way I'd been dreaming about for so long. In my wildest imagination—and it had gotten pretty wild in all the fantasies I'd had about her over the years—I never would've come close to knowing just how good it would be.

There was kissing and then there was this. Nova's inhibitions seemed to have been obliterated by either lust, or alcohol, or both, and she was giving me everything she'd been holding back the previous times this had happened. Her chest was fused to mine, her hands clawing at me as desperately as mine were clawing at her.

It took her no more than a few minutes before my trunks were hitting the floor. With my heart in my throat, I decided to return the favor, tugging the strings of her bikini top free before I died. Okay, so I didn't really die, but as that scrap of material fell away from her body and I separated my chest from hers for a moment to let it happen, I felt like I might've died because this was definitely heaven.

Her nipples were hard little pebbles against my chest, her skin sweet and warm. I drank from her mouth like a guy that had been thirsty forever. When she finally lifted my trunks over my rock-hard dick, I stepped out of them, naked as the day I was born and still very much in a state of disbelief.

In the back of my mind, I kept waiting for something to happen. Either, I was going to wake up and find out I'd been dreaming again, or we were going to have to cut this short. All that just added to the wild urgency of the experience.

I hooked my thumbs into the waistband of the tiny mini skirt she'd put on over her bikini bottoms, sliding it past her ass and taking the swimsuit with me.

I wanted nothing more than to savor these moments, but I couldn't slow down. Not while it felt like there was some kind of clock ticking down, about to chime at any moment to signal that we were out of time. I ran my hands over every exposed part of her skin, memorizing the feel of her under my fingertips and so turned on that I was already right on the edge.

It made me feel a little bad until I realized that it felt like our entire lives had been leading up to this. Every look, word, and touch we'd exchanged since I'd been twenty years old had been foreplay for this moment, and besides, I wasn't going to lose it until I'd finally gotten to see, feel, and taste every last inch of her.

Nova trembled in my arms, moaning into my mouth again as she leaned into me. Suddenly the overwhelming urge to protect her swept through me again, mingling with the lust to make me feel like some kind of primal beast that needed to satisfy all her needs at once.

It was crazy, but that was no surprise. Nova had been driving me crazy since the very first time I'd seen her in that same damn bikini at seventeen years old.

Without breaking the kiss, I walked her back to the bed and laid her down, but I didn't follow her onto the mattress. Not yet.

Instead, I stood next to it, my eyes roving over her naked body and my heart pounding so hard that I heard it in my ears. Nova dressed made me wild. Nova undressed? I swallowed hard and prayed to the gods of sex and endurance.

She was so fucking perfect that it made my heart and my cock ache simultaneously, which was odd. My heart usually stayed out of it when I had a woman naked, but this was different.

Nova's torso was shaped like an hourglass and her breasts were so damn full even though she was lying down. Her skin was soft and silky smooth—everywhere—and her nipples were a dusky pink, small little nubs that begged me to taste them.

While I stared at her, she did the same to me, breathing as hard as I was as she let her eyes linger on every part of me. "Shit, Nova. You're sure about this, right?"

In response, she tucked a toe behind my knee and smiled as she nudged me toward her. "I'm sure. Are you?"

"Fuck, yes," I groaned, finally climbing onto the mattress with her and kissing her lips before moving on to her jaw, her throat, and her chest.

When I clamped my mouth around the first nipple, she moaned out loud and scraped her nails against my skull, holding me to her. Her back arched and her legs hooked around my ass. I could feel the heat of her against my shaft in this position and I moaned too, so fucking ready that everything in me felt like it had reached a breaking point.

I nipped at that hard peak in my mouth to distract myself, then ran a hand up her silky thigh and trembled when I felt the wetness. "This isn't going to last long."

"Nope," she agreed huskily. "We've got all night, though. I want you, Carson. Now. Everything else can wait."

"Fuck." I wanted so badly to ignore her, but I couldn't. Her voice had been a plea—and that was when I realized that I didn't have any condoms. My wallet was at our cabin, all the way on the other side of the lake.

When I paused, Nova groaned. "You don't have one, do you?"

"No." I swallowed the bitter disappointment rising within me, but when I finally pulled away to look at her, she was smiling. "What?"

"It looks like I'm more presumptuous than you. Because I have one. I have three, actually."

I nearly jumped for joy. "Three?"

"A whole box," she said slowly, drawing out each word. "All for you. A girl can hope, right?"

"And a guy can be really fucking grateful." I kissed her again, hard and fast until I wrenched my lips away from hers. "Where are they? This is probably already risky."

I felt the precome leaking out of me, my body desperate for hers. She glanced at the nightstand. "In the drawer. Quickly."

"You don't have to tell me twice." Moving as fast as I could, I sat up and found the condoms exactly where she'd said to look. Then I ripped one open and rolled it on before positioning myself between her thighs.

My tip nudged against her entrance, and she let out a loud moan. I lowered my body down on hers and looked into her eyes. "This is it, Nova. If we do this, there's no going back."

Her fingers ran up the length of my back and she pushed them into my hair, bringing my face closer to hers again. "I don't want to go back, Carson. I'm ready to move forward. With you."

She wrapped her legs around my hips and used the muscles in them to push down, guiding me into her one euphorically agonizing inch at a time. Sinking into Nova was like nothing I'd ever experienced before, and looking deeply into her eyes while I did it was intense. More intense than anything I'd ever felt.

Her lips parted, but her eyes never left mine. Not even when I brought my mouth to hers once I was fully seated. She kissed me gently, with so much feeling that mini-explosions went off inside my soul that triggered movements in my body.

With my gaze still glued to hers, I started rocking slowly at first, only picking up speed when she did. "Nova, you're so fucking amazing."

I didn't have the words to describe how she made me feel, so I left it at that. She nodded and kissed me again before she murmured her response against my lips. "It's perfect. It's so beautifully perfect."

As she said it, she started spasming around me. Her impossibly tight channel got even tighter as her muscles contracted. "Carson, I'm close."

She clung to me like she would never let go. I dragged my lips across the column of her throat, trying to soothe her as my hips kept thrusting and my own orgasm raced toward me. "Let go, baby. I'm right there with you."

"I can't—" She started shaking, then smashed her mouth against mine when the climax hit.

I went off like a geyser at the exact same time, emptying myself into the condom so hard that my ears rang and my blood stopped flowing. In the aftermath, I stayed on top of her for a long time, panting and kissing her everywhere my lips could reach until she finally stopped thrashing underneath me.

For the first time ever, I felt the need to take care of someone after, so I whispered soothing words to her as her body relaxed. Then I kissed her eyelids and her cheeks before I slid out of her. "I'll be right back. I'm just going to get a cloth and take care of the condom."

She nodded jerkily, her eyes still closed. "Come back soon."

"As soon as I can," I promised as I climbed off the bed. My legs were heavier than they should've been as I stumbled to the bathroom.

After doing what needed to be done, I cleaned her up gently and then got back into bed with her, pulling her into my arms and kissing her temple as she nestled into my side. "Nova?"

"Hmm?"

"You okay?"

I felt her lips curving into a smile against my throat. "I'm all good, Carson. I'm great, actually. You?"

"Relieved." I ran a hand up and down her back, stroking her hair and twining a lock of it between my fingers. "That was a long time coming. Do you want to talk about it?"

"Not right now," she said softly. "Sleep first, then talk."

"Okay," I agreed, my brain still too numb to think. I closed my eyes, breathing her in as I drifted off to sleep.

I woke up the next morning alone, butt naked, and eager for another round, but the fact that I was alone said that wasn't going to happen. Groaning as I rolled over in her bed, I got up and tracked down my clothes, pulling them on as I wondered what to do next.

I heard voices filtering up from outside, so going out the window wasn't an option. Even if I could figure out a way to climb down that didn't involve a one-story drop. Resigned to having to use the door like a normal person, I really fucking wished I didn't have to sneak out—or leave her bed at all.

Last night had been the best sex I'd ever had, and more than that, it had been one of the best nights of my life. I was never going to forget it and I was definitely not going to be getting over it anytime soon.

Sighing, I cracked open the door and glanced up and down the hallway, feeling like a damn cat burglar. It dampened my mood a little but not much. With the memories of Nova's body underneath mine and her moans echoing in my ears, nothing was going to bring me down today. I was on top of the world.

Until I got downstairs and saw Ryan outside.

I swallowed hard as the guilt finally set in. He and Vance were cleaning up with Jessie and Harriet, and while I knew I should probably go out there and join the effort, I followed my nose to the kitchen first.

The smell of coffee and bacon drew me there, and when I saw Nova and Cassidy standing around the island, I decided I'd help them instead. Still walking around like a creeper who didn't want to be seen, I stayed light on my feet and stuck close to the wall, wondering how I was going to pretend like I'd only just gotten here when I was still wearing yesterday's clothes.

A low murmur of voices came from the kitchen. I could hear Cassidy and Nova talking. "So, you and Ryan, huh? How did that go?"

"So good," Cassidy replied softly but dreamily. "He really isn't such a bad guy, you know. In fact, there are a lot of things he's not bad at *at all*."

Nova's giggle turned into a groan. "I'd rather not hear about those things. Thanks, but no thanks."

"Who am I supposed to rave to, then?" Cassidy asked playfully. "You're my best friend. One of your primary duties is listening to me talk about boys and sex."

My eyebrows shot up as immense relief coursed through me. On the one hand, I was surprised to hear that Cassidy and Ryan had spent the night together, and on the other, I was very fucking relieved that he'd been so wrapped in her that he probably didn't know I'd disappeared with his sister.

I really hadn't been sure he was going to go for it with Cassidy, but I was glad he did. What puzzled me more was that she was talking about it to Nova so openly. He was her brother.

*Don't girls have the same rules we do about that kind of thing?*

Evidently, however, they didn't. Nova let out a long, disappointed sigh. "How about a compromise? We can talk about it, but you don't give me any details about the sex. I don't need to hear any of that, as long as he made you happy."

"Oh, he made me happy, alright. He made me happy *soooo* many times all night long." Cassidy's laughter rang out until it abruptly cut off after a soft thwack. "Ouch. What was that for?"

"The details," Nova said with amused exasperation in her tone.

I reached the kitchen. The girls finally realized I was there and shut up. Cassidy beamed at me, immediately pushing herself away from the stove and handing over the spatula she'd been using to cook the bacon to Nova.

"I'm sure you guys can handle this. I'm going to go... somewhere else." She laughed and gave me a sassy wink when she passed me on her way out.

I chuckled, waiting until we were alone again before turning to face my girl "How are you feeling this morning?"

She gave me a shy smile, her face clear of any makeup and those eyes so soft and vulnerable that I wanted to pull her into my arms and never let go. *This can't have been a one-time thing.*

"I'm good," she said quietly, glancing over my shoulder. "We probably won't be alone for long, so we can't really talk about it, but how are you?"

"Better than ever," I said, moving a little closer and checking that we were still alone before I glanced back at her. "Listen, I just want you to know that—"

"Nova, how's that bacon coming?" Ryan asked and his voice sounded like it was coming from right outside the kitchen.

*Fuck.*

"It's almost done," she called back. "Just a minute."

I sighed. "We'll talk later."

She nodded, giving me one last smile before she turned her gaze back down to the pan in front of her. Everything in my being begged to go over there, but instead, I filled a mug with coffee and tried to make it look like I'd just arrived.

I grinned at Ryan when he walked in. "Hey, man. What happened to you guys last night?" I asked. "I had the whole cabin to myself. It was weird. What would've happened if I'd gotten scared?"

# 31

## NOVA

After breakfast and a ton of cleaning up, the girls and I were finally alone again, lounging around the pool. Jessie had her phone in her lap where she lay with only her legs in the sun, another cocktail on the table next to her as she texted with Vance.

Harriet was on her stomach in the full shade of a patio umbrella, scrolling through emails and pretending that she didn't notice the eye rolls we were all giving her whenever she looked up. I loved my friend, but she really needed to learn how to disconnect.

Amber was on the other side of the pool, her whole body in the sun as she tried to soak up as many rays as she could before we left tomorrow night. As I looked around, I realized how lucky I was to have had this weekend with them. It'd been great catching up and shutting out the world.

Not so great was how I currently felt about hooking up with Carson. Last night, with the sun setting over the lake and the pleasant buzz of alcohol in my system, it had felt impossible to resist the attraction.

I didn't regret what we'd done, but I was conflicted. Cassidy sat next to me with a book in her lap, but when I let out yet another heavy sigh, she finally glanced at me. "Okay. Out with it. What's bugging you?"

"Carson," I said, keeping my voice down but also knowing that the others were so wrapped up in their own worlds right now that they probably weren't listening. Even if they were, it would be okay. These were my friends.

It was just that I'd really prefer to confide in only one of them at a time, and Cassidy was closest to me these days. She was also the only one who'd seen Carson and me together consistently since he'd come home, so I figured she had a bit more insight into our situation at the moment.

She pursed her lips at me. "Why is he bugging you?" Her eyes suddenly went wide. "Was it not good last night? Did he do something wrong? Does he have a bent carrot? I keep seeing commercials about that."

"No," I said quickly. "Nooooo. It's not that."

The tension that had been tightening her features melted and she smirked at me. "So it's bugging you because it was good?"

"It was great." *Still an understatement.* "It's just, uh, it didn't feel like a hookup."

She frowned. "If it didn't feel like a hookup, then he definitely did something wrong."

A blush burst out across my cheeks, racing down my neck and making even the tips of my ears feel hot. "Not like *that*. Let's just say it exceeded my expectations. By a lot, but it didn't feel like a hookup because it felt like more, which is why I'm conflicted today."

Her eyes narrowed and confusion set in. "Were you expecting it to feel like only a hookup when it's been years in the making? Just yesterday, you told me that you like him, so obviously, it was going to feel like more. Have you spoken to him at all about what it meant?"

"Nope." I sighed and raked a hand through my hair. "We didn't get around to it, but I don't know, Cass. It just feels like it's one thing to crush on him and maybe even to hook up with him casually, but actually falling for him? Trying for something more?"

"Isn't that what you said you wanted, though?"

*Why, yes. Yes, it is.* I squeezed my eyes shut, trying to make sense of all the thoughts racing through my head. "I want it. I just don't know if I can have it. Or if I should have it. He's Ryan's—"

"If you finish that sentence by saying that he's Ryan's best friend, I'm going to stop you right now. I thought we'd established that Ryan doesn't get a say in this. Don't get me wrong. That boy rocked my freaking world last night, but that doesn't mean I'm suddenly on his side. You do you, Nova. If that means that you do Carson, then so be it. Ryan will have to adapt and survive."

I doubted my brother was going to see it that way, but that didn't mean that she didn't have a point. I just had to learn to accept it—and to face my own feelings instead of hiding behind Ryan's.

At the end of the day, the guys came over again for dinner, and my heart skipped about a million beats when Carson walked in. His dark hair was tousled and windswept again, but I'd heard from Jessie that they'd spent the day racing around on the lake.

Wearing navy blue shorts and a fitted white T-shirt, he was so gorgeous that I wanted to jump on him and claim him as my own. It definitely didn't help that I now knew what it felt like to be claimed *by* him as well.

My entire body filled with heat as his eyes met mine, those greens so much more vivid today than I'd ever seen them before. For a moment, our gazes locked. My nipples strained against my bra, my breathing quickened, my heart raced, and my panties caught fire.

A slow grin hooked on Carson's lips, like he knew exactly what was happening inside me and couldn't have been happier about it, but then my brother walked into my field of vision and it all crashed and burned.

Ryan smiled as he accepted a beer from Jessie, I tuned back in to the girls' conversation about our plans for Memorial Day tomorrow. As I turned away from Carson, Cassidy resumed the argument she'd been having with Amber before the guys had arrived.

"You'll get a better tan on the boat than on the deck," she said. "Besides, I'm willing to bet that I'm a better water skier than Ryan, and I can't wait to see him trying to beat me."

"Actually, I need to head home in the morning," he said, glancing at me with an apologetic smile on his face. "So do you, sis. I'm afraid our time here has come to an end. Mom and Dad need us to get back."

Disappointment raced through me. I'd been planning on staying with the girls until tomorrow night and was hoping to spend some more time with Carson. When I glanced at him, I could tell he was disappointed too but he hid it fast.

"Okay," I said, trying to mask my true feelings about it by forcing myself to sound conversational. "I guess we've had our fun. I want to stay, but if they need us at home, they need us at home."

Ryan nodded, perking up as he uncapped his beer. "Hey, at least we've still got tonight, right?"

Giving me a wide smile, he headed outside with Vance and the others, and I made to follow them until Carson wrapped his fingers around my wrist and pulled me aside. Looking around, he leaned in closer, the faint scent of bergamot and spice wafting from him as he penned me in against the wall. "I had a great time with you this weekend, Nova."

"So did I." My eyes flicked up to meet his. My heart raced again when I realized his lips were only inches away from mine. "Let's just hope what happened doesn't end up making you leave again."

A smirk ghosted across his lips and he shook his head, glancing around before he leaned in even closer to speak against my ear. "I'm not going anywhere, baby. I'm exactly where I want to be."

With that, he pushed away from me, winked, and walked away, leaving me trying to catch my breath. I let the wall hold most of my weight. *Damn. That was surprisingly hot.*

Unfortunately, it was also the last time I got to speak to him that night. We never seemed to be able to find another minute alone, and though I wanted to talk to him about what all of this meant, I resigned myself to having to do it when we got back home.

Early the next morning, Ryan and I drove home from the lake together, the sun only rising when we were already about halfway there. Sipping on my takeout coffee, I stared at the mountainous landscape, wishing I was waking up to the lake again.

"You had fun this weekend?" Ryan asked, his mind obviously in the same place as mine. "I have to admit, I did. There's just something about the water that helps me relax."

I turned to arch an eyebrow at him. "The water, huh? I'd have thought Cassidy helped you relax more than the boating did."

He chuckled but released one hand from the steering wheel to mime zipping his lips. "I don't kiss and tell, but nice try."

I shrugged. "I didn't ask you to tell, but I would like to know that you don't plan on hurting her."

"I'd never do that," he said irritably. "I know we've grown apart a bit, but shit. You know me, Nova. You know I'd never mess with someone's feelings. That being said, Cassidy and I talked. She knows where we stand and I'm not having this conversation with you."

"Touchy much?" I teased, rolling my eyes as I shook my head at him. "You're a prude, you know that?"

"I'm not a prude," he retorted, but he laughed anyway. "Okay, maybe I am, but it's weird talking to you about this stuff." He dragged in a deep breath before he glanced at me. "Prude or not, I did notice you looking pretty cozy with Carson. What was that all about?"

"Nothing much, but why would it be a big deal if anything was going on between us?" I asked, using the opportunity to talk to him about it.

As expected though, he balked. "That's not going to happen."

"Why not?" I ground out. "Hypothetically, if there was something going on between me and Carson, why would it even have anything to do with you?"

For the first time when speaking to me about this subject, Ryan didn't just get mad. He also couldn't leave, so this really was the best time to ask for the answers I'd been curious about for so long.

"Do you know the kind of life he lived before coming home?" he asked, glancing at me with a soft but wary expression in his eyes.

Turning his head back toward the road, he shoved a hand

through his hair, inhaling deeply. His jaw hardened like he was trying to stop himself from being sick.

I stared at him, surprised by the question but also by the fact that he seemed to be keeping his cool, which was unexpected. I shook my head. "I don't know much about it, other than he played in the NFL, was pretty good at it, and stuck to it until he decided to retire."

"Pretty good?" Ryan made a face at me. "You know better than that, Nova. The guy is a living legend."

"Okay," I said slowly. "So what? What does that have to do with anything?"

"Everything," he said emphatically. "He was dating models and actresses, traveling all over the world in the off-season and probably spending more money on one night in a club than you and I on groceries in a month. With a life like that, do you really think he's going to settle down with a small town girl who runs a bakery? Do you even think he's really going to make a life for himself in Silver Springs?"

"I don't know." I swiped my tongue across my lips, my mouth and throat suddenly drying out. "He sure seems determined to make a life for himself here."

Ryan nodded. "I know, but that doesn't mean it's going to last. He can build the best damn house in the county and still get bored of country living and small town girls real fast. He could head back to any big city any day and only come to his nice country house once a year to spend the holidays with his mother. We don't know what's going to happen, but don't let him suck you in."

I was tempted to tell him that Carson and I had slept together just out of spite. Clearly, Ryan thought I was too *small town* for a guy like Carson, but he might have felt differently if he'd known what happened between us. Unease in my gut kept me from speaking up, though.

Now that he'd put it that way, I was starting to wonder if I'd misjudged my brother's motivations. Maybe he wasn't trying to keep me from getting with Carson simply because I was his little sister.

Maybe he really was worried about me getting hurt if Carson ended up realizing that life in rural Wyoming wasn't for him anymore.

*Am I just a good time to Carson now? A conquest? Does he only want me because he "can't" have me or because things ended the way they did way back when?*

Ryan left me to my thoughts, not saying anything more on the subject and not needing to. If he'd been trying to plant a seed of doubt, he'd certainly succeeded and that seed had grown into a massive bush by the afternoon.

We got home. Our parents were working on the farm, and we joined them, helping out with the things they'd called us home for. When they invited us with them to the big Memorial Day BBQ in town, I declined. My doubts were now huge and insistent, nagging at me and refusing to let up for even a moment.

My family left for the BBQ and I went to the bakery, hoping that working would distract me, but it didn't help at all. Late in the afternoon, Carson called me, but for whatever reason, I didn't even reach for the phone to pick it up.

I just let him go to voicemail as my brain screamed at me that I needed to get a grip. I knew Ryan had probably just been trying to keep us apart by saying what he had, but it still stung.

*Why would Carson want a girl like me after all the stunning women he's been with in the past?* The simple answer was that he wouldn't.

Not forever anyway.

To mess around with, maybe.

But to have and to hold? There was just no way that was happening. Believing that it might was tantamount to me allowing my heart to be broken. I loved myself too much to let that happen, but I also hated the knowledge that Ryan had been right all along.

Carson and I weren't meant to be, and the sooner I convinced myself that was true, the better. For all our sakes, I had to fstop this thing in its tracks.

As much as it sucked, that was what I intended to do.

# 32

## CARSON

Back at my mom's house after leaving the lake early myself, I looked down at my phone. Nova hadn't answered my call, but I figured she was busy on the ranch. They had come home early for a reason, after all, so I didn't think too much of it.

Firing off a quick text instead, I asked her if we could talk soon. Then I looked up as my mom walked into the living room. "Hey, baby boy. How was the weekend?"

I got up and pressed a kiss to her cheek. "It was great, thanks. How was the BBQ?"

Mom laughed and patted her stomach. "I probably won't eat again until Independence Day, but it was worth it. I thought you were driving back in the morning?"

"We were going to, but I took Vance's truck. He'll come back with the girls tomorrow. I guess I'm all laked out for now."

"Laked out?" she asked as she lowered her head to one side, her gaze sweeping across my face like she knew something else was going on. "It looks more like *lucked* out to me."

"What do you mean?"

She smiled, chuckling as she inclined her head toward the kitchen. "I think you lucked out by finding a girl you're smitten with, and you being home early has something to do with her. You know, I saw the Murphys at the BBQ. They mentioned Nova and Ryan arriving home this morning. This wouldn't happen to have anything to do with that, right?" She grinned and pulled a jug of homemade iced tea out of the fridge.

I rolled my eyes. "You don't have to look so delighted about it. I'm not smitten."

She barked a laugh. "I know you, darling. I can see those stars in your eyes, and as it happens, I know exactly who put them there. Tell me about her. Did something happen this weekend? Are you two seeing each other now?"

"Nope. I saw Nova this weekend, if that's what you mean, but there's nothing to get excited about." I was lying through my teeth, but I'd always been pretty good about keeping my mouth shut when I needed to, and right now, I needed to.

Mom was already so invested in the idea of Nova and me getting together. Since Nova had apparently stopped taking my calls—maybe, anyway—this didn't seem like a good time to get Mom even more excited about it.

She exhaled deeply through her nostrils, staring at me with narrowed eyes before she filled a glass for each of us. "Now why don't I believe that?"

"I don't know, but it's true. Vance is trying his luck with one of Nova's friends, so we saw them around a couple times, but that's it, Mom."

*Well, that, and I think I might want to marry her, but hey, whatever.* I jolted as that thought ran unbidden through my mind. *Marry her? What the fuck, man?*

Mom lifted an eyebrow at me, then shook her head and seemed to accept that I wasn't going to give her the details she was after. "I ran into Coach Mason at the grocery store this morning."

"You did?" I grinned, glad for the change of subject but also genuinely interested in hearing about how the high school football coach was doing. "How is he? I haven't seen him for years. The last few times I've gone to the school, he hasn't been around."

"He's always so busy," she said. "He's good, though. We talked about you."

I shrugged and smirked at her. "I figured. What's not to talk about? I'm one of his greatest success stories."

She chuckled. "I love you, my dear boy, and you're absolutely *one* of his success stories, but let's check that ego a bit. You're in your mother's house. I changed your diapers not so long ago."

I laughed. "It's been a few years, but I get it. Always keeping me humble. Thanks, Mom. Why did Coach talk about me, then? If you weren't bragging and he wasn't either, why bring me up at all?"

"Well, he's putting on a summer camp for football and he mentioned he could use a hand. I told him I'd ask you if you'd be willing to help out."

A different kind of excitement than what I'd been feeling about Nova zapped through me now. "That's right up my alley. I'll talk to him tomorrow after I'm done at the library. That could be fun."

"He'll be grateful," she said cheerfully, handing over my iced tea before she slid her phone out of her pocket. "I've got a few calls of my own to make. Don't stay up too late, baby."

I chuckled. "Of course not, Mom. Wouldn't want to stay up past my bedtime on a school night."

Her laughter drifted out behind her as she walked to the living room. I headed to my bathroom, grabbed a quick shower, and got my laundry from the weekend done after. All night, I watched my phone but I didn't hear back from Nova.

In the morning, when I still hadn't heard from her, I finally started getting a little bit anxious. Needing to work off the excess energy coursing through me, I drove down to the gym and found Vance already there.

He grinned when he saw me. "Guess what?"

"You got engaged to Jessie yesterday," I said, deadpan.

"No. What the hell?" He grunted, adding another weight to the bench press machine. "Shit, man. Talk about stealing my thunder. Now my news seems weak."

"What's the news?" I asked as I eyed the weights he'd already added. "Are you trying to kill yourself?"

"Nope. Just to set a new personal record. I can't let myself go now that we're not forced to push ourselves anymore." As he lay down, he wrapped his fingers around the bar and grinned again. "The news is that I put in an offer on a house this morning when the bank opened. I can't live at my parents' place forever and this place ticked enough of the boxes that I took the leap."

My chest tightened. "Wow. Congratulations. I can't live with my mom forever either, though she'd love that, but I still haven't found a place to call my own."

Vance huffed out a breath and braced to lift more weight than he ever had before. He lifted, and his voice was strained when he spoke. "Yeah, but I've been looking at houses while you've been too busy trying to help out the Murphys to pay attention to the property market."

I shrugged, but my chest was still a little tight with either jealousy or panic about accidentally living with my mother for the rest of my life if I didn't get a move on. "Fair enough. Maybe I need to balance those things a little better. Keep looking for a property while trying to convince them to let me help out."

Vance nodded slowly, balancing the weight for a moment to get a feel for it. He started lowering the bar. We were both quiet for a minute, but when he seemed to tense up halfway through, I took the weight off his hands.

"Maybe you were a little too confident there. I'll take some of those off for you." I pointed toward the weights. "We could also find out how much the middle-schoolers are pressing these days. That'd probably be more your speed."

"Fuck off, Drake. It's not like you could do any better."

"Want to bet?" I asked.

His eyebrows shot up as he nodded. "Sure thing, but not for money."

"What, then?"

"Information." He pumped his eyebrows at me and sat up. "You and Nova. I know something happened between you this weekend and I want to know what it was."

"What? No. I'm not talking about that. It's personal."

Vance scoffed back a laugh. "Since when?"

"Since now."

"Fine, but then you're going to keep spotting me and I won't give you a turn to show me up." He lay back down again, his brow furrowing with concentration. "So something *did* happen, then?"

"Yep, but it doesn't look like it's going to go anywhere."

"Why not?"

I shrugged. "I haven't heard from her since. I reached out, but I think this might've been a one and done thing for her."

"Or maybe she's just freaked out that Ryan will kill you both if he finds out." Having now had some time to get used to the weight, he started showing off a little, speeding up and doing well until I added a little extra pressure to the bar.

Vance started laughing when he realized and he couldn't lift the bar anymore. I put it back on the rack. A pretty girl nearby was watching us. I rolled my eyes as I nodded at Vance. "What a weakling, huh?"

Lightning fast, he swiped his gym towel off the floor and smacked me in the crotch with it. Pain streaked through me, and I doubled over, only barely aware of him smirking at the girl. "Who's the weakling now?"

I groaned but laughed through gritted teeth as I tried to breathe. "Thanks for that."

"Got to keep you faithful to your girl, man. If you're already trying to get with—"

"That wasn't what I was I doing," I protested, pain still radiating through me. "Not at all. Don't even think like that, or it's somehow going to get back to Ryan that I'm not serious about his sister."

"Are you, though?" he asked. "Serious about her, I mean."

I considered the question carefully before I answered, but the truth was that I already knew what to say. All the errant thoughts I'd had this weekend had already confirmed it for me. "Yeah, but I need to talk to Ryan about it. I just can't do that until Nova and I are on the same page. Since she doesn't seem to want to talk to me at all, it's a lot more complicated than I would like."

"Maybe it's for the best," he said. "You need to be really sure about what you want from her before you talk to her brother, man. If you're even a little bit uncertain while you're having that conversation, Ryan will smell it like a shark and chum."

"I know what I want," I said in no uncertain terms. "For starters, I don't want to sneak around with her."

"Yet that's what you've been doing."

"Yep, but no more. I want to take her on dates. All that stuff." *Ask her dad for permission to propose to her one day.*

I blinked hard at the second thought I'd had about marrying her in less than one damn day.

Vance laughed. "It sounds like you've got it all planned out, man. What's stopping you, then? Go talk to her and then tell Ryan that's the way it is."

"I've known that she's it for me since we were teenagers. The Murphys are the ones who are making it complicated. I have to show him I'm serious about her. I get that, but I need to get her to talk to me about it first."

Vance let out a low whistle as he motioned me toward the machine. "I think I'll give you a turn after all. It sounds like you need to blow off some steam a lot more desperately than I do. Your life is like a soap opera these days, man."

"I know." I swapped places with him and hoped that I wasn't about to buckle under the pressure. Although it wasn't the actual weight I was worried about so much as the emotional weight.

*Who knew being back in tiny Silver Springs would be worse than running onto a football field as a veteran in the NFL? Not this guy. That's for damn sure.*

# 33

## NOVA

Carson showed up at the library again while I was volunteering, and my spirit sank when he walked in and sat down on the beanbag next to mine. Mrs. Norris smiled happily at him, handing over a copy of the story I'd been reading today and then hanging back to watch us do our thing.

We couldn't quite fall into the same rhythm as before though, often interrupting each other and then pausing awkwardly while we tried to figure out who was going to read what. It was awful. Afterward, I couldn't wait to get out of there.

Sliding my purse over my shoulder as soon as we were done, I nodded goodbye to Carson and took off, hurrying out to the parking lot and hoping he wouldn't come after me.

But he did.

I was almost to my truck when a large hand landed on my shoulder, and my body's reaction to the touch told me exactly who it was. A tingle shot down my spine, warming me even as I tried to break free of his grasp without making it obvious that I couldn't stand to have him touching me right now.

When I spun to face him, that faint trace of bergamot drifted to my nostrils, reminding me of the way he had smelled after our night together, and none of that helped my situation.

"What?" I snapped, then cleared my throat and dragged in a deep, calming breath. "I mean, what do you need, Carson? How can I help you today?"

"Well, you can stop acting like I'm trying to sell something to you," he said with confusion drifting like clouds into his clear green eyes. "I just wanted to ask if you'd like to have lunch with me?"

"Oh, uh, I can't." I grasped for an excuse but I suddenly couldn't come up with anything except the usual. "I have to go help my parents and do some baking. It's a busy week. Busy, busy week. Goodbye, Carson."

He fixed me with a look that made my feet forget how to move. I swore I even saw some hurt in his eyes. "Are you avoiding me for some reason?"

*For some reason, huh? Yep. I am. For some reason.* "No. Why would I be avoiding you? There's nothing to avoid."

I flashed him a tight smile and backed away toward my truck as soon as I remembered how to move. Carson wasn't having it, though. He followed me, effortlessly matching my pace even if I had been trying to rush away.

"Please just wait," he said, getting ahead of me and then turning to stand right in my path. As that gaze hooked on mine once more, he slid his hands into his pockets and dropped his head to one side, eyes never leaving mine. "Did I do something wrong, Nova? Did I hurt you, or make you mad somehow?"

"No. It's none of that." I waved him away and tried to step around him, but I didn't stand a chance. The guy saw the feint coming from a mile away and once again easily kept up with me.

"What is it, then?"

"It's nothing, Carson," I snapped as exasperation flowed through me.

As I looked into those confused eyes, I wondered if he truly had no idea what it was about or if he was just pretending. I didn't know why he would be, though. Or why he seemed hurt, for that matter.

"What happened between us didn't mean anything, did it? So stop it. I know it didn't mean anything to you. Acting like it did is just a little bit cruel, to be honest."

His face scrunched up, his nose wrinkling as he shook his head. "What?"

"*What?*" I threw the question right back at him, but the only thing it seemed to do was make him mad, too.

"What do you mean by that, Nova? Who do you think I am?"

Before I could stop myself, the words shot out of my mouth. "Someone who dates models and actresses, not plain, boring girls like me."

Carson's throat worked, his jaw dropping open. The anger left him and the confusion came back full force. He frowned, then barked out a laugh. "Are you serious right now? You can't be, right? This has to be some kind of a joke."

"It's not." Tears pricked at the backs of my eyes, but I pushed through them. He wasn't going to leave me alone until we'd had it out, and right now, all I wanted was for him to leave me alone. "I'm dead serious, and I'm fine with it. So what do you want from me? A good time? Because we've already had that and it's over now, so just..." I trailed off, collecting my thoughts before I continued, still looking him straight in the eyes and hoping like hell that he couldn't see the tears threatening to fall. "If you did it out of pity because my family's broke and you're bailing us out—"

He scoffed as he took a step closer. "That's not what it was about," he said, an underlying fierceness in his tone I'd never heard before. "In fact, that might just be the biggest bullshit ever. Where the hell are you getting this from?"

Before I could give him an answer, understanding suddenly sparked in his eyes and he snorted. "Oh, I get it. You've been talking to Ryan, haven't you?" Clearly annoyed, he shook his head. "What else did he say, Nova? What other lies did he plant in your head?"

"Nothing. It wasn't him. I've just been thinking and it doesn't make sense otherwise."

"Bullshit," he repeated. "The actresses and models thing came from him. I know it."

I tossed my chin up in the air, my eyes narrowing as I came to my brother's defense. "So what if it did? Does that mean it's not true? You haven't been with actresses and models?"

"No, I have been. In the past, which is behind me. As it should be. He's the one who doesn't seem to be over it."

"Maybe that's because he knows you," I retorted. "He knows that you're going to leave again. That's what you do, isn't it? You leave."

"That's not fair," he said incredulously. "I left once, Nova. One time. To play in the fucking NFL and you both knew that was the plan. I didn't blindside anyone or make any promises I didn't keep, and it's not like I kept coming and going. I left to go do what I was always going to do, and now I'm back in the place I was always going to come back to."

I didn't know what to say to that, so I didn't say anything. Carson, however, seemed to be on a roll. "I really hoped you knew me better than that, Nova. For a minute there, I even thought that you were one of the people who knew me best."

Annoyed flames flickered in those eyes, but it was all underscored by the hurt that was still there. "Have you forgotten that I offered to buy your portion of your family property to save your bakery and, hopefully, the whole ranch with it? Do you honestly think I would do that just to get into your pants?"

So many responses swirled through my head, but I swallowed them all and my cheeks burned with shame. Had I forgotten that? Did I think he would?

Yes and no.

I had forgotten, but I really didn't think he'd done it to get into my pants. We were talking about a great deal of money and a guy like Carson didn't have to spend a penny to get into a girl's pants if that was all he wanted.

The truth was that I had let Ryan get to me, and then my thoughts had spun out from there. I didn't say anything, just standing there staring and trying to figure out how to even begin to respond in a way that made sense. Carson started moving toward his truck.

"I'm coming to your place later." He pointed right at my chest, the muscles in his forearm and bicep rippling with the movement. "You better be there, Nova."

It was then that I realized he was leaving. In the middle of all this, he was walking away. I frowned, wanting to go after him but not knowing if that was fair considering that I'd been the one trying to run away just a couple minutes ago.

"Where are you going?"

He shook his head and climbed into his truck, driving away without another word. I didn't know what had just happened, but I knew I'd made a mistake in thinking that our hookup hadn't meant anything to him.

While it did all kinds of amazing things to my insides to know it had meant more to him too, it also made me that much more worried. Falling in love with my brother's best friend wasn't my style. Or at least, I'd never have thought it was.

Crushing on him as a teenager had been different. In a way, it was kind of expected that a younger sister would, at some point, develop feelings for her older brother's hot friend, but we weren't teenagers anymore and this wasn't just a crush.

Whatever it was, it felt like it had wormed itself into my soul in just a few short weeks, and I had no idea what to do with that. Because from here on, it wasn't innocent anymore. We'd crossed a line on the weekend, and with Carson coming over tonight to talk, I knew we were about to cross another.

If he could forgive me for my momentary lapse in judgment—and, of course, if he actually wanted me for some unfathomable reason—then we were about to be something. Something that we would have to tell Ryan about.

I was a little dazed as I drove home and wondered what he had in store for me tonight. There would be talking. I knew that. Talking about what had happened, what I'd thought until just a few minutes ago, and then, there would be *the talk*.

The one about what we were going to do now, and I had no idea how to have that talk. I glanced at the clock on my dashboard and winced. I didn't know what time he'd be coming, but I probably had no more than six hours before he'd be there.

Which meant I had no more than six hours to figure out if I was going to risk Ryan's wrath or if I was going to say goodbye to Carson for good. *Shit, that's not nearly enough time.*

Sixty hours wouldn't have been enough, but six?

I drove straight to the bakery and started baking, churning out more pastries in one afternoon than I ever had, but when I finally headed home, I still had no idea what I was going to do—and I had a lot less than six hours now to decide.

# 34

## CARSON

*ctresses and models.* I scoffed down laughter as I sped to Moe's to have a drink with Vance. *Who knew that was going to come back to bite me in the ass?*

Maybe I *should've* known, but I never thought anyone would actually care. I'd been young, single, and trying to get over the nagging feeling that I'd left behind the best girl I would ever find. It had never crossed my mind that the same girl would now throw that in my face as an excuse not to try something with me now.

Somewhere deep down inside, I could see where she was coming from. What I didn't understand was why she was insecure about it. Why she seemed to think that she was just a plain, boring country girl.

That was the part that had pissed me off more than anything else. Nova was unlike any other woman out there. Her strength and tenacity, her determination and her heart.

There was no one else out there like her, and I'd looked. I'd tried for a long time to find someone who made me feel even a fraction of what she did and I'd failed. Miserably.

The girl was gorgeous, funny, smart, and she didn't take any shit. *What's not to love about any of that?*

Parking in front of Moe's, I climbed out of my truck and breathed in the scent of frying chicken wings and fries coming from inside. My stomach grumbled, but even that couldn't distract me from the turmoil brewing within me.

I strode into the bar to find Vance at the table on the deck at the back, a cold beer and a basket of wings in front of him and another mug waiting for me. I dropped into the seat opposite him, wrapping my fingers around the icy glass immediately and taking a long sip.

"I'm going to buy some of the Murphy property," I declared as an opening statement once I'd swallowed the beer.

My friend blinked hard at me before his eyebrows shot up. "Wait. Are you serious?"

"It's time."

"Time?" He frowned. "Time for what?"

"I have feelings for Nova," I admitted, my heart skipping at saying the words out loud. "Real feelings. I know you thought it was all about finally hooking up with the one who got away, but it's not. I want more with her, Vance."

"Okay," he said slowly, surprising me by not trying to talk me out of it again. "If you still feel that way, then I guess that you've been right all along. It's not just about getting what you didn't have back then, but I think you're in over your head with trying to buy the property to get with her."

"I would've done it for her anyway," I said firmly. "Even if things were different."

"Why, though?" he asked, genuinely curious. "Why are you so intent on saving that ranch?"

"It's the right thing to do and everyone around here knows it. I'm not going to sit around waiting for it to happen anymore. They're one of the founding families and they've been here forever, and I promised to come home and take care of my community. That includes them. Hell, they're a cornerstone of this damn community and so is Red Stone Ranch. I'm not about to let some developer get his hands on it."

A slow grin broke out across his lips. "You know, I really believed you right there. You made it sound like it has nothing to do with either Nova or Ryan."

I took another sip of my beer and shrugged. "Truth be told, it doesn't. I mean, I'd hate to see them lose the houses and the property they love so much, but at the end of the day, this is also about what's best for the town. Nova's market is providing an income for a lot of people, all of whom stand to lose everything if a mall pops up where the market used to be."

"On the other hand, putting up condos for rich out-of-towners brings more money to local business owners."

I nodded. "Sure, if the rich out-of-towners support the local businesses, which they won't if there's a mall full of chain stores they can pop into. Plus, if they're buying condos out here, they're not staying at the dude ranches, the motels, or the cabins set up as holiday rentals."

"Fair enough," he said as he picked up a chicken wing. "I guess that same developer has already bought a bunch of other properties in town. Let him bring growth using those, right?"

"Exactly. I'm not against development happening around town in general. I just think the Murphy property will be a huge loss if it's no longer the Murphy property."

"I agree, but I still think you're in over your head. Ryan and Nova are notoriously stubborn and they know you're trying to buy the place to help them. If they wanted you to do it, they'd have given you an answer already."

"Then I guess it's a good thing neither of them hold the title to the place," I said, knowing what I was risking but prepared to do it anyway. "I can't allow this friction between Nova and me or Ryan and me to impact my decision anymore. Besides, maybe if I finally go ahead and put my money where my mouth is, she won't get things so twisted about me."

"What? I feel like I missed something." His eyes narrowed as they met mine. Then he glanced down at his chicken wing and bit into it.

While he chewed, I filled him in on what Nova suddenly thought about me. Repeating it all made me even more confused than I had been back at the library. We had a great time at the lake, and now that we were home, she'd taken fifty steps backward. It just didn't make any sense to me.

Vance's brow furrowed while I spoke. Then he grunted when I got to the end, his head shaking as he tried to process it. "Did you guys talk about anything like that at the lake? I mean, where did it come from?"

"Ryan," I said on a loud groan. "He got into her head and then things snowballed from there. I've set her straight, but I'm still not sure if she's going to let it go. She seemed so completely convinced that it'd meant nothing to me that I don't actually know how to change her mind."

"You don't think that maybe it's time for you to let it go?" he asked cautiously. "Ever since we've been back, you've been fighting for this girl and I know you said you want more with her, but it's starting to feel like you're trying to force the issue. When does fighting for her become forcing something into being that just can't work?"

"I don't know, but I feel like I'm still fighting," I said honestly. "I have to keep fighting, Vance. I'd love to be able to let it go and pursue any of the women who've shown interest since we got home, but I just can't do it. I haven't been able to rustle up even a touch of interest in anyone else."

"So it's Nova, huh?" He grinned as he lifted his eyebrows at me. "Better you than me, bro. Even if you win her over, you've still got to work on Ryan, and that's not going to be easy."

"I know, but it'll be worth it." There was no doubt in my mind about that. I wasn't usually the type to sit around talking about my feelings, but with her, I couldn't seem to stop. "She's it for me, Vance. I don't know how I know it, but I just do. That knowledge has haunted me for ten fucking years and I've tried to get away from it. I've tried to bury it in football, and money, and sex, and alcohol, but nothing has worked, so I'm ready to fight now."

"To keep fighting, you mean." He picked up another chicken wing. "I don't have any more sage advice for you, but I'm here if you need me for anything, okay? I'll even go in on the ranch with you if you think it might help."

"Thanks, but having both of us involved will just piss them off. It's bad enough that *I'm* trying to help, but I'm afraid it'll send us back to square one if you offer them your money too."

He chuckled. "Do you think they know how much we made?"

"No," I said honestly. "Neither of us have said a word about it. Ever. I don't know about you, but I never even told my mom how much my first offer was, let alone the amount I ended on."

"Same here." He tore into his chicken wing and spoke around it. "It felt wrong to be throwing out those numbers when we knew that so many people around here have always been struggling."

"Exactly." I nodded and finally picked up a wing of my own.

I ate in silence, devouring my basket, and Vance did the same. Once we were finished eating, we both went back to our drinks and he looked at me again.

"I can practically see the wheels turning in your head. You've got a plan. What is it?"

"I'm going over to her place tonight," I told him, my tone brooking no argument. "I'm going to tell her that I'm doing this, whether she and Ryan like it or not and whether she and I are a thing now or not. Frank said that George had approved whatever offer he made him in principle, which means that I need to sit down with George and Mara to hash out the details."

"Well, at least you've already made that deal with Ryan."

"Yep. As long as we keep Frank out of it, he's still happy. As far as I know."

Vance grimaced. "He might not be so happy about it anymore, once he finds out about you and Nova."

"Again, this has nothing to do with that. That's personal and this is business."

"For them, those two things aren't entirely separate. Not when it comes to you, and that ranch, and you buying the ranch, and also visiting his sister on it. It's all tangled up in each other."

"That may be true, but that's why I need to speak to George and Mara about it. I've been going through Nova and Ryan because I felt like I owed it to them, but I need to get this done before Frank brings George an offer from someone else."

"What happens if you do it and Nova never wants to speak to you again because of it?"

I drew in a deep breath. "I don't know. I'm hoping I never have to find out."

"Okay, man. You've got my support, but be careful. There's a chance this girl might shoot you down and you're wasting your time with her."

"Just another risk I'm willing to take," I said decisively, and it was true. I was going to help her family regardless, but when it came to having Nova in my life, there was nothing I wouldn't do.

No risk that wouldn't be worth taking.

Now if only I could make her and her stubborn brother see it that way, maybe things could finally get on track for all of us.

## 35

## NOVA

The sun had set and I still hadn't heard from Carson. On edge, I sat on my front steps and stared into the distance, but there still wasn't so much as a puff of dust that let me know there was a car on its way up. I sighed, dragged my fingers through my loose hair, and inhaled deeply before I got up.

Sitting around waiting for a man wasn't quite my style. Not even if I had severely offended that man and owed him a serious apology.

He'd told me to be here when he arrived, but it was starting to look less and less likely that he was even coming, and I'd never done well listening to instructions anyway. Finally making my decision, I wiped my sweaty palms on my jeans and got up, heading in the direction of Ryan's to talk to him.

I didn't know where Carson had gone after he'd left the library, and the not knowing was starting to drive me a little bit crazy. Considering he'd been pretty pissed when he'd left, I was just hoping he hadn't mouthed off about it to my brother and that I hadn't unwittingly derailed their friendship in the process.

Feeling like I was walking a tight rope, I knocked on Ryan's door before pushing it open to find him working in his shop in the converted barn he lived in. He looked up and shut off the table saw he'd been working with. "Hey, Nova. What's up?"

Well, at least he didn't seem pissed at me. "Nothing much. I just wanted to come check in with you. Any news about the ranch today?"

He shook his head. "I haven't seen Mom or Dad. You?"

"Nope. Mom was heading to town the last time I saw her this morning and I think she said that Dad was with the hogs."

"So he's burying his head in the sand again." Ryan groaned. "Damn it. I really thought he was done with that."

"I don't think that's what he's doing," I said carefully. Ryan sent me a questioning frown. "Dad was ready to accept Carson's offer from Frank, even if Carson hadn't actually made an offer. That means he's come around to the idea of selling a piece of the property. We were the ones who kicked up a big stink about it. I think he's waiting for us to tell him whether to go ahead."

"Maybe." Ryan cocked a hip against his work bench and folded his arms, but his expression was soft as he looked at me. "I talked to Carson about it over the weekend and he's serious about buying a part of the property. We made a deal to keep Frank out of it."

"That sounds good." I shifted on my feet, unease sweeping through me. I forced myself to keep looking directly at him instead of averting my gaze. "So, uh, you spoke to Carson about it over the weekend, but you didn't talk to him again today?"

"No. Why?" He frowned. "You think he's changed his mind?"

I shrugged. "It's always possible. You know how he is, always going from one thing to the next."

"What?" His frown deepened. He gave his head a quick shake and blinked hard before frowning at me some more. "No. I don't know that about him. I might not be happy about him having to bail us out, but I trust him, Nova. He's also the only option we've got if we want to keep the ranch. Why does it suddenly sound like you're not so sure?"

"It's not that," I said tentatively. "It's just, do you think he's really going to do it?"

Ryan nodded. "I'm not sure who you were talking about when you said he's always going from one thing to the next, but that's not the Carson I know. He set his sights on football when he was five years old and he took it all the way. When he makes up his mind about something, he doesn't waver and he doesn't go on to the next thing, Nova. He never has."

My heart thrummed in my chest. "Are you sure about that? Like you said, he is our only option if we want to keep the ranch. What if we make him angry and he decides against helping us?"

"It won't happen. He's not *that* guy, and I thought you knew that. He's the guy who can be so pissed that he can't see straight and he'll still do whatever it is he said he was going to do. Why are we talking about this? Did you piss him off?"

I blinked innocently. "No, I'm, uh, I was just wondering if you'd heard from him."

"I haven't, but it's not like I speak to him every day." Ryan took a closer look at me, his features knitting before he blew out a heavy breath. "What are you not telling me, Nova?"

"Nothing," I lied, but it wasn't easy.

Ryan knew Carson better than most and I was dying to talk to him about the conversation we'd had earlier and get his take on it. But given that he was the one who'd insisted Carson wouldn't settle down with a small town baker in the first place, maybe that wasn't such a good idea after all. I was just torn about what to do, and my brother had always been a good sounding board.

Sure, these days, we definitely weren't as close as we used to be, but he'd always been there for me, and that hadn't changed. I needed him to be there for me now, and knowing that he wouldn't support me on this hurt.

He wouldn't support me if I decided to break down the walls I'd put up to keep Carson out. They were new walls, and breaking them down wouldn't be particularly difficult, but despite everything Cassidy had said, I still didn't know if I could get Ryan out of the way.

Those two sides of me were still at the war, the younger sister who respected her brother and didn't want to hurt him, and the woman who knew he shouldn't be so involved in her love life.

After a lifetime of being protected by him and trusting him

implicitly, it went against the grain of my being to ignore his feelings about this—if there still was a *this*. I didn't know if Carson had finally given up on me after what had happened today.

My brother leveled a puzzled look at me. "Are you okay? You seem a little off tonight."

"I'm fine." *Liar, liar. I wonder if my pants are about to catch fire.* "I just wanted to tell you that I'm okay with it if you want to date Cassidy. I know she's my friend, but it wouldn't be weird for me."

He just smirked, soft laughter bubbling out of him. "I'm not sure what you're talking about."

"I'm talking about the fact that I'm not as territorial as you are," I said, my tone sharper than I'd intended.

Ryan's smirk faded, a heavy breath falling out of him before he cocked his head at me. "Is there anything else? I need to finish this before I go to bed."

I stared back at him, wishing that he'd just open up about his true feelings regarding Carson and me. He hadn't gotten mad when we'd talked about it on our way back from the lake, but he'd definitely made sure I knew how he thought Carson saw me. *If I tell him he was wrong, would he believe me? Would he give us his blessing?*

I doubted it.

Even though I desperately wanted to have the conversation with him, I shook my head and waved goodbye before I turned and left his place. On the walk back to my own, I considered why I hadn't just ripped off the band-aid and told him that I wanted to be with his friend if I still had a shot at it.

But that was where the problem lay.

Right then, I didn't know if I still had a shot. There was no sign of Carson, and night had fallen properly now. After the way he'd left me earlier, I didn't know what to think.

The day felt unfinished when I walked into my house and headed upstairs to my bedroom to get ready to go to sleep. A certain turbulence inside made it difficult to imagine even getting into bed right then, not to mention how unlikely it was I would actually manage to get any sleep.

Going through the motions, I kept hoping that the turbulence would ebb. I knew it wouldn't leave altogether, but if it could just give me some space to breathe, maybe I could make it through the night without having to be institutionalized in the morning.

I brushed my teeth and washed my face, putting on my lotion before I changed into my pajamas, but my nightly routine didn't settle me. I kept twitching at the slightest sounds, on high alert just in case any of them turned into the rumble of a truck's engine.

None of them did. Owls hooted, and every once in a while, I heard a cow, but that was about it. I sighed as I headed back downstairs in the hopes of finding something mind-numbing to watch on television.

As I reached for the remote, however, I finally heard a truck pulling into my driveway. My heart lurched and leaped. I hurried to the front door and opened it just in time to see Carson turning off his engine.

I waited for him in the doorway, uncertainty weighing me down as I watched him approach. As soon as he was on the steps, I looked into those green eyes and wondered why his hair was so messy, but I didn't ask.

Instead, I got right down to business. "Listen, if you're going to withdraw your offer, I get it—"

"Nova, are you ready to talk about what this is going to look like?" he asked, cutting me off and staring intently into my eyes.

I frowned. "What do you mean?"

"Me and you," he said simply, then walked around me and stepped inside.

I was too shocked to say a word. This was really happening now. Carson and I were finally going to have *the talk*, and while a burst of excitement shot through me, I was also still scared.

Whichever way it went, this talk was going to be a turning point in my life. It was either going to be the moment we decided to get together, or the moment we decided to walk away forever.

I, for one, had no idea which of those options would be better in the long run.

# 36

## CARSON

Nova was stubborn and tough, but she also got in her head a lot. Ryan must have said some things that made her think I was only after a fling. Something fun for a bit that would never lead to more. I needed to make her see he was wrong about me.

Her brother, who was like a superhero to her, had misjudged me and my feelings for her and he was way off base in his assessment of what was happening between us. *And that's not going to be easy.*

As I walked into her cozy little cottage, I was determined to prove it to her, though. *Easy or not, here I come.*

Nova looked adorable in a pair of pale purple pajamas, the shorts real short and the shirt a sleeveless top that revealed a distracting amount of side-boob. Once she shut the door behind us, I glued my eyes to her face, refusing to get sidetracked.

"Have you given any thought about what you and I are going to look like?" I asked again.

She strode to her kitchen and started making tea. "I don't know, Carson. Why don't you tell me what you've got in mind, and we'll take it from there?"

I braced my hands against the stone countertop and watched her fussing with cups and sugar, wishing she'd just fucking look at me. But I didn't press her.

This woman had a mind of her own and telling her what to do wasn't going to end well for me. Besides, she didn't have to look at me as long as she listened. I breathed through the need to see her eyes while I said what I was about to and simply laid it all out for her.

"I want you, Nova. I want to have breakfast with you in public and kiss you whenever and wherever I want. I want to hold your hand and fall asleep next to you at night. I don't want to pretend you're not all I see when you walk into a room." I smiled, even though she couldn't see me. "Nova, I want to ride jet skis with you."

Her shoulders stiffened before she shook her head. "We can't be together, Carson. Everything you're describing sounds like a relationship, but you and I can't have that."

"Why not?" I challenged. "Because of Ryan? Because of the ranch? Give me just one legitimate reason why we can't have what we've both wanted for so damn long."

"Well, for starters, yes. Because of Ryan," she murmured. "He'd freak out and I don't know if he'll ever get over it, but you're also buying half the damn ranch to save my family from financial ruin. It's just too complicated, Carson. There are so many ways we can end up getting hurt—and only one way we don't."

My heart cracked in my chest but I wasn't giving up. "What we have is real and it's worth fighting for. I don't know why you can't see that, but I sure as hell do, and I'm not leaving until you do too."

With the tea still brewing, she finally spun to face me, her cheeks flushed but not with embarrassment or arousal. Unless I was very much mistaken, they were flushed with anger.

Her eyes narrowed to slits and tears welled on her lower lids. I realized she wasn't just angry. She was on the verge of sobbing. I had no idea why.

"That's what you said before, Carson." Her voice wobbled as she planted her own palms against the counter, clearly bracing herself for a fight. "You told me that you had real feelings for me, but then Ryan found out and you left."

"You knew I was going to leave, though," I argued, really not understanding why we were talking about the past at all right now. "I never told you that I was going to stay."

"No, you didn't. All you said was that what we had was real and that you were never going to forget me, but you did. As soon as Ryan saw us together, you forgot all about me. Suddenly, you were so focused on his feelings that mine didn't matter. You didn't think we were worth fighting for back then. So what makes things different now?"

"You're not in high school anymore," I said emphatically. "I'm not the college student about to get drafted whose entire future can be stripped away if someone posts a damn picture online of me kissing a girl who hasn't even graduated yet."

She stumbled back a step, but I wasn't done yet. "My feelings for you have always been real, Nova. Hell, if I could've married you back then and taken you with me, I would've done it in a heartbeat, but again, you were in high school and you had dreams of your own that didn't involve becoming the teenage wife to a college ballplayer with an uncertain future."

"That's not what happened," she whispered. "That's not why you left."

"Isn't it?" I asked, my face collapsing in on itself as I breathed hard. "From where I was standing, that was very much part of it. Sure, Ryan finding out was part of it too, but we were at different phases in our lives. That was a massive issue to him that doesn't exist anymore."

Crossing her arms, she held her chin up and her gaze on mine. "From where I was standing, it wasn't like that at all. What I saw was a guy who'd been telling me everything I wanted to hear, and I had such a crush on him that I fell for it. I fell for it hook, line, and sinker, and I know you didn't make me any promises about a future together, but shit, Carson. The way you were talking, you sure made it seem like you were always going to feel that way. Fast forward to five minutes later, and you're defending yourself against Ryan, jumping in your truck, and speeding away."

My heart pounded in my chest. I wanted to yell and rage that it hadn't been that way, but to her, that was exactly what it had been. I couldn't argue with the way she'd experienced it any more than she could argue with the way I'd seen it back then.

Inhaling and exhaling slowly, I tried to calm the fire inside and took a few steps around the counter, trying to gauge her reaction to me coming closer before I closed the distance between us. Her nostrils flared when she noticed I was moving toward her, but she turned toward me instead of backing up.

"We're adults now, Nova. You're an adult." I stopped when we were only a foot apart. "I'm sorry that I hurt you back then. I'm sorry that I gave you reasons to doubt me. I know it doesn't make it better, but that was never my intention. My feelings for you were as real then as they are now. The only difference is that then, I didn't have much of a choice about what to do with them. Whereas now, we've both got choices. I'm here and I'm not going anywhere."

Her eyes bounced between my own, doubt still written in the crease between her brows and the slight parting of her lips. "What if you get bored of Silver Springs? Of me? You can afford to go anywhere in the world without having to work another day in your life. You've had women who are worldly and sophisticated. Women who can afford to go on those adventures with you and who won't be missing their little corner of countryside every minute they're away."

"Do you really think I'm going to get bored of you?" I asked softly, gently, and disbelievingly. My head shook, and I reached for her face as I finally took that last step closer. "Silver Springs has always been my home as much as it yours, Nova. I had to go away for a little while because I couldn't do the job I wanted to do from here, but I'm back now. For good. I promise. If I wanted to travel, I'd have done it. I wouldn't be here right now."

I bowed my head with my eyes fixed firmly on hers. "As for getting bored of you, that's never going to happen. I know I made you feel like I forgot about you after I promised I wouldn't, but I didn't. Not even for one day. I could never forget about you. If I'm more than just someone to hook up with for the summer, then I'm in. I'm all in."

She turned a little red, so I asked again. "Is there something here, Nova? Or am I losing my mind for thinking that there is?"

My heart thudded against my ribs. She stared at me without answering. Her silence was an answer in itself, I thought. Then she leaned into me. Pressing up on her toes, her arms wound around my shoulders and she pushed her fingers into my hair, pulling me down until my mouth met hers.

She kissed me with her whole body, her torso melting into mine as she hung onto me, even bringing one of her legs up to hook it around my thigh. I groaned, relief, joy, and a whole different kind of tension coursing through me.

As I kissed her back, I closed my eyes, but not just because I was kissing her. I sent up a prayer of thanks to whomever had intervened on my behalf. I let go of her face to wrap my arms around her waist. I held her to me and lifted her clear off her feet.

I spun us around, so damn happy that I couldn't stand still. She giggled. I grinned against her lips, breaking away from them for just a moment to look into her eyes. "Is that a yes?"

"That's a yes. There's something here." She slanted her mouth over mine once more, still smiling.

She kissed me like she was never going to stop. I was okay with that. I was already wondering how we were ever going to leave her cottage again now that it was finally official.

*Well, sort of, anyway.*

Deciding to figure it out later, I picked her up and gently laid her on the sofa. She pulled me with her, and when she started tugging at my shirt, I grinned and lifted my arms to let her take it off.

I kissed her again, spreading her legs apart with my hips to make space for myself between them. Then I reached for the hem of that cute pajama top of hers and made quick work of tossing it with mine on the floor.

After all these years, Nova and I were finally together, alone in her cottage with a whole night ahead of us to make up for the time we'd lost, and I was planning on putting it to good use.

I had no idea how to be a boyfriend or what she would expect from me going forward, but that was the beauty of all this. These kisses? They were just the beginning of a whole new story for us, and I was really fucking excited to see how it was going to end.

# 37

## NOVA

One thing I'd learned since Carson had been back in town was that he'd grown into a remarkable man since he'd left. That boy who had whispered sweet nothings to me a decade ago had kept his word after all, but he was delivering on those promises as a man who made my knees weak and my heart flutter.

All afternoon, I'd worried that I'd wrecked the deal. That my temper tantrum had cost us the farm. It looked like maybe Ryan had been right after all, though. Carson hadn't tucked tail. He hadn't called my brother in a fit of rage and he'd shown up at my house just like he'd said he would.

He pressed kisses along the length of my torso, his hot, firm lips setting fire to my insides. I ran my fingers through his thick hair and wondered if this could really be it. *The talk* had gone much faster and smoother than I'd ever imagined possible. It was difficult to believe that, after everything, all it had taken was him saying *this is what I want* and laying his cards on the table.

He made it clear he wasn't looking for a fling and that what he felt was still real after all this time. My doubts and the insecurities I'd had these last few days had been eradicated. *Communication really is key. Who knew?*

Carson hooked his fingers into the waistband of my pajama pants and swept them off my legs, taking my panties off at the same time. His fingertips brushed against my legs with the movement and I shivered, needing more of him.

Carson had blown my mind the other night at the lake, making me orgasm harder than I ever had. At the same time, he made me feel the things I thought I'd never feel. I was feeling all those things right then. My body was overheating, but my heart was on fire too.

He kissed my stomach and the insides of my thighs, making me ache with need, but I also felt my heart swelling. It felt so full that I didn't know what to do with it.

*Oh, holy cow!*

My train of thought crashed into solid rock and exploded when he sucked my clit into his mouth. A cascade of pleasure raced through me. His long fingers wrapped around my thighs, and he opened the most intimate part of me. His groan was a deep rumble in his chest as he licked a hot path right through my slick folds.

My muscles tensed up and my back arched. I squeezed my eyes shut and tried to control my breathing. Nothing had ever felt as intimate as this, having Carson Drake's face between my legs. I was enjoying the intimacy almost as much as I was enjoying what he was doing to me.

With his lips sucking at my clit and his fingers teasing at my entrance, I gave myself over to the sea of sensation, letting it carry me away. My toes curled and I moaned his name. With a start, I almost clapped my hand over my mouth to stop the sound, but then I remembered that it was just the two of us and that I could be as loud as I wanted, and that made it even better.

"Carson, yes!" I moaned, my hands burrowing into his hair and my nails pressing into his scalp. "Yes!"

I trembled and shook, so close that I could almost taste the pleasure rocketing toward me. I held on to his head, my hips rolling. The precipice suddenly arrived and I tumbled over it.

He slid a finger into me, hooking it in just the right way to touch that special spot I'd needed pressure on. My climax thundered through me, and I might have screamed, but I didn't know or care as waves of continuous ecstasy dragged me under.

Breathing hard, I finally managed to open my eyes as the bliss subsided. Blinking his face back into focus, I reached for him, needing to kiss that concerned frown out of existence. I smiled lazily as I pulled him to me, my eyes on his.

I looped my hands around the back of his head. "What are you so worried about?"

At the sound of my voice, the frown eased and he smirked at me. "You. I thought you'd stopped breathing for a minute there."

"I did," I admitted huskily, pushing at his shoulders so I could get out from under him. "Your turn."

"Not yet." His voice was strained and impatience burned in his eyes, but he didn't seem to be rushed as he stood up and held out his hand. "Come with me."

"I'd love to," I teased, still a little breathless as I placed my palm in his. "We can't do that standing next to each other, though."

He chuckled and shook his head as he tugged me toward the stairs. "We're going to your bedroom."

"Sofa not good enough for you?" I asked as we ascended the staircase

In a flash, he laid me down on my bed and crawled onto it. "No, it's not good enough for you," he murmured. "This isn't some cheap fuck. I thought it would be better to do it right."

"And that means on a bed?"

He shrugged, another smirk curving on his lips. His head descended to mine. "For now, yes."

He kissed me again and my heart and soul went wild. Then my body realized how very hard he was against my stomach. Carson was a big guy in general, but I'd still been stunned when I'd seen his cock for the first time at the lake.

I was stunned again now as I wriggled out from underneath him and rolled us over to pull his jeans off. He kicked off his shoes and lifted his butt so the pants could come off, and then there it was.

In all its glory, his dick stretched proudly toward his belly button, curving slightly and thick enough that my insides were already tingling to have him fill me up again. Transfixed, I wrapped my fingers around the base of his shaft and relished the groans that spilled out of him.

I started stroking up and down. Carson lay back on the bed, letting me play with him. He shut his eyes and hooked a shapely bicep behind his head. "Be gentle with me, Nova. I'm already worked up."

"You and me both," I muttered, staring at the wetness shimmering on his exposed tip and feeling my own core heat in response.

Eventually, I realized I was just being cruel to us both at this point and I resolved to continue my exploration later. I grabbed the condoms from my nightstand. There was one left in the box after our adventures at the lake, and Carson's heated eyes followed my movements as I opened it and rolled it on.

He groaned and tensed until it was in place. Then he took my hands and helped me balance with one leg on either side of his hips. "It's you, Nova. You're it for me. You always have been."

*Wow. It's not quite an "I love you," but it's pretty damn close.*

I held his hands, lowered myself down on him, and looked into his eyes. Mine filled with tears. "You're it for me too, Carson. I've known it since I was sixteen and that's never changed."

He wound his fingers more tightly around my own. His hips moved as he pulled me down for another kiss. It was deep and hard but meaningful and passionate all at once. As we kissed, our bodies came together over and over again. He stretched me out and filled me in all the right ways. His mouth fused to mine and his powerful hips thrust with the perfect rhythm.

I lost all sense of time as he moved inside me. My entire being hummed with a feeling of rightness and belonging I'd never felt before. When my next orgasm hit, he crushed his lips to mine and came with me, holding on to me for dear life. He kissed me all the way through it. Afterward, he stayed in me as long as he dared before going to take care of the condom and coming back to take care of me.

Once he climbed back into bed, I cuddled into Carson's side, unable to stop myself from wanting to be as close to him as I could possibly get. Glancing up at his strong features in profile, my eyes dragged across the dark stubble on his jaw and the movement of his Adam's apple as he swallowed when he looked at me.

He smiled lazily, amusement and something softer sparkling his eyes. "What?"

I shook my head without lifting it from his chest. "I don't know. I guess I just can't believe that we're really here."

He chuckled and pressed a kiss to the top of my head. "It's pretty crazy, right? Amazing, but crazy."

"Is it, though?" I asked quietly, twining my fingers together on top of his heart and resting my chin on them as I stared up at him. "Are we crazy for trying this?"

"No. What's crazy is that it's taken us this long to do it," he said earnestly. "I guess the only thing that matters is that we finally made it."

"Yeah. Maybe." I exhaled a deep breath through my nostrils, worry sinking back in now that my head was clearing. "You and I were never really the problem, though. I mean, we were, but my brother is the bigger problem. So what are we going to do about that? If we're serious about trying this, we can't hide it from him forever."

"We won't," he assured me with another smile. "If I wasn't naked, I'd go talk to him right now."

My heart jolted. "Uh, well, no. I don't think that's a good idea. In fact, maybe we should just take it slow."

"Take it slow?" He arched a teasing eyebrow at me. "It took us ten years to have the *what are we* conversation, Nova. Glaciers move faster than we have."

I chuckled. "I know, but what I meant is that maybe we don't have to worry about Ryan right now. Maybe we just work things out for ourselves before we involved him."

Carson sighed. "You just said we couldn't hide it from him forever."

"Not forever, no, but maybe for another couple weeks? Just until we've figured things out ourselves?"

"What's to figure out?" he asked, and I could tell he would rather just clear the air with my brother now. "We know what we are, right?"

"Do we?" I wasn't trying to be funny. I just really didn't know. "Are you my boyfriend? Are we serious? Are we exclusive?"

"We're exclusive," he said immediately. "I am your boyfriend and it's serious. There. Have we covered everything?"

I laughed softly. "Just about, but you still can't tell Ryan until I'm ready, okay?"

He groaned. "Any idea when that might be?"

"No, but it won't be long. I just need to work out what to say to him, is all." I shut my eyes for a moment, my head still spinning with everything that had happened just today. "A few hours ago, I didn't even think you could be interested in anything real with me, and now here we are. I just need a second to get my ducks in a row."

He nodded and rolled onto his side. "Okay, baby. I can give you that. Of course, I can, but in the meantime, when can we move forward with me buying part of the property?"

I sighed, my head shaking even as I smiled. "You haven't let that go?"

"Nope. I'm going to do it. I guess I was just hoping that I wouldn't lose you while I was at it."

My heart skipped a happy beat and I hooked a leg over both his thighs, trying to get as close to him as possible. "I'll arrange for you to meet with my parents privately to make the sale, but do you think we can stop talking now?"

He gathered me in his arms and pulled me on top of him, grinning against my lips. He was already hard again. "We can definitely stop talking, but at some point tonight, we're also going to have to sleep."

"Who needs sleep?" I tucked my hair behind my ears and gave him a wicked smile before I started pressing open-mouthed kisses against his throat. "I only need a few hours, but if you want to sleep, go ahead. I'll have fun all by myself."

"Hell, no," he growled, then flipped us over and pressed me against the mattress. "I think we've both had our fair share of *having fun* by ourselves. If it's all the same to you, I'd rather have my fun with you from now on."

My laughter morphed into a moan when he sucked my nipple into his mouth. My legs fell open to wrap around his hips, and my eyes shut as pleasure streaked through me. Things were far from settled between us, but at least now, there was an *us*.

After everything we'd been through to make it this far, I had never been more certain that this was the way it had always been meant to work out.

# 38

## CARSON

Football camp was awesome. I was surprised by how much I liked helping the new generation hone their skills. As a kid myself, I'd often felt a bit of pity for the coaches. Despite how deeply I respected them, I had wondered how they'd ended up coaching instead of playing.

*I guess now I know.*

I had done my playing, but I still loved the game and this was an incredibly satisfying way of remaining part of it. Grinning, I jogged off the field and waved at a few of the boys who were taking off after the day. I made my way to my truck, only for the grin to fade when I saw Ryan waiting for me.

My friend looked disheveled, his dark hair sticking up in all directions and his features resigned, like the life had been sucked right out of him. My heart constricted and I frowned, kicking my pace up to close the distance between us faster.

"Ryan, what happened?"

He pushed away from my truck and sighed. "I just wanted to let you know in person that things have changed. My parents are considering another offer for the ranch as a whole, and I think they're likely going to take it."

"Shit," I breathed, all the air in my lungs suddenly gone.

Ryan grimaced as he nodded. "I wanted you to hear it from me before word gets out. They only told me about it this morning, but it's a good offer and they wanted me to know that they're giving it some real thought."

"I'm sorry, Ry." I shook my head, rocking back on my heels as my mind raced. "Do you think I should counter? Would that help? At this point, I'm not sure what else to do."

"It's a lot of money, Carson. I appreciate that you want to help, but this goes way beyond what we talked about. It's in my parents' hands now. I'll let you know as soon as I hear anything."

"Thanks," I muttered, feeling defeated. I couldn't even begin to imagine how he was feeling, and Nova had to be devastated. "You're sure there's nothing else I can do?"

He blew out a heavy breath. "We've just got to let this thing run its course, man. Dad knows exactly how Nova and I feel about it, and he and Mom aren't fully convinced that they're ready to say goodbye to the ranch, but it's a numbers game now and they need to make a decision they can live with."

"Tell them that my offer is still on the table," I said, needing to make sure that they knew I wasn't just going to walk away.

George and Mara both liked me, but this was serious business that went beyond my relationship with their family. Like Ryan had said, they had to make a decision they could live with and it might be easier for them to sell the ranch as a whole than to cut it into pieces and sell one of those to me.

I'd wanted to help, but I couldn't push this issue too much. Not if there was another good offer on the table. It was their family property and they needed to do whatever was right for them.

"Thanks, man," Ryan said. "I'll let them know, but you may want to prepare yourself for them to turn it down."

"Whatever happens, at least we'll know we tried," I said, moving around him to the driver's door of my truck.

Ryan nodded and sent me a wave before he walked away, but he hadn't gotten more than a few steps before I called to him. "Wait!"

He turned, looking at me over his shoulder with a quizzical expression on his face. "What's up?"

My heart pounded. I'd meant to tell him about Nova and me, but as I looked at him now and remembered the promise I'd made to her, I sighed and shook my head. "Do you want to go get a drink later?"

"I'll let you know," he said, a tired grin spreading on his lips. "It depends on what's happening at home when I get there."

"Okay," I agreed. "Keep in touch. Vance and I are meeting at the brewery at six if you're interested in joining us."

He checked his watch and nodded, then took off, leaving for real this time while I wondered if I should've just done it. Sure, I'd told Nova we could keep our relationship from him for now, but with every minute that went by, I felt more and more guilty about lying to him.

On the other hand, he had more than enough on his plate and this was hardly the time to add another huge weight. In the end, I climbed into my truck and headed home to grab a shower before I met up with Vance, all the while thinking about how Ryan had had the decency to come to me to tell me about the other offer.

He had wanted me to hear it from him in person, which made me feel even worse about what I was hiding from him. I knew he should hear it from me that Nova and I were together now, and the longer we waited, the higher the chances that he found out from someone else.

It was still weighing heavily on my mind when I walked into the brewery, joining Vance at the bar and nodding at the bartender to bring me a draft. As he filled up a glass from the tap, Vance turned to frown at me.

"You look like hell," he said cheerfully. "Care to tell me what happened this time? Your life has more drama than a soap opera these days."

I groaned and brought my head down to bang my forehead softly against the counter. "It's not that bad, is it?"

"It totally is. I love it."

Lifting my gaze to his, I speared him with an exasperated look but gave him the update on the Murphy ranch. "George and Mara are thinking about selling it as a whole. They've got an offer on the table and Ryan wants me to be prepared for them to take it."

He let out a low whistle. "Wow. I never thought they'd willingly sell that place. Do you really think they're going to do it? What does Nova say?"

"I don't know. I haven't spoken to her about it," I admitted. "She and I worked things out, but now it feels like we're out of the frying pan and into the fire. I mean, we're together, but we still can't tell Ryan about it, or go out in public, or do any of the things normal couples do."

"So basically, nothing has changed?"

I shrugged, gratefully accepting my beer from the bartender and taking a long sip before I responded. "Technically, *everything* has changed. We agreed to make it official. We just can't act like it."

"So nothing has changed," he repeated before he chuckled. "If a relationship falls in a forest and there's no one around to hear it, does it even make a sound?"

"Our relationship isn't falling. Whatever that means. It's just..."

"Complicated?" he finished for me.

I nodded. "Something like that. I guess I just thought that when we finally talked everything through, we'd get to be together for real, but now she's dragging her feet and I get it. I do. I understand that she doesn't just want to drop this bomb on her brother's head, but it's not like I'm asking her to marry me tomorrow."

He cocked his head at me. "What *are* you asking her to do?"

"Just to give it a real shot. Do it right," I said. "It feels like we can't do that until it's out in the open, though. We're still sneaking around. Still lying. The only difference is that at least now we know where we stand with each other, but that's it."

"That has to be a relief, though," he said. "Knowing where you stand with her is a definite step forward from wondering what she wants and if you're ever going to find out."

"Yeah, I guess." I spun my glass slowly between my fingers, watching the bubbles rise in the amber liquid before I looked back at him. "A long time ago, I came home for a visit just after the season wrapped for the year."

"Okay?" He frowned. "What does that have to do with anything?"

"I always used to fly my mom out to visit me instead because our schedule was so insane, but that time, I came home, and while I was here, I went to Moe's."

"Ah. I get it. You came home and you saw Nova. That's how it ties into what we were talking about before?"

I nodded. "It was the first time I'd seen her in years, but I didn't speak to her. I didn't want anyone to know I was here, so I kept a low profile and sat in the corner outside wearing a ballcap and sunglasses. I just wanted to get out of the house for a minute, you know? I didn't want to make a big splash."

His eyes widened. "So you watched her like some kind of stalker?"

I scoffed down a laugh. "No, it wasn't like that. I saw her sitting inside with someone, but I couldn't see who it was. Eventually, just when I'd decided I'd go say hi after all, some of the people around their table moved and I saw a guy."

"You saw a guy?"

"Yep." I inhaled deeply through my nostrils. "I asked my mom about it when I got home, and she told me he was Nova's college boyfriend. They'd been dating for a couple years and he moved here briefly to be with her after they graduated."

"What? I didn't know she had a boyfriend."

I shrugged. "She hasn't mentioned him at all, but I thought they were going to get married. At the time, it sounded like that was what everyone thought."

"Everyone, or just your mom?" he asked.

I chuckled dryly. "Everyone. The few times I spoke to Ryan during that time and managed to find a way to bring up Nova, he told me about the boyfriend. A while after that visit, that was also how I found out they'd broken up. The guy had left her, from what Ryan told me."

Vance narrowed his eyes. "What are you trying to say here, Carson? Why the trip down memory lane?"

I drew in a deep breath. Closing my eyes for a moment, I wondered about it myself. "The last few days, I just keep thinking about that visit and remembering how I felt when I saw them together. I would've been fine if she'd moved on. I would've been happy for her, but I knew they had broken up years ago and that she was still single, and I guess part of me was hoping that I'd have a shot if I came home, you know? That I would get a second chance."

"That's exactly what happened, though. Isn't it? You guys are together now, so this is your second chance."

"In a way, sure. We still have an obvious connection, but now Nova's got all this other stuff going on and I don't know how to help her or how to make her see that I want this for real. I just can't stop wondering if she wants to keep it from Ryan because she thinks I'm going to leave again, or if it's because she doesn't think I'm serious about her."

Vance listened to me patiently, and when I was done, he leaned forward a little, his expression uncharacteristically serious. "Look man, I know you've got it bad, but maybe think about letting her go. At least for a while. None of us are going anywhere anytime soon, and if you think she's not ready, that she's still skeptical about relationships, or that she's got too much going on, maybe you should consider telling her that you'll wait until she's worked it all out."

Before I could respond, a group of women came up to us, giggling and jostling each other as one tentatively held out a sharpie. "We're so sorry to bother you, but could we have your autographs?"

*Fuck. This has to be the worst timing ever.*

Vance and I had gotten used to these kinds of interruptions though, and we both switched on that charming, carefree persona and pretended that they hadn't just butted in to something.

I grinned at one of the women closest to me and nodded. "Sure thing. What are your names?"

The girl descended on me like a fly to honey, especially flirty as she practically shoved her friend out of the way and came to stand so close to my side that she was almost in my lap. Thankfully, I'd been trained in the art of putting someone down gracefully and I did it without hesitation.

Scooting back a bit under the guise of asking the bartender for some napkins and another pen, I busied myself signing my name. I thought I'd dodged the bullet, but what I hadn't realized at the time was that Amber was at the brewery and that she'd seen the whole thing—and that from where she had been standing, the charm and the grinning hadn't looked like a well-trained bit at all, but like two guys who were interested in the women they were talking to.

# 39

## NOVA

In the kitchen at the bakery, I was putting the finishing touches on a few wedding cakes for next week. This was the first year I'd expanded my services to include weddings, and it was killing me. I wished I could hire a second, or even a third, assistant to help me out, but all of my income was going back into the ranch to keep it afloat.

Which meant I had to grit my teeth and get this done. No one was coming to save me. Wiping my brow, I added a few shards of tempered chocolate to the top of the first cake going out and tried my best not to get overwhelmed by the amount of detail that still had to go into it.

When the door swung open, I sent up a quiet prayer that Cassidy had somehow felt my desperation and had come to offer her assistance, but it wasn't her. My brother strode into the kitchen instead, filthy from having been out in the field all day. My spine snapped straight.

"How's it going?" he asked.

At the same time, I jutted a hand back toward the door. "Nope. You can't come in here looking like that. Get out and I'll meet you out back."

He exhaled harshly and pretended to be offended. "Fine. Jeez. It's not like I was going to get dirt all over the cakes."

"These things are so delicate, they might get dirty if you so much as look at them. Get out. I'll be there in a minute."

Ryan chuckled but saluted me and left, and I turned back to the cake I'd been busy with, my heart pounding as I held my breath, waiting to make sure it had survived the encounter. When it didn't suddenly collapse or melt, I heaved out a sigh of relief and quickly stowed it away in the freezer before going to meet my brother.

He was leaning against the back wall of the building, his features forlorn as he stared at the mountains in the distance. My heart lurched and flopped around in my chest like a dying fish.

*Something's wrong.*

"What is it?" I asked.

He turned to look at me, defeat and remorse in his eyes as he shook his head. "Dad has been dragging his feet about making the sale to Carson, and Frank showed up at their house today. He pitched an offer from a developer for twice as much money. I think this is it, Nova. I think we're going to lose the ranch."

I blinked hard, my entire soul freezing over as I stared at him in silence, unable to breathe, speak, or even think. "No."

"Yes," he said gently, pushing away from the wall and striding over to put his hands on my shoulders. "I know this is a huge blow, but there's nothing else we can do. If Dad decides to take this offer—"

"Carson will match it," I said immediately. "We can call him. We can—"

"We can't," he countered patiently. "We can't ask this of him, Nova. It's completely out of the question. It's too much. We're going to have to cut our losses and hope—"

"No," I said firmly, my head shaking hard and fast. "No, we can't do that. I'll speak to him. I'll ask. You don't have to do it. We'll pay him back."

Ryan squeezed my shoulders tenderly, his eyes softening as he bent his knees to look directly into mine. "Is this really what you

wanted to do with your life, being tied to this place and always struggling to keep our heads above water?"

My eyebrows mashed together, my heart still feeling like it was in
the throes of death. "What are you talking about? How could you
even ask me that?"

"Just think about it," he said, gentle but insistent. "Dad's getting
old, Nova, and it's starting to show. He's better off retiring. I can start a
contracting business and you'd get to start all over. The bakery would
do so well in town and you'd be able to hire the extra help you need."

My throat suddenly felt like it was closing up as my emotions got
the better of me. I couldn't believe what I was hearing from him. I'd
always imagined our whole family growing up and old here, my kids
running between my house and my parents' place all day, every day.

I knew for a fact that Ryan wanted that too, so what the hell was
he thinking? He didn't want to leave. Maybe he did want to start a
contracting business, but there was nothing preventing him from
doing it right here.

"This is our home, Ryan. We need to fight for it." Both of us
loved this ranch, and if it were totally up to us, it would be a
booming business with an event venue and the works. He and I
could make it into that if given the chance, but we'd never get it if he
gave up.

He stared deeply into my eyes, and I could see the pity in his
expression. "Don't get your hopes up, little sister. I think we need to
be realistic about this."

"I *am* being realistic," I snapped as I took a step back. "I'll talk to
Carson about it if you don't want to, but he'll do it, Ryan. He'll do it
and we'll pay him back. That was the deal, right?"

"I've already told him, Nova," Ryan said in a hushed voice,
sounding pained as he broke my heart. Again. "He already knows
there's another offer on the ranch and he said to tell Dad that his
offer is still on the table, but that's it. He didn't say he'd buy the whole
place outright."

Surprise rattled through me. My feelings for Carson had definitely distracted me from the issue at hand, but I could lose my home

and my bakery if he couldn't, or didn't, want to help, or if Ryan wouldn't allow him to. I couldn't let that happen.

It was time for me to step up and I planted my hands on my hips, lifting my eyebrows at my brother. "Did you ask him to buy the ranch outright, or did you just wait for him to offer?"

"We can't ask him to—"

"Maybe *you* can't, but *I* can." I started walking backward, shaking my head at him as I held his gaze. "I'm done letting *the boys* handle all of this. I'll see you later."

"Where are you going?" he called as I spun around and dug my keys out of my back pocket.

I hit the unlock button on the fob and the lights on my truck flashed. "I'm going to talk to Mom. Stay out of it, Ryan. I've got it from here."

Without waiting for him to argue, I climbed into my car and drove to our parents' house, relieved when I saw Dad's truck wasn't parked outside. That meant he was still working on the ranch, and for once, I'd have some time to talk to my mom alone.

"Hello?" I said as I pushed their front door open, letting myself in and shutting it silently behind me. "Mom, are you here?"

"I'm in here, baby," she called.

I followed the sound of her voice, then stopped dead in my tracks when I walked into the kitchen to find that she'd unpacked every cabinet and was on her hands and knees, washing the shelves and doing God only knew what else.

I arched an eyebrow at her, my gaze sweeping across the room before it settled on hers. "Mom? What on earth are you doing?"

"It was time for a cleanup," she said, her eyes too wide and her cheeks flushed. "If we're going to be moving out soon, we need to get a head start. We've got lifetimes worth of stuff in this house and we need to start sorting through it all."

She was obviously stressed and I walked in slowly, sinking to my knees in front of her and taking her hands. "You're not moving out yet, Mom. Let me get us some water and we'll talk, okay?"

Jerking her chin in a nod, she hung her head and closed her eyes, breathing in and out deeply. I got up and went to pour us each a glass of cold water. Once I had our drinks, I went back to her and helped her up. Then I led her to the backyard and sat her down at the table in her favorite spot in the garden.

Tears filled her eyes as she looked around, taking in the flower beds that surrounded us and the tall trees that she'd planted here with her own two hands. "I'm so sorry it's come to this, honey."

"It hasn't come to anything," I said reassuringly, leaning back in my chair and trying to keep my voice even. "Why don't you tell me what you're thinking? Where's your head at?"

"It's time for your father to retire," she said shakily. "He just won't admit that the business has run its course and that he needs to let you kids take over. Hell, we could sell off a few parcels of land and nothing would change, but the land that has the most value is what's been built up."

"Which is your house, mine, Ryan's, and the bakery." I sighed as I took a sip of my water and tried to hide how badly my hands were shaking. "The land Carson has offered to buy."

My mother nodded, wiping away the tears from her eyes. She drew in another breath and offered me a sad, apologetic smile. "I'm sorry, baby. I shouldn't offload all this onto you. You just caught me at a bad time. I'm assuming Ryan told you about the other offer?"

"A few minutes ago," I said before I blurted out, "I'm seeing someone."

She blinked rapidly a few times before she schooled her expression and smiled a happier smile this time. "Are you? I'm glad to hear it, baby. It's good that you're finally letting yourself think about love and relationships again rather than just focusing on work. Who is it?"

I shook my head. "I can't tell you that, but I can tell you he might be able to help. If you'll let him."

"It's Carson," she concluded, her smile growing into a full-blown grin. "It's about damn time, honey. I can't say I'm surprised."

"You might not be, but I am. How did you know?"

She laughed softly, her earlier misery making way for excitement. "I remember how in love you used to be with him. Now he's back and suddenly you're seeing someone who can help? It has to be him. You know, I always thought you two would be end game."

"End game?" I gaped at her. "I'm not sure why you thought that. Ryan is going to be livid. He'll never let us live happily ever after."

Mom waved a hand dismissively. "He's just protective of you, Nova. That's all it is. He doesn't want to see you get hurt and he definitely doesn't want to acknowledge that you're a woman now. If you explain to him how you've always felt about Carson, he'll understand eventually."

I wasn't so sure about that, but if even my mom thought that my brother would get over it in time, maybe I was making too big a deal of his reaction. "Maybe you're right, but let's keep it a secret for now. Do you think Dad will sell to Carson once he finds out?"

"I think you need to do what you think is right and focus on your own life instead of worrying so much about Dad and Ryan." She leaned forward and took my hand on the table, squeezing it as she nodded at me. "I love you, baby. Things are going to work out the way they're supposed to, okay? We're all going to be okay in the end. We just need to trust the journey life takes us on."

I wound my fingers around hers and squeezed them in return, not saying anything else for a long minute. Maybe we needed to trust the journey life took us on, but that didn't mean that I had to sit back and just let things happen.

We were going to be okay in the end. I had no doubt about that. I just wasn't about to let *the end* be that we lost the ranch when we still had options available to keep it. I wouldn't go down without a fight and *the end* wasn't here just yet. Until the final whistle blew when Dad put pen to paper, I was in it to win it—or to keep it, as the case may be—and I still had a lot of fight left in me.

Now I just had to hope that Carson did too, and that his legendary determination would count in my favor this time.

# 40

## CARSON

Trying to decide the best approach to the situation at Red Stone Ranch, I lay in my bed and watched as the sun rose outside my window. I'd hardly gotten any sleep last night, but I wasn't tired. I was amped, my brain awake and alert as I considered my options.

The first thing I had to do was to find out what Nova and Ryan really wanted from that place. What they envisioned doing with it if it was to become theirs. In the time I'd been back, there had been so much talk about all the potential it offered and how they had so many plans that George just wouldn't let them realize, but I still didn't really know what any of those plans entailed.

Ultimately, I agreed that the property had massive potential. There was enough land to do a lot with it, but I needed Nova to just tell me what she wanted, which seemed harder than it sounded. I also had to talk to Ryan about whether he even wanted to stay there, or if he wanted to move on.

So far, most of my discussions about it had been with him, but in retrospect, something seemed off about him, and it was making me wonder if it was pride standing in the way of him opening up to me about it, or if it was because he was trying to help his family but was ready to leave the ranch. I never would have thought it was a possibility, but the guy had sacrificed everything for that place and that family.

Maybe he had decided it was time to live his own life. I wouldn't blame him for it.

As the sun broke free of the horizon and started rising in the sky, I rolled out of bed and got ready to coach football camp for the day, happy for the distraction it would provide. The Murphys were still on my mind as I showered and got dressed.

It was still way too early to leave, but I headed downstairs anyway, hoping that I was up before Mom for once so that I could make our breakfast. Of course, as soon as I hit the stairs and smelled pancakes, I knew I was already too late.

I walked into the kitchen to find her standing behind the stove with a whole stack of pancakes already done. I grinned and went over to brush a kiss to her cheek. "I was hoping I'd get to do this for you for a change. What time do you get up?"

"Why? Are you going to set an alarm just to beat me to it tomorrow morning?" she teased and motioned toward the coffee machine. "It's already locked and loaded. All you need to do is push the button."

I shook my head. "I should be ashamed that I'm letting you do all this for me. I'm a grownup. At some point, I'm pretty sure I'm supposed to start taking care of you."

"If that's true, we haven't reached that point yet," she said, winking as she flipped another pancake. "Besides, you do take care of me. Take that machine, for instance. I might've put the coffee in it this morning, but you're the one who bought it. Same goes for the ingredients for the pancakes."

"Yeah, but I'm staying here for now. It's only fair that I pay my own way."

She scoffed. "I'm your mother. You don't need to pay for anything and you're welcome to stay here as long as you like."

"Thanks, but I can't do that." I hit the button for an espresso and waited as dark liquid filled the little cup she'd already placed in position. Cocking my hip against the counter, I looked at her, wondering if she was really okay with us going back to the days of her cooking my breakfast and doing my laundry. "You'd tell me if you wanted me to get out, right? I still don't mind renting a place until I find a property to build on. I didn't think it was going to take me this long when I agreed to stay with you."

"You'll find something when you find it," she said easily, sliding the next lot of pancakes onto the waiting plate before she ladled more of the mixture into the pan. "Just so long as you make sure that you're saving up some money to build said house and have a family someday. You've been so busy focusing on what the town needs that I'm starting to get scared that you've forgotten that you still need to be able to live."

I chuckled, shaking my head at her. "Don't worry, Mom. Financially, I'm all good."

She glanced up at me, arching an eyebrow. "Only financially, huh? What's going on, Carson? I feel like I haven't spoken to you in weeks, but it's been at least that long since you've gone to look at any properties or since I've heard you talking about settling down."

"I still want that," I said honestly. "It's just that the idea of it seems to be getting further and further away."

"So what's on your mind?" she asked after flipping the pancakes and scraping the last bit of batter left in the bowl into her ladle. "Something's going on with you. Why is the idea of a house and a family getting further and further away? That's what you came home to do, so it should be feeling closer than ever, not further."

I shrugged. "To have a family, I need someone who wants to build it with me and I've hit a snag as far as that's concerned."

"A snag?" Mom frowned. "What happened to Nova?"

"How do you know I was talking about her? Maybe there's someone else."

Mom scoffed. "Please. There is only her. We've spoken about this, so why don't you just tell me about this snag instead of trying to pretend like you've got eyes for anyone else?"

"Fine. I don't. There is still only her. She's the only thing on my mind and the only one I want, but I don't know. She's hesitant."

"Well, of course, she is, honey," Mom said wisely, shutting off the stove once the last of the pancakes were done. "Let's sit down and you can tell me why she's hesitant while we're eating. Maybe I can help."

Taking the plate with the pancakes from her, I carried it and my coffee to the breakfast nook. Then I grabbed butter and syrup and set that down too before joining her. All the while, I thought about what to say about my situation with Nova.

For a guy who was supposed to be keeping quiet about it, I'd now told Vance and I was about to tell my mom. I didn't know if Nova had told anyone, but if she had, we were getting dangerously close to everyone finding out before Ryan, and he was going to hate us even more for that.

Mom smiled as I blew out a frustrated breath, unsure what to think about the fact that she wanted to keep it quiet in the first place. "You know how much I love Nova, sweetheart, but she's a complex girl. That's one of the reasons why I love her so much. She's independent, she follows her own heart, and she works damn hard, but if you're not willing to be patient with her, then maybe she's not the girl for you after all."

Everything in me rejected that statement. My stomach tightened into knots and my heart stammered. "It's not that I'm *not* willing to be patient. I am. I have been. It's just that every time I think we've taken a step forward, she goes and takes fifty steps back. It makes me wonder if she even wants this at all."

"She does," Mom said confidently. "I was always surprised that you two didn't get together back in high school. You were so in love with her and she was so in love with you."

"I wouldn't go that far," I grumbled. "I might've been in love with her, but she didn't feel the same way."

"Oh, yes, she did." Mom laughed softly, her head shaking as her eyes glazed over with a memory. "I remember watching her at your games. She always pretended she was there for Ryan, but he may as well never have been on the field for all the attention she paid her brother."

"Well, he's the only one she seems to be paying much attention to now," I said.

Mom tilted her head to the side as doubt splashed across her features. "She's not the only one, my dear boy. I think you're both too worried about Ryan. He's a big brother. Of course, he's protective, but he will survive once he finds out the truth. I bet he even expects it. Suspects it, at the very least."

"It's more than that." I sighed, then told her for the first time what had happened between us all back in the day.

To my surprise, she laughed again. "Oh, my sweet boy. Is that what you're afraid of? That he's going to punch you again?"

"No. I'm afraid he's never going to forgive either of us, and I think Nova's scared of it too."

Mom slid a couple of pancakes onto her plate, silent while she fixed them with all the trimmings before she finally looked back at me. "You don't know whether or not he'll forgive you. I'm sure he will, but I'm also sure neither of you will ever forgive yourselves if you don't work this out. Talk to her, sweetheart."

"I thought I had."

She chuckled. "If you had, you wouldn't think it. You'd *know* it. Try again, and this time, take the time to really listen to her before you get... distracted."

My eyebrows shot up when she winked at me. "Mom!"

Her head dropped back as she started laughing and shaking her head at me all over again. "Don't you *Mom* me, Carson Drake. I was young once too. I know how these things go, but promise me that the next time you talk to her, you'll keep your wits about you and use your head. Nova loves her family, but she also loves you. If you two really try, you can work out all these other things and finally give me those grandbabies I'm waiting for."

"What if we can't?"

She held my gaze, the humor melting away as a profound sadness filled her eyes. "That's not an option, Carson. You listen to me and you listen well. Do not let her slip through your fingers. If you love her like I think you do, then you cannot allow her to push you away. Not for anything, but least of all for her brother."

"I'm not sure that's my decision to make."

She sighed and reached for me, her eyes intent on mine as she tightened her grip on my hand. "I don't know if Ryan will forgive you two for being together, but aside from you two not forgiving yourself if you don't try, just remember that Ryan won't forgive himself either if he ever finds out he stood in the way of both of your happiness."

I stared back at her, not sure if she was right about that one, but then she released my hand and gave me a meaningful look. "He wants her to be happy, Carson. It might take him some time to accept she's found that happiness with you, but if there's one thing everyone knows about Ryan Murphy, it's that he puts his family's well-being above everything else. He will learn to live with it, but it'll kill him if he learns he's responsible for breaking his sister's heart. Or that he's responsible for her breaking it herself."

That much, I knew was true. Ryan would kill me if I hurt his sister, but if he found out that *he* did? I just didn't think he'd be able to forgive himself. Or me. Or her. It was just another complication to add to all the other complications I had to work my way through, but Mom had made a few good points. I needed to sort this out and I would find a way to do it. Even if I had no clue right now where I would even start.

# 41

## NOVA

While I was running errands in town, my phone rang and I fished it out of my purse to find Carson's name on the screen. I smiled and my heart skipped, but then I remembered that things were still tense between us.

As it turned out, the beginning of our relationship wasn't all sunshine and rainbows. We weren't in some kind of honeymoon phase where it was just us, a bed, and lazy mornings spent drinking coffee, talking, and laughing.

Instead, what we got was me trying to navigate my family's troubles while he coached football camp and tried to give me the space I needed to do what I had to do. The smile faded from my lips as I answered the call. Anxiety made me jittery. Was this the call I'd been waiting for?

"Hey, you," I said, trying to keep my tone light even as I gripped my phone real tight so that it wouldn't slip out of my trembling hand. "What's up?"

*He's going to tell me that it's over. That he doesn't want to hide and doesn't want to be with someone who's asking him to.*

"Hey, yourself," he said, his voice surprisingly warm. Not at all like someone who'd called to break up with someone else. "Do you think you could come over to the high school real quick? Vance and I are here, and if you've got a minute, I'd really appreciate it if you could meet me here."

*Maybe he wants to do it in person. Crap.* "Um, okay. What's going on? At least tell me if it's good or bad."

"It's good," he said easily. "At least, I think it is. Where are you?"

"A few blocks away. I had to come into town to do some things. Do you want me to meet you now?"

"The sooner, the better."

I breathed out, nodding even if he couldn't see me. "Okay. I'll be there soon. I just need to run to the post office, then I'm all yours."

"I like the sound of that," he said, lowering his voice. "I really like the sound of that. See you soon, Nova. I can't wait."

With that, he ended the call and my heart soared again. *Okay. Maybe he doesn't want to see me just to break up with me in person. It sure didn't sound like it.*

Pressing my hand to my chest in an attempt to regain control of my heartbeat, I popped into the post office to send a parcel to my aunt from my mother. Then I hurried back to my truck and drove straight to our old high school.

As promised, Carson and Vance were already there, both wearing shorts with official-looking blue and yellow T-shirts with the high-school's eagle emblazoned on them. I smiled at the sight of them back in Silver Creek Eagles gear after so long.

After hopping out of the truck, I made my way across the field. Carson ran drills with the current teenage football team. All hot and sweaty when he finally looked up, he grinned when he saw me and started in my direction immediately.

Those smiling green eyes met my own. His shirt stuck to his arms and abs, and all those pearly whites were being flashed right at me. My mouth went dry, my palms suddenly sweaty as a horde of butterflies took charge of my stomach.

"Thanks for coming." He stopped just short of me and put his hands on his hips as he tried to catch his breath. "Have you got any plans today?"

Still having a hard time focusing, I bit my lip and let my gaze roam over his gorgeous face before it dropped to those broad shoulders. "That depends on what you had in mind."

He barked out a laugh, pupils dilating a little. "Not that, but I'm available later if you want me to come over."

His voice was rougher than before, but when I realized this hadn't been a booty call—or a breakup—I fished my mind out of the gutter. "Okay. We'll talk about *later* later, but what did you have in mind for now?"

"Do you remember any of your high school soccer drills?"

*What?* I frowned deeply. *Well, if that's not a sudden change of subject, I don't know what is.*

"Why?" I asked. "Maybe some, but definitely not all."

"You kept playing in college, right?" He jabbed his thumb at a group of forlorn teenage girls moping at the far end of the field. "Their soccer coach didn't show up for the first day of camp and it sounds like it'll be canceled if they don't find a new one."

I sighed. It was hot as hell and I hadn't played a lick of soccer in years, but he was right. I'd played all through high school and college, and I'd been pretty good. If it had been me sitting on that field back in high school, faced with the possibility that camp was about to be canceled, I'd have been upset and praying for anyone to step up.

Between that and the way Carson was looking at me, I nodded. "Let me see what I can do. I can't promise I'll be any good at it, but I'll try."

"Thank you," he said emphatically, opening his arms until he seemed to think better of it. "I'd better not hug you right now. I'm pretty sure I stink."

"That's okay." I walked up to him, winding my arms around his neck and pulling him close, not minding the scent of fresh sweat at all as he wrapped his arms around my waist and held me for a second.

In that moment, it felt like everything was right between us. Like we were okay and like nothing could tear us apart.

But then the shrill shriek of a whistle pierced the air and Vance laughed. "Get your ass back here, Drake."

"I should never have let him have a whistle," Carson muttered into my hair, squeezing me tight. He finally let go and flashed me another grin. Then he started jogging backward, his eyes still on mine as he ran a hand through his hair. "Call me later?"

"You got it." A girly thrill shot through me. My heart fluttered and my lips begged to smile.

As I held his gaze, I let the smile break free. He nodded, looking at me for just another second before he finally turned and headed back to the football players. When it was just the two of us, even when we were surrounded by people like we had been just then, our connection was so real and so alive that it made me wonder why things felt so difficult between us sometimes.

There were all these moments when us being together felt as natural as breathing, but then the world forced itself back into focus and *poof!* That connection didn't mean a single damn thing and our relationship felt as doomed as ever.

Watching him from the corner of my eye, I crossed the field to the girls, finally forcing myself to forget about the guy and do what I'd apparently come here to do. The high school soccer team gave me a collective frown as I smiled and offered them a halfhearted wave.

"Hello, ladies. I'm Nova Murphy and I'm told you're in a bit of a predicament."

"Who?" One girl's frown deepened, but another suddenly smacked her friend's shoulder and stepped closer to me.

Her eyes were curious as she looked me over. "Nova Murphy, as in *the* Nova Murphy?"

I swept my tongue across my lips, not having any idea what she was talking about. "I don't know about that, but I've never heard of another Nova Murphy in this town, so..."

"So you're *her*," yet another girl said excitedly. "You're, like, a legend at school, Nova. You led your team to the championships in your senior year, right? I heard you even got a scholarship to play for Oklahoma U."

"Uh, yes. I did." I'd just had no idea anyone knew or cared about that. "I guess I *am* her, then."

The first girl flushed, extending her hand toward me. She apologized. "I'm so sorry, Ms. Murphy. Coach Dell didn't even tell us she knew you. We didn't know you were going to coach the camp. I'm Annie Locke. The captain."

"It's nice to meet you, Annie. To be fair to Coach Dell, I didn't know I was going to coach the camp either. I just got a phone call a few minutes ago, but if you'll have me, then I'll stand in for the day."

"If we'll have you?" She grinned. "We'd love that. Who called you?"

"Carson Drake," I said, glancing at the man in question and trying not to drool at the sight of his ass in those pants as he bent over to demonstrate something.

"Of course, you'd know him." Another girl sighed dreamily. "All our local legends probably know each other. Does that mean you know Vance Abrams too?"

"Yep, but we're not here to talk about boys. We're here to work." I turned my attention to them, my tone sharp. I dropped my purse on the field and folded my arms. "Alright, ladies. You're going to have to listen up because I don't have a whistle and I don't like yelling, but let's get started."

As I ran them through practice, exhilaration flowed through me. All my worries were washed away in its wake. I was loving every second of this, and when I looked over my shoulder to see Carson watching me with a smile on his face, I loved it even more.

I really didn't know how he always seemed to know what I needed and how he found a way to give me just that, but he did. He really was something else. I just had to hope that I didn't lose him because my mind was constantly someplace else. If I did, I wasn't sure I'd ever get another chance.

All I needed was a little more time to figure out how to have it all —my home, my job, and my love. *I just need a little more time. Please let him give me that. Please don't let him give up on me just yet. Just not yet.*

# 42

## CARSON

.

After camp wrapped for the day, I waited for Nova to finish making arrangements with the soccer team and then I grinned at her when she finally came walking up to her truck. "You have fun today? It sure looked like you were."

"I did, actually," she said thoughtfully. Then she blinked it all away and looked at me. "How about you? It looked like you were putting the boys through their paces."

I shrugged, but I couldn't stop the smirk that tugged at the corners of my lips. "We've been doing that every day. What's the point of camp if they don't get something out of it? They didn't sign up to laze around."

"Maybe not, but I also don't think they signed up to be tortured," she teased. "You heading home?"

I pushed away from her truck, deciding to try this one more time. "I was hoping to be heading out to a late lunch with you. What do you say? Will you let me buy you a sandwich? If anybody asks, we can tell them it was about camp."

Bracing myself to be turned down again, my eyebrows shot up when she nodded instead. "Sure. I'd love that. I just want to go home and take a shower first. I feel like I've been dipped in a vat of lava sweat." Her eyes finally broke away from mine, traveling to my damp hair first and then to my fresh shirt. "You've already showered?"

"Yeah, Vance and I hit the locker rooms earlier. I wanted to wait for you to finish up anyway and you were still busy, so I figured I'd use the time productively."

"Want to tag along with me, then?" she asked, surprising the socks off me once more. "You can have something cold to drink at my place while I shower, and then we can go get lunch. I've been wanting to talk to you anyway."

"Sounds good." It sounded pretty fucking great actually. More like we were in a relationship and less like two people bumbling around in the dark, trying to meet each other halfway while they were in two different rooms.

Nova smiled and walked around me to get into her truck, even taking my hand and squeezing it as her smile turned sweet and sexy all at the same time. "I missed you."

"I missed you too," I said, my voice suddenly husky with a combination of surprise and attraction. "I'll meet you there."

At her house, she left the door open for me and went to grab a quick shower, emerging in a T-shirt and shorts, her wet hair falling down her back. She was a sight to behold like this, and I found myself suddenly clamming up a bit when I felt those sparkling blue eyes sweep across my face. My usual charm was nowhere to be found as I tried to remember my mom's advice to talk to her instead of getting *distracted*.

"I'm surprised you didn't tell me to get lost," I said, voicing the first thought that came to mind. "How are you doing? Should I take it as a good thing that I'm here? What did you want to talk to me about?"

She blinked, clearly pretty surprised herself. "How am I doing? No one ever really asks me that. Not the way you just did, anyway. It's the usual '*how are you*' stuff, but I never feel like they actually want to know how I'm doing."

"I do," I said quietly, feeling bad about not having asked her that myself in a long time. I walked up to her, taking her face in my hands and looking into her eyes. "You're taking on so much, Nova. It hurts to see you stretched so thin and to know that I'm adding to the stress."

"You're not." She let her hands drift to my shirt, running her fingers up along my sides until her palms were resting on my chest. "I didn't mind coaching today. It was fun."

"I wasn't talking about that. Don't get me wrong, it was great to see you looking so happy for a change, and you really did look happy on that field today, but I was talking about the situation between us."

"That's the one good thing I've got going for me right now." Eyes on mine, she let out a deep breath and stroked her fingers over my heart. "I owe you another huge thank you."

"You do?"

She nodded. "I really was happy today, and once again, I have you to thank for it. So thank you."

I let my hands drop to her hips and flexed my fingers as I held her, letting her know that I wasn't going anywhere. "Do you think you'll be able to keep coaching them?"

"I'm going to try to make it work, but between the ranch and the bakery, I'm not sure it's going to be sustainable."

She seemed so sad that the question just shot out of me. "Why do you keep working on the ranch?"

Surprise flickered behind those eyes again. "Excuse me?"

"You heard me, Nova." I kept my voice soft and gentle, but I really did want to know. I *needed* her to tell me, in fact. "The truth, if you don't mind. Don't tell me that you're obligated to do it. Why are you still working so hard on this ranch when everyone else seems to have given up?"

It took her a beat, but then she dragged in a shuddering breath, took my hands, led me over to the sofa, and sat me down with her. "I've always envisioned my future here. I've got my bakery, sure, but it took me years to open it and I don't want to lose it now that it's finally doing so well."

My breath stalled in my lungs. This was exactly what I'd been hoping to get out of her today, and now here she was, telling me without even having to be begged to do it. "What else?"

"What else what?"

"What else did you envision in your future here?" *Tell me, Nova. Please don't shut down on me now.*

Her tongue came out to wet her lips as she thought about it. "Dad would never go for it, but I'd really like to open an event venue. We could open a Christmas tree farm, hold weddings and parties, and even have an inn or a bed and breakfast. We don't have to rely wholly on cattle, but I want to revamp the way we go about selling even that. I told you about the subscription boxes, and I have so many other ideas. It's just that Dad doesn't want to let go of times that are long gone, even if I know we could make it work."

As she described it, I finally saw the whole picture the way she did, the thriving ranch with so many different businesses all booming under her management. "That's exactly what your family needs to do, I think. Diversification is the only way to go these days. Where is Ryan in all of this?"

"He hates change," she said, and with those words, I finally understood why my friend had been having such a hard time.

Ryan hadn't wanted things to change after high school. He had to stay home to help his family, but he also chose not to go away to college. He even turned down that scholarship and watched us move on without him. All so things wouldn't change, and now, he didn't want his friendship with me to change if Nova and I got together.

All of these things were suddenly so obvious that I couldn't believe I hadn't ever thought about it that way before. As much as he wanted to save the ranch, he also just didn't want things to change, and if they had to, it had to be his way or the highway.

Expand the farming operations—or go big and find a new home. I grunted at the force of all these realizations as they hit, and my eyes flew wide open. Nova seemed amused, smiling even as a sense of sadness clung to her.

"Why does it feel like you just had an epiphany?" she asked.

"Because I did," I admitted, feeling like she'd just yanked a sheet of thick wool away from my eyes. "Can it really be that simple? He just hates change."

She shrugged. "That doesn't mean that he's not capable of it. He'd just rather things change as little as possible."

"So then how is he taking it so easily that your parents might sell the whole ranch?"

"You think he's taking it easily?" She snorted as she tried to hold back her laughter. "He's not, Carson. He's a wreck. I don't think he's stopped working long enough to sleep for even an hour all week and I know he'll support me in whatever business I want to start here, but that doesn't mean he wants the same things."

"He's told me that he's got a lot of ideas for the place himself, though."

She nodded. "Even Ryan knows that something has to give. In a way, he's exactly like Dad. Ryan just isn't stuck in the same past Dad is. He wants to move forward, modernize, expand, and diversify, but not quite as radically as I'd like to do."

My heart tripped over itself, but for once, I wasn't going to let Ryan stand in my way with all this. "Well, I think that you're right. I think everything as you envision it is exactly what you need, and I want to invest in your business ideas. I'll support you all the way and I don't care what it costs. Just put a plan together and I'll start pulling strings."

"Are you serious?" she asked. "You can't be. I mean, I know we've been talking about you buying the ranch and that was what I wanted to talk to you about today, but—"

"I'm dead serious, Nova. This is a much better plan than me just buying a part of your property. It's an actual business investment, which I've made a lot of at this point. If you can put these ideas on paper and follow through, then I really think it'll work."

Her eyes moved from one of mine to the other, but I could see she was trying not to get excited just yet. "You know, I promised myself I was going to step up and talk to you about saving the ranch, which this would do, but now I'd like to know something else."

"Yeah, what's that?"

"Would you still have thought that my ideas are good if you didn't want to get into my pants?" she asked, completely deadpan.

I laughed and reached for her hands again. "Contrary to what everyone around here seems to believe, I know the difference between good business and romance, and I don't confuse the two with one another."

"You don't?" she asked softly. "You seem to be doing just that right now."

I stroked my thumbs across her knuckles, my gaze drinking in the vulnerability in her eyes and the hope as she stared back at me. "I would've wanted to do this for you either way, and I really want to help your family, but what you just described is exactly what I've found successful ranchers these days are doing. I've been looking into it for weeks and all my research has pointed to using the property for different things."

"Diversification," she said slowly. "That's the only way to go these days, huh?"

"Yep." I smiled and released one of her hands to brush a lock of wet hair behind her ear. "You've already proven that you're a great businesswoman, Nova. You have a knack for it, and if you can start all these, with the help you need on a property you love, I know you'll make a success of it. I'd be stupid not to want in on that. It'd just be an added bonus that it will also give me an excuse to speak to you more often."

"Is this supposed to be romance or business?" she joked breathlessly. "It sounds like a bit of both to me."

"Well, maybe I was wrong about not combining them," I murmured as she wrapped her arms around my neck.

Nova beamed at me before bringing her mouth right to mine. "I'm going to kiss you now."

Before she could do it, I did, kissing her and pushing her back down on the sofa. Mom had warned me not to get distracted while we were talking, but we'd talked.

Nova seemed okay with me giving her the money she needed for business ideas that I honestly believed would work, and that meant we had a plan to save the ranch and to stay together while we were at it. Just this morning, I hadn't been sure if either of those things were possible, but now, it felt like a whole new world of possibility had opened up to us.

One in which Nova and I changed the entire town for the better, created dozens of new jobs, and brought in people from all over to stay, to attend functions, and hopefully, to support the local people. I grinned against her lips as I pulled back a little bit.

"If we're going into business together, does that mean you're finally going to take me up on posing for the videos for the subscription boxes?"

"I don't know," she teased, her voice breathy as she pushed her hands under my shirt. "I think I'm going to need to inspect the merchandise. Thoroughly."

"Inspect away," I groaned as I let her sit me up and climb into my lap. "Inspect as much as you want. I'm all yours anyway."

Nova smiled and repeated my words from earlier right back to me, making both my heart and my cock swell like they never had before. "I like the sound of that. I really, really like the sound of that. As long as you know that I'm all yours too, Carson. That still hasn't changed and it's not going to."

# 43

## NOVA

Our kisses quickly turned into more, and I couldn't stop smiling as my heart raced and my body ached for his. I knew I should've jumped at the opportunity to have him invest in my ideas instead of jumping *him*, but right then, he was all I wanted.

Him. Us. Together.

It seemed more important than everything else, and as always, the world melted away as his lips moved against my own. I let my feelings for him consume me. He made me feel like I mattered. Like nothing mattered more than us.

Logic took a backseat as I pulled off his shirt, eager to finally have the opportunity to explore him the way I'd always wanted to. I scooted off his lap, sank to my knees between his, and moved my hands to the waistband of his shorts.

Carson watched me intently but didn't stop me when my fingers hooked into the elastic and I started pulling down. He even lifted his butt for me to pull them off, and I was thrilled when he was naked in front of me for the first time in days.

I knew that wasn't such a long time, but it had been such a tense, stressful few days that it had started feeling like I was never going to get to be with him again. Butterflies raced around my stomach. I lifted my eyes to his, holding his gaze as I ran my hands up and down the length of the muscles in his thighs. I ran my hands all the way up to his crotch and let the backs of my fingers brush against him.

"Fuck, Nova," he groaned, lids growing heavy. "How is it that you always get me so worked up so damn fast?"

I shrugged a shoulder, took one of his hands, and put it on my breast. "I don't know, but you do the same to me."

A quiver rippled through all those powerful muscles when I wrapped my fingers firmly around his shaft. Carson's lips parted, his eyes more hooded than before. He massaged my breast in one hand and gripped the armrest of the sofa with the other.

"Are you done with your inspection yet? I'm not sure how much more of this I can take."

I wagged a finger at him, not picking up the pace of my stroking. A moan caught in my throat when I looked at my hand wrapped around his thick shaft and saw the wetness glistening at his tip.

Leaning forward, I brought my head down and sucked him into my mouth. My sounds of pleasure mingled with his as I licked him everywhere. He hit the back of my throat and I eased back, my hand working with my mouth until I felt him swell.

He tried to pull back, and when that didn't work, he grasped my shoulder, but I still didn't move. I'd been wanting this for too long, and now I wanted to taste him just as he'd done so many times with me. My name and a few curses started spilling from his lips. Then he let out a loud roar and came, shooting his release into my mouth. Breathing raggedly in the aftermath, he shook his head at me when I finally smiled up at him.

"You're a bad girl, you know that?"

I brought my hand to my chest, feigning innocence as I batted my lashes at him. "Me? I didn't realize that was bad. I thought it was pretty good, but I guess you'd better show me what happens to bad girls."

*God, I can't believe I just said that.*

A slow, lazy grin spread on Carson's face and he sat up a little, beckoning me to him. I scooted up again and he positioned me on his lap once more. He gripped my hips and ran his fingers along the waistband of my shorts, making a shiver of need shoot down my spine.

He quickly removed my pants and watched me closely as he ran his hands up and down my thighs. "Bad girls have to let me watch them come. All of it. Keep your eyes on mine, Nova."

"Or?" I asked between panting breaths. "What are you going to do to me if I don't?"

"Depends," he rasped out. "Do you like being spanked?"

A spark shot through me. "I wouldn't know."

"Let's find out soon. Like maybe if you don't look at me, but otherwise, we'll find out after, okay?"

I jerked my chin in a nod, so wet that I felt slick between my thighs even though his hips were between them and I couldn't squeeze them together. Carson finally brought his hands up. His fingers of one hand rubbed through my folds while he used the other hand to hold me open.

A loud whine slid out of me, but I never stopped looking at him. Not when he started drawing circles around my clit or pushed a finger into me. Not when he tightened those circles or found the most amazing rhythm. Not when I felt the orgasm rapidly approaching.

Not even when I dropped my forehead to his and whimpered his name when it hit. My body jerked into his hand. My hips thrust and bucked. Pleasure dragged me under and made me see stars instead of his eyes.

The orgasm took forever to subside, and when it did, I looked at him again to see that he'd already produced a condom from somewhere. After easing me back gently, he rolled it on, lifting me up on my knees and asking a silent question. I nodded. I was sure I wanted this. I always wanted this.

Always wanted him.

"I'm never going to say no to you, Carson," I whispered, my throat too dry to talk as I kissed him. "It's always going to be yes. I'm always going to want everything with you."

As I said it, I lowered myself down over him, still so sensitive that my nerve endings exploded with pleasure even as I just fed him into me. All the while watching me carefully, he held me close and started moving, only not looking at me when we were kissing.

His lips were firm and hungry on mine. His whole body was tense with restraint as we found our rhythm together. This time when I went over the edge, he was right there with me and it made the orgasm that much more intense to know that my pleasure had triggered his.

After, we got dressed but quickly ended up tangled together on the sofa again. I giggled as he lay on top of me, tickling my ribs with his forehead pressed to mine. "If that's your idea of an inspection of the merchandise, you can do one any time you'd like."

"Is that so?" I laughed. "How am I ever going to go to—"

Just before I finished the sentence, my front door burst open and we both practically jumped out of our skins. I clung to him, only pushing away when Ryan's face suddenly appeared in my field of vision. Ryan's very pissed-off face, glaring angrily at us as his jaw worked and his hands formed fists at his sides.

Shit. There was no way I could explain this as anything other than what it was, but more than that, I didn't want to lie to him anymore. I'd asked Carson for time and he'd given it to me, but I was ready for my brother to know the truth.

Even if he didn't seem at all ready to hear it.

# 44

## CARSON

Sitting up, I met Ryan's death glare full on and stood, making sure to keep Nova behind me. I didn't think he would hurt her, but he was going to take a swing at me and I didn't want her getting caught in the crossfire.

Mind racing, I couldn't come up with any excuses for the position he'd just found us in. This was *not* the ideal way for him to find out the truth, but he wasn't stupid. We were busted and I'd been wanting to talk to her about telling him sooner rather than later anyway.

Ryan's jaw ticked as he glanced between us. His shoulders were rigid with rage, his cheeks flushed, and his lips parted. I didn't want to make any sudden movements, but I was ready to block a punch if I had to. I just didn't want to come across as being defensive.

"Ryan," I said, slowly raising my hands to show him my palms. "Clearly, we need to talk. Do you want to sit down? I'll get you a drink and we can—"

"That's my sister," he spat, practically hissing. "You know how I feel about you two being together."

"Yes, I do, but I'm not going to apologize. We're not kids anymore, Ry. I know you want to protect her, but you don't have to protect her from me."

He scoffed, taking a menacing step closer as his fists tightened. "I don't have to protect her from you? That's rich, coming from the guy who left a string of broken hearts behind in every fucking city he's ever lived. Including this one."

My heart hammered in my throat. *What does he mean by that? I didn't break Nova's heart back then.*

Since I was trying to diffuse the situation though, I knew better than to argue with him. We could hash that out another day.

"Nova isn't any other girl, Ryan. Not to me. What I feel for her is real and—"

"Bullshit," he snapped, taking another step closer and getting right in my face. "Unless you can stand there and tell me right now that you're going to marry her, you haven't changed. You're not going to settle down. You're going to hurt her and I'm going to be left to pick up the pieces."

"I will never intentionally hurt her," I said confidently, needing him to believe me. "We haven't talked about marriage yet, and if we do, that's a conversation I'll have with Nova before I have it with you. I respect her too much to make decisions for her."

"You respect her?" He sneered. "After what I just walked in on, you really want me to believe that you respect her? You want to fuck her, Carson. That's not respect. That's lust."

"Ryan, I—"

With a loud roar, he pulled his fist back and took that swing I'd been waiting for. My arm flew up and I blocked him, feinting to one side before I ducked to dodge the punch. He let out something like a war cry and came at me again, and from the corner of my eye, I saw Nova wince, her eyes filled with tears as she watched us.

"Okay, that's it," I said firmly, straightening up and giving him a not-too-hard shove toward the front door. "We're taking this outside."

"Why? You don't want her to see you lose?" he taunted as he stumbled back, even though I hadn't shoved him that hard.

Catching himself on her dining-room table, he regained his balance but strode to the door, rushing down the stairs outside before spinning around to face me again. "That's my fucking sister, Carson. I don't want you anywhere near her, but you just can't stay away, can you? You have to have her because she's a challenge. Because you just have to have everything. You can't leave anything alone."

"She's your family, I get that," I said, inhaling deeply in an attempt to remain calm. "She's not your property though, Ryan. She belongs to herself and she makes her own decisions."

"Not this time." His temper escalated and he advanced on me quickly, his legs eating up the space between us as he threw another punch.

This time, I didn't duck or try to block it. I knew I owed him one, so I let him have it. His fist landed. Pain exploded across my jaw and cheekbone and my head snapped back. I lost my footing for a moment, staggering a few steps back before I managed to stop myself from falling on my ass.

Blood poured out of my nose and I was definitely going to have at least one black eye, but I blinked hard to keep focused, ignoring the taste of hot metal in my mouth as I threw my arms out to my sides. "Are you happy now? Is that what you wanted? Is this what you need to feel better about me *taking everything* from you?"

I knew I shouldn't be calling him out, but shit. That was what all this was about, wasn't it? For a couple months now, I'd had a feeling that his resentment of me came from someplace deeper than just having caught me with his sister, and now I knew for sure.

He snorted, breathing hard as he circled me, clearly looking for an in to take another swing, but he wasn't going to get it. I'd given him that one for free, but he wasn't getting another. "What I want is for you to get the fuck off my family's property and never come back."

I hadn't realized that Nova had followed us outside until she spoke up. "This is my house, Ryan. I need *you* to leave."

When I glanced at her over my shoulder, she was standing at the top of the steps that led to her front door, looking miserable with her arms crossed and those tears still swimming in her eyes. Ryan's gaze darted to her at the same time mine did, and his eyebrows shot up.

"You want *me* to *leave*? Fine. If you want to act like every other sl—"

"Don't you dare call her that," I snarled. "I know you're pissed, but don't call her names, Ryan. You can never take that back."

"I'm speaking to my sister," he snapped without looking at me, his gaze now firmly focused on her. "You know what he is, Nova. So, what? You're just going to throw yourself at his feet like every other fucking woman in this town? You're going to let him use you and then toss you away?"

She opened her mouth to respond, but he didn't let her. "I thought you were better than that. I thought I could trust you. Both of you."

"This isn't about trust, Ryan," she said in a shaky voice, but she was standing up for herself and I admired that about her. "It's about you needing to accept that I'm an adult with as much of a right to make my own choices as anyone else. He's not using me, but even if he was, it would've been up to me if I was going to let it happen."

"You have no idea what you're saying," he hissed, teeth clenched and eyes narrowed to slits. "Don't let him fool you. He's like a leech who'll take everything you have to offer and suck you dry before he leaves without looking back."

My jaw dropped open and pain seared through me again at the movement, but I couldn't help it. I was struck dumb by what I was hearing from him. "What the fuck, man? What have I ever taken from you?"

"Leave, Ryan," Nova insisted, crossing her arms tighter. She nodded in the direction of his place. "Just go. Calm down and we'll talk more later."

He rolled his eyes, chest still heaving. He shook with fury, muttering a few choice words under his breath as he finally turned and stormed away. I watched, stunned, unable to believe what had just come out of him.

As soon as he was gone, Nova rushed down the stairs and came up to me, holding up her hands but not touching my cheek. She swept her gaze across my face, obviously trying to assess the severity of the injury. "I'm so sorry. I can't believe he did that. Again. Come on inside. We'll get you some ice."

"Thanks, but I'm okay," I said, pushing past the pain as I stared into those worried blue eyes. "I'll be fine, but I have to go."

"Go?" She frowned. "Go where? At least let me help you clean up before you leave."

"This is nothing," I said soothingly, trying not to wince. It hurt like a bitch, but I already knew he hadn't broken a bone. "It's just soft tissue and swelling. I've taken enough hits in my life to know when it's serious and this isn't. I'll clean up at home. Talk to you later?"

She blinked a bunch of times in rapid succession, mouth opening and closing. The furrow in her brow deepened and she looked at me again. "Are you sure? Your nose is bleeding. Just let me get you something to help with that."

I pinched the bridge of my nose. Pain stabbed through my entire face from the point of contact. Tipping my head back, I patted my pocket and felt my car keys still safely tucked inside. "I'm really sorry, Nova, but I do have to go. I'll call you. Promise."

Knowing she was probably confused as hell right now, I reached for her hand and, being careful not to get any blood on her, tugged her closer. "I'm going to chase him down. After everything he said, we need to talk."

She nodded against my chest and pulled away to walk me to my truck. "Yeah. Okay. I understand. Go talk to him. You're sure you're okay, though?"

"I'll be fine." I pressed a kiss to her forehead and climbed in behind the steering wheel. Silently cursing him, I waved goodbye to his sister and took off.

Halfway to Ryan's house, however, I decided against going after him right then. I wanted to talk this out, but he probably needed more than a few minutes to calm down, and the last thing I wanted was to make it worse. Leaving the ranch instead, I headed home to clean myself up, happy that my mom wasn't there and I didn't have to explain the state I was in just yet.

As I ran cold water onto a washcloth, my head was still spinning. I'd known Ryan was going to be angry at us, but that level of rage had surprised me. Plus, I'd had no idea he somehow held me responsible for everything that had gone wrong in his life.

I didn't understand it at all, but at least now I knew. I blew out a heavy breath and wrapped my fingers around the porcelain rim of the sink, wondering just what the hell I was supposed to do now. All this time, I'd been worried that Ryan finding out how I felt about Nova was going to derail a friendship that had just been getting back on track, but that didn't seem to be the case.

If that was really how he felt about me, I wasn't sure there was anything worth salvaging there, but on the other hand, he was my oldest friend. I didn't know where any of that had come from, but if he resented me so much, then surely the least we could do was have a conversation about it.

I glowered at myself in the mirror, wondering for the first time if I'd made the right decision by coming home. I wanted to be here. I wanted to have the life I'd envisioned and I wanted to have it with Nova while supporting her in making all her dreams come true.

But shit, with Ryan feeling the way he did, I wasn't sure Nova was ever going to be all in with me. My second chance might well go up in flames. I still had my mom and the community, but my heart was with Nova, and if I didn't have her, it might be too painful to stick around here where I would see her all the time. The wound would never heal.

# 45

## NOVA

Feeling awful about what had just happened, I went back into my cottage and called Cassidy, hoping like hell she'd be able to come over. I didn't reach out often because I happened to think I could solve most of my problems alone, but not this.

Not today.

All those things Ryan had said kept rolling through my mind. The look on Carson's face when my brother had seen us was front and center in my brain. I'd never meant to come between them, but I had —and I didn't think there would be any coming back from it.

Not anymore.

With tears pressing at the backs of my eyes, I gripped my phone and nearly gave up hope before Cassidy finally picked up. "Hey, babe. How are you? Please don't tell me you're working and need help."

"No, it's not that," I said, my voice shaking. I sank down on a stool in my kitchen, staring forlornly out the window and wondering if I'd just ruined everything. "Could you come over? Ryan, uh, he just found out about Carson and me, and it did *not* go down well."

"Shit." I heard the scrape of a chair against tiles. "I'm on my way. Give me fifteen minutes. Pour yourself a drink and then stay right where you are. I'll be there soon."

She ended the call after I heard a door slamming, and I drew in a deep breath as I put the phone down on the counter. Following her instructions to pour myself a drink, I poured one for her as well and carried both glasses out to the deck overlooking the river.

A short while later, my front door creaked open and I froze until I heard her voice. "Nova? Where are you?"

"I'm out here."

My blood began flowing again now that I knew neither of the guys had come back. I sat up a little straighter, half embarrassed by the tears flowing down my cheeks and the mess I was. Cassidy gave me one look when she appeared in the doorway and then pulled me up into her arms, not caring that I looked like shit.

"That bad, huh?" she asked into my hair as she gave me a hug. "Well, at least now he knows. Was there any blood spilled?"

She asked the question as a joke, but her body tensed against mine when I nodded. Pulling away, she frowned, her eyebrows arched and jaw slack. "What, are you serious? There was blood?"

"Carson's," I said softly. "He said he was okay, but he left before I could even help him clean up, so I'm not sure if he really is."

"Ryan got a hit in on Carson?" Her frown deepened. "I'm surprised. I kind of thought an NFL quarterback would be faster than that."

I sat down, reached for Cassidy's drink, and handed it over. Then I brought mine to my lips. "Carson let Ryan punch him. I'm pretty sure he felt like he deserved it, but again, I don't know for sure because he left. He wouldn't even let me give him ice or a cloth to clean up."

"Did he say where he was going?" she asked cautiously. "Maybe he was just a little humiliated and didn't want you to see him hurt."

I pulled my shoulders up again. "Maybe. I honestly don't know. He said he was going to track Ryan down, but I don't think that would've been a good idea so soon after the fight, and I'm also not sure if he actually did it. I also don't know why he would've been humiliated. It's not like I've never seen him hurt before. I used to go to every last one of his games. Seeing him take hits was part of the package."

"Yeah, but that's not really the same thing." She reclined in her chair, her brow furrowed as she looked me over. "You're okay, though?"

"I'm fine." I waved her off. "Shaken but physically okay."

She pursed her lips at me. "If that was true, you wouldn't have called, so talk to me, girl. I know you're okay physically. Neither of them would ever hurt you like that, but you're obviously still hurt, so tell me what you're thinking."

"I don't know." I sighed and ran my hands through my loose, slightly knotty hair. I'd never even gotten around to brushing it after my shower. Then things had happened with Carson and now it felt kind of impossible to believe that it had all been such a short time ago that I still hadn't brushed my freaking hair. "My brother is an asshole who seems to think I'm incapable of making my own decisions. He also came this close to calling me a slut." I held my fingers about an inch apart.

"You should've seen him, Cass. He was completely beyond reason and totally irrational. The only reason he didn't call me that was because my boyfriend, who apparently will never settle down with me because I'm not good enough, stopped him before he could get the word out. The same boyfriend who fled from me like his ass was on fire after."

Her mouth dropped so far open that it looked like she was about to unhinge her jaw. "He called you a slut?"

"He was about to," I muttered. "It seems the only way I can be with Carson is if I am one. Either that, or just another girl who's willing to open my legs to a guy who will never have real feelings for me."

She scoffed. "That's ridiculous. He said all that?"

"Pretty much." I dragged in a deep breath through my nostrils and closed my eyes. "I don't know what to do, Cass. When it's just me and Carson, I'm so sure that it's right, but it feels like there's always something that's tearing us apart."

"Ignore the noise," she said wisely. "That's all it is. Noise. The only thing that matters is how you feel. Hold on to that, and everything else will fall into place eventually. Do you want me to talk to Ryan? He might see things differently coming from me. I'm sure as hell not going to keep going on dates with him if he's going to be like this with you two."

"You've been going on dates with him?" I asked disbelievingly. She nodded and I took a huge sip of my whiskey. "Fucking hypocrite. I don't want to ruin what you guys have got going on, though. I just wish he would see things from my point of view for once."

She sighed. "I remember what those guys were like in high school. They were a trio. A tripod. I never thought anything would get between them."

"Neither did I," I admitted. "Ryan seems to blame Carson for everything, though. It just doesn't make sense. He's been bitter ever since they left, but he's the one who decided to stay."

Her expression softened and she hesitated before she leaned forward a bit, taking a few more sips of her own drink before she said anything. "I don't want to defend what he did or what he said to you. Rational or not, he shouldn't have done it."

"Preach."

She chuckled, but there was a deep sadness in her eyes as she stared back at me. "That being said, Carson does carry some of the blame. So does Vance."

"What do you mean?" I asked slowly, struggling to see where she was coming from. "I know you knew them back then, but I was there, Cass. No one influenced Ryan to turn down that scholarship. Not even our dad."

"I know, but Carson and Vance went and they left Ryan behind."

I frowned. "Surely, he knew that was going to happen when he decided against going with them. I mean, were they supposed to take him with them as their mascot? What good would that have done? He wanted to stay here, on the ranch. He didn't want to leave."

"Oh, he wanted to," she countered gently. "He wanted to so bad, but he didn't feel like he really had a choice. Your family needed him here and he told me that even if he'd gone, he probably wouldn't have done very well because his heart wouldn't have been in it."

My own heart ached with sympathy for my brother. "That's still not Carson's fault, though. Or Vance's."

"No, but I wasn't talking about them leaving him behind here when they left. Obviously, they all knew that was going to happen, but Ryan never thought they would forget all about him once they had their fancy lives in the big city."

"They didn't, though." Even as I said it, I knew that wasn't entirely true. "Did they?"

She shrugged. "I don't know, but I do know that he hardly ever heard from them. He knows they were busy. So was he. Growing apart is natural under the circumstances, but they also hardly ever made an effort to see him when they were in town. They left him behind in more ways than one, and now they're back and they just think they can all pick up where they left off?"

For a long minute, I kept quiet, processing everything she was saying and unable to respond. It dawned at me that there really were two sides to this story. "Don't stop seeing him, Cass."

She shook her head, that sadness growing even more profound. "I'll think about it. It kills me to see history repeating itself with those two on one side and Ryan on the other, but that's no excuse for taking it out on you. For calling you names and refusing to even consider the possibility that Carson could be good for you."

I squeezed my eyes shut, trying to wrap my head around all the different points of view and emotions tangled up in this. I loved my brother, but I also loved Carson. Carson, who wanted to support me no matter what. Who wanted to stand by me despite the shit he knew he was going to take for it from my brother. Carson, who understood me and made me feel like no one else ever had.

Yet, Ryan was my blood. My family. My only sibling. I couldn't just ignore that. Once again, I felt like I was at a crossroads. I had to decide whether to follow my heart or to stay true to my blood. It was an impossible decision, and one I had no idea how to make. Especially not now that I was finally starting to understand that things were a hell of a lot more complex than I'd ever realized before.

My mother and even Cassidy had been wrong. I was starting to think that if I chose Carson, Ryan would never get over it. I really would lose my brother, and I just didn't know if I could live with that. Even if the thought of losing Carson for good might just actually kill me.

*Damned if I do, and damned if I don't.* I sighed. *Being a grownup really sucks sometimes. Does anyone want my subscription to adulthood? Because I'm pretty sure I'm done with it now.*

# 46

## CARSON

Vance had finally closed on a house and was actively moving into it. I hadn't been there just yet, but he'd sent me the link with the address just this morning, and now seemed like as good a time as any.

Bloodied and bruised, I showed up with a six-pack of beer, a succulent plant in a pot, and a pile of brand-new towels under my arm. He opened the front door when he heard me pull up and he grinned—until he saw my face.

His eyebrows rose as high as they could go. He sprinted over to me, took everything I'd brought along out of my hands, and gave me a serious look. "What the hell happened to you, bro?"

"Ryan," I said as if that one word explained it all. "I cleaned up. Does it still look that bad?"

He snorted and stepped aside to let me precede him up the flagstone path that led past a little fountain toward his front door. "If that's what you look like after you cleaned up, I'd hate to know what you looked like before. I think your nose is still bleeding."

I twisted to motion at all the stuff he was carrying. "Mom says you can never have enough towels and that single guys never have any that are in decent shape, so they're a housewarming gift from her.

The plant is from me. Apparently, those aren't easy to kill. The beer is from me too, but that's just because I wanted one and I wasn't sure you'd stocked up yet."

Vance chuckled and showed me inside. He deposited all the gifts on the kitchen counter and spread his arms open wide. "Fine. If you don't want to tell me why Ryan did that to you, allow me to give you the grand tour."

"I'm good with that." I waited for him to break open the six-pack and hand over a beer before I followed him through the spacious, open-concept design of the lower level of his new house.

Hardwood floors barely made a sound beneath my feet, the ceilings were high, and there were lots of large windows that offered spectacular views of the mountains and farmland surrounding the property. Vance grinned when he saw me looking around, pumping his eyebrows. "Yeah, I know. I did good. It's nice, right?"

He inclined his head toward the right, where a sprawling entertainment area took up one whole side of the house. It was covered in boxes, but he'd already mounted a massive flatscreen TV on the wall and a few bottles of booze sat on the bar in the far corner.

"This is what I like to call the Fun Zone," he said happily. "Many parties will be held here, but I'll wait until you're healed before I invite you. Don't want people thinking this is some kind of fight club."

I groaned. "It's not that bad. Seriously. It was one punch."

"Tell that to your nose." He pointed to the right, where a family-style kitchen and dining area took up the other side of the house. "It's also got a huge pantry, a wine cellar down that way, and a formal sitting area that I'm going to turn into a home cinema room."

"A home cinema room?" My face scrunched up before I could stop it and pain trickled through me like thousands of needles being stuck into my skull. "Ouch. Don't do that. Don't say stupid shit. I can't keep my face from screaming the subtitles of the stuff I'm not actually saying."

He laughed. "A home cinema is a necessity. Come check out the outside area. I've even got a pool, man. It's awesome."

"What's upstairs?" I asked once I'd seen the expansive backyard with the pool that definitely needed a bit of work.

He shrugged. "The bedrooms. Where the magic will happen."

"Oh, so by magic, you mean the disappointment?" I joked.

He tutted his tongue at me but then led me to a bench that had been built into the deck outside. Giving me a long onceover, he blew out a heavy breath and cocked his head at me. "Your stay of execution is over. Out with it. What did you do to Ryan to deserve that?"

"He caught me with Nova," I said.

Vance's eyes flew wide open, and he doubled over laughing. "Jeez. It feels like I just went back ten years. What the hell, Carson? You couldn't stop him from doing it again?"

"I could. I just didn't. Felt like he deserved a free shot."

Vance shook his head. "Another one? Methinks not, man, but okay. So what now? Are you still seeing her?"

"Yeah, for now." The pain in my chest was a lot worse than the pain in my face when I thought about breaking it off with her. "If he's going to keep putting himself between us, I'm not sure how long it's going to last. I really don't want it to end, but I'm starting to wonder if I'm crazy for even thinking it could work between us."

"You're not crazy." He winked at me. "Crazy in love, maybe, but not, like, batshit crazy. If you know what I mean."

"Whatever kind of crazy it is, I don't know what I'm going to do. You should've seen how upset she was after the fight. It did something to me. I don't want to keep doing that to her."

"Then maybe you should keep your distance for a while," he suggested. "That family has too much going on right now. Give 'em some time to figure their shit out. Let Ryan cool down and then, when all that has happened, sit him down and talk to him instead of letting him walk in on you getting naked with his sister."

"We weren't getting naked," I protested. "We'd actually just gotten dressed again."

Vance groaned. "So he interrupted the lovey dovey cuddling after? Somehow, I feel like that's even worse."

"It's not." I thought about Nova on her knees between my legs and what he would've walked in on if he'd been just a few minutes earlier, and that would've been much, much worse. "You really think I should keep my distance?"

He nodded slowly and moved his gaze back to the mountains in the distance. "It doesn't need to be forever, but you owe him some time to get used to the idea of you and Nova together as adults. Both of us owe him a lot more than that, but it's probably a good place to start."

I snorted. "I just let him hit me, like, two hours ago. I doubt I owe him anything else."

Vance arched an eyebrow at me. "In case you've missed it, he's not happy with us. At all. Can't say I blame him."

"You can't? Because I do. He seems to blame us for everything, but—"

"But nothing. You kissed his sister and left. I left with you. We stayed away for a decade, hardly ever made time for him, and now you're back, kissing his sister again, and his family is in all this trouble despite the sacrifices he made. He has a right to be pissed."

"None of that is our fault," I said. "Except the kissing. That's my fault, I guess, but it's not just a fling, Vance. It's more than that. I just don't know why he can't see it that way."

He shrugged. "Maybe he will, but he's going to need time."

"Nova is stressed out enough already." I sighed deeply as I thought it over. "This isn't going to help, is it?"

"Nope."

"So I'm keeping my distance," I decided out loud, not liking it but knowing he was right. "The last thing I want is to cause her pain. I want her to be happy." I didn't want to be away from her for any period of time, but at this point, my presence in her life was just making things worse. "I'm still going to help her, though."

He groaned. "What part of keeping your distance do you not understand?"

"I don't have the luxury of keeping my distance when it comes to the business end of things," I said, shaking my head. "George is going to accept that other offer if I don't do something. Neither of the

Murphy siblings can change that, and neither can Ryan's feelings about me. I need to help her while I still can. If I wait, their dad will sell the ranch and there won't be a damn thing we can do about it."

"Wait," he said slowly, drawing out the word. "In the past, it was all about helping *them*. The *family*. Now, all of a sudden, it's only about *her*?"

"No, it's not like that," I explained. "You know how much I've been wondering how I can help them and how I don't want them to lose the ranch, but then I realized that what I wanted to do before would've been tantamount to a handout."

"Which is what we've all been saying, but I'm glad you finally realized it."

My eyes rolled. "They were going to pay me back, which is why I didn't see it that way, but I don't know if I ever believed they would actually pay me back. Which got me wondering what all these big plans for the ranch are."

"I've wondered the same thing," he admitted. "Big property like that has got a lot to offer in the right hands."

"Exactly, so I asked her."

"You did?"

I laughed. "You don't have to sound so surprised. I have learned a thing or two about investing."

"Sure. Keep telling yourself that."

"I will. Thanks, dick."

We laughed.

He brought his beer back to his lips but gave me a pointed look before he took a sip. "So, what are the plans? Anything that might work?"

"Yeah, I think so." I laid it out for him, and excitement stirred inside me. Sure, things were a bit of a clusterfuck on a personal level with the Murphys right now, but this was business, and Nova's plans were solid. "If I can help her by investing in legitimate businesses, it won't be a handout and I'd get to support her in doing what she was meant to do. It's the best of both worlds."

"If it works, it could be a huge moneymaker for the ranch and the town." Vance paused. "Have you spoken to your financial advisor about it yet?"

"No, but I'm going to. I'm looking at putting some serious money into this, so I can't just swipe my card and hope for the best."

He gave me a conspiring look. "If you need someone else to invest, hit me up. This is a really good opportunity, even without the personal connection."

I chuckled, and pain exploded across my entire face, making me feel like my bones had caught fire. "Again, you don't have to sound so surprised, but I'll let you know when I've spoken to my guy."

"Do," Vance said easily, leaning back and looking out at his spectacular new view again. "I know you've had a bumpy landing, but it's damn good to be home, isn't it?"

I took in the sprawling green fields and the mountaintops jutting into the clear blue sky. "Yeah. Yeah, I guess it really is."

The knot that had been in the pit of my stomach since earlier evaporated. I hadn't made a mistake by coming home. This was where I belonged. I would work things out with Ryan or I wouldn't, but I had meant it when I'd told Nova I wasn't going anywhere. I was home now, and I was here to stay.

Even if her brother would never like it.

# 47

## NOVA

After a sleepless night of tossing and turning, I got up early and made sure everything was squared away at the bakery before I headed out to soccer practice. Cassidy had assured me she'd be okay alone as long as everything was baked and ready when she got there, and I had happily agreed to let her manage the store for the time being.

Soccer had been good for me yesterday and I was looking forward to another day on the field. Especially after that damn fight.

It didn't hurt that I would finally get to see Carson once I got to the school. I didn't know if Cassidy had spoken to Ryan yet, but I hadn't heard a word from him—or from my supposed boyfriend. Unease churned through me as I drove to the high school, hoping against all hope that he'd be there for football camp by the time I arrived.

If I could just know that he was okay, maybe I'd feel better too, but to my great disappointment, there was no sign of him when I showed up. Vance was on the field, running drills with the boys all by himself.

I tried to shove down the bitter disappointment as I climbed out of my truck and made my way to the girls. They grinned as I approached them, and after saying good morning, I blew my brand-new whistle and pointed to the equipment shed.

"We're going to need cones. Three rows. Line 'em up and divide yourselves into groups. After you warm up, we're going to do weave drills."

"What's that?" one of the girls asked.

Another groaned. "We have to dribble the ball with the inside and outside of our feet, circling right and left around each cone. Am I right?"

"Yep." I smiled at them. "Get used to these, ladies. I happen to think it's one of the best basic drills there is."

I blew the whistle again and the girls took off toward the shed. Leaving them to it, I crossed the field toward Vance. He was watching the football team warm up with a happy grin on his face, but it dimmed a little when he noticed me approaching.

"Good morning, Nova."

"Good morning," I said hesitantly. Vance and I had never been super close. In fact, we'd never talked much at all, but he was Carson's best friend and the only person around who might be able to tell me where the man of the hour was this morning. "Please just tell me he's not too hurt to be here."

Vance frowned, then seemed to realize what I was talking about, and he chuckled as he shook his head. "It'd take a lot worse than that to keep him away. He just had a few errands to run, but he'll be here tomorrow."

"Oh, okay."

He must've seen the desperation for information in my eyes because he took pity on me and clasped a hand on my shoulder. "He's fine, Nova. I swear. I saw him yesterday after the fight and he's all good. He went to the bank up in Crystal Springs today to talk about some money stuff with the manager over there."

"Oh."

He sighed and looked into my eyes. "You know, he was raving about your business ideas yesterday. It sounds like that's what he's gone to talk to the bank about, and honestly, I would've jumped on it too if you'd come to me. You've got a good head on your shoulders, Murphy. Never let anyone make you doubt that."

My eyebrows inched up as I stared at him. "Carson still wants to go through with that? I thought for sure that he wouldn't want to after everything that happened between him and Ryan."

"That's personal, and this is business." He scowled suddenly and blew his whistle, then barked instructions at a few of the boys before he turned back to me. "It's good business. He's going through with it."

I drew in a deep breath, relieved, but also still worried. Peering up at Vance, I decided to push him for more information. He had seemed relatively open to talking to me about it so far. "Is he okay? You said you saw him, and that he's fine, but is that really true? He..." I trailed off, clearing my throat before I finally found the words. "He didn't want me to help him yesterday and I haven't heard from him at all. I thought I might, but I haven't and I'm just worried."

"Don't be," Vance said, his attention split between me and the team. I knew I should be getting back to practice myself, but there was no way I would be able to focus the way I should without knowing.

When I didn't walk away, Vance glanced back down at me. "Is there anything else?"

"I, uh, yes." I held his gaze, uncomfortable but also not about to let that stop me. "If you saw him, that means you spoke to him, which also means you're a step ahead of me. He didn't want to talk to me at all after it happened, and at this point, I have no idea what's going on with him."

He shifted on his feet, gaze still flicking between me and the boys. "We've got a whole field full of teenagers we're supposed to be coaching here, Nova."

"I know, but the girls are setting up cones and the football players seem to be doing okay getting their asses kicked without you even being there, so the sooner you tell me, the sooner I'll let you get back to torturing them."

"I'm not torturing them," he protested. "I'm getting them in shape for the season."

"Either way, I need to know how Carson's doing. Not just his nose but *him*. How is he holding up?"

Vance was clearly reluctant to talk to me about this but also realized that I fully intended on standing my ground until he told me. Eventually, he heaved out a deep breath and looked at me again. "Ryan, Carson, and I have been friends for a long time."

"I know."

"Ryan said some pretty crazy stuff to Carson yesterday, the way I heard it."

I nodded. "I know that too."

"Then you should also know that Ryan has never wanted you and Carson together."

I held his gaze, not ashamed but still feeling pretty darn guilty. "I do know that. Thanks, but I still don't know how Carson is doing right now."

"Honestly?" Vance shook his head, his eyes suddenly far away as he shrugged. "All this stuff with Ryan is weighing him down. Your brother has a good heart, Nova, but so does Carson, and at this point, he doesn't know what the right thing is to do. Every move he makes seems to hurt someone, and he doesn't want that."

"Yeah, I get that." I nodded at him and started backing away. "Okay. Thanks, Vance. I appreciate you telling me and I'm sorry for the role I'm playing in all this drama."

He chuckled. "It's not your fault. It's no one's fault, really. It's just a whole bunch of circumstances that are making things a lot more complicated than they need to be."

I wasn't sure about it not being anyone's fault, but he sure was right about how complicated it all was. I turned my back on him and jogged over to the soccer team. Trying to focus, I demonstrated the drill and then watched the girls as they tried it, but I couldn't stop thinking about what Vance had said.

Knowing that the stuff with Ryan was weighing Carson down so much made me feel worse than ever. Ryan and Carson had their own issues to sort out. I got that. For starters, I now knew that Ryan felt betrayed by both Carson *and* Vance for the way they'd apparently forgotten about him after they'd left.

But that didn't involve me. How Ryan felt about Carson and me being together and the effect it was having on Carson? *That* involved me. They could sort everything else out on their own time, but I was starting to realize that I might lose Carson if I didn't stand up for him to my brother.

Ryan had no right to decide who I could and could not date. Whether he liked it or not, Carson and I had something that wasn't easy to find.

Our kind of chemistry and connection were rare, and it was precious, and I was pretty sure it was the reason why no one else had ever measured up for either of us. I couldn't let that come second anymore.

It deserved to be prioritized. With everything else going on, I hadn't realized just how much I had been neglecting it until now. *No more, though.*

Ryan could rant and rave at me as much as he liked. He could stomp his feet and bang his fists on his chest. Hell, he could really be a stubborn ass and never speak to me again, but I needed to set him straight about a few things.

I lifted my chin as resolve grew in my chest. I'd been a bystander in all of this for too long, feeling too guilty to do much, but that was over now. I was going to stand up to my brother and I was going to do it soon—before Carson started thinking that he didn't mean enough for me to make my voice heard or that I didn't want this as much as he did.

I wanted it at least as much, if not more, and I wasn't going to let anything stand in the way of that anymore.

This time, no matter what, Ryan was going to listen to me and I wasn't going to be deterred by any temper tantrums. I was going to tell him how I felt, and if he didn't like it, then that was his problem. Not mine. Not anymore.

# 48

## CARSON

Having decided to take matters into my own hands, I drove out to the ranch to talk to Nova's parents. After I'd hit up my money guy to make the funds available, I'd called Mara and made an appointment, and they knew I was on my way.

Ryan was going to fucking hate me for going over his head like this, but I needed to take action. I couldn't let his resentment stop me from moving forward with this, so here I was, pulling up to his parents' house and wondering how they were going to take my offer.

I opened the door, nerves swirling through me as I thought about how much was at stake. This wasn't just a game or even a season at risk. If I failed here today, Nova's whole life could change course. Generations of their family's hard work and sacrifice would be lost with the property.

No pressure or anything.

I dragged in a deep breath as I strode up to their front door, but before I could knock, Mara opened it. She looked so much like Nova that it made something deep inside me ache with longing. It had only been about twenty-four hours since I'd last seen her, but even that had been way too long.

I'd never been needy in a relationship, but I felt off-kilter all of a sudden. Like I needed her with me right now just to regain my balance. But there was a reason I hadn't called to tell her I was coming, and that reason hadn't changed.

*Get it together, Drake. There's too much riding on this for you to turn into a lovesick fool right now.*

Mara smiled and gave me a quick hug. "I have to admit, honey, this is quite a surprise. Is everything alright? You sounded so serious on the phone."

"I know. I'm sorry. I didn't mean to alarm you." I hugged her back, then stepped out of her embrace and followed her into the house.

I'd all but grown up in the place. All the furniture was still exactly where it had always been and the delectable scent of Mara's cooking still hung in the air. I wasn't sure why, but it always smelled like vanilla, lemon, and homemade cookies in here.

The only thing that had changed since I'd been a kid was that there were always some new pictures on the walls. Pictures of Nova and Ryan as adults now joined the memories Mara liked to have in plain sight.

The pressure on my insides mounted. If I couldn't convince the Murphys today to take my offer, this would all be gone. They'd be moving on and the house would probably be unrecognizable one day soon.

My breath stalled in my lungs at the thought of never coming here again. *So many memories.*

I didn't know how they could stand the idea of losing this place, but I sure couldn't. Mara gave me a sad smile when she noticed me looking around.

"It's good to have you back in our home, Carson," she said softly. "We've missed having you around."

"I'm sure you haven't missed having to feed three teenage boys instead of just one," I said, trying to keep my tone light.

She chuckled. "Well, maybe not that part so much, but I kind of enjoyed cooking for you all. It always makes a mother feel good when the kids enjoy her food so much that there's never any leftovers."

We walked into the living room where George was already waiting. He got up to shake my hand, his hair so silver these days that very little of his natural deep brown remained. "Carson, it's good to see you, son, but I'm a little confused as to why you needed to see us so urgently. Have a seat."

After I released his hand, I sat down on the chair he motioned me into and prepared myself to jump right into the pitch I'd spent all night and all morning rehearsing. "Thanks for agreeing to see me on such short notice."

"Of course," he said. "What's going on?"

"Ryan told me you've received an offer for the ranch as a whole, and I wanted to speak to you about another option."

"Another option?" Mara asked as she came into the room carrying a tray of lemonade in glasses. "What other option?"

She glanced at her husband, but he shrugged. George's skepticism shone in his eyes as he looked at me. "If there was another option, I'm sure we'd have been aware of it by now."

"No, sir. This particular option only became available earlier today after I spoke with my financial advisor."

He cocked his head, reluctant, but rolled his hand to show me to continue. I drew in a deep breath, gratefully accepting the lemonade from Mara but not taking a sip yet. "I want to invest in the property."

Mara sat down and gave me a curious look. "Well, we know that, honey. You want to purchase the part of the property Nova's cottage and the bakery are on. Ryan's told us all about that already."

"That was the offer that was on the table previously, but this is a different offer. An offer to invest rather than purchase."

She frowned. "Invest? Invest in what?"

"The businesses Nova wants to start here," I responded.

George sighed. "I'm not sure a bigger bakery and coffee shop are going to cut it, son. We don't want her to lose her businesses either, but she'd be able to move those into town if we sold."

"Sure, of course, but if you agree to let me invest, it wouldn't just be in the existing business. It would be in all the different ventures she's got in mind for the future."

"Like what?" Mara asked. "She's mentioned a few things to us, but nothing that we think will generate enough income to allow us to keep the property. It's all a bit of a pipe dream, isn't it?"

"I don't think it is," I said respectfully. "I've done extensive research and I asked my financial advisor to look into it as well. He agrees that if the ranch is developed to its full potential, it would be a sound investment that would allow you to not only keep the property, but to profit from it again as well."

George exhaled slowly. "Developed to its full potential, huh? Considering that you're talking about Nova's plans, I know you're not thinking of breaking it all down to build a resort, so what do you have in mind?"

"When I spoke to her, she mentioned a few ideas, like starting a Christmas tree farm and opening up an event space with venues, as well as a few orchards that could double as outdoor options for weddings and parties. She would also be able to expand on the bakery, open a restaurant instead of just having a coffee shop, and complement it all with accommodations. Either a B&B, or cabins, or something like that. You could also still have your cattle, George, but Ryan could help you upgrade and modernize. My financial advisor will also send over a few ideas for increasing meat sales, and then, of course, there would still be the hogs and the horses."

"You want to do all that and still keep the livestock?" he asked, clearly not quite onboard with the plan yet. "I'm not sure how that would work, son."

"Nova is going to prepare a business plan that lays it all out, sir, but in short, you'll still be a rancher. Ryan would have sections of the property for the farming operations he has in mind, and Nova would start and manage the rest of the businesses."

George's eyes were firm on mine, searching as if he was looking for something he couldn't find. "What do you get out of this? My understanding from Ryan was that they were going to pay you back if you purchased that section of the property, but if you're just going to be giving us money to start all these businesses and upgrade the things that are already here, what are you expecting in return?"

"Not much," I replied honestly. "I just want to see you thriving."

"It's an investment, George," Mara said. "I'm sure he'll receive a percentage of the profits as a return."

"The exact numbers still have to be worked out, but yes, probably. It'll be an investment in the businesses to be operated on the property and I'd be happy to take whatever percentage y'all are comfortable with."

"And we'd keep the property?" George asked thoughtfully. "As a whole?"

"Yes, sir."

He nodded slowly, then checked his watch and got up. "I'll consider it, and I won't sign anything until I've given you an answer. Thanks for coming to talk to us face to face, Carson. I appreciate it."

I stood and offered him my hand. He grasped it warmly, giving me a final nod before he released me and left, undoubtedly off to wrap up his chores in time for dinner.

Mara watched him go, her eyes so like her children's that I'd always felt like I knew her so much better than I actually did. Once the door shut behind her husband, she swung her gaze to mine and inspected my face, lingering on the blackish eye and my swollen nose.

"What happened to you?" she asked curiously.

I shrugged, not wanting to rat out her own son to her. "I had a disagreement with someone."

"Ryan," she said knowingly. When I frowned, she chuckled. "I'm his mother, honey. Nova's too. A mother always knows these things."

I held her gaze but was unsure how much she knew or what to tell her. "If it makes you feel any better, I deserved it."

"You two have always been rough on each other. Even growing up, you kept each other in line and made it very clear when you disagreed with one other. You always butted heads like brothers. Still do, apparently."

I looked back at her, seeing that maternal softness in her eyes even if she wasn't looking at one of her own kids. "Do you think George will really consider my offer?"

"Yes," she said simply. "He will. We both will."

"Okay. Well, then, I guess I'd better get going." I smiled at her. "Thank you for your time, Mara. It's always good to see you."

"You too," she said, rising to walk me to the door. "I should be thanking you, though. I know you're doing this for Nova. She never does anything for herself. Just as stubborn as her brother and her father. Thank you for having her back, Carson, and just so you know, you have our blessing."

I stared at her and nodded, something like hope blooming in my chest. Then George walked back in, waving in the direction of the paddock closest to their house. "Ryan's already out there, which means that you and I can sit back down and go over the numbers. Let's have a real discussion about it while you're here."

Surprised, I went back to my seat and thought about all the information I'd received from my financial people this morning. Mara moved to join us but stopped when Nova's truck pulled up outside.

George's eyes darted toward it, but Mara shook her head at him. "I'll get her and we'll leave you men to talk."

Strangely, I was grateful for that. Not because I thought she should *leave the men to talk*, but because having Nova in here right now would make things significantly more difficult for me. Plus, if Nova was here, someone might think that Ryan should be too, and he might come out swinging again.

It was starting to feel like I had a real chance of making a deal here, and he would definitely be a monkey wrench in the works right now. If his dad went for this, I'd go talk to him about it later. For now, I was glad when Mara went outside and left me with George.

"Alright, son. Talk to me," he said once we were alone.

Mentally rolling up my sleeves, I leaned forward and forced myself to shut out everything else. Right here and right now, the only thing that mattered was this.

# 49

## NOVA

There was nothing quite as frustrating as being ready to stand up to someone and not being able to find them. That was the position I was in. I had searched high and low for Ryan but didn't find a trace of him anywhere.

Out of sheer desperation, I went to my parents' place, not really thinking he'd be there at this hour, but it was about the only place I hadn't looked for him yet. As I parked outside their house, I saw another truck parked around the side and I frowned.

*Is that Carson's truck? It can't be. Can it?*

My heart clawed its way to my throat. I climbed out of my truck and ran into my mom instead of my brother on my way into their house. "Hey, baby. Let's go for a walk?"

I craned my neck in an attempt to see past her, but she stepped in my way and took my arm, leading me firmly in the opposite direction. I glanced at her, so damn confused that I let her pull me away. "What's going on, Mom? Have you seen Ryan, and was that Carson's truck?"

"Ryan is rounding up the herd for Daddy, and yes, that was Carson's truck," she said excitedly. "That's why I don't want you going in there right now. I want them to be able to talk business without any stubborn mules getting in the way."

"Okay, Mama. You're going to have to back up a minute. What business are they talking about? Carson's not pressing charges against Ryan, is he?"

Mom laughed as she shook her head. "No, honey. It's nothing like that, but thanks for confirming my suspicions. Carson sure wasn't eager to snitch on his friend. I ought to wring Ryan's neck for doing that to him, though."

*Well, I don't disagree with you there.*

As we walked through the garden, realization dawned on me. "Wait, if he's not here to talk about that, is he here about investing?"

I could practically see the stars in her eyes as she nodded and beamed at me. "He said something about making a deal before we accepted the other offer, and he and Daddy have been talking almost ever since."

My feet faltered, Disbelief made me feel lightheaded. "Daddy's actually listening to him?"

"He sure is," Mom said, using her grip on my arm to pull me back to the table in her favorite spot out here. "Carson told him about all the ideas you have, and that even his financial advisor thinks they could work."

My head spun as I sat down. "I've told you about those ideas dozens of times, but you never thought they would work before. What's changed?"

"Well, we've got an investor now, honey," she said gently. "Even Dad has become inclined to believe it's time for a change, but starting businesses like that requires capital. A lot of it, which is money we just don't have."

"Ryan mentioned looking for investors before, though," I said, inhaling deeply and hoping the fresh air would clear my mind. "He told me Daddy said no."

"Well, that's because your father didn't want a bunch of rich strangers coming out here telling him how to run a business he's been running his whole life. Plus, it could've taken years to find the right people to work with. It's kind of like a marriage in that sense. You can't just take money from the first person you meet."

Hope suddenly streaked through me like a lightning bolt. "Does that mean you think there's a chance he's going to take Carson as an investor?"

"I sure do." Tears of joy filled her eyes as she nodded at me. "This might just be the opportunity we've been praying for, honey. Dad could sort of retire and let Ryan manage the ranch without us having to leave. With money like Carson's, we could start turning a few of the old barns into venues right away. We'd have to see about the upgrades and everything else, but I think—" Emotion clogged her throat.

I reached for her, winding my arms around her neck and burying my face in her hair, on the verge of tears myself. I'd been happy when Carson had said he'd be willing to invest, but I hadn't thought there was a real chance of Dad accepting it.

Especially not just like that, but if they were still in there, then maybe we really did have a chance. Mom hugged me back, holding me for a long time before she pulled away to look into my eyes. "All of this is because of you, baby. Thank you."

I hugged her again, not really knowing what to say. Once I let her go, she and I sat in the garden in silence, waiting with bated breath for Dad and Carson to emerge. When they did, they stopped on the porch and shook hands, and then Carson turned and strode toward his truck.

He looked a little like he'd gone through a meat grinder, and I felt awful. Mom smiled at me as she got up. "I'd better go check in with Daddy. Tell Carson thanks from me."

She took off and I jumped up, jogging over to intercept Carson before he climbed into his truck. He blinked hard when he saw me. There was something dark in those vibrant green eyes that I hated seeing there.

"Your dad is going to accept my investment," he said, but his voice sounded off. Hollow almost. "He's excited."

He didn't reach for me or look at me in any special way, and where there should have been joy and relief in my very being, there was only worry, and it was getting heavier by the minute. "What's going on, Carson?"

"I know a few contractors who can start working next week. I called them on the way over here just in case. Your dad has their phone numbers."

"Okay, that's great, but I wasn't asking about that."

Slowly moving his gaze away from mine, he looked around the property like he was sizing it up. "By fall, you could have a few new income streams. Hopefully, you'll be ready for the winter wedding and event season. It's kind of hard to imagine this place teeming with people all dressed up, but it's going to be good for you."

I lifted my arms to hug him, but he took a deft step away and shook his head. That worry within me suddenly got so heavy that it felt like my chest was about to be crushed. "Carson?"

He hesitated, his eyes filled with remorse and regret when he finally brought them back to mine. "Maybe us getting together wasn't such a good idea after all, Nova. I understand your hesitation now. I, uh, I won't bother you anymore."

"What?" I took a step closer to him, feeling like his words were slicing me open. "You're not bothering me, Carson. You could never bother me and I wasn't hesitant."

He gave his head a slight shake. "No, you were hesitant, and I really *do* get it now. You were right all along. Ryan is never going to accept this and he's going to keep getting between us. You need to focus on your family. They're going to need you, and if all these businesses are going to work, you're going to need them. That can't happen if you and Ryan are constantly fighting, and if I stick around, you will be."

"No. That's not—"

"It's okay, Nova." For the first time today, he managed a small smile when he looked at me. "I don't want you getting hurt. Not because of me." He pulled in a big breath of air, filling his lungs with oxygen before he started toward his truck again. "I'll see you around, Nova. Good luck."

He climbed into his truck and I watched him drive away, knowing that he wasn't coming back anytime soon. My heart shattered, and pain seared through me, hurting me in places I hadn't even known could hurt.

Tears spilled down my cheeks, and I wrapped my arms around my torso to hold myself together. I kept praying he would come back. That he would suddenly turn around and hear me out, but when his truck disappeared around the far bend, I knew it really was over.

My mouth dropped open and a soft sob spilled out of me, but the sound triggered a much more primal response. Anger.

*Ryan* was responsible for this. It was his fault that Carson thought we didn't have a chance. If it hadn't been for my boneheaded brother, my heart would still be in one piece.

Heartbroken and pissed off wasn't a good combination for me, and I spun on my heels, this time intent on not stopping until I'd found the asshole. As it turned out, he was done with the herd and I found him in one of the barns.

I walked in, and the jerk had the nerve to narrow his eyes at me when he saw who it was. "Nova? You here to apologize?"

"No, I'm here to talk, and for once in our fucking lives, you're going to listen to me." I stopped a few feet away from him. When he realized I was crying, he looked shocked, then worried, but before he could say a single word or ask a single question, I lit into him. "You had no right to storm into my house yesterday or to pick a fight with Carson for being with me. It's not cute anymore, Ryan. It was uncalled for even when I was in high school, but now? Now it's just plain unacceptable."

He scoffed, standing his ground now that he knew what it was about. "Date whoever you want, Nova, but stay away from my friends. No doubt he's the one who made you cry anyway, so I guess I don't have to be worried about that anymore. There's a whole world of people out there for you. It's not my fault you went after the one guy who was always going to hurt you, so don't take your anger at him out on me."

"It's not him I'm angry at," I yelled, feeling my cheeks heat and my heart race. "I'm twenty-seven years old and I get to decide who I want to be with. I don't need your input or your permission, and I sure as hell don't need you barging in on private moments and trying to break the guy's damn nose. He hasn't hurt me. *You* have."

Ryan shook his head at me. "I haven't even seen you today, little sister."

"No, but you have ruined any kind of friendship you might've had with Carson and whatever relationship you could've had with Cassidy, for that matter. Oh, and you also ended my relationship with Carson, so I guess we've got that in common. We've both lost him."

"Don't bring Cassidy into this," he snapped, but he looked struck by my words.

I huffed out a breath through my nose. "She's already in this, *big brother*. You might not have realized it before now, but she doesn't take kindly to this kind of shit. Unlike you, Cassidy believes in love. Believes in respect, and integrity, and even when she doesn't believe that someone's doing the right thing, she'll fight like hell for their right to do it. In this case, though, she believes that Carson is right for me because she's not blind and she doesn't insist on sticking her head in the sand. The way you've been acting is revolting and she knows it."

As he opened his mouth to respond, I started backing away, my heart still in pieces and my insides feeling strangely empty now that I'd told him everything I'd been holding back for so long. I spun to leave, but before I stormed out, I gave him one last look. "Carson is investing in the ranch. You should thank him for saving this place. Just, you know, be sure to show some fucking gratitude. As of about twenty minutes ago, you and I owe him everything we're about to have."

# 50

## CARSON

I looked through the rundown farmhouse on the outskirts of town with Vance. Having officially fired Frank for a second time, my new realtor turned to face me, smiling but seeming nervous as he tried to assess my feelings about the place.

"It's a real fixer-upper," he said. "Like I mentioned on the phone, I do other, newer listings, but nothing with this kind of acreage. I know this is a lot of work, though. Maybe more than you're willing to take on?"

I shrugged. "Let me take a look around. I'll let you know."

The guy literally bowed as he left us, hurrying back to his car outside.

Vance arched an eyebrow at me. "You're seriously considering this place? It's a dump, and it's only two bedrooms. Why don't you just buy something new, or go back to your original plan and build? Or is that why you're looking at this? Are you going to tear it down and build here?"

"No," I said, my head shaking. "I don't know actually. I might eventually tear it down or do something else with it, but it's fine for now."

He made a confused face at me. "It is?" Pointing up, he tilted his head back. "That's a hole, Carson. In the ceiling. Right through the roof. I don't really see how that's going to be fine."

"I'll get someone to fix it," I said, really not able to bring myself to care.

I started heading toward the tiny kitchen and he fell into step beside me. "Okay, that's enough. What happened? I know you didn't get into it with Ryan again. There are no new bruises on your face. Is it his parents? Did they turn you down?"

"Nah. They're taking the money. You're officially looking at the guy who's investing in the dawn of a whole new era at Red Stone Ranch."

"Wow, that's awesome." He grinned. "Congratulations. Is that it, though? Are you sad because it's going to cost you more than you thought it would or is there something else going on?"

I shrugged, my gaze roaming around the kitchenette and living area. I finally told him about the other possibility I had on the horizon. "I'm rethinking my retirement."

"Whoa. What the fuck?"

"I'm done on the field, but there are a few opportunities for me to become a broadcaster, which is something I think I could be good at."

"Wow, that's huge." Disbelief shone from his eyes and his jaw went slack. "Just the other day, we were talking about how good it was to be home. What the fuck happened?"

"This will still be home. Even if I do take one of the jobs I've been offered, I'll always come back here. It would just mean being gone for a while at a time, which means that, for now, I'll only need a place to land. Nothing fancy. Besides, a two-bedroom place is right up my alley if I'm going to be a bachelor forever."

Vance groaned and sank to his haunches before he darted a glare up at me. "I can't believe this is happening, man. Nova broke up with you. Is that it?"

"Nope."

"What then?"

I sighed, trying to ignore the pain that radiated from my very blood when I told him the truth. "*I* broke up with her."

His face went ashen. He straightened back up and clasped my shoulder. "I'm sorry, man. I wouldn't have suggested that you keep your distance if I thought you were going to take it as having to break up with her."

"That's not why I did it." *God, why does this hurt so much?* "It just wasn't meant to be right now. I told you how upset she was after the fight the other day, right?"

He nodded. I blew out a heavy breath, feeling like my lungs had grown too small to keep it in there anymore. "If I didn't end it, she just would've kept on getting upset. Every time Ryan and I saw each other, he would've come at me. Ultimately, she's the one who would pay the price for it. I just realized that I couldn't do that to her."

"I'm sorry, bud. That sucks," he said sympathetically. "It doesn't mean you have to be a bachelor forever, though. There are plenty of other women out there without surly older brothers. Many of those women even live in this town. You don't have to leave."

"I'm not leaving. At worst, I'll be commuting," I reasoned. "I'm happy to be back. I really am. I just need to reassess some things."

"Broadcasting?" he asked, cocking his head at me. "Funny. I've never heard you talking about it before."

I shrugged. "I wasn't thinking about doing it before, but now?"

He sighed. "I could ask Jessie to set you up with one of her friends? Another friend. Not Nova, obviously. I know you're not ready to start seeing someone else, but maybe you just need to be reminded there are other fish in the sea."

"Thanks, but no thanks." I didn't hesitate to turn him down. "I haven't forgotten that there are other women out there, or that they don't have surly older brothers, or that there is life after Nova romantically. I'm just not interested right now. I've only ever felt that spark with her and I'm tired of chasing it."

All true.

With hindsight being twenty-twenty and all, I'd realized that I'd been chasing that spark for a decade. I'd searched far and wide, and yet, I'd only found it again when I'd come back here and reconnected with her. I wasn't thinking of giving broadcasting a try so I could go search for it someplace else.

Eventually, maybe I would, but for now, I just felt like I needed something to fill the void. Vance followed me through the rest of the house, not looking any more excited about it when we left than he had when we'd arrived.

"Are you sure about this?" he asked. "I kept waiting for something to jump out at me, but it didn't happen. There's just no real potential here, man. Not that I can see, anyway."

"Yeah, I know," I replied. "It's perfect. I'm going to make an offer. It's a good-sized property and I'll have someone fix it up while I'm going through the motions to secure a sports broadcasting gig back in LA."

"Don't give up yet, bro. Please? You've got a lot going here and I know you've been through the wringer with the Murphys since we've been back, but there's more to being home than just them."

"I know, which is why this will still be home."

He climbed into the passenger seat of my truck, but when I headed toward his place, he shook his head. "If you're serious about broadcasting and about making an offer on that place, we need to go get a drink to celebrate."

I barked out a dry laugh. "You really want to go out to celebrate me getting a house that's practically falling in on itself?"

"Hey, it's a fresh start. Besides, you said you'd get someone to fix it up. You're also about to embark on a whole new career path. It's not something I thought you'd ever be interested in, but if you are, then that's something else we need to drink to."

I wasn't in the mood at all, but I let him convince me and eventually drove to Moe's instead. All day, I'd been waiting to feel something inside, but it felt like I'd had everything that should've been in there ripped out.

Of course, that changed when we walked into Moe's and I saw Nova there with her friends. She was at the bar, not exactly laughing or looking like she was having a good time, but she was there, and suddenly, my heart and soul were back.

But they were gray and stormy. Just not feeling right.

Bitterness swirled through me like acrid smoke. I knew it wasn't fair, but in that moment, I was pissed at her. Pissed for letting her get under my skin when it should've been clear from the very beginning that we could never be together.

"Maybe we should try another bar," Vance muttered when he saw who I was staring at. "The brewery? I really liked that—"

I shook his hand off my shoulder. "We're not leaving."

He let out a deep, pained groan. "Alright. If you insist on torturing yourself, then I guess that's your business."

Without a word, I walked to the other side of the counter and signaled to the bartender that we wanted two beers. He brought them over, and Vance paid him before leading me away. I knew he was trying to keep some distance between Nova and me, but it wasn't helping.

All that emptiness I'd been feeling was still filled with all kinds of negative shit I'd never felt before. Underneath it all, there was also regret, and longing, and even fucking uncertainty. *So much uncertainty.*

I had never felt as uncertain about absolutely fucking everything in my life as I had since I'd come back to Silver Springs. Feeling even more bitter than I had before, I watched her from across the bar.

Vance started talking to me about something, but I wasn't listening. Wasn't even pretending. I was too busy trying to hear what Nova was saying to her friends, even though I knew that there was no chance of it happening.

The sun was setting outside. Happy hour was starting. Moe's was getting fuller by the minute. There was way too much chatter and laughter in the air for me to hear her all the way from over here, and yet, I was borderline itchy just for that. Just for the sound of her voice.

Somehow, seeing her wasn't enough. I wanted to hear her. Feel her. Shit, I even wanted to smell her.

"Carson?" Vance broke into my thoughts, a concerned frown between his brows. "Are you okay? You look like you're going to be sick."

Before I could lie and tell him I was fine, a man approached her. A young guy. Probably around her own age. He walked right up to her like he had every right in the world to get close. Then he leaned in, smiling flirtatiously, and said something that made her look at him.

Only vaguely aware that Vance was still with me, I suddenly saw red. The itch won, and before I even knew what I was doing, I was up, across the bar, and standing between them, glowering at this guy I'd never seen before and defending the honor of a woman who wasn't mine to defend.

Not so long ago, Vance had told me that I wasn't batshit crazy. That I was just crazy in love. But as I stood there, ready to beat this guy to a pulp for just smiling at her, I had a feeling he'd been wrong. Some time between now and then, I'd lost it. I'd gone completely fucking insane and the worst part of all was that I wouldn't have had it any other way.

# 51

## NOVA

Carson appeared out of thin air. I had no idea where he'd come from, but one minute, Andy had been in front of me, and the next, I found myself staring at Carson's broad back instead. He was breathing hard, his shoulders rising and falling fast and his spine ramrod straight.

Biceps flexing, he crossed his arms, and the next thing I knew, poor Andy deflated like a balloon and slunk away. Carson hadn't even said anything. All he'd done was stand in front of me, and yet, it seemed like he'd scared Andy half to death.

My heart went wild in my chest, righteous anger taking control of my pulse. I scowled at his back. *The nerve of this guy.*

Not two days ago, he'd told me he would see me around like I meant nothing more to him than some distant neighbor he only walked past every once in a while, and now here he was, scaring away a friend who'd only been trying to talk to me.

Indignation fueled the anger building in my belly and my scowl deepened. I didn't know what to think but I didn't want to let myself get my hopes up that it had meant anything either. Part of me wanted to believe it did, that he hadn't wanted another man talking to me because he still wanted me to be his, but I couldn't let that part win.

Focusing on the anger and indignation instead, I acted on instinct and smacked Carson's arm so hard that my fingers stung. "What the hell do you think you're doing? That guy went to high school with me. He's harmless, not that you should care."

Carson turned around slowly, blinking like he was coming out of a trance and wasn't even sure what he was doing here. His gaze met mine, those greens so electric and alive with emotion that for one foolish moment, I thought he was going to tell me that he'd made a mistake.

My heart skipped and my soul reached for his. I felt like the world was finally about to turn right way up again. I knew I shouldn't forgive him too easily, but I didn't know if I was strong enough not to. All I wanted was for him to realize that Ryan didn't have to be in our way. That I would shove him out of our way myself if he tried to come between us again.

Before I could even think about offering my forgiveness, Carson opened his mouth and all that hope came crashing down around me at the lame excuse he offered. "You looked like you needed help."

"I didn't." I hadn't been prepared for how much it was going to hurt to be so close to him again, but the pain of it took my breath away. I struggled for air, my lungs not wanting to function if it meant breathing in his spicy scent, and I stumbled back to put a few feet of space between us.

Once I was what I thought would be a safe distance away, I folded my arms and glared at him. "I was fine. I *am* fine. You should go and enjoy your night. There are plenty of women here who would love some attention from the famous Carson Drake."

A shimmer of pain crossed his eyes, and I wondered why the hell we were even talking if it was hurting us both so much. I blinked away tears, feeling so damn foolish for thinking that he might've come over in an attempt to apologize. To win me back.

My throat started closing up, completely clogged with the sobs I was fighting as I stared at him through narrowed eyes. "Go, Carson. I didn't ask for your help and I didn't need it. Just go. Please."

Almost like it was an involuntary movement, he took a step closer to me, invading my personal space and making me want to reach for him. That pain in his eyes was so raw that I almost started hoping again, but I gave my head a hard shake even as he frowned at me like he didn't understand the words coming out of my mouth.

"I don't want any other women, Nova," he said, sounding so damn sure that my heart broke a little bit more. "I don't care who wants my attention. I don't want theirs."

"Yeah, well, evidently, you don't want mine anymore either, so I'm still at a loss for what exactly you're doing over here."

His dark eyebrows tugged together, confusion written across his furrowed brow. "You think I don't *want* you anymore?"

I scoffed, hating that *this* was the conversation we were having after *the end*. It made me feel pathetic. Like I was fishing for him to say, "Of course, I want you, Nova. I've always wanted you and I'm never going to want anyone else."

Silently berating myself, I lifted my chin in the air and hoped with everything in me that he didn't see the tears swimming in my eyes. "You made yourself pretty clear the last time we spoke. You don't want to be with me. It wasn't a good idea, remember?"

"No." He shook his head over and over again, squeezing his eyes shut before opening them again. "That's not why I broke it off. It wasn't because I want to be with other people. Do you?"

*What I want is to not answer that question.*

The truth was so damn obvious and it was staring him right in the face, but if he couldn't see it, if he couldn't see how much this was hurting me precisely because I *didn't* want anyone else, then he wasn't looking hard enough. And that wasn't my problem. I wasn't going to beg him to take me back.

I nearly cried with relief when my phone started buzzing in my pocket. *Saved by technology.*

Breaking eye contact with Carson, I finally felt like I could breathe again. I reached for it, thinking it was Cassidy and planning on telling her where we were so she could join us, but it wasn't her. It was my dad.

My heart suddenly stammered, my very bones suddenly knowing

that something massive had gone wrong. Dad didn't just call to chat or to check in.

"Hello?" I pressed the finger of my free hand into my ear in the hopes that I'd be able to hear my father. "Daddy? What's wrong?"

"It's the bakery, Nova! It's on fire!"

For just a second, I thought I'd misheard him. What he'd said couldn't possibly be true, but when he ended the call without saying anything else, I knew the worst had happened.

My entire body started shaking. Fear unlike anything I'd ever felt swept through me. I'd put my heart, soul, blood, sweat, and tears into that place. It was part of me, and if it burned down, I had no idea what I would do.

*No! I can't lose it! It's not going to be gone.*

Panic raced through me and my hands shook so badly that I dropped my phone. My blood drained out of my whole head and not just my cheeks. Frantically looking around for my purse, I almost forgot about the phone until it was dangling right in front of my face.

"What happened, Nova?" Carson asked as I snatched the device from between his fingers, his green eyes burning intensely into mine. "Is it your dad?"

"The bakery is burning." Those were the only words I could get out before I started running, pushing through the crowd as fast as I could, but they weren't moving as quickly as I needed them to.

A strong arm wrapped around my shoulders and I glanced up, seeing that Carson had come to my rescue once again. As soon as he did, people suddenly started jumping out of our way like they were feeling the urgency of the situation. When I saw the look on his face, I understood why.

I didn't know what *I* looked like right now, but Carson sure looked serious. His jaw was clenched so tight that his teeth were at risk of cracking. His posture was rigid and his eyebrows were mashed together. He looked like a man on a mission.

I was still hurt by him. Still angry. But in that moment, gratitude overwhelmed me. I let him rush me out of there, and I didn't protest when he ran us to his truck instead of mine. "I'll drive. Get in."

Throwing open the door, I practically dove inside and he was behind the steering wheel not a second later. Tension thrummed in the air as he turned over the engine and slammed the truck into reverse. Gunning it out of the parking lot, he put his foot down and got us to the ranch before the fire trucks had even arrived.

Neither of us said a word on our way over, but Carson's movements were jerky with stress and I couldn't stop repeating my new mantra in my head. *It's not gone. I'm not going to lose it. It's not gone.*

Dad and Ryan were already there when we raced onto the ranch, and I fell to pieces when I saw the plume of black smoke leaking out of my beloved bakery. Carson hit the brakes, tires skidding to a stop on the gravel. He twisted toward the door and yanked it open before he glanced back at me.

"Stay safe, Nova." Then he was gone, running to Dad and Ryan who were trying to put out the flames.

Dad tossed him a spare fire extinguisher. I wanted to go help, but shock held me immobile. For what felt like the longest time, I just sat there, staring at the glowing red inferno devouring the place that was my sanctuary.

Numbness spread from the core of my being to my limbs, my extremities, and even my tongue. Dad, Ryan, and Carson each held a fire extinguisher and they were bravely fighting to keep the flames contained, but to me, it felt futile.

This wasn't some kind of stovetop fire or a candle that had only just engulfed the table underneath it. It was a full-blown structure fire. Flames licked the ceiling inside the building and the smoke rising from it got thicker and thicker.

I hadn't even climbed out of the car yet, but I could already feel the heat. It was blazing. The kind that could roast a human being like a Thanksgiving turkey but in much less time.

My gaze flicked up and I saw the illumination from the fire lighting up the night sky. This was my worst nightmare come to life and what made it even more terrible was that the three men I loved most in the world were right in the path of that thing.

A loud crash rang out from inside and one of the windows

exploded, sending shattered glass flying out in a strangely beautiful, sparkling rain. I shook so hard that I couldn't breathe. Sobs rolled through me as I finally jumped out to help.

Dad, Ryan, and Carson had fallen back when the explosion had happened. They exchanged glances that said they'd realized what I'd known all along. Fighting this fire with a few extinguishers and a lot of grit wasn't going to cut it.

The bakery was lost. The best we could do now was to hope the flames didn't spread.

# 52

## CARSON

The sound of sirens pierced through the roaring noise of the fire. The blaring came closer with every beat of my heart, and yet, I already knew they were too late. A portion of the ceiling had just collapsed and the rest of the building probably wasn't far behind.

At this point, the firefighters would put it out to prevent it from jumping to the surrounding landscape, but the bakery was beyond saving. Despair trickled into me, and I fell back, getting into position next to Ryan to aim my extinguisher at the embers that were being spat toward the permanent market stalls.

We were trying to stop the fire from reaching even more fuel, which the wooden structures Nova had erected for the original market vendors would certainly provide. Working together to fight the fire, Ryan and I were in sync once more, as if we could read the other's mind and knew exactly where to go to provide backup, but not even that helped.

The blaze was out of control, and at this rate, it would be a miracle if it only took the bakery with it. With a loud honking of horns, the fire trucks finally arrived. The firefighters hit the ground running, throwing open hatches and seamlessly taking their places.

Watching them was fascinating until I remembered what they were here to do and who this place belonged to. A thud at my side alerted me to Ryan setting down his extinguisher, and I did the same. Our work here, however useless it might've been, was done.

As I looked around, I saw that we'd at least managed to save the market stalls scattered around, but the rest was definitely a total loss. I turned toward my friend and my heart wrenched at the look of utter devastation on his face.

Ryan's cheeks, neck, and brow were smeared with black and shiny with sweat, his jaw slack and his mouth twisted in pain as he watched the firefighters fan out. They were calling out to each other, running with hoses and trying to contain the blaze, and I sent up a prayer that they would manage to do it before it engulfed the entire ranch.

George ran up to Ryan, as filthy and heartbroken as his son. Together, they strode toward the fire captain and I turned, frantically looking for Nova. She wasn't in my truck anymore, the cab of it lit enough by the fire that I could see it was empty.

My heart tripped over itself. Horror spread through me. Had she somehow tried to make it inside? The pain of that thought threatened to bring me to my knees. My chest squeezed with unbearable pressure and my entire body was on high alert.

I never stopped looking for her, though. Never gave up hope that she was still somewhere outside here with us.

The tiniest flash of movement behind the truck caught my eye and I sprinted toward it and skidded on the dirt as I circled around back. And there she was. Safe and sound, her hands clamped over her mouth with tears streaming down her cheeks as she watched a group of strangers trying to save not only her livelihood but her home.

Without hesitating, I wrapped my arms around her waist, hauled her closer to my chest, and held her up. Her knees buckled and her body shook but not a sound escaped as she stared at the devastation.

I just held her, not saying anything for the longest time. My chin rested on top of her head and I kept her tightly gathered in my arms.

She didn't try to get away from me. Didn't tell me to shove off or even really seem to realize that I shouldn't have been holding her.

Instead, her fingers wrapped around my forearms and dug in like she was trying to keep me close. Like she needed me to stay exactly where I was.

The fire cracked and roared. Various alarms and shouts came from the fire trucks. But somehow, it was all distant. Even the intense heat seemed to be separated from us by some kind of invisible barrier.

*Also known as shock.*

It was only when I saw approaching movement in my periphery that I finally snapped out of it. The world crashed back into focus. The sounds were suddenly deafening, and the acrid scent of smoke in the air was so much thicker now than it had been before.

The movement turned out to be Ryan running toward us. I let go of Nova, keeping a hand under her elbow to steady her but needing to put some space between us before Ryan threw me into the flames. I didn't know if he'd go that far tonight, but emotions were running high.

"Are you okay?" I asked her as we both glanced at her brother jogging over to us.

Those blue eyes came up to meet mine, so wide and sad that I almost reached for her again. Instead, I just squeezed her elbow to let her know I was here and that I wanted to support her.

"I'm okay," she said quietly. "I'm fine. Thank you for your help."

Ryan skidded to a stop in front of us, breathing hard. He shoved his hands into his damp, matted hair. "Captain Adams thinks they're going to be able to contain it. I'm so glad we cleared a parking lot for the market. If we hadn't..." He trailed off, his head shaking before he tipped his face back toward the sky.

Ash was raining down on us, but he didn't even seem to notice it. When he looked at us again, his gaze dropped briefly to where I was still holding Nova's elbow, and he definitely noticed that, but he didn't say anything, looking up into her eyes instead.

"Are you okay? You stayed back, right?"

"I did and I'm fine. Or at least, I'm not hurt. You?" She looked at both of us as she asked the question, her own face dotted with black ash. The worry in her eyes was intense. "You were much closer to it than I was."

Ryan reached out and pulled her into his arms, giving her a tight hug. "I'm fine. I'm fine. I'm okay. Don't look at me like that. I'm not about to drop dead."

"I'm okay too," I said, itching to pull her into my arms next when he released her, but still not wanting to risk igniting his temper in addition to everything else.

"Where's Dad?" Nova asked, craning her neck to look past her brother. "I thought he was with you."

"He was, but he's still with Captain Adams," Ryan said, quickly adding, "He's not hurt. They're not checking him out or anything. He's just talking to them."

She jerked her head in a nod. "And Mom? She wasn't down here, was she?"

"No, she's up at the house. We should call her. She's bound to be out of her mind by now." With that thought in mind, he pulled his phone out of his pocket and did just that, taking a few steps away from us to talk to Mara.

I turned back to Nova, my gaze sweeping across hers. The shock finally started to subside, and my heart ached. "Are you sure you're okay?"

"No," she said honestly, her voice finally cracking as emotion overwhelmed her. Her eyes moved toward the burning building, a fresh sheen of tears welling on her cheeks. "That place meant everything to me, Carson. It was my dream come true, and I know we can probably rebuild, but it just won't be the same."

*Fuck it.*

I tugged her into me before wrapping my arms around her. Ryan finished up on the phone, but even he didn't have any objections about it when he came back to find me holding her.

"I just don't understand how it happened," she said miserably, letting me hug her for another moment before she stepped out of the circle of my arms and looked at her brother. "Have the firefighters said anything? I've been trying to imagine how it could've started, but I just don't know. Did I leave an oven on? A stove?"

Ryan and I exchanged a glance, back on the same wavelength as I saw the darkness of my own thoughts staring back at me from his eyes. We didn't have any evidence, but I'd been thinking about it since she'd told me what was going on and I didn't think this had started with an oven.

He swept his tongue across his lips, slowly moving his gaze away from mine as he glanced at the building. "I have a feeling this wasn't an accident."

"What do you mean?" she asked, shock making her voice several octaves higher. "You think someone did this on purpose?"

"I think we should leave and let the firemen do their jobs," he said. "But yes, I think it's possible."

She arched a questioning eyebrow at me, and I nodded my agreement with him. "They'll know more soon. We should get out of their way, but it didn't look like that blaze started in the kitchen, Nova."

We all piled into the truck.

"We could be wrong," Ryan said reluctantly. "At this stage, it's only a feeling, but Carson is right. It didn't look like it started in the kitchen. Either way, we'll only know for sure once the firefighters do."

Behind the steering wheel, I took one last look at the dying flames, and unease sank like a stone to the pit of my stomach. Something bad had happened here tonight, and it hadn't necessarily been only the fire.

Someone had done this, and if they'd gone this far, there was no telling what they would do next.

# 53

## NOVA

I sat on the sofa with my mom, holding her hand and leaning into her side. Dad, Ryan, and Carson spoke about the fire. Carson had driven us here, to my house, with my father in his own truck, and my mother had been waiting.

I hadn't even heard Ryan telling him where to go. It was like my head was too foggy right now. My ears were ringing slightly and everything in my body was just too sluggish to pay much attention. I felt like I was zoning in and out of consciousness without ever actually losing it at all.

Mom sat steadfastly by my side, her thumb stroking the back of my hand as she listened to the men talking. I listened too. Or at least, I tried, but every time I blinked, I saw the flames destroying everything I'd built and I lost focus again.

For once, Ryan and Carson were obviously on the same side and acting like friends again now that they had a common enemy—either a faulty gas line or someone who had intentionally started the fire.

It was bad enough to know that the bakery was gone, but the thought that someone had burned it down made me sick.

That was where the real shock had come in. It was why I still couldn't quite focus and why I was so loopy that everyone kept sending me worried glances.

"It's not the gas line," Ryan insisted, standing around the kitchen counter with Carson and Dad.

All of them were still covered in soot, but it didn't seem to be bothering them much. Mom had offered to fetch them all a change of clothes just after we'd arrived, but I hadn't even heard any of them responding to her.

*Then again, I'm definitely not hearing everything that's being said tonight.* Narrowing my eyes into slits, I hoped I'd be able to stay focused for this part of the conversation. It seemed important that I did.

Dad cocked his head at my brother, not disagreeing, but also not looking as convinced as Ryan sounded. "How do you know? These gas lines are old, son. All of our infrastructure is."

Ryan shook his head. "I was there when Eric did the upgrades while we were doing the revamp. He knew that building was going to become a bakery and he was careful."

"It might not have been anything he did," Dad reasoned. "The problem could've come from somewhere else."

"I don't think so, George," Carson said, taking Ryan's side just like he had been all night. "It's not impossible, but it just didn't look like it'd started anywhere near the gas line."

My father was pale under the smeared ash, his eyes wide and his face betraying his exhaustion, but he didn't back down. "That's what you both keep saying, but there's just no way either of you can know for sure."

"What do *you* think?" Ryan challenged him. "Do you honestly think it was an accident?"

"I don't know." Dad released a heavy breath. Specks of dirt in his hair stuck to his fingers as he dragged them through it. He glanced at his hand, his expression haunted. "All I know is that if you two are right, we've got bigger problems than we think."

Mom squeezed my hand, her eyes on her husband. I knew she wanted to take him home and get him cleaned up and to bed, but we were waiting for the sheriff. Apparently, Captain Adams had told Dad the police would want to take our statements tonight.

Carson and Ryan stood shoulder to shoulder, seeing eye to eye for the first time in a long time. Neither of them seemed to be carrying a grudge tonight, and for that, at least, I was grateful. Watching them fight that fire together like they could hear each other's thoughts—and now seeing them put everything else aside in a time of crisis—reminded me of how they used to be.

More like brothers than friends.

Maybe Cassidy had been right the other day. All this drama was just noise, but for Ryan and Carson's relationship. I sighed. All of that seemed so damn insignificant right now, and yet, I knew it wasn't. I knew how much it meant that they were putting it aside for me tonight, and I appreciated them both for it.

A sharp knock at the door made Dad stiffen. He glanced at the guys. "Stay put. I'll let him in, but let's hear what he says before we start slinging wild theories at the man."

Ryan sighed heavily and Carson didn't look too happy either, but they both nodded when Dad kept staring at them. Once he had their agreement, he glanced at me and his expression softened. "Are you going to be able to talk to them tonight, honey? We can give our statements and ask them if you can go do yours at the station in the morning."

"No," I said, steeling myself for what had to be done. "I'll do it now. It's fine."

Mom squeezed my hand again. Dad opened the door and stepped aside for Sheriff Dawes to enter. The man went to the same church as we did, but he wasn't all kind and smiling now like he usually was on Sundays.

Dressed in his uniform with his gun on his belt and graying scruff on his jaw, there wasn't a hint of smile. "George. Mara." He greeted my parents with a nod at each, then turned to Ryan and Carson. "I understand you boys did a good job keeping the fire under control until the fire department arrived."

They exchanged a glance, but the sheriff had already turned

toward me. "After I get your statements, I'll need to ask you a few questions, Nova."

"Of course." I cleared my throat and nodded, scooting forward on the sofa and releasing my mom's hand. "Would you like something hot to drink before we get started?"

I couldn't help myself. The small-town hospitality was infused in the blood that ran through my veins. Especially when it came to older people and authority figures—both of which he was.

He shook his head at me, though, the lines on his face seeming deeper tonight than they had been even on Sunday. "Thank you, but I won't take up too much of your time. I need to get back down to the station and get started on the paperwork."

"Whatever you need," Dad said, his voice gruff and tired. "Go ahead."

The sheriff nodded at him, then had quick conversations with Carson, Ryan, Mom, and Dad. He jotted down notes and told them he'd be contacting them with more questions, and then he came to sit down across from me.

His dark eyes intently focused on mine, and my pulse spiked. As he regarded me for a long moment without saying anything, I swore I saw suspicion shining back at me. I frowned and the sheriff cocked his head in response.

"You've been having some money troubles around here, am I right?"

Ryan tensed and Carson reached out to grab his shoulder when he started forward. Both of their faces were suddenly set in hard scowls, and Dad's head reared back like he'd been smacked.

"What is the meaning of this, Joshua?"

He exhaled deeply, glancing at my dad with an apologetic shrug. "I'm sorry, George, but it needs to be asked."

I felt like a freaking criminal, but I held his gaze evenly when he looked back at me. "All of that has been sorted out, and not by setting fire to the bakery. Realistically, burning down the bakery would only set us back more. It's been an extremely lucrative business and the money we'll get from the insurance won't cover the very real losses we're going to suffer every day that I'm not open."

"How do you know that?" he asked. "How do you know how much your insurance will cover?"

I let out an incredulous, humorless laugh. "Because it's my business, Sheriff Dawes. There's nothing I don't know about it. I realize that you have to ask what you have to ask, but with all due respect, you're wasting your time if you're going to keep going down this road."

He gave me another long look before he nodded. "I'll look into it and call you if I have more questions. How does that sound?"

"Fine," I replied, doing my best not to snap at an officer of the law. "Is there anything else?"

"Did you leave anything on in there this afternoon?" he asked.

Once again, the question really pissed off Ryan and Carson, and both of them surged forward. Only a hard look from my dad stopped them from interrupting. I sighed and ran my hands through my hair repeatedly, honestly trying to remember if I'd shut everything off this afternoon like I always did.

"I have a routine, sir," I said honestly. "It's the same thing every day and I never vary from it. Part of that routine is a final round to make sure everything is off. The stoves. The ovens. Everything. Between the safety issues and budgetary constraints, I just can't afford to do it any other way."

The sheriff made another note and stood up, giving me a final nod. "Alright, then. Thanks, folks. I'll be in touch again in the morning."

"Sheriff?" Carson took a step forward with his jaw hard but he forced himself to be polite. When the man looked back at him from the door, he continued. "Why did you start with that question? The one about the money troubles, I mean. A cash flow problem doesn't start a fire."

"No, it doesn't," the sheriff agreed easily before looking at me again. "People who have cash problems sometimes do, though. The fire department has noticed something suspicious. It might be arson, but we'll know more in the morning."

With that, he left. Mom and Dad hugged me goodbye before they followed, both of them looking completely wiped out after all that. Once they were gone, Ryan glanced at Carson and tipped his head toward my porch. "Can we talk?"

"Sure," Carson said, sending me a confused look before he followed my brother out the door.

I had no idea what Ryan wanted to talk to him about either, so I couldn't help even if I wanted to.

My brother's voice filtered in from outside once they started their private little chat. It was quiet enough around here tonight that I heard most of it. "Look, I don't like it, but I'm worried about Nova and I want you to stay with her."

"Me? Why? I mean, I will if she'll let me, but why don't you stay with her?"

Ryan muttered something I couldn't hear, but I caught the last part. "—angrier at me than at you. If I stay, I'll only make it worse."

A few seconds later, he strode back into my cottage, eyes cloudy with worry when they met mine. "If it's okay with you, Carson is going to stay here tonight. Make sure everything's okay."

I jerked my chin in a nod, still sitting on the sofa where I'd been with Mom and not really knowing what to do or say about any of this. "Sure. That's fine. I don't need a babysitter, but I'm too tired to argue."

"Good." He crossed the distance between us quickly, pausing for a second before he pressed a kiss to my forehead. "Try to get some sleep, sis. We'll figure it all out tomorrow. Don't worry, okay?"

I grumbled something in response, but not even I was sure what I'd said or what I'd meant to say. Instead of trying again, I merely waved at him. He left and Carson came back in, shutting the door behind himself.

"Can I make you some tea?" he asked, clearly a little uncomfortable as he hovered right near my door, not coming any closer but looking directly at me. "Earl Grey, right? You're upset. That's what you like when you're upset?"

"You remembered?" I all but whispered, so exhausted that my bones felt heavy. Somehow, he was still making my heart beat faster. "Yeah, that would be great. Thanks."

Alone with him for the first time in a few days, I should've been trying to talk to him about us. About Ryan and how I finally stood up to him, but I couldn't bring myself to add more stress to this day.

Carson made the tea in silence, then brought it to me but didn't sit down. "Do you mind if I grab a quick shower? You don't happen to have any more of Ryan's laundry, do you?"

I accepted the cup gratefully as I nodded. "Help yourself. It's folded in the hamper in the bathroom."

"Thanks." He turned around and strode down the hall before I could say anything else.

While he showered, I stayed exactly where I had been all along, sipping the tea and wondering if my brain would ever function fully again. Carson walked into the living room again not long after, and he sat down with me this time, but not close enough that we were touching.

A pang of longing shot through me and I let out a soft groan. "You really don't have to stay with me."

At the same time that I said it, he spoke too. "None of this is your fault, Nova."

Our eyes met and he smiled at me, motioning for me to go ahead, but I shook my head no and nodded at him instead. He sighed, eyes locked on mine. "Can you think of anyone who would come after your family like this?"

My heart flipped. "No, not really. We don't have any problems with anyone that I'm aware of."

His features hardened. "Except for Frank. You might not have a problem with him, exactly, but he sure has a problem with *you*. I wouldn't put it past him to do something like this after trying so hard to get you to sell to him."

My head spun so violently I swayed with it. Carson gave me a soft smile as he got up. "Why don't you lie down? We don't have to talk more about this tonight. I'm going to go check on what's going on at the bakery, but I'm coming back, okay? I know you don't need a babysitter, but after everything that happened tonight, I do."

"I know you're just trying to make me feel better," I murmured as I dragged the throw off the back of the sofa and covered myself with it. "Thanks, though. I'll see you later."

"Sure, Nova. See you later."

My eyes closed as soon as he was out the door. I started realizing he might've been right.

Shocked, sad, and completely and utterly exhausted, I fell asleep, unable to fight it for even just a minute longer.

# 54

## CARSON

Wiped out after all the excitement of the night, I got back to Nova's place about an hour after I'd left, opening the door slowly and as quietly as I could. All the lights were still on but the woman herself was fast asleep on the couch.

I watched her for a bit, not walking in just yet for fear of waking her. Her face was pale. Slight purple bruising under her eyes was an obvious sign that she hadn't been sleeping so well recently. I hadn't noticed it before, but with the lights having been dim at Moe's and then having been distracted by an actual fucking fire, I wasn't surprised.

*I guess that makes two of us that have been struggling to sleep.*

I drew in a deep breath and finally moved inside, locking her front door silently behind me. After digging through some of the debris with the firefighters, I was filthy again and I went to grab another shower and donned a fresh pair of shorts.

When I came back out, she was still sleeping. Her golden blonde hair fanned out against the sofa as she lay on her back with her mouth slightly open. I smiled, comforted by the fact that she was sleeping so well after the night she'd had.

The only thing left to do was to switch off the lights and put her to bed. No way I was leaving her on the sofa and taking her bed.

Nova let out a soft snore and I smiled again, hoping I wasn't about to bother her too much when I moved her. Going back to the sofa, I carefully slid one arm under her knees and hooked the other behind her neck, then lifted her gently against me.

She stirred and made a happy noise as she burrowed into my chest, breathing me in as a whisper escaped her. "Carson."

The sound of my name on her lips when she was asleep—and the fact that she sounded so happy while she said it—made my heart clench. *This girl.*

Holding her tighter, I carried her upstairs to her bedroom and laid her down. I looked again and saw her eyes were open. "I'm so sorry. I didn't mean to wake you. Go back to sleep, sweetheart. I'll be right downstairs."

She shook her head lazily, her eyes on mine. She scooted up to make space and then patted the mattress. "Stay with me. Just for a little while."

I knew I shouldn't do it, but I climbed into bed with her anyway. Didn't even try to resist.

In the dark of her bedroom with only silver moonlight shining in through her window and with her by my side, it felt like everything was going to be okay again. It was just for a moment and then it was gone, but when she lifted her head to rest it on my shoulder, I wrapped my arm around her and held her close, hanging onto that moment for as long as I could.

Neither of us said anything at first, and I was convinced she'd fallen asleep again until she suddenly spoke up. Her voice was soft and husky with sleep, but there was no missing or misunderstanding what she said.

"Do you really not want to try this anymore?" she asked, tilting her head on my shoulder to look up at me.

"No, I'm sorry, Nova." My heart cracked as I glanced down at her, not sure this was the right time to have this conversation but we needed to have it. "I'm so sorry for the way I ended things. If it means anything, I didn't want to do it."

"Then why did you?"

I breathed out, trying to find better words than what I'd used before. Obviously, I hadn't been nearly as clear with her as I'd thought I had been. "I felt like it was the right thing to do."

"Why?"

"It just felt like the odds were stacked against us and that being together was doing more harm than good."

She rolled over to face me. "What does it matter now? All I had was the bakery and that's gone, but in a way, losing *you* felt even worse."

Her eyes bounced between mine as she tried to explain. "It sounds so silly when I say it like that, but I guess losing you put things in perspective for me. No matter what else is going on in my life, I want to be able to share it with you. If I can't, it just feels incomplete. It feels like I'm waiting for my real life to start, and I'm tired of waiting, Carson."

"So am I." My heart thumped in my chest. I looked into her eyes and leaned forward, stroking my fingers into her hair to push it back. Then I kissed her.

As soon as my lips touched hers, a bolt of desire tore through me. There had never been any denying that I wanted this girl, but after everything she'd just said, I didn't just want her—I wanted to ravage her. Claim her. *Possess* her. And I wanted it to be for good.

In the back of my mind, I knew that our main problem wasn't solved yet. Ryan wasn't going to magically come around just because the bakery had burned, but I didn't want to stop. Being apart from her hadn't felt right. It'd felt like I'd torn off half my limbs and was just drifting around, waiting for them to be reattached.

I couldn't live that way and it didn't sound like she could either. Rolling her underneath me, I parted her soft lips with my tongue and slid my hands along the length of her arms until my fingers wrapped around hers.

"Carson," she sighed into my mouth. Her body writhed under mine when my hips started moving against her.

So hard, I was liable to lose it before I even got her clothes off, but I forced myself to hold it together. I pressed her hands against the mattress and undressed her slowly, savoring every inch of creamy skin that I exposed. In response, she pulled off my shirt and shorts, her eyes and mouth never leaving my own unless it was absolutely necessary.

I'd fucked a lot of women in my life, but this wasn't that. This was making love and it was so much better that I was suddenly as nervous as if it were my first time, which it was in a way, but my hands even shook as I rolled off her panties, my mouth dry and my dick aching.

*At least that part is familiar.*

Yet, as much as I was way out of my depth here, I didn't break the moment, looking straight into her eyes. She pulled off my underwear and wrapped her legs around me. I lowered my head, slanting my mouth over hers once more and holding her face in one of my hands while reaching for a condom in her nightstand with the other.

I'd left some here before. When my fingers brushed against the smooth surface of the box, I could've shouted with relief. *Thank the gods, they're still there.*

For the briefest, craziest moment, I considered leaving it and asking her to let me knock her up, but I didn't want it to happen that way. Nova wanted the traditional love story, which involved a ring and a wedding before a baby and a stroller.

I wanted to give her everything, in the exact order in which she wanted it, so I made quick work of putting on the condom. I felt like I was surrendering my soul to her when I sank inside her heat. Nova's mouth was gentle against mine as she kissed me like there was nothing we couldn't do as long as we stuck together—and in that moment, I believed her.

I was in love with Nova Murphy. Absolutely and irrevocably in love with her. Even if I had to take a punch for it every day for the rest of my life, I would do it. As long as I got to spend the time before and after it happened loving her.

# 55

## NOVA

Waking up the next morning, I felt Carson tucked around me and I smiled. I hadn't even opened my eyes yet, but I was already smiling because he was here. He'd stayed. I hadn't been sure that he would, and knowing that he had made me feel like we'd turned over a new leaf.

Staying right where I was, I cuddled up against him and hugged his forearm draped around my waist. He was still fast asleep. With his eyes closed and his handsome features relaxed, he looked younger, more innocent. More like that boy I used to know.

My heart skipped as I rested my forehead against his, feeling like this really was it this time. I'd already stood up to my brother, but I'd do it again if I had to. My mom knew about us and I was pretty sure she'd have told my dad by now, but even if she hadn't, we were closer to a real relationship than we'd ever been before.

We were making it happen and I was ready to grab the bull by the horns—or my brother by the balls—until he relented. Still smiling, I gave Carson a soft kiss on the cheek before I slowly started sliding back, extricating myself from him to surprise him with breakfast in bed.

I rolled over, hanging my legs off the side of the mattress before I slowly got up, but that was when reality hit me. I couldn't bring him breakfast in bed. The bakery had burned to the ground last night and I needed to get down there to see the damage with my own two eyes now that morning had come.

A heavy weight settled into my heart as I stood there watching the sunlight creep over the top of the mountain to wash the grazing land in early morning light. I stood in front of my window for a while, just looking out at the ranch and everything we'd come so close to losing.

*But we're still here. We're still standing.*

The bakery was gone, but the rest of it was still here and so was I. So was Carson. Devastated as I was, I needed to get on with it, so I grabbed a quick shower and dressed in simple shorts and a T-shirt. Then I put on my sneakers and jogged down to the bakery, making a mental note to go pick up my truck from Moe's later today.

The rhythmic pounding of my feet against the dirt soothed me. The fresh breeze on my face cleared the cobwebs of shock and sleep, allowing me to start thinking about the future. A future with Carson and the rebuilt bakery, hopefully right here on this very ranch.

By the time I turned the final corner between my cottage and the bakery, I was wide awake and buzzing with energy to get started. The heaviness in my heart was still there and the tasks ahead were daunting, but the run had helped. I'd never given up before and I wouldn't do it now.

Much to my surprise, Ryan was already there when I arrived, sitting on the bed of his truck and staring at the burned-out husk of the building that had been left behind. He looked up when he heard me, waved me over, and gave me a tentative grin. I stopped and rested my arms on the side of his truck.

"Did you get any sleep?" he asked.

I nodded, noticing the bags under his eyes and his messy hair. "I was wiped out. You? It doesn't look like it."

He chuckled but shrugged. "My brain didn't want to shut off. It kept me up half the night and I spent the other half trying to decide what to do about the thoughts I was having."

"Yeah?" I cocked my head at him, leaning against his truck now as my knees started getting numb.

An acrid scent still hung in the air down here, and with every breath I took, I was reminded of what I'd lost. Even though I wasn't facing what had remained of the building, I was painfully aware of it.

Ryan patted the open space next to him on the back and extended a hand toward me. "Come on. I'll help you. You look like you need to sit down."

"I think I do." I smacked my palm into his, let him help me up, and then sat down next to him, just staring at the blackened char that just yesterday had been a bustling business. "It's crazy how much things have changed in less than twenty-four hours, isn't it?"

"Yeah, it really is," he agreed before giving me a sidelong look. "Hey, uh, I know you're going through a lot right now, but can we talk?"

"Sure, as long as talk means talk and not fight, I'm up for it." I faced him. "What's up? Is this about whatever was keeping you up last night?"

He jerked his chin in a nod, the look in his eyes suddenly far away. "Did Carson stay with you last night?"

I exhaled sharply, my defenses immediately springing up. I narrowed my eyes. "Yes, he did. You asked him to—"

Ryan put his hands up in surrender, leaning back. He shook his head. "No, Nova. That's not why I asked. I'm glad he stayed."

I blinked hard. "What?"

"I'm glad he stayed," he repeated, saying the words slower this time. "I thought it might be time we talked about why I had a hard time accepting you guys being together."

"I know why."

"Just let me talk, would you?" His blue eyes were firm on mine, and there was a hint of pleading to them. "I promise this isn't going to go how you think it is."

"It's not?"

He shook his head. "Look, you're my little sister and I don't want you to get hurt. That part remains true, but there is some stuff you don't know yet and I want to tell you about it."

"Okay," I said slowly, dragging out the words. "What is it?"

He inhaled so deeply that his chest rose. He kept it in for a moment before releasing it and swiping his tongue across his lips. "I busted my ass to make sure you still had a chance to chase your dreams and I know how hard it is to give those up. Hell, I did it and I've always wondered what I could've been, but I've never regretted the choice I made."

"You didn't? It sure seems like you regret every day."

"I don't. That's not regret, Nova. It's worry, and stress, and the *what ifs* taking control, but it's not regret. It can never be regret. Not when I know that I did the right thing by staying and helping to keep this place afloat while you went to college."

"Would you have stayed if it hadn't been for me?" I asked, needing to know if I was the reason he'd abandoned his dreams. It was suddenly sounding like I was.

Ryan nodded and the squeezing sensation in my chest receded.

"Dad hasn't been able to do it all for a long time, Nova. Before we were old enough to help, he had Gramps. Then he died and we were there. It's too much for one person. I don't think I'd ever have been able to leave him to deal with it all alone. This place means just as much to me as it does to you."

Guilt I hadn't even realized I'd been carrying around lifted off my shoulders and I inhaled deeply, feeling like even my lungs were suddenly expanding more easily. A smile broke out across my face and I bumped my shoulder into his.

"I guess that really is what we both want for our futures, then. To be tied to this place. For a second there, I thought maybe you wanted to leave."

He chuckled. "Me? Never. Maybe eventually, I'll go exploring for a bit, but this will always be home. That also circles us back to what I originally wanted to talk to you about."

"Oh, that wasn't it?"

"It was part of it, but the other part is about Carson," he said.

When I opened my mouth to tell him again that I didn't want to fight, he arched an eyebrow at me in warning. "Just hear me out."

"Fine."

"I don't want you to get hurt and I'm worried that Carson will up and leave again," he said, gaze fixed on mine. "I remember how hurt you were the first time, and I know you like to pretend that it didn't hurt because you always knew he would be going back to college after that summer, but it broke your heart when he left."

I sniffed. "Only because you drove him away before the summer was even over. I still had two more weeks with him."

"I knew he was in line to get drafted," Ryan said with a gravity in his voice I hadn't been expecting. "When I drove him away, I did it knowing that he had a real shot, Nova. I overheard a conversation between the coaches one day. It happened by accident, but I couldn't unhear what I'd heard and I knew the NFL people had been sniffing around him."

My eyes widened. "Do you really think that's an excuse? Everyone knew."

"You're not listening to me," he said urgently. "This wasn't just about knowing that he had the talent to make it. I knew that they were already looking at him and I'd seen the way he looked at *you*. I'm not blind. I knew you two had feelings for each other long before I caught you kissing, and the way he looked at you?"

Ryan sighed before he refocused on me. "He'd have given it all up to be with you, Nova. I couldn't let that happen to him, or to you, for that matter. So I did what I had to do to separate you, thinking that it was the right thing to do, and not only because I thought it was creepy my baby sister was hooking up with a dude in college."

My heart stammered, but as I stared back at him, I knew that this was the truth. Him not wanting us to be together back then had run much deeper than I'd thought, and honestly, I was suddenly grateful to him for doing it. I'd been mad at him for such a long time, and all the while, he'd done it so Carson wouldn't have given up his dreams for me, a fact that I'd never have been able to live with if I'd ever found out.

"Thank you for finally being honest with me," I said softly, my voice and my breath stolen by the weight of his revelation. "What about now, though? You don't want us to be together now either, but I'm going to be with him, Ryan. I need you to be okay with that. We've both been miserable for long enough."

He let out a harsh exhale before he nodded. "Yeah, I know, but what if he leaves again? What if another opportunity comes along? A guy like that has to be getting a lot of offers to do a lot of different things, and none of those opportunities will be in Silver Springs. He's the guy who chases his dreams, Nova. He's got the balls to do it and I don't want you getting left behind again."

"I won't be, but if I am, then that's on me. At the end of the day, it's all on me. Whatever happens, positive or negative, I won't stay in this purgatory just because you're uncomfortable."

"It's not just that I'm uncomfortable, Nova. I'm worried. If he leaves—"

"Then maybe I'll go with him," I said firmly. "The only thing tying me down to Silver Springs is the ranch and it sounds like all our problems are going to go away soon anyway, so maybe if Carson chases a new dream, I'll join him. I'll go and do some exploring of my own. Would that be the worst thing in the world?"

He stared at me for a long time before he finally shook his head. "No, I guess it won't be."

"Exactly." I reached for his hands, giving them a soft squeeze as I looked him right in the eyes. "I want you to consider this your official invitation to get onboard with me and Carson. It's time to let go of all these animosities, Ryan. They're toxic and they're poisoning you."

He didn't say anything, but I took that as a good thing. Since he seemed to understand, I decided to push even further. "You owe Carson an apology if any of us really want to be able to move forward."

The fire chief showed up before Ryan could respond, climbing out of his bright red SUV with what appeared to be an investigator in tow. My brother and I both climbed off the truck and extended our hands to shake with the officials.

"This is Mr. Rickman," the fireman said. "He's the arson investigator assigned to this case. We'd like to take a look around if that's
okay with you, Ms. Murphy."

"Of course." I glanced at my brother once the men started walking
toward the bakery. "I'll be back when they're done. Then we'll keep
talking."

"Actually," he said, clearing his throat. "Will you be okay staying
here alone for a few minutes?"

"This is probably going to take longer than that. I'll be fine. I'm
just going to be hanging out while they do what they need to do."

"Is Carson still at your place?"

Excitement zapped through me as I nodded. "I think so. He was
still sleeping when I left, but you're only allowed to go there if you
promise me there will be no more fighting."

"I promise." He eyed the officials for a moment before he looked
back at me. "Don't answer any weird questions, okay? The normal,
run of the mill stuff is fine, but if they start asking the same stuff that
the sheriff did last night, Dad said to call him."

"I've got this," I assured my brother, inclining my head toward his
truck. "Go find him, Ryan. I'll call Dad if I need any help, but you
need to go clear the air. There's good coffee in the cabinet next to the
mugs, and if it comes down to it, the good whiskey is in there too."

Ryan laughed as he backed away from me. "Thanks. Love you, sis.
Call us if you need us."

"I won't," I said.

I watched him go with a sense of relief so strong it was almost
dizzying. After all this time, all the fights, and all the fear, Ryan had
come around. That felt like a dream come true in and of itself, and
the joy of realizing it was so intense that not even the fire could take it
away.

The bakery was gone, but it could be rebuilt. It was a setback, but
it was temporary. What Ryan was about to do, however, would be
permanent. If he had really made his peace with Carson and me
being together, then there was nothing standing in our way anymore.

We could be together, out in the open, for real, and if that was true, then not even arson or the person investigating it could bring me down today. This really was the first day of the rest of my life, and I wasn't about to start it feeling dejected or defeated.

Instead, I was going to look at this as an opportunity to start again and to do it even better this time.

## 56

### CARSON

The sound of movements downstairs woke me up, gently drawing me out of a dream I'd been having about being in Nova's bed after making up with her. I sighed groggily, opened my eyes, and wished that it had been more than just a dream, but when I looked around and found myself in Nova's bedroom, I grinned.

*Shit, it was real.*

My grin widened. I got up and pulled on my boxers, kind of sad that I couldn't wake her up with an orgasm but also not opposed to the coffee I could smell brewing. A lazy morning drinking coffee with my girl didn't sound too bad either. I crept softly to the kitchen to surprise her.

The surprise was all mine. I stopped short and the grin melted off my face when I saw Ryan instead of Nova in the kitchen.

He glanced at me and heaved out a heavy breath, his head shaking as his eyes settled on mine. "Go put some clothes on so we can talk about how this is going to go."

I groaned, turned around, and headed back upstairs, mentally preparing for a fight as I put his clothes back on. Mine were still in the washer, so not only did I have to face Ryan instead of Nova this morning, but I had to do it while wearing his fucking clothes.

*Not the way I want to have this discussion.*

As I walked back downstairs, I went over the arguments I'd been formulating in my head for months, but when I got to the kitchen, he simply poured me a cup of coffee and pushed it over to me. "When I said to stay with her last night, I didn't mean in her bed."

"Where else was I supposed to sleep?" I asked wickedly. I was probably stirring the pot, but hell, he'd just caught me waking up in his sister's bed. The shit storm was already coming. I wasn't going to tiptoe around my feelings for Nova anymore.

To my utter surprise, he didn't seem angry. He didn't laugh at my joke, and he definitely wasn't amused, but he didn't punch me or throw coffee in my face.

He sat down across from me at the counter with a coffee of his own, watching the steam rise from the surface for a moment before he sighed. "There's an arson investigator at the bakery, so it looks like they really don't think it was an accident."

"Shit." I squinted, wondering if I should share my suspicions about Frank with him as well. "Has Nova got any enemies I don't know about? Competition in town or something?"

He gave me a pointed, exasperated look. "This isn't a bake off gone wrong. And you've been back long enough to know she's the town's golden girl. Everyone loves her. She's like the female version of you. No one is going to burn her bakery down."

"Yet, it seems that someone did," I said evenly. "Do you think it could've been Frank?"

"I don't know, but the thought has crossed my mind. I just don't know why he'd have targeted the bakery. If he's pissed off with my dad for saying no to the deal, why didn't he just set fire to the ranch?"

"The bakery is easily accessible from the road," I reasoned. "He could've been hoping it would spread. Or he could've chosen it because he knows that's where most of the money is coming from at the moment. Without the bakery, your parents are in deeper shit than ever before. If he doesn't know I'm going to invest in the ranch, he probably figured it would cripple you and force you to sell."

"I didn't think about it like that." He paled a little. "You don't think he'd come after Nova here, do you?"

"I don't know, but I doubt it. The bakery was the money-maker. She's the brains behind the operation, but it's not like she can keep the ranch in the black out of her kitchen here."

Worry still sped through me at the possibility, though. I bit my lip, gripping my mug harder in an effort to stop myself from jumping up and going after her. Ryan glanced in the direction of her front door like he was considering doing the same thing, but then he turned back to me and shook his head.

"She's with the fire chief and the investigator. She'll be fine. As soon as she's done, I'm sure she's going to race right back here to make sure your head is still attached to your body."

I faced him head on. "You can take as many shots at me as you want, but I'm not backing down again, Ryan. I can't. She's it for me, and I know you don't believe it, but I'm done trying to fight it just to spare your feelings."

"Yeah, I've heard that before. From Nova." He took a small sip of his coffee, his eyes never leaving mine. "You're serious about her?"

"Yes," I said without hesitation. "She's the one, man. She always has been, and while I'd appreciate your blessing, I'm not waiting until I get it anymore."

"I've heard that too," he said, letting out a long breath before he finally nodded. "Yeah, okay. I'm onboard. You have my blessing."

My eyebrows shot all the way up. "For real?"

"For real," he said, gritting his teeth but not looking like he was lying or trying to make a joke about it. "Just don't hurt her again. I know she acts all tough, but she's got a really small, really soft heart, Carson. You've broken it twice and I know that I had a hand in it both those times, so I'm willing to give you one more chance, but if you fuck it up?"

He didn't answer the question, but he didn't need to. In reality, he was only giving me one real shot at this, but one was all I needed. I was going to make this work. Come hell or high water, I wasn't going to mess it up now that we finally had his support.

Ryan was doing his best to make peace, and while part of me still wanted to tear him a new one for all he'd done to keep us apart, I simply nodded. "If I fuck it up, you'll rip off my balls with your bare hands?"

"And banish you from this fucking town forever. Not even the hero-worship you've got around here will survive the damage I'll do if you hurt her."

"Got it," I said, and I really did. If I hurt her, I'd rip off my own balls and exile myself. I wouldn't wait for him to do it for me. "Thanks for coming over here to talk to me about this, man. It's really been weighing me down to feel like I betrayed you. For what it's worth, I really tried to stay away from her."

He scrunched up his face as he regarded me from across the counter. "You didn't try too hard, it seems."

"Trust me, if I could've chosen who I had these feelings for, I wouldn't have chosen your baby sister. It wasn't a choice, Ryan. That's the whole point. It's never been about the fact that she's your sister or that she was the one I couldn't have. To me, she's Nova, the most amazing woman in the world and the only one I can't live without."

"So you're telling me that your love for her was just so strong that you couldn't stay away?" He gave me a dubious look.

I shrugged and nodded. "Yeah, I guess that's exactly what I'm telling you. I didn't choose her to be the one that I felt this way about, but I do feel this way about her, and because of that, I will choose her. Every time and above everyone and everything else."

He frowned. "It wasn't a choice, but now it is?"

"Something like that," I said, giving him another shrug. "I took a lot of hits to the head, okay? I can't explain it any better. It's just that I've learned over these past few weeks that when push comes to shove, I will always choose her, even if I didn't decide to fall for her, and I sure as hell didn't pursue her just to piss you off."

He managed a small smile. "That's good. She deserves someone who will put her first. Why did it take you this long to do it?"

I choked on my coffee, incredulous laughter bubbling out around the liquid. "What? That's ridiculous. I've always put her first."

"No, you haven't," he said pointedly. "There was football and the NFL, and me, and all sorts of shit."

"What, you'd rather I didn't worry about what you thought at all?" I scoffed. "Forgive me for trying to be a good friend."

"A good friend never would've stared at my sister in a bikini, looking like his eyes were about to fall out," he said. "I've had your number for a long time, Drake. You might've thought you were fooling me, but I knew about it the very first time you realized she wasn't a baby anymore."

"Bullshit. I have a better poker face than that," I argued. "Besides, you'd have jabbed my eyes out if you'd really noticed me staring at her."

He scoffed, but there was amusement lighting his eyes now as he shook his head. "Maybe I should've jabbed out your eyes. I wanted to. And also, it's not your face that gave you away. Swim trunks aren't good at hiding what's underneath them and we were young. It was more difficult to control it back then."

I pretended to gag. "You knew I had a hard-on for her? That's what you're saying?"

He winced. "Unfortunately, yes. I did know that. Although, at the time, I was desperately hoping it was for someone else."

I sighed. "To be honest, so was I. When I said I never meant to betray you, I was being honest, man. It took me by surprise too, these feelings I have for her. It's not like I was trying to fall for her."

"Did you though? Did you really fall for her? It's not just about the chase, or sex, or whatever?"

"It never has been," I said honestly, getting up and holding out my hand for him to shake. "Can we agree to let bygones be bygones?"

He left me hanging for so long I was convinced he wasn't going to shake my hand, but then he got up and smacked his palm into mine. "They're bygones, but if you break her heart again, I'll make you disappear."

"What happened to ripping off my balls and banishing me?"

He shrugged as he tightened his grip on my hand. "That was before I really had a chance to remember those first times I saw you noticing her. Now that I have, banishing you without your balls doesn't seem good enough. You'd find some way to still make something of your life, so making you disappear seems to be a better option."

"I don't doubt it," I said. "For now though, we need to worry about the bakery and what's going on down there. There's no risk of me breaking her heart today, but if they really suspect arson, there might be other risks we need to be aware of."

He put more coffee on, then pulled three to-go mugs from a cabinet. "You know, having you around to help me protect her might not be so bad. At least I know that she's got one person watching her back. It helps that I know it's a person I can trust to keep her safe."

"You've got that right. I won't let anything happen to her, Ryan. I swear."

His eyes lingered on mine. "I know, but we might have our work cut out for us. On the other hand, if we don't get some caffeine in her soon, it might be the people from the fire department who are in trouble. Let's go. I want to talk to the chief personally before he leaves."

So did I.

After helping him fix the coffees, I drove down to the bakery with him, glad to be moving past old grudges. Ryan was a formidable enemy and he was tenacious as fuck. So was I. Especially when it came to protecting the people we loved. The two of us together? Whoever had done this wasn't going to get away with it.

That much, they could be absolutely fucking sure of.

# 57

## NOVA

Carson, Ryan, and I left the sheriff's department three days after the fire, all of us tense about the outcome of the investigation but relieved to have given our updated statements. After all the questions we'd been asked, it had become clear that the investigators needed to know about any possible enemies or recent disputes.

We'd sat on it for a couple days since we didn't have any evidence, but we'd all gone through every other encounter we'd had with everyone else in and around the town, and nothing else made sense. The only person who had a bone to pick with us was Frank, so we'd finally gone to the authorities with it.

After all the conversations we had, we came up with two possibilities. If Frank didn't know about Carson's investment, burning the bakery down would put pressure on us to sell. With no money coming in, we'd have no other choice. Alternatively, if Frank *did* know Carson was investing, maybe burning the bakery would make Carson pull out. Or maybe he'd simply wanted to make us hurt. Whatever his twisted motives, Frank had to be the culprit.

When we stepped out of the police station and into the sunshine,

Carson squeezed my hand and slid his sunglasses back on. "You doing okay?"

I shook my head, sliding my own sunglasses over my eyes. "I'm not going to be okay until they arrest him, but for now, at least we know we've pointed them in the right direction."

Ryan didn't even grimace at us for holding hands. His gaze dropped to our entwined fingers before he gave me a reassuring smile. "They'll get him if he's the one responsible for this. Just keep your chin up and your eyes open."

"Yeah, you too," I said, frowning when he stopped walking. "Where are you going? I thought we were all headed out to lunch."

"I can't. I've got that contractor coming in to talk about building a new bakery and I've got to fill Mom and Dad in about this morning before I meet with him. Have fun, though."

Carson grinned at him. "Oh, we will."

Ryan groaned. "Too soon, man. Too soon. Just promise me you two will stay in public, with chaperones, and not make me an uncle any time soon."

My cheeks flushed, but Carson shrugged at him. "I don't make promises I can't keep. You don't need me to be there for the contractor, right?"

"Nope. I only needed your money to pay him, and now that I've got that, I can take it from here." He smirked at his friend. "You had it coming."

Carson laughed, not seeming offended in the least. "Yeah, I guess I did. Are you sure you don't want to join us for lunch?"

"Sorry," Ryan said, motioning at us and waving his hand in a circle at our chests. "I'm not sure I can stomach seeing this for more than an hour at a time just yet, and I really do need to get home. Mom and Dad will be waiting and that contractor is coming at one."

"Do you need me to be there?" I asked, amused as I glanced between them. "It's nice of you both to think that you need to be present for the meeting, but it's *my* bakery."

Ryan smirked at me. "Sure, it is, but I designed the building when we remodeled and I'm pretty sure it worked out well for you, so I'll take care of it again."

"Fine, but remember what we talked about last night. This design needs to be open to possibilities for growth in the future."

He saluted, then waved and strode toward his truck. Carson watched him go with a smile on his lips, only turning to lead me down the street once Ryan was gone. "He's taking this much better than I thought he would."

"He really is," I agreed. "I think I'm still waiting for him to change his mind. Every time you touch me in front of him, I wonder if he's going to snap."

Carson chuckled. "Nah, I think he's learning to live with it. So, what do you feel like for lunch?"

I lifted my free hand to check my watch and groaned. "Takeout from the Greek place on the corner? We have to be at the library in thirty for our reading session."

"Shit. Is it that late already?"

"Yep."

He only let go of my hand when we reached his truck. He opened the door for me, leaned in to plant a kiss on my lips, and shut it. As he jogged around the truck, I brought my fingers up to my still tingling mouth, smiling as I all but melted into the seat.

It had only been three days, but they had been three of the best days of my life. Now that we didn't have to sneak around anymore, Carson was proving to be quite a boyfriend. Without either of us having to get to work, we were spending almost all our time together.

So far, it had mostly been in bed, but I wasn't complaining. He helped out with chores on the ranch while he was there, and then we went back to my cottage, locking ourselves in and finally getting to spend some time as a couple.

It was great. He glanced at me as he climbed in behind the steering wheel. "God, that smile does things to me. Please tell me I put it there."

"Of course, you put it there." I turned to face him. "Are you staying over again tonight?"

"Is that an invitation?"

"Do you need one?"

He considered it for a moment as he got us on the road. Then he shook his head. "No, I guess not. I'm staying over again tonight, but I'd like to take you somewhere before we go back to the ranch."

"Okay. Where do you want to take me?"

"You'll find out soon," he said mischievously, then left me hanging all through lunch and our reading session.

By the time we'd been in his truck for another fifteen minutes after we'd left the library, the curiosity was just about to kill me. "Seriously, where the hell are we going?"

"To the house I'm buying."

I blinked back my surprise. "You found a place? I didn't know that! Why didn't you tell me?"

"I found it while we were separated, then the bakery burned down and that hardly seemed like the time."

"It's been days since then."

"Sure, but I've been *distracted*." There was a faint smile tugging at the corners of his lips when he said it.

We started slowing in front of what turned out to be a huge piece of land with a tiny, dilapidated house on it.

"This is it," he said happily, putting the car in park before climbing out and walking around to open the door for me.

I followed him out, looking around at the overgrown garden, the chipping paint on the walls, and the sagging gutters. "Really? This is the place you're buying? I thought you wanted to build. If you decided to buy something, I'm surprised it's not a mansion. This place certainly has character."

He took my hand again, leading me up a path of broken flag-stones to the front door. There was a garage, but I could see why he hadn't parked in it. The door was broken. The dark, gaping hole in it made me wonder what kind of critters had made their homes in there.

A shiver ran down my spine. "Seriously, this is a joke, right?"

"No jokes," he said as he produced a key and unlocked the door that had seen better days.

Inside, the place was dark, dingy, and dirty. Our footsteps echoed across the old tiles in the foyer, leading into what I assumed to be the living area. Carson and I had both pulled off our sunglasses when we'd walked in, and I turned to him. The crease between my eyebrows grew deeper as guilt gnawed at my stomach.

"Are you thinking of buying this place because it's the best you can afford now that you've given us so much money? This is too much of a sacrifice."

"No." He took my other hand in his as well and tugged me closer. My chest touched his and he dipped his forehead to mine. "A big, shiny house isn't going to make the town better and that's what I aim to do with the money I have. The investment I made in the ranch hardly made a dent, Nova. I'm okay. I'm not buying this place because it's cheap. I'm buying it because it has potential and because I'm not sure yet what the future holds."

"What do you mean?" My heart gave an aching pang. I looked into those gorgeous green eyes and suddenly realized what was coming. "You're leaving, aren't you? That's why you're not building the house you said you wanted when you first got back."

"I'm thinking about going into broadcasting," he admitted. My spirit would've sagged if he wasn't still holding me so tightly that it didn't feel like his way of breaking up with me.

"You'd be great at it," I whispered, not wanting to speak normally in case my voice gave away the pain growing inside. "It's just, uh, sad that it would mean you have to leave again."

"Hey, now," he said softly, nudging his nose against my own. "I'm going to come home, baby. To you, to our town, and to our families, and I want you to be here waiting for me when I do. I want you to be mine and I haven't accepted any gigs yet, so if you don't want me to go, I won't."

"No, it's not that." I tipped my head back and released his hands to wind my arms around his neck. "I want all the same things you want. I guess I just wasn't expecting you to leave again so soon."

As he spoke, he backed me up against a wall, his body hot and heavy against mine, and he looked straight into my eyes. "I'm not leaving you this time, Nova. We'll work out the details and the logistics, but even if I do leave town, I won't be leaving *you*."

Pushing me up against the wall, he caught my wrists and extended them above my head. Keeping a tight grip on them, he kissed me deeply. Shock still reverberated through my system, but with each stroke of his tongue against my own, I felt more reassured that it wouldn't be the same this time. With each item of clothing that we removed, I told myself we weren't going to let this break us apart, and when he sank into me, I held on to him tightly, silently promising him that I would support him in making all his dreams come true with the same fervor that he'd shown in his support of mine.

Together, there was nothing we couldn't do. I just had to keep my wits about me, not let my brother get into my head when he said "I told you so," and quite possibly, I would have to prepare myself to leave Silver Springs for short bursts of time.

As I came, he swelled deep inside me at the same time. Blind with pleasure, I kissed him again, knowing that we were still only just beginning. This wasn't the end. I absolutely refused to let this be the thing that finally put an end to us. With the bakery months away from even being open again and Dad and Ryan able to take care of the ranch together in the meantime, maybe it was my turn to be there for Carson for once.

# 58

## CARSON

When I showed up at football practice for the kids at camp, I was on cloud nine. It looked like I was going to get the house, Nova knew I was considering taking a broadcasting job and she was still with me, and the contractors were just about to start work on Red Stone Ranch.

The early morning air was warm as I strolled out onto the field. None of the kids or Vance had arrived just yet. I thought I was alone until I saw a figure striding out of the equipment shed with her arms full of cones, but even though her face was obscured by bright orange, I knew who it was.

No one else moved like Nova and no one else affected me the way she did. My heart rate spiked. My entire being was already reaching for her as I jogged over. I'd slept at Mom's last night after spending more than a week staying at Nova's, but I'd missed my girlfriend so much in the twelve hours since I'd last seen her that I wrapped my arms around her from behind and lifted her off her feet, cones be damned.

She squealed with laughter and dropped them to twist and wrap her arms around my neck, not seeming surprised to see me here. "Trouble sleeping?"

I hiked her up against my stomach and slid my hands around the bottom of her ass to hold her there. "Yes, it's funny, but it seems I've already outgrown sleeping alone."

"That *is* funny," she said, amused as she toyed with my hair and dotted little kisses across my forehead. "What's even funnier is that the same thing has happened to me at exactly the same time. Amazing how that works, huh?"

"Yep. Does it make me a horrible person that I'm happy you feel the same way?"

"I don't think so," she murmured against my skin, breathing me in before she pulled back and smiled. "If you are, then I'm a horrible person too, so we can be horrible together."

I chuckled. "Done. Let's just be horrible together, then. Can I help you put out the cones for the practice drills?"

"I'll be okay. You can borrow some of these to set up for your own practice, though. The kids will be getting here soon."

"Yeah, I know." I gave her a hopeful smile. "Do you think we've got time for a quickie in the locker room?"

She swatted my arm, but she seemed to be considering it until we heard a car pulling up.

I groaned. "Damn it. Later?"

"Later," she promised coyly, making me wonder what she was planning, but when I set her down on her feet and turned to find the sheriff walking toward us, my mind immediately left the gutter.

Nova tensed at my side, reaching for my hand without even looking at me. He tipped his hat at us, looking up and down the length of the football field with a fond grin.

"When I was a youngster, I was always here early," he commented lightly. "Kids of today, huh? Always sleeping in."

Nova gave him a curious smile, but she was still tense, her entire body rigid. "Practice doesn't start for about twenty minutes, sir. Is there something we can do for you, or have you come to watch the teams?"

"I'd love to stay and see what you've taught them all these last few weeks, but I'm here on official business," he said, looking at her. "Your father told me you'd be here, and I thought I should come tell you in person that we've had a break in the case."

"A break?" Relief surged through me, as she and I shared a hopeful look. "What break?"

"We arrested Frank Louison for arson," he said, suddenly smiling.

Nova released my hand to clamp both of hers over her mouth.

I gaped at him. "Are you serious? Do you think the charges are going to stick? Did you find some evidence?"

The sheriff nodded, hooking his thumbs into his pockets and looking mighty proud of himself. "The charges will stick. I imagine he'll be paying for all the damages you suffered, once all is said and done."

Nova's eyes went as wide as I'd ever seen them. "Do you really think so? What about a trial? What happens if he's found not guilty?"

"He confessed, Ms. Murphy. We questioned him and presented him with our evidence, and he caved almost immediately," the sheriff said. "This won't make it to trial. He's sitting with his lawyer and the prosecutor as we speak. He wants to make a deal. We'll need your input into whatever deal the prosecutor wants to make, if they choose to let him make a deal at all, but he confessed. I thought you'd like to know."

"Why did he do it?" she asked, her eyes boring into his unrelentingly. "He has to have told you, right?"

The sheriff sighed as he grimaced. "It turns out that he was looking at selling your ranch to cover a ton of debt he'd accumulated over the last year or so. Some or other investment of his went wrong and your ranch was the best opportunity he could see to get himself out of that hole."

"This wasn't to hurt Nova?" I asked disbelievingly, gritting my teeth as my fingers rolled into fists at my side.

"What a slime ball," she muttered beside me, her head shaking even as she stretched out her hand to shake with the sheriff.

I could think way better things to call the guy than a slime ball, but there was a lady present.

Biting it back, I shook hands with him too, still unable to believe that the man had been willing to destroy a generational ranch because of his own foolishness. The sheriff tipped his hat at us again and chatted to some of the kids who had now arrived as he made his way back to his cruiser.

Nova and I remained exactly where we were for a long minute, ignoring all the curious looks we were getting from the teenagers. At this point, everyone in town knew about the bakery burning down and I was sure that most of the kids were assuming, correctly, that was what the sheriff had been talking to us about, but thankfully, they gave us a wide berth to process and started their own, individual warm-ups instead.

"We'd better get to it," Nova mumbled, looking slightly dazed as she watched the sheriff drive out of the parking area. "They'll be wondering what's going on."

"Let's tell them the slowest kid at practice is getting arrested," I said.

She laughed and slapped my arm. "We can't terrorize these children."

"They're teenagers. Nothing scares these little monsters. I'm more concerned about you. How are you feeling after hearing that? The guy wrecked your business for nothing."

She closed her eyes and breathed in and out deeply a few times before she looked at me again. "I'm not angry anymore. To be honest, I just feel kind of bad for Frank. He must've been really desperate and I understand what that feels like."

Awe and admiration rolled through me at the sincerity shining in her eyes. Her kind heart and her willingness to forgive someone who didn't deserve it had been my saving grace more than once, but I couldn't believe she felt like that even about a low life like Frank. She really was too good of a damn person.

I wrapped my arms around her, holding her until I felt my own anger starting to subside. "I've got to say, I'm really impressed with you. I definitely wouldn't have taken that news so well. It's not even my bakery, and I'm not taking it that well. If we weren't standing here together right now, I'd have been on my way to that police station to break his teeth."

She chuckled into my shirt, holding on to me and looking into my eyes. "I'm just happy that this chapter is over. Frank has been arrested. The case is closed. Work on the new bakery is starting soon, and more importantly, Ryan is getting used to us. We won, Carson. Frank lost. Life in prison is going to break more than just his teeth. Let it go."

With that, she smiled and sashayed away from me, giving a sharp blow of her whistle to draw the girls' attention. I shook my head, a grin on my lips. How had I gotten so lucky? After practice wrapped for the day, I was definitely taking her out to celebrate and then I was going to worship at that woman's altar all night long.

I really was the luckiest man alive, and tonight, I was going to tell her exactly how I felt about her.

# 59

## NOVA

Ryan walked into Moe's with his arm around Cassidy. I smiled, glad they seemed to have patched things up and that they were back to being happy. I cuddled deeper into Carson's side, leaning into him. My brother and my best friend headed over to the bar before they came to join us.

Vance sat across from me and he made a gagging noise when Carson turned to press a kiss to my temple mid-conversation with him. "Have I told either of you lately how much I hate being fifth wheel? You guys are too sweet, and so are Ryan and Cassidy. Y'all are going to give me cavities."

"Don't be a dick just because it didn't work out with you and Jessie," Carson said. "I had to watch you make out with her a bunch of times and you didn't hear me making any smart-ass remarks."

"Just because I didn't hear 'em doesn't mean you didn't make 'em," Vance said with a wink at his friend.

"Who's a smartass?" Ryan asked as he and Cassidy sat down next to Vance. "If it's Nova, then yes. I agree. If it's Carson, then I'd leave the 'smart' out of it. He's just an ass."

Carson laughed and good-naturedly flipped him off. Vance shook his head at them both. While the boys bantered, I reached over to squeeze Cassidy's forearm since I couldn't get close enough to give her a hug.

Keeping my voice down, I tilted my head toward my brother. "Is everything okay now?"

"It's all good," she said quietly, sliding her eyes to the side to glance at him and smiling as she looked back at me. "He told me about the talks he had with you and with Carson. I'm glad he finally took himself out of the equation, but I'm also glad that you two finally stood up for yourselves and realized that he should never have been such a big part of it to begin with."

"True, but I like to think that it all worked out for the best." I reached for Carson's leg under the table and wrapped my fingers around his thigh. He pressed it against mine immediately and I tried to hide a secret smile, but then Cassidy arched an eyebrow at me and I blushed. "What?"

"Nothing," she said, laughing. "I just wouldn't let your brother catch you feeling up your boyfriend right in front of him."

I rolled my eyes at her, then deliberately tracked my gaze down the length of her arm to where it disappeared under the table. "I'm not doing anything you're not doing. Except for the fact that my hand is on his leg. I don't even want to know where yours is."

"On his leg," she said adamantly, then turned when Vance said her name. "What now?"

"We were just talking about your parents' lake house," he explained. "Jessie was nice to me while we were there."

Ryan nodded. "Maybe if you'd been nicer to her once we got back, she'd still be around. Where'd she go anyway? Did you run her out of town or something?"

"No," he lamented. "She went off on some internship program. It really wasn't anything I did."

"Which is why it's time for you to move on," Cassidy said like it was some kind of sweeping declaration. "I have the perfect girl for you to do it with."

"Do it?" Vance asked, waggling his brows.

"Move on," she said.

He nodded. "Right."

While Cassidy told Vance about this perfect girl—Ms. Norris, the librarian's daughter who would be coming home from college soon—I ran my fingers along the length of Carson's thigh and settled in with my drink. Looking around the table, I wondered if this was going to be our new group. The people we hung out with as a couple and those who would eventually stand up with us at our wedding, provided we made it that far.

Our evening was filled with lighthearted banter. Afterward, Carson drove me home. My brother didn't even flinch when we said good night, he was so absorbed in Cassidy and trying to convince her to let him drive her home.

Carson chuckled as we climbed into the truck. "Do you think those two are going to work out?"

"I don't know. I used to think so. Then I thought they definitely wouldn't, and now, I'm just not sure. I guess we're going to have to wait and see."

"Well, at least our turn for will-they, won't-they is over," he said happily and got us on the road. "You were driving me crazy in there tonight with this."

He demonstrated what he was talking about by running his fingers lightly over the inner seam of my jeans, and my pulse spiked. "Shit, I'm so sorry. I wasn't even thinking about that. I just wanted to be touching you."

"I want you to be touching me." He dragged his fingertips almost all the way to the apex of my thighs. "Let's just agree that until we know your brother is fully over the urge to punch me when he sees us together, you won't touch me *there* when he's around."

I laughed, the sound husky in the dark truck. "What was it that you said before about making promises you can't keep? You're mine now. I'm way done with holding back because of him, but I will promise that I'll try to dial it down in public."

Carson groaned, fingers skating along my inner thigh and making me burn for him. "As long as I can do the same, I'll find a way to live with it. It might involve getting it on in public restrooms, though. What's your stance on that?"

I spread my legs a little wider, feeling wilder than I ever had before but also knowing that I was safe to explore this new side of myself with him. "We can try it. Then I'll let you know what my stance is."

He glanced at me and frowned. "You've never tried it before?"

I shrugged. "Some people prefer beds."

"Are you one of those people?" he asked cautiously. "It's okay if you are."

"I don't think I am, but my ex definitely was. Lights off, socks on, and in bed." I'd never mentioned Max to Carson before, but he didn't seem surprised by it.

"It's no wonder it didn't work out," he said, his voice growing rougher by the second. "New rule. No more beds until we've christened every other surface in your house."

He cupped my pussy over my jeans and my hips bucked. My lips parted and my cheeks grew hot. "I can get behind that. I think. No beds at all?"

"Later, maybe." He turned onto the ranch and drove up to my cottage without letting go of me. Then he hauled me over his shoulder and carried me inside.

After kicking the door shut behind us, he set me down in front of my kitchen counter and flicked open the button on my pants. His pupils were so dilated there was barely a hint of green left. He knelt in front of me, slid down my zipper and then removed my shoes before peeling off my pants and my panties.

The lights in my living area were on, but he didn't seem to give a damn as he picked me up by my hips and deposited me on my kitchen counter. I lay back, and he pulled up a stool and sat down between my legs, one of his feet kicked up on the rung like he was settling in for a casual conversation.

Instead of talking though, he smirked at me and spread my legs open wide. His gaze lowered to where I was exposed to him before he leaned forward and licked me. Just like that. No hesitation. No being shy about it. He just licked me.

At the first touch of his hot tongue against my core, I cried out. He sucked my clit into his mouth, and my hips nearly came off the counter. "Holy fuck, Carson!"

He hummed against me and tightened his grip on my thighs to keep me down and then he really went for it. My muscles tensed, my body starting to shake. He slid a single finger into me and started working it along with his mouth.

I couldn't believe we were doing this right here, where anyone could walk in and see it. We'd done it on the sofa the other day, but at least we'd been shielded from the door by the sofa itself. Now, however, if anyone were to burst in here, they would find me spread eagle on the surface where I prepared my breakfast.

While I knew it wasn't *that* depraved, the thought of it all kicked my arousal up another notch. When Carson's teeth grazed across my clit again, his finger pressing on just the right spot inside me, I lost it. Pleasure flooded through me, racing from my core and curling my toes, as I shook and moaned.

He licked me through it, cleaning me up. Then he slowly made a show of taking off his clothes—while I was still on the damn counter.

I watched him with hungry eyes as he exposed those washboard abs and broad chest and shoulders. My gaze drank in the ridges and valleys of his torso, then followed his fingers deftly opening his jeans.

Flicking them open, he left the denim hanging off his hips and stepped right up to me. Biceps bulging, he leaned over and held himself right above me. "This counter is the perfect height. You good with this?"

I nodded wildly, my head practically bouncing, and he kissed me. Tasting myself on him, I wondered if it was normal to like feeling like I'd marked him with my scent. When he deepened the kiss, my thoughts scattered and I wound my arms around his neck, kissing him back and deciding that I didn't care if it was normal.

I liked it and that was the only thing that was important. Abruptly breaking the kiss, he straightened up and pushed off his pants and underwear. Chest heaving with labored breaths, he grabbed a condom out of his wallet and rolled it on.

Pushing myself up on my elbows, I watched as the latex slid over his hard length, my mouth practically watering for it. He positioned himself at my entrance. He pushed inside, his eyes never leaving our joining bodies.

"Fuck, that's hot." He brought his thumb back to my clit and drew circles around it, and he withdrew and thrust in again.

I sat up a little further, moaning when I realized he'd been right. The counter really was the perfect height for him and it really was fucking hot. Transfixed by what I was looking at, I felt pleasure starting to build deep inside me all over again. Sensation got the better of me. I was not only feeling it this time, but seeing it too, and it was incredible.

"Come for me, Nova," he commanded. "Now."

As if my body had been waiting for the order, the floodgates opened deep within me, and I spasmed, biting my lip and trembling. I flexed my legs around his ass, forcing him to bury himself deep inside me when he came. Carson roared and tossed his head back, his hands grasping my hips so tight I was pretty sure he was going to leave marks, but I didn't care. The sight of him like that was branded in my memory and I was never going to be able to look at him again without being on the brink of an orgasm.

*God, he's so damn sexy. And he's all mine.*

I collapsed against the counter, breathing hard in the aftermath and feeling like my bones had been liquefied. He stayed still until he recovered enough to take care of the condom. Then he came back, gathered me up in his arms, and wordlessly carried me to bed.

Climbing in naked beside me, he pressed the sweetest of kisses to each of my eyelids and then to my mouth. His head hovered just above mine and he smiled. "Nova?"

"Hmm?"

"We're doing that again later," he murmured. "Everywhere."

"You've got yourself a deal." I pulled him to me and kissed him again. Then I fell asleep in his arms, feeling like everything was finally right in the world.

# 60

## CARSON

"As you can see, it's been neglected these last few years," I said to Daniel, the contractor, as I walked into the house with him.

I'd just closed on it earlier this week, but I was eager for the work to get started. One of Daniel's teams was also helping build the new bakery, and another was starting to turn some of the old barns on the Murphy ranch into venues.

Nova was up to her ears in renovations and construction, and I was helping out where I could. It was good to be busy and I really wanted to get this house livable.

Daniel arched an eyebrow at me as we stood in the center of the small living area, his eyes dark with doubt. "*This* is where you want to live?"

"Eventually," I responded. "Sooner rather than later would be good. I need to get out of my mother's house, man."

He laughed. An old friend from high school, he'd assured me that he had enough people he could call on to tackle another project, but I wondered if he was regretting that now. "You could've told me you'd bought a tear-down. I'd have called it a shell, but I'm not sure the structure counts as that. One more big storm and the whole thing could come down on your head."

"It's that bad?" I asked, rubbing the back of my neck as I eyed the bits of plaster on the floor that had fallen off the walls and the cracks I could see in the ceiling. "Never mind. It's that bad. What was I thinking?"

"Probably that you wanted to get out of your mother's house," he teased before the expression on his face grew serious again. "I'm not going to lie to you, Carson. This is going to be a big job. Do you want to tell me what you've got in mind here?"

I shrugged. "Honestly, I haven't really had time to think about specifics. I've been looking for a property to build on, but there's nothing suitable on the market right now, so I figured this was the next best thing. Salvage what you can and let me know what to do with the rest."

He nodded slowly, his gaze sweeping around the place once more. "Okay, I'm giving you homework. I'm going to have my assistant send you some links. Look at them, and let me know which style you prefer. After that, you and I are going to sit down and talk about design. I'll get a team of guys together for you while that's happening, and I'll get them in here to start with the cleanup while we figure out a miracle. Good thing I like a challenge."

"Make the guys local and use as many as you can," I said.

He gave me a sidelong glance. "I've heard you were on a mission to help the town. You sure you only want locals? We might need to wait for some of them to finish on other projects, but I'll get together as many as I can."

"Only locals but county-wide is fine," I replied, sliding my hands into my pockets and rocking back on my heels. "I like windows. If that helps. Lots of natural light."

He groaned. "You've spent way too much time in the city, but sure, I can bring in natural light. Would you like some green juice to go with that?"

I flipped him off. "Just the natural light is fine. Thank you."

He laughed, pulled out his phone, and readied the camera. "I'm going to take a look around and get some pictures. You can either hang out or leave me with the keys and I'll get them back to you."

"I'll hang out," I said. "I still need to get a feel for the place myself."

As he nodded and walked away, my phone rang. I headed into the overgrown garden before I took the call. When I saw my old agent's name on the screen, my blood chilled a little bit, but I picked up, not yet having the answer I knew he wanted from me.

"Paxton, how are you, man?"

"I'm doing well. You?" He didn't wait for a response, always too busy for small talk as he continued in his brisk, efficient tone. "The network is still waiting on your answer about that sports broadcasting gig, Carson. I can't stall them forever and word has gotten out that you might be interested. I'm juggling offers here, but you need to let me know where your head is at."

"I'll have an answer for you soon," I said. "I just need to talk to someone first."

"Call me back as soon as you can." He hung up and I sighed.

I headed back inside and dropping the keys on the kitchen counter. "Daniel? I have to leave after all. Keys are in the kitchen."

"No problem, man," he called from one of the bedrooms. "I'll call you with an update as soon as I have one. In the meantime, remember to take a serious look at those links we're going to send you."

"I'll do that." I walked back out into the sunshine, but my blood still felt a little cold. I had to find Nova to talk to her about this, but I didn't know what to say.

As luck would have it, I found Ryan first, overseeing work in the bakery. He grinned when he saw me walking in. "Hey, Mr. Investor Man. You coming to check that we're not squandering your money?"

"Of course," I joked. "I wanted to make sure you hadn't taken it and run off to a tropical island."

"I seriously considered doing that, but in the end, I decided to stay for another week or so. Cassidy has to have her nails done before we leave."

I laughed. "She's already washed her hair, then?"

"Yep." He pumped his eyebrows at me, then cocked his head, those blue eyes suddenly fixed on mine. "What's up? You look stressed. Did something go wrong with the house? I thought you were taking Daniel out there today."

"I did, but it's not that." I took a look around. "Is Nova here? I was hoping to talk to her."

"She just left," he said, frowning deeply with his eyes still locked on mine. "One of the builders called with a question about the wedding venue, so she went over to the barn. What's going on?"

"Don't freak out, but I got offered a job in sports broadcasting and my agent is pushing me for an answer," I rushed out, needing him to have all the information before he jumped to conclusions. "Nova knows I'm considering it, and even if I go, I'm not moving away."

Ryan's jaw tightened and his posture went stiff. He drew in a deep breath, rolled his neck, and then looked at me again. "I think we better sit down for this."

Showing me to a break area with a bench under a tree out back, he sat down and propped his elbows on his knees. "So you *are* leaving again?"

"Maybe, but like I said, I wouldn't be moving away if I take it. My home base will still be here. I'll just be commuting back and forth."

"Nova knows about this plan?"

"It's not a plan." I looked him square in the eyes. "It's an offer I got while she and I were apart and I've been toying with the idea of taking it. I told her about it as soon as we got back together."

He scratched the side of his neck. "I was afraid this was going to happen. It's why I didn't want you guys to get together. You're always after the next big thing, man. I—"

"The only big thing that matters to me is Nova," I said firmly, not even bothering to let him finish the thought. "There is no *next*. There is only her. If I take this job, it will be with her full support, or it won't be at all. I won't leave if she doesn't want me to."

He scowled. "You can't put that on her. If she thinks she's keeping you from making your dreams come true, obviously she's going to tell you to go, but she might come with you if you asked her to."

My heart rate kicked into a higher gear, suddenly racing. "Do you really think so?"

His eyebrows twitched, but he nodded. "Yeah, I really think so. You told her you were considering this but you haven't asked her to go with you?"

I blew out a heavy breath. "I wanted to, but I haven't done it yet. With everything going on here, I'm scared she's going to feel obligated to stay and help."

Ryan sat up. His gaze was completely serious with that protective gleam simmering behind his eyes again. "I'm going to tell you something now that I should've told you ten years ago. Nova loves you. She isn't going anywhere. If you leave, as long as you come back to her, she'll wait for you, but if you want her to come with you, she'll probably say yes."

"She loves me?" I couldn't believe I was hearing this from him instead of his sister.

He scoffed down an incredulous laugh as he nodded. "Of course, she does, but don't take advantage of her love, Carson. If what you said is true and you'll be commuting with this as your home base, then she'd be here often enough to check on the progress of the renovations while all the changes are happening. Otherwise, she'll be here waiting for you every time you come home, but don't guilt her into going or staying. Do *not* take advantage."

"I would never." I inhaled deeply, trying to calm my rapidly beating heart.

As I looked back at Ryan though, I knew he truly believed what he'd said. I could see how much he hated that he'd said it to me at all, which meant it had to be true. His sister loved me and he still wasn't a big fan of it, but at least he was accepting it.

This was also his worst nightmare come true, him accepting us together only for me to be thinking of leaving again. I reached out and clamped a hand around his shoulder. "I'm not going to hurt her, bro. I swear. I'm not leaving. I'm not running away from her or from home. I'm not bailing. Trust me."

"I'm trying," he said. "Go talk to her, but if you hurt her—"

"You'll make me disappear." I smirked. "I'm not going anywhere, Ryan. I'm not going to hurt her, but I will go talk to her. You going to be okay if she decides to come with me for a while?"

He rolled his eyes, finally relaxing again. "I'll be great. It would be nice not to have her under my feet while the construction is happening."

I knew he didn't mean it, but I also knew he would be okay. He would be fine without her for a couple months at a time and he and I would be fine too. If he was already joking about it, then our friendship would survive this.

Relieved, I let go of his shoulder and strode back to my truck, intent on asking her to come with me after all. She loved me. I loved her. If I did this, then of course I'd want her there with me. I wouldn't let the fear of her turning me down keep me from at least floating the idea.

*One Murphy down, one to go. Fingers crossed her brother knows her and her heart as well as he thinks he does.*

# 61

## NOVA

After I left the barn, I went back to the cottage and started baking. I'd stored a crate of strawberries at my parents' house and I was now going to use the last of them to surprise Carson and his mom with the pastries they loved.

*Thank goodness he's over at his place today.* I'd been meaning to bake these all week, but we were rarely apart these days. As much as I loved being with him, it was kind of hard to surprise him when he was right there while said surprise was going into the oven.

Humming under my breath, I switched on the radio in my kitchen, donned an apron, and got to work. Making the dough was second nature to me and it made me feel all warm and tingly to be back in the kitchen, baking for those I loved.

This was how I'd started and, undoubtedly, how I would end when the time came. Simply baking what I felt like for people who weren't paying me for anything in particular. It was weird, but getting back to my roots and the basics for a change felt good.

If anything positive had come out of the bakery burning, it was this. Well, this and all the time I was getting to spend with Carson now that I didn't have to be running a business full time while still doing my chores as well.

Even so, I was looking forward to re-opening day and I was very excited for everything we were going to be starting on the ranch as soon as construction was done. For now, I was happy with the breathing room and ecstatic with life in general at the moment.

It really couldn't be any better. I smiled, thankful that all the drama and the storms had died down—and then Carson walked into my house. It took one look at his face for me to know that my brief time of peace had come to an end. My spirits sagged, and my heart dropped to my shoes.

"What is it? What's wrong?" I abandoned the rolling pin and walked around the counter, embracing him and not giving a damn that I was getting his shirt covered in flour. "You look like you're going to be sick, but you're weirdly happy about it, but also worried. What on earth is going on?"

He chuckled, hugged me tight, and kissed the top of my head. He pulled back, spotted the crate of strawberries on the counter, and flashed me a hopeful smile. "I thought you said all of those were gone."

I groaned. "It was supposed to be a surprise. That's why I didn't tell you there were any left, but you're going first. What's going on with you?"

The look in his eyes was a mixture of caution and hope. "We need to talk about that broadcasting job I mentioned to you the other day. I need to make a decision about it, but I need you to know that I meant what I said the other day. I'm not leaving you, not even if I take the job."

My breath got stuck in my lungs. I'd known he was considering taking the gig, but I'd been hoping that we'd have more time together before he needed to take off. Staring at him now, I looked into those bright green eyes and imagined only seeing them on video calls for a couple months at a time and it made my insides ache.

Everything inside me hurt at the idea of him leaving so damn soon. "I think you'd be great at it."

He sighed. "You've already said that, baby. I don't really care if I'd be any good at it. What I care about is talking about what it would look like for us if I take it."

Realizing that he was weighing his options based on my opinion, I pushed past the hurt and shoved away the disappointment. It would all be back with a vengeance later, but I couldn't let him turn it down just because I was worried about not seeing him for a little while.

"You should do it," I said evenly, lifting my chin and looking right into his eyes. I couldn't hold his gaze, though. I averted it and pretended to have to watch the dough while I kneaded it instead. "It's a wonderful opportunity for you and a logical step after you stopped playing professionally. The fans would love to see you."

"Nova," he said, but I still couldn't look at him. There were tears welling in my eyes and I didn't want to hold him back. "Nova. Look at me, baby. Please?"

"I can't." I squeezed my eyes shut and inhaled deeply. Then I finally lifted my gaze to his and let out a huff of sad laughter. "I'm sorry. I didn't want you to see this. Don't let the tears stop you, Carson. I'll get over it. You'll be back soon, right?"

*Sure. Once or twice. Then the commute will become too tedious.*

The stool he'd been on scraped against the floor as he pushed it back. He came over to slide his arms around me. Chest to chest, I felt the heat of him and got enveloped by the scent I loved so much. In that moment, I couldn't imagine being away from him for even a day.

"I will always be back and it will always be as soon as I can, but if you want to, I want you to travel with me."

My jaw dropped and I tilted my head back so I'd be able to see his eyes. "Are you sure?"

He cracked the tiniest grin as he nodded. "I'm very fucking sure. I want you with me, Nova. Always. But I also understand that you have obligations here, and if you say no, then that's okay too. It wouldn't mean that we're over. We'd just be long distance for a little while at a time, and it'd suck, but we'd make it work."

I pulled away from him a little more, turning my head to look at the ranch stretching out beyond the kitchen window. That view had been what I'd woken up to almost every morning since my parents had brought me home from the hospital, and it was an amazing view.

During the time I'd spent at college, I'd missed it every single day, but I wouldn't be leaving it for years this time. If I said yes, if I followed my heart and went with him, I'd still get this view to come home to often.

So many thoughts shot through my head all at once. I stared at my mountains in the distance, the puffy, ice-white clouds in the beautiful blue sky, and all the green in between. *Would the ranch be okay without me? Would my family cope with all the renovations if I wasn't here to help? Was it fair to expect them to?*

I didn't know the answers to any of those questions, but as Carson kept gently holding me, not pushing for an answer and waiting patiently for me to sort through it all, I realized that for the first time in a long time, I had a bit of breathing room.

Just a few minutes ago, I'd had that exact thought. I'd forgotten about it when Carson had walked in, but I finally had some space to be me without worrying about all the responsibilities of being part of a family who owned a ranch.

The bakery wouldn't be opening for months. The venues were on about the same timeline. In the meantime, the only thing I would be doing was overseeing work and helping out with the chores, but with Carson's investment in the property, Dad was going to be hiring a couple ranch hands anyway.

We'd finally gotten through to him that he couldn't keep the same pace as ten, twenty, and thirty years ago. He needed help, and so did we.

All of which meant that right at this very moment, there was absolutely nothing holding me back. Bringing my gaze back to Carson's, I wound my arms around his neck and smiled. "Thanks to you, I've actually got the time to follow my dreams right now and the only dream I want to follow is being with you."

A dazzling light came on in his eyes and his eyebrows lifted. "Is that a yes? You'll come with me?"

"It's a yes," I all but squealed, pushing up on my toes to meet his lips. "It's a hell yes."

He swept me clean off my feet, his tongue diving between my lips and scattering my thoughts. He kissed me like his very existence depended on it. Wrapping my legs around him and tightening the grip of my arms, I laughed when he started carrying me out of the kitchen.

When I broke the kiss to ask him where we were going though, he surprised me with the intensity of the look in his eyes. "I love you, Nova."

My heart skipped, then started beating so fast at the sound of those words. Happy tears suddenly filled my eyes and the widest smile I remembered ever smiling broke out across my lips. "I love you, too, Carson. God, I can't believe I finally got to say it."

He let his forehead rest against mine, breathing me in. He let out a deep noise from the back of his throat. "Tell me about it, but I don't think I'm ever going to be able to say it enough. Or to hear it enough. Say it again."

"I love you, Carson Drake."

He let out another noise, then started moving again, faster and more urgently than ever before. With the tears still in my eyes and my heart still racing, I clung to him and laughed. "Where are we going? What's our first stop?"

"Our bedroom, then LA"

My heart skipped about ten more beats. "*Our* bedroom?"

"Yep. I'm all in, Nova. Besides, it's not like we're going to rent separate places once we get there, so we might as well make it official."

As sudden as it was, there was logic to his madness. Besides, I didn't want it any other way. "*Our* bedroom, it is. Whatever will we tell our parents?"

He chuckled against my hair and started up the stairs, one hand on the barrier and other holding me firmly to him. "We'll tell them whatever you want, my dear. I know what I'd *like* to tell them, but it might be a bit soon to start talking about that."

My heart soared and I shut my eyes briefly. I wasn't quite sure when or how it had happened, but my life right now was everything I'd ever wanted it to be and more. I never would've imagined it was possible to be this fulfilled, this happy, and this safe in the knowledge that this man, the only one I'd ever truly loved, was really going to be my happily ever after.

# EPILOGUE
## CARSON

A few weeks after I'd started my new job, I was walking around my house in Silver Springs. The renovation was just about wrapping up and I honestly couldn't believe how much they had gotten done in such a short space of time.

All the back walls were gone, replaced with stackable glass doors that let in the natural light I'd wanted. The interior had been completely redone. From walls, to floors, to fittings, it was all brand new and modern but still cozy.

At this point though, I wasn't even sure why I was doing this anymore. I'd bought the place and it had needed to be fixed up, but I sure as hell didn't want to move in here anymore. I'd been staying with Nova whenever we were in town and her cottage felt more like home than any other place ever had since leaving my mother's house ten years ago.

Nova and I were both happy at her place, and I was seriously wondering what to do with this house. Like clockwork, Ryan showed up, grinning. He walked in and let out a low whistle. "Wow. I've been meaning to come out here to take a look at what they've been doing with this place, but this is amazing. It doesn't even look like the same house."

"Yeah, I know. It's crazy, right? Daniel's team has performed a miracle here."

He nodded his agreement, and his features were slack with surprise as he kept looking around. "Very true. If you've got some spare time between doing videos for Nova's subscription boxes, you should consider giving him a shout-out on social media. I'm sure you've got a few new followers now that you're a big-time broadcaster."

"That's not a bad idea, actually. I'd have to talk to him about it before I do it, but if it'll help his business, I'm in."

"Of course, it's not a bad idea. I only have good ones."

I laughed and gave him a droll look. "Are you sure about that? Because I vaguely recall you using a singing telegram to invite Stacey McGaffin to the Valentine's dance in the seventh grade. That definitely wasn't a good idea."

He groaned. "When are you leaving again? To think, I was excited about having you come home."

"Only next week. Sorry, bro."

He walked further into the house and took a closer look. "This place really is something now. When are you moving in?"

"I don't know," I said honestly. "More accurately, I don't know if I am. Do you want it?"

"You want to give me your house?"

I shrugged. "Not give it to you, but let you live in it? Sure. If you want to."

"Thanks, but no thanks. Maybe someday, but for now, I'm happy in my own place. You could talk to your mom about offering it to the church? They're forever looking for housing for people who have fallen on hard times. It could be a halfway house of sorts."

"That's not a half bad idea," I said. "Keep going, man. You seem to be on a roll with the ideas today."

He chuckled and pretended to dust off his shoulder. "It's not just today, Drake. What can I say? I'm just that smart."

"Yeah, okay." I laughed and opened the fridge. I'd brought some beers over earlier just in case, and now I was glad to have them. I offered him one and cracked open my own. "How are things going on the ranch?"

"Really well," he said, looking more relaxed than I'd ever seen him. "Construction is in full swing and we're definitely going to have a couple venues ready for the winter wedding season. The upgrades to the farming side of the operations are also coming along. Dad is having some issues getting used to the technology, but even he has said that it'll help. A lot."

I nodded. "That's good. Nova mentioned it was going well, but the details she's been giving me are about stained-glass windows in the chapel and the type of tables she's ordered for the bakery. I haven't heard much about the upgrades or any of that."

"Well, you're home now and you're practically living with my sister, so you might as well come check it out later when you get back."

"I might just do that. Thanks." I watched him for a moment before I drew in a deep breath. "Are you okay with that? Me practically living with your sister?"

He sighed. "I think I'm getting used to it. I mean, it'd be naive of me to think that you're not living together when you're away from here, so it doesn't really matter that you're also doing it when you're here. Speaking of which, how's that going, her traveling with you?"

"It's been great so far," I said honestly. "I'll be flying out to games during the season to do the commentary though, and once the bakery is up and running again, Nova won't be able to be out there with me all the time."

"So what's going to happen then?" he asked conversationally, not seeming at all worried anymore that I was suddenly going to up and leave for good.

I shrugged. "It's a for-now thing, but she'll travel with me when she can and I'll be here when I can. I'm going to try to go down to the local level soon though. That way, I'll be able to be here full time with Nova but I'll still be broadcasting."

"Good luck with that," he said. "You don't think it'll be a demotion?"

"Nah, not really. To be honest, I'd rather be here. I haven't been away from a big city for that long, but being back there has been overwhelming. I'm ready for the quiet life and I can't do that while I'm there, but I'm also really enjoying commentating, so local level gives me the best of both worlds."

"Look at you, all happy to be settling down and shit," he teased. "Never thought I'd see the day."

I'd been waiting for an opportunity to mention something to him, and there would be no better chance than the one he'd just given me. Bracing myself for a Ryan Murphy Shit Storm, I dug my hand into my pocket and wrapped it around the box I had with me at all times these days.

"Yeah, uh, now that you've mentioned me settling down, there's something I need your help with."

"Sure," he said, still relaxed as he leaned against the counter. "What do you need?"

"I want to propose to Nova," I said, pulling out the box and handing it over. "I know it's quick, but I've loved her for over a decade and I can't imagine my life without her now. I'm not asking for your blessing, but I would appreciate if you could help me plan it."

For his part, Ryan didn't seem to be shocked at all. He simply took the box from me and flipped open the lid, checking out the ring I'd bought the last time I'd traveled for work without Nova.

He whistled between his teeth. "Now that's a rock," he said as he inspected the platinum band with the brilliant cut diamond inlaid in it. "Okay, I'll help. What is the plan?"

I broke it down for him, thanking my lucky stars he hadn't freaked out. Ryan and I had been getting back on track recently and part of me had worried that this would throw us off course again.

With that not being the case, I felt surer than ever that this was the right thing to do. I knew I could wait, but I didn't want to. She and I had already spent more time apart than I'd ever wanted to and now that we were together, happy, and going strong, I didn't want to waste any more time not being official.

A long time ago, before I'd left Silver Springs that fateful summer when I'd kissed her for the first time, I remembered looking at her one day and having a fleeting thought about making her my wife. It had been over ten years since, and somewhere in the back of my mind, that thought had always been there.

Nova and I had waited long enough. If it had been up to me, I'd have asked her as soon as I got back to the cottage, but it wasn't only up to me. She'd always dreamed of getting married and having a family, and I knew the proposal was the first step toward making that dream a reality.

I wanted to give her the life her dreams were made of, so to my mind, that started by giving her a proposal she would never forget. And that was where Ryan came in. As long as he didn't think I was too crazy once I finished laying it out there for him.

The End

# ABOUT THE AUTHOR

Hey there. I'm Weston.

Have we met? No? Well, it's time to end that tragedy.

I'm a former firefighter/EMS guy who's picked up the proverbial pen and started writing bad boy romance stories. I co-write with my sister, Ali Parker, but live in Texas with my wife, my two little boys, my daughter, two dogs, three cats, and a turtle.

Yep. A turtle. You read that right. Don't be jealous.

You're going to find Billionaires, Bad Boys, Military Guys, and loads of sexiness. Something for everyone hopefully.

# OTHER BOOKS BY WESTON PARKER

Wedding Bells Alpha Series:

Say You Do

She's Mine Now

Don't You Dare

Promise It All

Give Me Forever

Faux Series:

Fake It Real Good

Fake It For Money

Fake It For Now

Fake it For Real

Fake It For Love

Fake It For Us

Fake It For Wealth

Fake It For Good

Fake It for Fame

Fake it for Fortune

Fake it for Glory

Fake it for Him

Searing Saviors Series:

Light Up The Night

Set the Night On Fire

Turn Up The Heat

Ignite The Spark Between Us

Bad Boy Greeks Series:

Fake It For Me

My Favorite Mistake

Pretending to be Rich

Standalone's:

Hometown Hottie

Maybe It's Fate

One Shot At Love

Caught Up In Love

Let Freedom Ring

Maine Squeeze

Between The Sheets

Follow You Anywhere

Take It All Off

Backing You Up

Give Me The Weekend

Come Down Under

Going After Whats Mine

Fake It For Me

My Favorite Mistake

Heartbreaker

My Holiday Reunion

Spring It On Me

Airforce Hero

Brand New Man

Pretending To Be Rich

Good Luck Charm

Captain Hotness

All About The Treats

Show Me What You Got

Come Work For Me

Trying To Be Good

Have Your Way With Me

Love Me Last

My Last Chance

My First Love

My Last First Kiss

Made For Me

Hot Stuff

Take It Down A Notch

My One and Only

Desperate For You

Take A Chance On Me

Fair Trade For Love

We Belong Together

Dropping The Ball

Standing Toe to Toe

Pay Up Hot Stuff

Love Your Moves

The Billionaire's Second Chance

Runaway Groom

Showing Off The Goods

All Good Things

Bad For You

Printed in Great Britain
by Amazon